ZOMBIE
APOCALYPSE FIGHTBACK

Chronos Macchina

http://fug.io/za!

ZOMBIE
APOCALYPSE!FIGHTBACK

Created by Stephen Jones

With

Guy Adams

Anne Billson

Peter Crowther

Paul Finch

Amanda Foubister

Neil Gaiman

Nancy Holder

Paul McAuley

Reggie Oliver

John Llewellyn Probert

Michael Marshall Smith

Peter Atkins

Pat Cadigan

Les Edwards

Jo Fletcher

Christopher Fowler

Brian Hodge

Roz Kaveney

Lisa Morton

Sarah Pinborough

Robert Shearman

Simon Strantzas

and Lisa Tuttle

ROBINSON

RUNNING PRESS
PHILADELPHIA · LONDON

Constable & Robinson Ltd
55–56 Russell Square
London WC1B 4HP
www.constablerobinson.com

First published in the UK by Robinson,
an imprint of Constable & Robinson, 2012

A copy of the British Library Cataloguing in Publication
Data is available from the British Library

UK ISBN: 978-1-78033-465-3 (paperback)
UK ISBN: 978-1-78033-655-8 (ebook)

1 3 5 7 9 10 8 6 4 2

First published in the United States in 2012 by Running Press Book Publishers

US ISBN 978-0-7624-4598-1
US Library of Congress Control Number: 2011939127

Running Press Book Publishers
2300 Chestnut Street
Philadelphia, PA 19103-4371

Visit us on the web!
www.runningpress.com

Printed and bound in the EU

Designed by Basement Press, Glaisdale
www.basementpress.com

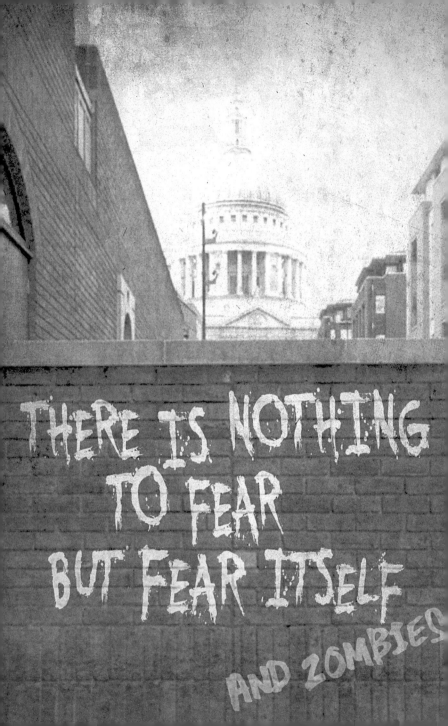

THE NEWS OF BRITAIN

GREAT BRITAIN'S MOST PATRIOTIC NEWSPAPER

FRIDAY, JANUARY 13, 2012

40P

OLYMPICS CANCELLED!

NO GAMES FOR POVERTY-STRUCK BRITAIN

THE NEWS OF BRITAIN EXCLUSIVE

by Staff Reporter

THE 2012 OLYMPIC GAMES have been cancelled after a furious row between all-party MPs was quashed by the Prime Minister and his Coalition Deputy.

The Olympic Games preparation has already cost Britain £7.8 billion – that's £3.5 billion *over* the initial £5.3 billion budget announced in 2005.

The Prime Minister, speaking from his £750 million private yacht *Austerity*, moored alongside his close friend Roman Abramovich's own £485-million *Eclipse*, gave a statement just a few hours ago.

He said, "Britain cannot afford to waste another penny on what is, in effect, a huge and costly white elephant. The Olympic Games serve no real purpose other than to drain the national purse. At a time when we are struggling to get the country back on her feet, we must surely all agree that wasting untold billions of pounds on what is, at the end of the day, nothing more than a few weeks' meaningless entertainment for the wealthy few, would be reprehensible.

Turn to Page 2 and 3

OLYMPICS CANCELLED! NO GAMES FOR POVERTY-STRUCK BRITAIN

Continued From Page 1

THE PM CLAIMED his unprecedented announcement was the only thing to do in the current economic climate. "As your Prime Minister, it is my hard duty to take these decisions for the good of all. The infrastructure already built will be put to good use, and I am already in discussion with a number of prominent bidders to sell off the various parts of what would have been the Olympic Park to those who will bring much-needed cash and employment back into the country.

"At the same time, we will be looking again at that valuable land currently designated for use as wetlands and a nature park. At this time we must all agree that the plight of the homeless must come before a few birds and water rats, and so the Deputy Prime Minister is introducing a new Planning Special Powers Act in the House which will allow our hard-working construction companies to get on with the job of rebuilding Britain without letting inessential red tape get in their way.

"While we are reforming the planning laws, we will also take the opportunity to deal with the recent riots by introducing the Police Special Powers Act, which will allow the brave men and women of Her Majesty's Constabulary to get on with their jobs keeping Britain safe, knowing that they themselves will be also safe. Details will be released shortly.

"We will be announcing more measures designed to bring Austerity Britain kicking and screaming into a brave new world, but I will end with one further announcement which I am sure will make up for any disappointment about cancelling the Olympic Games.

"I have decided that we will nonetheless celebrate all that is great and good about this country with a Festival of New Britain, and we have earmarked a number of sites in South London for this purpose. This will additionally enable us to remove the so-called 'haunted' church of All Hallows in Blackheath. There is no room in a modern Britain for rumour and myth that hold back the tide of progress."

The Prime Minister refused to answer questions, but promised a full statement on his return from his annual four-week holiday.

The Leader of the Opposition reacted angrily, saying, "The whole country's gone stark staring mad! To give up the prestige – not to mention the financial opportunities – represented by the Olympic Games for some little street party in South London? The Prime Minister will have some hard questions to face on his return."

But he admitted that he had already put in a bid for the Velodrome, originally planned to be run as a VeloPark by the Lee Valley Regional Park Authority after the Games. •

Cursed Church To Be Festival Site

The "cursed" church of All Hallows, Blackheath, has been the subject of several recent television documentaries. It was originally built by the so-called "Zombie King" architect Thomas Moreby, one of black magician Nicholas Hawksmoor's apprentices, allegedly for supernatural purposes, although much of the building was destroyed when fire raged through the church in 1850. Reports of hauntings date back beyond that, to its earliest days, and it has appeared in recent episodes of *Most Haunted* and *Supernatural U.K.* – although a spokesperson confirmed that the latter will not now be broadcast after one of the guest stars, Surita Mehmet, 13, suffered a stroke during filming.

Miss Mehmet, one of the child-stars of the reality TV show *Who's Afraid of a Big Bad Ghost?* and just cast in the remake of *In the Mouth of Madness* as the daughter of Mrs Pickman, is still in a coma, although doctors at Lewisham Hospital, South London, are hopeful of a complete recovery eventually.

Cameraman Eugene O'Barry, 37, who has been with *Supernatural U.K.* since Series One, claimed Surita Mehmet's stroke was not natural – that she was scared half to death. He told *The News of Britain*, "I've been filming woo-woo shows for a decade or more, and I swear to God I've never been more scared in my life. No wonder the little girl couldn't take it – she's not even fourteen years old yet.

"When we did our research, we found out the old Central Line extension to Hobbs End actually runs under that cursed church – and everyone knows those stories about the apemen of Hobbs Lane, and the insect Martians, and the horned Devil – we were going to do a separate show on Hobbs End Station, but I think that's gone for a burton now! It's not bad enough you've got some Satanist architect buried in a secret crypt somewhere beneath All Hallows, but now you've got devil-dwarfs running along the tunnels underneath as well?

"Surita walked off the set twice – she's not like that normally; she's a true professional to work with, a real sweetheart, not stuck-up like some I could name. But she said she couldn't stand the stench, and she was right: it was really foul, like a rancid sewer. It wasn't there all the time though, but when it did appear we all had to down tools. No way we could work with that stuff filling our mouths and noses.

"Another time Surita said she'd heard something tapping and knocking, but whenever we went to look, there was never anyone there. Then when she had that stroke, Surita screamed and she swore blind she'd seen this deformed hunched-over creature *disappear* into the walls – the camera had been recording, but it showed nothing of course – but that happens all the time on *Supernatural U.K.* There's usually something we can do to show what's going on, and I guess we'd have found a way if they'd aired it.

"And then there were the bugs – I've been in some dumps, but I swear: they were *huge* – and when they bit you, you really bloody felt it, I tell you."

O'Barry, 39, said Surita collapsed after filming a segment in the crypt near where Moreby's body is supposed to be hidden.

"She went white as a sheet and screamed so loud I swear I thought every piece of glass in the church would burst – then she started patting herself all over, as if she was being bitten by a million insects – and then her eyes went red as blood and rolled up into her head. The doc said she'd had a stroke, but when they opened her blouse to check her heart I saw her chest was covered with bite marks that got all swollen and bruised right while I was watching.

"'The director, he didn't realise I was still rolling, otherwise he'd have stopped me, but I wanted to see if I could work out what'd scared Surita so badly. I like the kid – thought it might help if I could tell her what she'd seen was really quite normal. But when I watched it back over the monitor I got terrified myself – I could see Surita's clothes moving as if something was trying to get out, and I swear I saw the shadows of some enormous insect on the walls – but when I turned to look, there was nothing there. You wouldn't get me back to that place, not even for a million quid." •

Mr O'Barry suffered a fatal heart attack three days after this interview. Surita Mehmet is still in hospital, where her condition is said to be "worsening". The director, K.M. Newman, has apparently disappeared.

The Underground Line From Hell!

The London Underground – the Tube – contains the oldest section of underground railway in the world. The Central Line – originally known as the Central London Railway – was opened in 1900, running from Bank in the City of London to Shepherd's Bush in West London. It was nicknamed the Twopenny Tube, both for its flat fare and the cylindrical shape of its tunnels; later on the whole system came to be known as the Tube.

Former Underground worker and expert Stephen Benaron, 87, explained that to minimise the risk of subsidence, the routing of the tunnels followed the roads on the surface and avoided passing under buildings, following strong protests from, amongst others, the Dean and Chapter of St Paul's Cathedral.

"I think they were afraid their buildings would tumble down because of the extensive underground works involved," he explained. "It was a common fear; we often had clergymen especially writing impassioned letters to the directors begging them to put 'their infernal lines from Hell' somewhere else. I remember when I was young, not long started on the Central, this one rector – somewhere near Greenwich or Blackheath, I think – claimed our works would release some 'Zombie King' – we never paid much mind to crackpots like that. Wherever you go you'll always get protestors – look at the whole Festival of Britain thing: the government tries to do something good for the country and all you get is people bitching."

Originally the line served thirteen stations and ran for around six miles. After a rejected proposal to turn the line into a loop, it was extended in 1908 at the western end to Wood Lane, for the Franco-British Exhibition, and at the eastern end to Liverpool Street Station.

It was extended several times more, although a number of planned additions – including the Hobbs End exchange – were never completed, some for lack of finance, and some, including Hobbs End, according to Mr Benaron, because of fear of unearthing something dangerous.

"The Home Office tried to suggest that unexploded bombs from the Second World War were behind the decision to stop work at Hobbs End, but there was a great deal of newspaper and radio coverage at the time. First of all some skulls of pre-human 'ape-men' believed to be some five million years old were discovered, and then the Army stepped in when the archaeologists found something they couldn't explain, and that set off a lot of spooky goings-on in the area, including mass hallucinations of a great horned Devil that experts later put down to a gas leak.

"I met a retired policeman some years ago – he'd been a PC at the time – and he told me the whole area was cursed, and had been for centuries – he was absolutely adamant that none of the newspaper reports came anywhere near the truth of what happened at Hobbs End.

"Whatever the reason, that branch of the line was never extended, and the station itself was sealed up, keeping whatever secrets it might hide well beyond reach. Mind you, I hear stories like this all over the Tube – after all, there are plenty of abandoned stations for the spooks to hide out in, and miles of dark tunnels for them to creep about to do their worst. It's interesting that you'll never see a cat around Hobbs End, even now. They do say cats can sense the Devil – or maybe they just can't abide the sewer smell you sometimes get there."

Now, at forty-seven miles and serving forty-nine stations, the Central Line has the longest length of track in the Tube. The Hobbs End extension has never been opened. ●

To: Simon Wesley, Histological Epidemiology, Hospital of Tropical
Diseases & Medicine, NW1
From: Prof. Margaret Winn, UCH London
Subject: All Hallows Church

Dear Simon,

I really appreciated you returning my call, and was sorry to have missed it. I've been trying to get back to you, but things have been crazy here – I'm actually typing this under the table while I'm sitting through yet another pointless government presentation on the New Festival of Britain preparations. Mascot costumes of great British figures. I want to throw up.

Simon, I'm being smeared by my own department, and it's over a breach of guidelines involving something that should, in my opinion, be made public knowledge.

You remember we talked about the current excavations at All Hallows Church, Blackheath? I was trying to work out why plague victims might have been buried there, and whether the excavations constituted a public health hazard. Diane Fermier at the London Metropolitan Archive kindly provided me with details of the 17th century boundary lines surrounding the park and church, and we turned up some anomalies.

Basically, there were reburials at the church overseen by a Hawksmoor architect called Thomas Moreby, who seems to have been involved in all manner of Satanic tomfoolery. I'm having trouble making sense of it all, but there are people who clearly believe he had plague victims buried for a purpose of his own. Moreby thought that those who had died of the plague would rise again if "expos'd to pure humours". I know it's hogwash, but in a funny way he was right – if the plague remained in their bodies after death, it was dormant but technically alive.

Apart from the possible health hazard, I thought that stopping the disinterment might give the archaeological team time to find out more – unfortunately it all has to be done right now in order to meet the targets set for the New Festival timetable.

Needless to say, my suggestion of stopping has been met with cries of outrage from the usual coterie of Health & Safety jobsworths employed by the council to keep information away from the general public.

But here's the odd part.

I talked to the site manager, Michael Brooks, and he told me that he was instructed to move any human remains he found into separate bio-hazard containers. This was ostensibly so that archaeological experts could sift through the material, but I contacted the team in charge of the site and they told me they knew nothing about this.

I wouldn't bother you if I didn't think there was a very real danger of contamination stemming from the excavation. You know far more about this sort of thing than I do, but I'm starting to doubt myself and need to canvass as many opinions as I can before I find myself locked out of my own office (I'm not kidding, someone has been going through my papers).

We're talking about a disease that has lain dormant for four and a half centuries. We know the ground conditions at All Hallows (damp clay with a low oxygen/high acidity content) were good enough to preserve bodies, but there's obviously a big difference between preservation and bacterial reanimation.

Most of the LMA's documentation is in the form of parchment maps, so I can't mail you any of our additional findings, but I've sent you a drop box of related material, including some background information on Moreby, a series of letters transcribed by my old schoolfriend Evelyn Hunt over at the Royal Society of Arts, and some clippings from newspapers of the time. If you get a chance to look through it, any help you can give me will be greatly appreciated.

I'm fighting this corner on my own.

Best,
Margaret

To: Prof. Margaret Winn, UCH London
From: Simon Wesley, Histological Epidemiology, Hospital of Tropical Diseases & Medicine, NW1
Subject: All Hallows Church, Blackheath

Dear Margaret,

Sorry we keep missing each other. It's a bit of a coincidence you writing to me about this, because most of the senior technicians here have been away on a course for the past week. You might be interested in what they were being sent off to study: "Emergency Procedures for London in the Event of An Unidentified Pandemic". When they say "unidentified", it tends to mean "of unknown origin", i.e. something not stemming from Avian Flu or Bovine spongiform encephalopathy. Of course, it might be a coincidence – I couldn't attend, but colleagues say there seemed to be a specific agenda behind the chosen subjects covered.

I've only had a quick look at the material in your drop box, it looks fascinating and I hope to get onto it more later today. Let me reply to your specific query, though.

Is it possible for a germ to survive that long in London soil? Absolutely.

Why don't we all get sick every time somebody digs up a graveyard? Hundreds of excavations are undertaken in the capital every year, and we always insist that a set of precautionary guidelines is followed.

Have we ever found a reactivated (i.e. active & aggressive) germ in excavated landfill?

No.

The reasons for this are pretty simple. Most germs simply aren't robust enough to survive exposure, and we are genetically different now. Plague germs have been known to survive a long time in stable conditions, but it's highly unlikely that they could breach the human immunity chain. For one thing, the bubonic plague was passed by blood and sputum; it was never air-activated. This fact alone protects the population, disregarding a wide variety of other factors. Europe now lives within a global community. This has made us vulnerable to some new diseases, but has brought immunities against a host of others.

However, the fleas that spread the plague were surprisingly efficient at carrying toxins. We were recently able to show the presence of around 100,000 *Yersinia Pestis* germs in <u>a single flea</u>. That's the germ behind the Black Death. Here's what it will do to a human.

Immediately after a bite occurs, symptoms such as headache, body aches and fever appear. Lumps arise, especially in the lymph nodes and lymph vessels. Once the pathogen has entered the bloodstream, it quickly spreads out to all organs and becomes a life-threatening sepsis via toxins. Now, you get enough fleas, and it might look as if a corpse has indeed started to rise, so perhaps your Thomas Moreby wasn't that wide of the mark.

I've lately been hearing rumours about further government interest in this subject, and if you really think someone is monitoring your enquiries, I suggest we meet face to face in the future, just to be on the safe side.

Give me a call as soon as you get this.

Best,
Simon

▼ From: *A Biographical Dictionary of British Architecture* (RIBA publications, 1936):

Moreby, Thomas James (?1702–?1803) pupil of Nicholas Hawksmoor (1661–1736) qv. Worked with him on several London churches, notably Christ Church, Spitalfields and St Anne's, Limehouse. Designed All Hallows, Blackheath (1736), in Hawksmoor's late Baroque manner. Later in his long life he adopted the fashionable "Gothick" style and did much work for Sir Francis Dashwood at Medmenham Abbey. A specialist in grottoes, follies, mausolea and vaulted subterranean chambers for country houses. In his last years he devoted nearly all his energies to esoteric studies. Said to have died in a riot, or incarcerated in Bedlam. Details uncertain. Married. No issue.

▼ Manuscript fragment of Boswell's *Life of Dr. Johnson*, omitted from the published version, found among the Boswell Papers at Malahide Castle.

(July 1782)

Johnson and I took boat from York Stairs to where, in the Doctor's own immortal words,
"Greenwich smiles upon the silver flood"
—and from thence, as was our wont, we rambled on, till we reached the environs of Deptford. Finding ourselves in Hob's Lane, Johnson stopped abruptly and shook his great frame as if shivering from the cold, though in all conscience it was a very humid evening.

Boswell: *Why do you halt and shudder so?*

Johnson: Why, sir, I know this place of old, and it is a wicked place. Sir, it is thoroughly damned and abominable.

I looked around in some amazement at my mean but seemingly quiet surroundings. The lane held several dwellings of unequal size and elegance, but we were stopped before a building of some refinement which I knew — to my shame — to be Mrs. Hackett's establishment. It was then that I recalled that some years previously my friend had investigated with other men of science and learning some disturbances that occurred in this very lane.

Boswell: Is this not the site of the Hob's Lane Ghost, sir?

Johnson: Ghost, sir! There was no ghost, sir!

Boswell: Then it was an imposture?

Johnson: I did not say that. There are more things in Heaven and Earth, and in truth more things under the earth than ghosts. It is true that the natives of this place vulgarly took it for a ghost, for they had not the wit to conceive aught else. They are all blockheads about here, sir: blockheads or rogues. There was much talk of the dead gnawing at each other's bones beneath the ground and suchlike. I will say only this: that what some of us heard and one man, to his great ill-fortune, saw, was no phantasm, but something Hellish. And if ever a man received sure and certain knowledge of the torments of the life to come, the everlasting gnashing of teeth, and the punishment of the damned, it was I upon that night, sir, in Hob's Lane.

I would have pressed my friend further on the matter, but he would not have it, and so we rambled on. Those who are curious on the matter of the "Hob's Lane Disturbances", as they were called, I would refer to an article in the Gentleman's Magazine of March 1777. As we continued our walk, we came presently to the church of All Hallows which is on the road to Blackheath. Johnson stopped once more outside the wall that surrounds its graveyard and contemplated the edifice, a work of the celebrated architect and savant Thomas Moreby.

Johnson: This, I venture to think, is a very ill-favoured building.

Boswell: But you must own, sir, that its architect, Mr. Moreby, a pupil of the great Hawksmoor, is a man of some genius.

Johnson: Genius, sir! If there is such a thing as evil genius, then that I grant you. I verily believe that he built this edifice not as a monument to his Blessed Saviour, but as an insult to his Sovereign Maker. If ever a man cast a stone in the very face of God, that man is Thomas Moreby.

Boswell: Why — are you acquainted with him in person, then?

Johnson: I have been. It was in connection with the Hob's Lane affair. We had some words and, thinking to persuade me to his way of thinking, he revealed an intimate matter concerning my late wife Tetty and myself that I alone should know.

Boswell: But how did he acquire such information?

Johnson: By damnable sorcery, sir! By converse with the dead! There is no other explanation.

Boswell: But what was it, concerning Hob's Lane that he sought to persuade you of?

Johnson: Why, sir, to "let the sleeping dog lie", as he put it. He told me of things that slumber beneath the earth, that gather wisdom and strength in darkness but must not be troubled in their midnight vegetations. But, said he, there will come a time when their master shall summon them, and the dead will arise and conquer the earth.

Boswell: Why, what is this?

Johnson: Foul and blasphemous nonsense, sir!

Boswell: They say his Treatise on the Flea is a most curious and learned work.

Johnson: It is nothing but a farrago, sir, an olla podrida of magotty headed metaphysical nonsense. He would have us believe that the flea is a great instrument of regeneration. "Sir," I said to him, "I have an abomination of fleas. My poor cat Hodge was my most loved companion for many years, and the only objection that I ever had to this excellent creature was that he was much inclined to harbour the flea. I verily believe that if ever the Devil created any one thing on this earth it was the flea, and so I say to you: 'oak, oak!'" At which, I am glad to say, Mr. Moseby was much discomfited.

Boswell: But what is this "oak, oak"? *

Johnson: A magical incantation against the fleas, sir! From that instructive work, the Geoponica, by a Byzantine Greek of the seventh century. I had thought to put the words in my Dictionary, but wiser, or should I say more cautious, counsels prevailed. Nevertheless I do believe it to be a sovereign incantation against the flea and have often used it to my own most commodious satisfaction.

> This is yet another indication of my friend Dr. Johnson's contradictory character. He was by nature the most rational of men and yet there were certain superstitions that clung to his person as a burr does to a coat of broadcloth.

163c : Sup. -ώτατα X.*Eq*.6.1.
ὤφελλον, Ep. for ὤφελον, aor. 2 of ὀφείλω.
✳ ὤχ, ὤχ, a magical incantation against fleas, *Gp*.13.15.9.
ὠχεῖ, Egyptian name of ἀτράφαξυς, Ps.-Dsc.2.119.
ὤχνων (gen. pl.), dub. sens. in *POxy*.2146.11 (iii A.D.).
ὤχρα, ἡ, *yellow ochre*, Arist.*Mete*.378ᵃ23, Thphr.*Lap*.40, *PCair*.
Zen.764.13 (iii B.C.), Dsc.5.93, etc.   II. in corn, = ἐρυσίβη,

---

✳ From Liddell & Scott's Greek Lexicon (9th edition, 1968)

▼ From: *The Gentleman's Magazine*, March 1777:

UPON THE LATE DISTURBANCES IN HOB'S LANE

ON THE NIGHT OF Saturday the 1st of February 1777 many gentlemen eminent for their rank and character were, by the invitation of the Reverend Mr. Bacon, of All Hallows, Blackheath, assembled at the house of a Mrs. Hackett in Hob's Lane, for the examination of various noises supposed to be made by departed spirits. There had been much complaint in the neighbourhood of fearful and unnatural sounds emanating chiefly from beneath the earth. Many likened these noises to the cries of wild beasts, or to the groans of men in torment. All agreed that the sounds were to be heard most clearly in the environs of Mrs. Hackett's house, an educational establishment for young ladies. To the surprise of many, neither Mrs. Hackett nor her charges had added to the tumult of complaint, and so it was imagined by some that Mrs. Hackett's young ladies were the cause of the troubles. The Reverend Mr. Bacon and the other gentlemen who included the distinguished lexicographer Dr. Samuel Johnson sat rather more than an hour in Mrs. Hackett's parlour, and, hearing nothing, interrogated Mrs. Hackett who denied, in the strongest terms, any knowledge or belief of fraud on the part of her girls. Then a few of the company, as they stood in the entrance hall, did hear something which was like a groaning or rumbling, but so far off that none could tell whether it was coming from above or below.

A thorough investigation was made of the young ladies' rooms on the upper floors of the house and from them were recovered a number of items which might not generally be associated with the normal activities of young ladies at a seat of learning. Various musical instruments were discovered, including a trumpet, several kettledrums and a portable organ; together with manacles and chains, several pairs of riding boots, a curious leather seat on a rocking base, some whips and scourges for the taming of cattle or horses, spiked collars and a singular leather and brass harness that appeared to be designed for use by a human being rather than a beast. Mrs. Hackett claimed that all these objects were about to be employed in a theatrical performance of her girls' devising. Upon examination, the young ladies in question showed a disposition to be somewhat insolent towards the Reverend Mr. Bacon and his eminent companions, but no confession could be drawn from them. However, their general demeanour was enough to excite considerable suspicion among the company.

Only one other incident of note occurred. One of the Reverend Mr. Bacon's associates, Dr. Spufford, a medical practitioner, ventured on his own into the cellars beneath Mrs. Hackett's house while the others were examining the young ladies. On his return he appeared to be in a distracted state and spoke of "a great engine forever groaning" in the subterranean vaults and of monstrous forms "like those of giant insects" running to and fro in great spaces under the earth. Having spoken somewhat incoherently of these things Dr. Spufford was suddenly overcome and swooned to the ground. While attempts were being made to revive him, Mrs. Hackett vigorously denied that anything was to be found in her cellars apart from half a dozen old brandy barrels, and it was the vapours from these, the lady conjectured, that had been the cause of Dr. Spufford's wild imaginings. Notwithstanding her protestations, several gentlemen, including Dr. Johnson, insisted upon inspecting the said cellars, but found nothing noteworthy in them, apart from a singularly oppressive atmosphere which, they quickly concluded, was what had effected Dr. Spufford's seizure. It was, therefore, the general opinion of the remaining assembly that Mrs. Hackett's young ladies possessed some art of making or counterfeiting the noises heard, and that there was no agency of any higher, or lower, cause. Mrs. Hackett was accordingly admonished to keep her charges in better order before the company left.

It is with the deepest regret that *The Gentleman's Magazine* announces that Dr. Spufford has not recovered from his experiences in Hob's Lane and that the balance of his mind would seem to have been permanently affected. We understand that he has been removed to the country where he has been placed in the devoted care of his sister, Mrs. Eliza Whiteman.

Thomas Hudson pinxit 1762.

A TREATISE ON THE FLEA.

Thomas Moreby esq.
Ætat. 60

H. Oliver sculpsit.

▲ Frontispiece to *A Treatise on the Flea*, engraving from the portrait of Moreby by Thomas Hudson (1701–1779) – original now lost. The church tower in the background is believed to be that of All Souls, Blackheath.

*Verses by Gracious Permission addressed
to Sir Francis Dashwood, 15th Baron Le Despencer
by his Most Humble & Most Obedient Servant. Thos. Moreby esq.*

When *Satan* from the starry vault was hurl'd
He fell to earth and sought to rule the world,
And from his throne mid' subterranean fire
Now sov'reinty dispenses, now his ire.
There in the depths he marshals all his might
And *Gods Beneath* are summoned to the fight.
"All hail, great *Anarch*," cry they with one voice
"With dreadful clamour let all *Hell* rejoice!"
Then speaks their Lord "let not the trumpets bray
Before our Dark Designs have won the day.
Until our rule's supreme let none draw breath,
Nor triumph hold, till we have conquered *Death*.
All *Nature* answers to His fell command
Princes and priests are crushed beneath His hand.
But I shall conquer *Death*, and grant to all
Immortal Life, who answer to my call."
Thus spake the *Anarch*, and his stern decree
Went forth to put all peoples in his fee.

And still the cry goes out that *Death* shall fail
And *Life* in *Death* shall through the world prevail,
Essential Salts revivify the corse
And loose upon the earth the *Anarch Force*.
To this great end I dedicate my song,
All may be right, when all that's right is wrong.
In studies deep the midnight lamp I've burned
And now reveal the secrets I have learned.
I sing the *Flea* whose small and lowly mien
Shall through my *Science* dominate the scene.
And with this *Treatise* to all Men of Sense
Wisdom disclose, and Mysteries dispense.
O noble *Dashwood*, who in Caverns deep
Of Wycombe, sagest company doth keep.
Monarch of *Hell Fire*,[*] hearken to my lay
Approve me with your genius I pray.
Let sermons cavil, and let folly rant,
Unleash your Fire and castigate their cant;
Nor priest nor pedant dare objection raise
To what great *Dashwood* with his wit shall praise.
With wisdom from *Beneath* we'll strike the sky:
When *Life*'s consumed, then *Death* Himself shall die.

[*] Sir Francis Dashwood (1708–1781), wit and politician, who held
sessions of his infamous Hell Fire Club in caves on his estate at
West Wycombe, and later at Medmenham Abbey.

▼ Letters from Anna Whitby, daughter of Oliver Whitby, wine merchant of Cheapside, to her Cousin Miss Catherine Orlebar (Later Lady Melville, wife to the Lord Chief Justice of England) of Overton Court, Kent. The following letters were recently found in a sealed casket in an attic room of Overton Court. Attached to the casket was a paper in Catherine, Lady Melville's, hand with this inscription: NOT TO BE OPENED IN MY LIFETIME NOR IN THAT OF MY CHILDREN. The letters are here transcribed by Dr. Evelyn Hunt F.R.S.A. for the first time.

No.15 Cheapside
August 2nd, 1803

Dearest Cousin,

Your last letter gave me much pleasure, and excited – do not be astonished, my dear Catherine – a very sincere envy in me. You would chafe at the monotony and dullness of your life in the country, but to me it seems a <u>Sylvan Idyll</u> compared with the alarms and excursions of a town existence. London in high summer, as it now is, is a most abominable place, believe me. The putrid odours of waste that rise from every street and midden seem to hang in the air like a miasma. I would fain fly to your country retreat to be with you, dearest Catherine, and breathe untainted air, but business keeps my father in the town and, since poor Mama's death, he will barely let me from his side. This is doubly agitating since it prevents me from seeing my beau Melville of whom I told you in my last letter. Though poor, he is of good family, being the younger son of a Baronet. He eats his dinners in Gray's Inn and will, one day, I am assured, be a great man of the Law. Two days ago Father let me out in the evening with my servant Jane and we walked in Vauxhall gardens. There, by a previous secret arrangement, I was able to snatch a few stolen moments with my Melville.

Yesterday, my father brought to the house a man whom I had not met before, whether an acquaintance or business colleague of his I cannot tell. His name is Mr. Moreby. In appearance he is a very proper, gentlemanlike man whom I would put in his forties, though it is hard to tell his age. I cannot say that I like him, though I do not know why I do not, for he has a most courteous, if old fashioned, address, but Father seemed very anxious that I should make him welcome, and so I did. He has strong features and a very piercing eye with which he watched me avidly in intervals between talking over some business with my father. Presently he asked me where and when I was born. On being informed,

Mr. Moreby smiled, patted my hand – which I did not care for – and said: "I congratulate you, my dear. You were born under a most favourable conjunction." I did not know what he meant and would have asked him, only he turned his attention back to business with my father who, with a look and a gesture, intimated that I must leave the room. I do not like Mr. Moreby.

The servant has just come into the room conveying a message from my father that Mr. Moreby will be here once again, within the hour, and that I am to prepare to receive him. In haste therefore I finish this letter, hoping, nay entreating, my dearest Catherine, that you will write back to me directly.

Ever your loving and affectionate cousin,

Anna

<hr />

No.15 Cheapside
August 15th, 1803

My dearest Catherine,

I received your last letter with the greatest delight, and thank you most sincerely for it. You call your country gossip dull, but, believe me, Cousin, I rejoice at it. Would that my life were as dull! For, since my last letter, a number of incidents have occurred which fill me with the most profound alarm and agitation.

Mr. Moreby, of whom I told you in my last, began to visit my father's house almost daily, sometimes twice in a day. The ostensible reason for these calls was business – Mr. Moreby has a wide acquaintance among the nobility and has promised to secure contracts from them for my father to supply wines to them – but increasingly he has begun to pay court to me. I need not tell you how unwelcome his attentions have been. Not only to I find his person disgusting – albeit without definite cause – but, as you know, my heart is given elsewhere, to Mr. Melville. Mr. Melville is yet without fortune or gainful occupation, but we have given to each other those secret promises that only the heart can give, and we are prepared to wait until our union can be blessed with material security.

On several occasions my father left me alone in the front parlour with Mr. Moreby and would not allow me to escape. Mr. Moreby, it is true, conducted himself perfectly properly, for his manners are most gentlemanlike, but my unease grew on every occasion that I had intercourse alone with him. He takes a great interest in all my doings and has wormed from me all manner of admissions concerning my poor young life that I would barely have thought to confide even to you, or my Melville. When, in return, I asked some things concerning himself, I received the vaguest and most vapid responses. I understand that he is an architect, and a man of considerable means, the possessor of much property in London, but beyond that I know nothing. When I sought, by the politest means possible, to enquire his age, I was met with nothing but evasion. Indeed, a warning look from him indicated that I should not pursue the matter further.

I told you in my last letter that I had thought him to be forty, but now I am less certain. He is a vigorous and active man with an upright bearing, but there is something about his lean face that appears worn, as if it were something very old that has been carefully preserved. The eyes, moreover, whose irises are of the palest grey, are, when not animated by some fierce, inscrutable passion, curiously dull and weary, like those of a very ancient and tired man. His hands are firm and strong but quite horribly cold. I dread his touch.

Yesterday evening, after Mr. Moreby had gone, I told my father that I did not care for Mr. Moreby and that henceforth I would not be left alone in his company. My father's response to this was very strange. He looked fearfully at me and then proceeded to beg me to continue to entertain Mr. Moreby. I told him that I would not yield until he revealed to me the exact nature of his relations with this person.

As you know, Catherine, when my dear mother – your aunt – was alive, it was she who managed the wine business which she had inherited from our grandfather. Since her death, I was aware that there had been a falling off in its prosperity, but I had not known till now the extent of the decline. My father is not a precise man of business and he has a great weakness for cards at which he has sustained heavy losses. In short, I discover that he is greatly in Mr. Moreby's debt and that without this man's continued support we are all but destitute.

It was a most shameful and distressing scene. My poor father went on his knees and begged me to show Mr. Moreby some kindness. He even suggested that I should welcome his addresses as a suitor for my hand! When he saw the anger and astonishment on my face, he retracted this last proposal, but I could tell that he is full of fear.

What is this man Moreby that he should hold my poor father like an insect in his hand? And what am I to do? I have written to Melville explaining my peril, and now to you, dear Cousin. I know there is nothing you can do, but it is some small consolation to be assured that you understand and feel sympathy for—

Your most unhappy but devoted cousin,

Anna

Moreby House, Blackheath
September 13th, 1803

Dearest Cousin,

You will be surprised to hear from me after so long an interval, but you will be still further astonished to hear that I am married, and to Mr. Moreby! I am almost fearful to write this, seeing as I do in my imagination the look of reproach in your eyes as you read the above sentence, but bear with me, I beg you, and have pity on your most dejected and miserable friend.

The day after I had sent my last letter to you Mr. Moreby came to the house. I kept to my room, hoping to avoid seeing him altogether, but even there I could not avoid hearing him. My father and he were having a most violent altercation in the front parlour and the noise could be heard all over the house. Finally I heard my father come out of the chamber and into the hall at the foot of the stairs. He called up to me, requesting that I should come down stairs to meet Mr. Moreby who had something very particular to say to me.

Imagine, dearest Catherine, how my heart beat in my breast with apprehension, as I descended the stairs. Both men were standing in the hall below me. My father trembled like an aspen leaf, but Moreby was motionless, his pale eyes fixed upon me. I swear that he did not even draw breath during my descent. A curious smile distorted his lips.

Without a word my father ushered me into the parlour and then stood behind Mr. Moreby facing me while Mr. Moreby stepped forward and took my hand in his icy fingers.

"My dear, Anna," said he, "your father has kindly consented to grant me the honour of asking for your hand in marriage."

Picture, if you will, my consternation! It took me some little while to compose myself, and all the while I felt the eyes of Mr. Moreby upon me. It was then that I became aware of an element of uncertainty, even discomfiture in Mr. Moreby's look. He had some feelings, after all, of the kind we call human and, for all his air of invincibility, it hurt him to think that my senses were disgusted at him. This gave me courage, even though I could see my father standing behind him and staring at me with imploring eyes.

"Mr. Moreby," said I, "I am very sensible of the honour you have done me. I must own that it is very sudden, but I feel I owe it to myself, to my dear father and to you to give it my most earnest consideration. Allow me therefore the privilege of youth, that is: a little time for reflection upon your momentous offer. When you next have the goodness to attend upon me, sir, you shall have your answer."

I saw a mixture of relief and agitation in my father's face, and untrammelled annoyance in Mr. Moreby's. Nevertheless he bowed to me and bent over my hand as if to kiss it. I felt his icy breath on the backs of my fingers.

"I shall attend upon you in the forenoon tomorrow, then," he said.

"Pardon me, sir," said I, "but you are too hasty. Well was it said that the impetuosity of youth is as nothing to the impatience of old age—" At this Mr. Moreby glared at me with such ferocity that I was all but struck dumb. Nevertheless, I continued: "If you will have the goodness to be here in the forenoon of the day after tomorrow, I shall promise you an answer that will put you in no doubt as to my feelings on the matter." And with that I left the room.

At once I retired to my room and scribbled a note to Mr. Melville which I dispatched by my faithful servant Jane. The following day I asked my father if I, accompanied by Jane, might take a walk in Hyde Park that afternoon. My father was very reluctant, but I prevailed upon him by saying that my answer to Mr. Moreby depended upon my being given the freedom to reflect upon the decision he had imposed on me.

Accordingly at three o'clock I found myself in Hyde Park where a Post Chaise was waiting for me. With Jane who was carrying a few humble necessaries for the journey, I got in and was conveyed thence North to the village of Finchley. There, Jane left me and I was joined by Mr. Melville who had ridden from Gray's Inn. He entered the carriage and bade the coachman drive North with all speed.

I thought my happiness complete. Within two days we would be North of the border at Gretna Green where our Union could be legitimised. Mr. Melville took my hand and poured out to me the passionate longings of his heart while the Post Chaise rattled and bumped Northwards from Finchley.

But our elopement was short-lived. We had gone barely ten miles from Finchley and had not yet reached the outskirts of Barnet when my Melville, looking behind him through the back window of the carriage, drew my attention to three dark and cloaked figures on horseback fast gaining on our carriage.

"Highwaymen!" He said and put his head out of the window of the chaise to urge our coachman to make greater speed. Just then we heard a shot fired and a ball sang past Mr. Melville's head which he promptly withdrew into the carriage. Then another shot and we felt a kind of bump above our heads while at the same time the pace of the chaise seemed to slacken.

"By God, they've got the coachman!" cried Melville who, while the carriage was still in motion, climbed out of the window and onto the coachman's box to take over the reins. By this time, however, the horses had slackened their pace to a trot and the horsemen were upon us. The coachman, mortally wounded, tumbled off the box of his own volition. Melville put up a bold resistance but was knocked into a ditch by two of the riders to be left for dead. I do not know at this moment if he lives or not because presently the third man entered the carriage. I was seized, blindfolded, gagged and my hands tied.

My mind can recall mercifully little of that ride back South to my father's house. I know only that my captors were rough and uncouth. Their voices were barely intelligible, more like the groans of wild beasts than the articulations of rational beings. By the time I had been conveyed – still bound and blindfolded – to my father's house, rage had superseded despair. Then, as I lay where I had been thrown, on my bed, a kind of calm, cold and still, settled on my mind.

The following morning I was untied and the blindfold taken from my eyes. I realised that throughout the night I had been attended by two guardians whom I had never seen before, a man and a woman, large folk, slabby of face and dull of eye. I noticed that whenever I made to move they tensed themselves in preparation for an onslaught. Presently my father came into the room, his face a wreck of guilt and anguish so that I felt only pity for him.

With tears in his eyes, he explained to me that unless I consented to marry Mr. Moreby, he was ruined, and the rest of his days would be spent in the Fleet Prison for debt. He begged my forgiveness for the misfortune he had heaped upon me, but at the same time implored me to save him from ignominious destitution.

Coldly I told him that I would agree to his request at which he fell upon me with many tears and protestations of love, but I shook him off. I ordered one of the guardians who were still in the room to remove him from my sight. The man obeyed with heavy reluctance at the second time of my asking. Dry-eyed, I saw the look of despair in my father's face as he realised that my love for him had, by his actions, been extinguished for ever.

I will not tell in detail the days that followed. Mr. Moreby visited me once to tell me when and where I was to be joined to him in holy matrimony. I affected to show not the slightest emotion at his announcement and I saw that this displeased him.

And so, on Wednesday last in the afternoon, I was taken by my father in a closed carriage to the church of All Hallows in Blackheath where, by the Reverend Mr. Bacon, the ancient rector of that parish, I was united to Mr. Moreby. The only other person present at the ceremony, apart from Mr. Bacon, my father, Mr. Moreby and myself was a decrepit pew opener who was given sixpence to sign the register as witness. No organ played, no choir sang. I looked into the eyes of Mr. Bacon and saw only the feeble terror of solitary old age. He too was somehow in thrall to Moreby.

There was no wedding breakfast; there was no nuptial journey. I was carried at once to Mr. Moreby's house in Blackheath. It is a great place with many rooms, but singularly bare of furniture, pictures or of any common comforts. There appear to be many servants in the house but what they do is a mystery to me. I insisted that my maid Jane must be with me, to which Mr. Moreby, with a very ill grace, eventually assented.

And now, my dearest Catherine, I must trespass upon your delicacy and relate to you what passed between me and my husband when we retired to our chamber that night. It would not have been my desire to acquaint you with the secrets of the marriage bed – which, I doubt not you will soon discover for yourself and in happier circumstances than I – but I must, for it has filled me with strange forebodings.

There was at least a fire in the bedchamber and my Jane had seen to a warming pan. I had gone up to prepare for the groom's arrival with what apprehensions stirring in my breast you may readily imagine. I was preparing to offer up my maidenhood to a man that I abominated before all others.

I had waited some considerable time in my shift and with my hair combed and brushed by the faithful Jane when he arrived. I will not say he was drunk but there was brandy on his breath. Summarily he dismissed Jane who was all too happy to quit the scene. Then, seating himself in a chair, he bade me stand before the fire and remove my shift. His eyes never left me as I proceeded to do so. I asked if I could now get into bed, but he said I was not to do so but to walk to and fro, naked as I was, in the roseate glow of the fire. You will ask me why I obeyed him so readily, but he had a sword with him which he had drawn and was waving carelessly before me, its thin, polished blade and needle point glinting red and gold in the firelight. While watching hungrily as I walked to and fro before the fire he – I blush to recall it, dear Catherine – he proceeded to do what men do when, as I understand it, they wish to pleasure themselves. When this was done, a kind of dullness overtook him. He bade me put on my shift again and get into bed.

He rose from his chair and came to stand over me in the bed.

"You may wonder," said he, "why I do not cut off the flower of your maidenhead as is my right, but I have consulted our horoscopes. I am looking to a favourable aspect for our first congress. When Venus is in alignment with Saturn, then you must prepare yourself for the great moment."

"And when will that be, sir?" I asked in trepidation.

"It shall be when I tell you, my lady," said he sharply and quitted the room.

And so you may say, dear Cousin, that it is the stars which have hitherto saved me from the loss of my virgin patent. Yet every night since that first one Mr. Moreby has come to my room – I call it mine for my husband chooses to sleep, or not as the case may be, elsewhere – commanded me to walk naked before the fire and pleasured himself by this spectacle. You may readily imagine, dearest Catherine, the unspeakable humiliation which these nocturnal events occasion in my breast.

During the day, I rarely see him, and am not permitted to leave the house unless I am accompanied by at least one of his servants. These servants of his are a very curious breed. They are both male and female, large, lumbering, dull of eye and incoherent of speech. My maid Jane, who sees more of them than I do, tells me that they shun the light whenever they can and keep the windows of their quarters shuttered. Needless to say my Jane cares for them no more than I do. "It is as if they are of another race," she says.

One curious incident concerning them I will relate.

Though, I have difficulty in going out, I am given the liberty of the house and one of my few pleasures is to make use of Mr. Moreby's library whose shelves are filled with many curious volumes. One afternoon I was in the library, reading The Life and Opinions of Tristram Shandy which I had the delight of finding there, when I heard a curious noise. At that time of day the house is usually as silent as the grave: one can hear a mouse trot, or a fly fall into a spider's web. This noise appeared to come from behind that part of the panelled wall of the library on which hung Mr. Hudson's portrait of my husband. It was a kind of low, querulous mumbling sound like several old men quarrelling over a trifle.

I went over to that part of the room from which the noise came and listened intently, but could make out nothing distinctly. When I examined the panelling on which the portrait hung I observed a long straight groove in the wood, as if the portrait were concealing a secret door. A closer look revealed that the door could be opened by sliding down two small metal studs in the panel which released a bolt of some kind. The door swung open to disclose a short, dark passageway leading to another door at the end of it. The sound of mumbling was now louder.

I walked down the passage to the other door which was opened by the simple lifting of a wooden latch. I opened the door.

I cannot even now quite explain the mysterious horror which the scene I beheld excited in me. Perhaps I had best merely describe it to you. The room I had entered was entirely without windows and lit solely by a few smoky rush lights and a fire that burned in a tiny grate. The atmosphere was unbearably hot and stifling. My presence was not immediately noticed, so I was able for some moments to spy upon the scene unobserved.

At a long table in the centre of the room were seated seven people, four men, three women, whom I recognised as being some of Mr. Moreby's servants. They were in the process of eating a dinner, and the altercation, as I surmised, had arisen over who was to have the largest share of the food that was set upon the table. No cutlery of any kind was in evidence and they were eating it with their bare hands.

But the worst of it was the food itself. Imagine my revulsion when I saw that it was raw flesh, uncooked. What the flesh itself was I cannot say. I saw traces of smooth whitish skin, and some black skin too. It most probably came from a pig, though a most unusual one without bristles on its hide. When these servants were aware of my presence they looked dumbly at me but made no move. Two of them who had been tearing apart between them what looked like the upper thigh of a hog dropped the red flesh on the floor. It fell with a sound like a slap, and a splash of blood. The meat, whatever it was, must have been very fresh.

I turned and retreated through the door, closing it behind me. When I reached the library I bolted the panelled door. My heart raced; my breast heaved at the mysterious horror of what I had just witnessed.

While I was in that library I made one further discovery which may strike you as scarce credible, but which I assure you is true.

I have told you that on the panel which was a hidden door, there was a portrait of my husband by Mr. Hudson. What had struck me as curious was that though Mr. Moreby now looks scarcely older than his portrait, in that picture he is dressed in a very old fashioned suit of clothes. When I examined the picture more closely I discovered it to be signed and dated thus:

Thos. Hudson pinxit 1762

It was painted over forty years ago! And I had taken my husband to be now in his forties or fifties! Diligently I began to search the library for some clue to my husband's true age. At last I found it in the shape of a copy of his <u>Treatise on the Flea</u>. There was a frontispiece engraving of this very portrait and, in a cartouche below it, the following:

Thomas Moreby esq. Aetat. 60

Good heaven! The man was sixty in 1762! That means he is now over a hundred! What can this mean? Only conceive my astonishment and dismay!

The rest of the day I spent in dread that the servants might tell Mr. Moreby of my adventure in their quarters, but when he came to my room that night for his nocturnal amusement, he said nothing. I suspect that the servants too are afraid of my husband and that in any case they are too inarticulate and slow-witted to express themselves rationally. This may yet work to my advantage.

As I told you, my husband is seldom at home during the day, and I do not go about with him, but last week Mr. Moreby took me to see the mad folk in Bedlam. It was a curious spectacle which I have never beheld before, though I have often heard speak of. The unfortunate creatures are displayed, some in open rooms, some – the more dangerous – behind the bars of cells or in specially constructed cages. Here you will see men and women of every class and degree, some clothed in finery, others next to naked, but all distracted and most of them seemingly oblivious of the scrutiny which is directed towards them by their fashionable observers. But I have brought this subject up out of no idle intention to divert you with the sights of London, but for a purpose. What occurred there, dear Cousin, was most curious and, to me, strangely alarming.

As we were shown around the place by one of the asylum's custodians – a villainous looking fellow in all conscience and perhaps little better than his charges – Mr. Moreby was in his most animated mood and, as a man of Science, endeavoured to explain to me his theories of mental derangement which I cannot remember exactly but had to do, if I remember rightly, with "an imbalance of essential salts" or some such. Be that as it may, I remember that when we entered the first room where the patients were housed, he was talking of this. The occupants were all women, quite respectable and decently clothed if not in their right minds. Our guide, whose name was Jacob Sims, told me that they were ones who were "melancholy mad", and in truth they were very subdued and withdrawn in their behaviour. However, when they caught sight of Mr. Moreby, I noticed that a change came over them. They began to mutter fearfully together and withdraw into the corner of the room furthest from him. When, with a show of good humour, he approached them, they either cowered where they stood with a great show of terror, or scuttled away from him into another, more distant corner. My husband seemed quite undisconcerted by their reaction; indeed he laughed, remarking that "These distracted creatures at least recognise the presence of a Great One." Sims, our cicerone, expressed some concern, but Mr. Moreby put silver in his hand, and commanded him to show us more.

As we passed from room to room, their occupants offered the same reaction to Mr. Moreby. Then we came to a row of single rooms with barred doors like prison cells in which, we were told, the most dangerous patients were incarcerated. These people too cowered back onto their wretched straw bedding when they saw my husband pass. He paid little attention to these unfortunates until he came to one particular cell at the end of the row.

Having peered in, Mr. Moreby tapped on the bars with his cane and peremptorily commanded Sims to open it. Sims said that he dare do no such thing, for that particular cell contained the most violent and dangerous inmate in all Bedlam.

My husband turned on him with a venomous look.

"Do you know who I am? I could have you removed from your situation this very instant if I so wished. You will do as I command. I take full responsibility. No danger will come to any of us. I have a means of quelling the madness of these creatures. Open the cell door, damn you!"

Sims did as he was told without further argument.

The man who confronted us was squat and dark with a brooding insolence written on his countenance. When he saw Mr. Moreby he let out a sharp cry and began to grovel on the floor of his cell.

"I see you have come to your senses at last, Verney," said Mr. Moreby with a mocking sneer.

At this Sims was much amazed and asked my husband if he knew the patient, at which he received a sharp "Mind your business, damn you, you poxy turnkey!" All the while this Verney was crawling about his cell, searching in his straw and seemingly picking up small things in his fingers and eating them.

"What are you doing, Verney, you lunatic dog?" said Moreby.

"I have found the elixir of life!" Verney replied. At this he held up something between his thumb and forefinger so small that I could barely see it. It was an insect and, as I later ascertained, a flea. This he raised above his open mouth and, by crushing the creature between his digits, sprinkled a tiny drop of foul fluid onto his tongue.

Mr. Moreby, thrusting teasingly at him with the end of his cane, addressed him thus, in a low, sneering tone: "You have found nothing of the kind, damn your soul to perdition. You were vain enough to think you could steal secrets from me. But wisdom comes from within. Learn this, my idiot friend: a book, however great, is but a mirror: when a fool looks into it he sees only the ape's face of his own folly. If you are so wise, how is it that you come to be here in this cell?"

Such was the scorn and contempt in my husband's voice that I almost thought to pity this Verney who was by now cowering and snarling on the stinking straw of his bed. Mr. Moreby turned away from Verney and made to leave the cell, signifying to Sims that he should lock it as soon as he was out.

"Wait!" cried Verney. "Master, wait! I have something to show you!"

Mr. Moreby turned and, waving Sims aside, went back into the cell, holding a scented handkerchief up to his nose to abate the stench. Verney scrabbled in a great heap of foul straw and, to my astonishment, drew out a model in miniature of a building made from card and paper, a thing of exquisite workmanship. It was a temple or church, somewhat resembling my husband's design of All Hallows, Blackheath, but with more of the Gothick style about it. Verney's eyes gleamed as he held it up for our inspection, then, with one hand he removed the front of the building, in a single piece of card, to reveal the interior which, if possible, was even more perfectly fashioned than the exterior.

We all three stared in astonishment, but our surprise was not complete, for the interior of the temple appeared to be populated with miniature moving figures! At an altar, a tiny creature in a tabard of black cloth appeared to be officiating at some ceremony while on the altar, fixed by thin threads of cotton, was another animated creature waving its limbs in the air in an agony of helplessness. Further figures were dragging about wagons attached to them by threads. These wagons had in them images like pagan idols. Others, fixed to the floor, were waving very little needles, like swords, at each other. I looked closer. Every figure was a flea.

"How dare you steal my designs!" cried Mr. Moreby. The next instant he had snatched the model from Verney's hands, dashed it to the ground and trampled it into fragments. The lovely thing was now a piece of rubbish. Verney let out a howl like a dog in agony, and began to glare at my husband with bestial ferocity. Mr. Moreby retreated from the cell and Sims had just turned the key in the door before Verney sprang at the bars to get at us. Mr. Moreby laughed and thrust at Verney through the bars with his stick.

"Do not fret, my old friend," he cried mockingly, "you have all the time in the world to recreate your foolish little toy."

With a sudden movement Verney seized my husband's cane – which had a great amethyst bound with gold in its top – drew it through the bars, and, putting it up to his mouth, bit it in half, like a dog. I heard the wretched man's teeth crack in the execution of this feat. Enraged, my husband made to draw his sword but he was restrained by Sims who said: "Come away, sir! Come away! You have done enough!" With a very ill grace Mr. Moreby consented to go, and very soon we had left that dreadful place.

When we were in the carriage going back to Blackheath I asked Mr. Moreby who this Verney was.

"He was the maker of my architectural models. A good craftsman in his humble way, but he stole from me and left my employment without permission." There was a silence and then my husband put his face horribly close to mine and almost whispered these words at me: "I brought you to Bedlam, madam, not for your amusement, but for your instruction. Now you have seen what becomes of those creatures of mine who run from me."

One further thing, my dearest Catherine, I must tell you, before I despatch Jane with this letter. This house, which is virtually my prison, has few visitors but yesterday afternoon as I was coming down stairs after my rest I heard voices coming from the library. The door which opens onto the hall was ajar and I stationed myself so that I could see through it. None of my husband's servants seemed to be about so I felt comparatively safe.

Mr. Moreby was leaning carelessly against the mantelpiece and was talking to a stout woman in her middle years, with a painted face and a beauty patch above her right eyebrow. Her clothes were gaudy and cheap, and she had a most unladylike air about her. I wondered what her business was in my husband's house.

"We have kept an eye on her, sir," she was saying. "She does not stray from the house except to see her father."

"And that maid of hers?"

"What maid? You said nothing about a maid."

"Damn you, do I have to spell out every instruction? She has a little maid who may run errands for her. I want her watched as well, damn you. Do you understand, Mrs. Hackett?"

"I will oblige you, Mr. Moreby."

"And all is prepared for the October Sabbath?"

"The invitations are sent. All is in order, sir. But it seems a shame—"

"What are you talking about now, you damned old harridan?"

"Such a pretty face, and quite unmarked by the pox. I hid behind a pillar and stole a glance at her when you were in All Hallows. It's becoming harder by the day to find young girls like that, and her by way of being a lady too. She could make us a fortune."

"Hold your tongue, you old fool! You know not what you are talking of. October the 7th is the day. All the planetary aspects are favourable. It is a great work that I do, one of which you in your foul and petty world have no conception. Have you my money for the last quarter?"

At this moment I heard a servant entering the hall, and so I thought my best course was to make myself known. I opened the door and entered the library, feigning surprise as I did so to see my husband with another woman. Mr. Moreby's eyes flashed anger at me.

"My dear, do you never think to knock when you enter my library?"

"Sir," said I, "you are never at home during the day. Thus I did not expect to find you here, and in company too." Then turning to the woman, I said: "Madam, I believe I have not had the pleasure of your acquaintance till now."

In the curtest possible tones Mr. Moreby performed the introductions: "Mrs. Hackett – my wife, Mrs. Moreby."

"Charmed, I'm sure, ma'am," said Mrs. Hackett attempting a curtsey with a dreadful simper.

"Mrs. Hackett runs an educational establishment for young ladies in Hob's Lane, hard by All Hallows."

"Wherein, I am sure, they are taught many elegant accomplishments," said I. Both my husband and Mrs. Hackett looked at me searchingly, but were met with the blandest of countenances. Young, I may be, unschooled in the ways of the world perhaps, but I am not a fool. I know a bawd when I see one.

I walked over to the table by the window, whereon lay the volume of <u>Tristram Shandy</u> that I was reading. I picked it up, explaining that this was my purpose in visiting the library; then, having begged them to excuse me, I quitted the room and went quickly up the main stairs. When I was on the first landing I turned to see my husband in the hall looking up at me enquiringly. It was a deep and penetrating gaze and I believe that had I let him hold my eyes for any length of time I might have revealed to him all the secrets of my heart.

Wednesday, 20th September

This letter has been a long one, for I am afforded few opportunities of sending it, as I intend to, by Jane who is the only person I can entrust with the task. But I am glad to have kept it back, for Jane came with some news just now which gladdened my heart immeasurably. My Melville is not dead! He was severely injured by the attack upon the coach and is still recovering. Now, having almost resigned myself to my fate, I am tormented by hopes of salvation. I send this to you at the same time as I send a letter to Mr. Melville in hopes that my two missives will find both of you in better spirits than

Your unfortunate cousin,

Anna

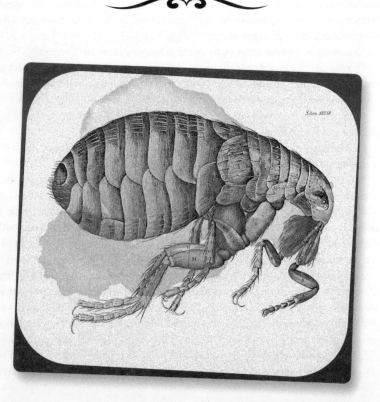

Moreby House, Blackheath
October 1st, 1803

Dearest Cousin,

One dreadful misfortune falls on another, not the least of which was Mr.
Moreby's dismissal of my servant Jane. He would give no reason for his
action, but I doubt not that Mrs. Hackett's spies were responsible. Moreover,
nearly all my father's servants have been discharged and replaced by
creatures of my husband Moreby. Only two ancient retainers remain, by one
of whom, my father's butler Spencer, I send this letter in fervent hopes that
it will reach you.

After overhearing the curious intercourse between my husband and Mrs
Hackett I became more than ever aware that I was being watched. This great
dark house in Blackheath is become a prison, and Mr. Moreby my principal
gaoler. Though he has on occasion allowed me to visit my father it is never
without an escort of one or more of his detestable servants. They have no
conversation, their persons are unpleasing to look at and the odour they exude is
become so unbearable that I am compelled to carry with me at all times an orange
stuck with cloves to dispel the foetid stench of decay. Such is its pervasive power,
indeed, that I can always tell when one of these loathsome creatures is in the
vicinity. Unseen and unheard, they yet announce their presence to my nostrils
which, I suppose, has its advantages.

I have become increasingly apprehensive about my husband's movements. I
have told you that during the day he was nearly always absent, but it struck me
as curious that I rarely saw him leave the house. We might meet at breakfast –
at which, I might add, he never speaks to me and scarcely eats – then I would
see him go into the library. In the course of the next hour it would become clear
that he had left the house for I would find the library empty, and the servants,
upon being asked where their master was, would mumble that he had "gone out".

Yesterday I determined to find a solution to this mystery. Having seen Mr.
Moreby enter the library shortly after breakfast I kept an eye upon the library
door without, I think, arousing suspicion from my husband's servants who are,
in all conscience, slow-witted blockheads to a man and woman. When above an
hour had passed, I went to the door of the library, opened it and found, as I had
feared, that the room was innocent of Mr. Moreby's presence. Yet there was
evidence that he <u>had</u> been there.

Two books lay on the table by the window, one open, the other shut. The
smaller of the two, which was unopened, was crudely bound in black vellum.
On looking inside I discovered it to be a kind of note book, hand written in a

very crabbed, antique style, mostly in black, but some in a dark red ink, like the colour of rust. The front page was inscribed in a great flourish <u>Liber de Nigra Peregrinatione</u>, which means <u>The Book concerning the Black Pilgrimage</u>. Underneath, the following had been scrawled in an orthography and spelling of over a hundred years back:

> "Accounte of a journeye, anno 1672, in which I, Amos Motherby*, visited the Black Cathedral in the Citie of Chorazin, and therein sawe many wondrous and terrible things and learned of the secrets that may not be known by the common herde of men. I took therefrom a companion, factotum, or as the vulgar have it, familiar and also many secret formularies concerning Essential Saltes and how the Essential Saltes of a man may be prepared and preserved in a depe and secret place, without any criminal Necromancy, so that, when expos'd to pure humoures, his shape may defie the worm and be rais'd up from whereinto his Bodie has been layed, to walk amongst his fellowes againe."

The rest of this book was mostly written in Shelton's short hand writing, or <u>tachygraphy</u> such as I have seen my father use in his journals and account books, but I felt no inclination to set myself to decipher it. Nevertheless, in looking through it, I came across one item of note. It was a drawing in black ink, crudely done, but most strange and alarming. It was of a creature, and whether it was human or not I cannot easily say. I might say it was half-human, for it was dressed in some kind of ragged robe with a cowl that covered most of its head. (Mercifully perhaps!) It appeared to be in motion, albeit of a crooked and shambling kind, and I did not care to look at it long. Underneath had been written the following in Latin:

> <u>Vera imago comitis quem apportavi ex urbe Chorazinis, nomine Anarchon, aut Ille qui Spectat in Caligine</u>.
> "The true image of the companion I took out of the city of Chorazin, his name being Anarchon or The One who Watches in Darkness."

I shut this book and turned my attention to the other volume on the table.

The second book was a printed folio which had been taken from a high shelf. It was Alexander of Pergamon's <u>De Morbis Siderum</u> (<u>Concerning the Diseases of the Stars</u>), a book of the fifth century after Christ, this edition printed at Genoa

---

* It may or may not be significant that Amos Motherby is an anagram of Thomas Moreby. Evelyn Hunt F.R.S.A.

in 1602. I speak as if I know the book intimately which I do not, but I have seen a similar copy to it in my father's study. He was poring over the book one day and, when I taxed him with it, he seemed vexed. With reluctance he told me that the volume was a prime manual of divination and that with it he could calculate the most favourable aspects for him to win at the gaming table. If this is so, then I can only conclude that it has served him very ill.

The book contained many tables with dates and planetary signs in them which struck me as of little interest, but there were passages in Latin in between them. One sentence in particular on the page where it lay open attracted my attention for it had been marked by a small red triangle in the margin.

Tertio die Novae Lunae, Saturno cum Venere conjugente, tum, sanguine virginis in die suae nativitatis, dominetur Daemon Anarchon, qui nonnunquam appellatur, Pulicarius, vel Magister Pulicum, cuius sub regno immane resurgant Dementes Mortui, etiamque Terra terrore contremebit. "On the third day of the new moon when Saturn is in conjunction with Venus, then, by the blood of a virgin upon the day of her nativity, the Demon Anarchon, often called 'Flea Bearer' or 'Master of Fleas', may rule, under whose monstrous reign the Witless Dead shall rise and even the Earth shall tremble with terror."

At another time and in other circumstances this passage might not have struck me so forcibly, nor made my heart beat violently within my breast, but I knew my Almanack. In four days from now there is to be a new moon, and three days after that on the 7th of October it is my nineteenth birthday, the day of my nativity. With trembling fingers I shut the book, then, recollecting that if he saw it shut, my husband would know that I had read the odious passage, I frantically searched through the book to find it again, and lay it open at the same page.

When I had done so I cast about me to think what I should do. I knew that I must get a message to you and to my Melville, but for that I needed permission from Mr. Moreby to visit my father. I looked out of the library into the hall and saw one of our footmen sitting dully before the front door. His eyes were open and as soon as he became aware of my presence they fixed themselves upon me with a kind of dogged watchfulness. I knew that I could not get past him. I had tried before and failed.

It then occurred to me that I must find the secret egress from the library which my husband undoubtedly used. I rejected the door that I had found the other day which only led to the servants' quarters and began to look for another way. I searched the panelling, but could find no crack or device which might indicate a door. It then occurred to me that one of the bookcases might be a door, the most likely being one which stood to the left of the fireplace with bare panelling on either side of it. It seemed secure. I then examined the books in the case. They were a dull collection, mostly of ecclesiastical volumes, unlikely to interest even my husband. One set of books, a three volume edition of Porter's Clavis Secretorum (Porter's Key of Secrets) appeared to be false. The three books were stuck together. Then I remembered that "porta" is a door. I tried to pull the object out of the bookcase but it would not move. Then I discovered that the front of the bindings appeared to be detachable. By further manipulation I contrived to lift up the front of the binding and disclose an empty space within, but not quite empty! There was a lever inside which I pulled down and by this manoeuvre the whole bookcase slid sideways away from the fireplace to reveal an entrance.

Confronted by my success, I felt even more apprehensive. The space that had been opened up to me was a mere passageway leading to a flight of stone steps which descended into darkness. I shut the bookcase door and went to find a candle to light my way.

When I came out of the library two of my husband's great lumpish servants, a man and a woman, were in the hall, mumbling together. On seeing me they ceased their colloquy and their eyes followed me as I went up stairs. This determined me to conceal my candle and the wherewithal to light it under my skirts as I came down stairs again. Their gaze followed me as I once more entered the library which, taking an extra precaution, I locked from the inside, placing the key in my bodice between my breasts, then, having lit the candle, I proceeded, with all trepidation, to descend the steps on the far side of the library's bookcase. At every step of the descent I stopped to listen for any sound but could hear nothing but my own beating heart.

Only conceive my astonishment, dearest Catherine, when, on reaching the bottom of the steps I found myself in a vast vaulted chamber, scarce a quarter of which my poor candle could illumine. On every side I was assailed with strange sights, for the place was filled with the most curious devices and objects.

If you have ever seen in some old engraving the depiction of an alchemist's den, then you will have some notion of what I saw. To one side was a great athanor or alchemist's furnace whose chimney must have connected with the library's fireplace. Around the vault on shelves and tables were ranged many great vessels and retorts of glass, and in a row of glass jars on one shelf I saw innumerable creatures and monstrosities suspended in a clear, somewhat yellow liquid: babies with two heads, fish with legs, the head of a man with a mouth in his forehead and other abominations which I cannot bring myself to relate to you. One vessel in particular attracted my attention. It was a great glass globe, suspended from the ceiling and filled with a liquid of the palest green. A number of creatures appeared to be swimming about in it, almost all head and virtually no body, propelled by long waving strands of what looked like hair, which was nearly white in colour, though with a faintly iridescent lustre. But it was their heads which troubled me most, for they were human heads, yet like the heads of very old men who had lived lives of terrible corruption and debauchery. As they swam by in that strange aquarium their eyes met mine and I think I saw understanding in them, and at the same time complete indifference. They glanced and swam on as though I had been a thousand miles away.

At the farthest end of the cellar there was one wall which was entirely covered by a series of wooden cupboards with wooden doors punctured by holes. From them a faint sound of scuffling could be heard. By this time, though I had not examined a half of what there was to be seen, I had had enough. Nonetheless, reluctant as I was to stay there, I had one essential task to perform which was to find the door that led out of this place.

And there it was: a great oak door in a gothick arch, like the door to a church, let into a wall which must have been the subterranean extension of the front of Mr. Moreby's house. Above the apex of the door was a little niche in which there was a statue in black marble. It was of a crouching figure in what seemed like a monk's robe with a cowl. The head within the cowl could barely be seen but what was visible – I am glad I did not see more – was not human, but resembled the magnified head of an insect. Emerging from the sleeve and clasping one thin knee was not so much a hand as a thing like the limb and claw of a crab, covered in coarse hairs. I was reminded of the figure I had seen drawn in the book of the Black Pilgrimage.

On the bronze plinth on which it stood was inscribed a single word in Greek script:

ΑΝΑΡΧΩΝ

—which I knew from what little Greek I had studied to spell the word "Anarchon".

So engrossed was I by this figure above the door that my hand was on the handle for almost a minute and I had not endeavoured to open it. I was about to do so when I heard footsteps approaching from the other side. I flew from the door and mounted the steps to a position where I might see and not be easily seen, extinguishing my candle as I did so.

The iron latch of the door was lifted and two men entered the vault, both carrying lanterns. The first was my husband, Mr. Moreby. I saw him suspend his lantern from a hook in one of the ceiling bosses so that the whole cellar was illumined. He removed his cloak and then paused for a moment, looking around and sniffing at the air as if he detected some alien presence.

However, he was distracted by the entrance of the second figure. This was one of his servants, a Blackamoor he called John Carrefour, the biggest and dullest of all that crew. His brow was protuberant and hung heavily over his small eyes and the thick senseless features of his face. His hands were like lumps of dough; his skin was of the same consistency and as black as night. He was bowed low from carrying something in a sack over his shoulder. My husband, having commanded John to set his burden down on one of the tables, took a long knife from a drawer and proceeded to rip open the sack. Inside were the naked corpses of two young children, a boy and a girl, between the ages of seven and twelve.

My husband contemplated the bodies in silence for a while, but I saw nothing in his face which indicated the smallest degree of pity or compassion. Carrefour too was looking at them, with unconcealed eagerness and appetite on his face – but for what? Slowly he edged closer to them.

Suddenly Mr. Moreby turned on John, brandishing the knife in his face.

"Keep away, damn you!" He cried. "You'll have your reward later." Then going to the cupboards on the far wall, he opened one of the doors and took out a portable cage, like an aviary, and carried it over to where the dead children lay.

At first I could not see clearly what was in the cage. It seemed to be a creature with long, ungainly legs, a heavy head, and a pale armoured body. If it had not been the size of a small dog, I might have taken it for an insect of some kind, perhaps a flea.

As soon as this thing, which I shall call a flea for want of a better word, came near to the two dead bodies, its limbs began to twitch in an agitated matter and I saw that the two great whiskers on either side of its head – I might call them antennae – began to wave up and down in eagerness.

With great care Mr. Moreby took the creature out of its cage and set it down on one of the children's bodies. The flea bowed its head then extruded from its mouth parts a long sharp instrument like a quill which, with a sudden decisive movement, it thrust into the child's breast. Like the rest of the flea's body the quill was a pale yellow colour and somewhat translucent, but then its colour darkened to a reddish brown, which colour then extended to the head of the flea and to the rest of its body. I could come to no other conclusion than that the creature was gorging itself on the dead child's blood.

I could watch no more and retreated up the stairs without a sound. Once more in the library, I slid shut the bookcase. My best course was to leave the room, but on going to open the library door I realised that I had locked it and that the key which I had placed between my breasts had slipped down deep into my bodice. While I was endeavouring to retrieve it I heard the bookcase begin to slide open. It was my husband. Alas, what must I do? I abandoned my search for the key and sank onto a nearby sofa where I pretended to be asleep.

Mr. Moreby's cold hand on my cheek roused me.

"What are you doing here, madam?"

"Why, sir, I came in search of a book and must have fallen asleep."

"Did you indeed, madam? And what book were you searching for, pray?"

"Paley's Evidences, sir."

"A wretched scrawl. Did you not hear me come in?"

"Why no, sir," said I in my most innocent voice. Mr. Moreby looked at me searchingly, then went to the library door and tried it. Finding it locked, he now recognised that he was in a dilemma: how could he unlock it without giving away the fact that he had come in by another entrance?

"Madam," said he, "why had you locked this door? I had to summon a servant to gain entrance."

"Why, sir, I did not wish to be disturbed by some foolish interruption from one of your creatures." I saw anger flash in Mr. Moreby's eyes, but for once I was not afraid.

"Give me your key, madam!"

"But, Mr. Moreby, you do not need it, for you must have had a key to enter this room."

"Damn your impudence, madam, give me your key! I never gave consent that you should have one."

"Sir, but you must excuse me. It is in a most intimate place, for I put it into my bodice."

"Then, madam, I shall have the honour of retrieving it for you." And with that he came up to me and thrust his cold hard hand down between my breasts. I felt the hand wriggling like a rat against my bare flesh, as it searched. At last he found the key and retrieved it. He went to the door and turned the key in the lock several times as if trying it out, but I knew his subterfuge. When he saw me watching him he came back to me and for a long moment scrutinised my face.

"Madam, have you seen more than you should have?"

I stared back at him with eyes of insolent vacuity. "And what is it, sir, that I might have seen that I should not?"

Mr. Moreby made no reply but turned on his heel and went to the door once again.

"In future, madam," said he, "you enter this room only with my express permission. Is that understood?"

I said nothing, but dropped a submissive curtsey. He may suspect all but he shall know nothing, and thus I may gain some small advantage.

Yet, for all my bravado, I know that I am in mortal danger and must quit this house for ever at the earliest opportunity. I am writing to Melville to plan our escape. Should I succeed, I will immediately write to you, telling you my situation; should I fail, then I am lost and I truly believe you will hear no more of,

Your most unfortunate but affectionate cousin,

Anna

October 6th, 1803
At Mrs. Miller's in Gallows Lane

My Dearest Cousin,

In haste, I must tell you of the most dreadful accidents that have befallen me. I fear I have little time left and must make good my escape soon or, verily, I do believe that I shall perish to satisfy the lusts and ambitions of that blaspheming Devil, my husband.

After our encounter in the library Mr. Moreby sought to keep me closer under guard than ever before. I begged him to allow me to visit my father again and yesterday he finally relented, provided that two of his servants went with me in the carriage. To this I agreed with a very bad grace.

When we were in the carriage I commanded the coachman that we go by Bond Street to buy some ribbon for my new bonnet. To this the servants put up many objections, but I silenced them by saying that Mr. Moreby would be most vexed with them if they thwarted me in this innocent desire for a little finery. Besides, said I, they could accompany me into the shop. This prospect seemed to please the poor dolts and so we set off for Bond Street. Once there, I went with them into the shop and spent much time choosing a suitable ribbon, so long that my escort became bored and indolent. Finally I made my purchase and walked briskly out of the shop with the dolts shambling in my wake.

Once in the street outside, and without waiting for them, I entered the carriage by one door and immediately made my exit through the door on the other side and into the street. By the time those poor blockheads of servants had realised what had happened, I was lost in the crowd. Having crossed Bond Street, I made my way to Hanover Square hard by, where a post chaise was waiting for me to take me to Mr. Melville's chambers in Gray's Inn.

Conceive of my delight and ecstasy when Melville and I were once more in each other's arms. I was determined that I should be his and no one else's, therefore I decided that I should yield my person to him that day so that, whatever might thereafter befall, my husband should not be the one to take my virginity.

I wish to deny Mr. Moreby the satisfaction of both his lusts and any more occult and diabolical design that he may have on me.

It was with some difficulty that I persuaded Mr. Melville of the necessity of his committing adultery with me – or, as he put it in his quaint lawyer's cant: "criminal conversation" – but I eventually succeeded. Indeed his reluctance on the matter does him very great credit: he is ever the man of honour. Further than that, my dear cousin, I need only say that though my apprehensions as to what was about to transpire had been inflamed by the advice that my late mother had given me shortly before she died, I was gratified to discover that what little of her counsel was not superfluous was wholly misleading. All was pleasure and satisfaction. Melville has made me the woman I wish to be and I feel the more enlightened for this particular "criminal conversation".

Shortly following the conclusion of that important transaction there was a knock at the door of Melville's rooms. I guessed that it was some deputation from my husband and bade my lover be on his guard. He told me he had a pistol and went to the door with it.

On opening it we found two persons standing outside. One was my husband's bawd Moll Hackett, dressed in her most vulgar finery, the other, a flunkey or punk of hers called Whiteman, whom I had seen once or twice lurking in the hall of my husband's house in Blackheath.

Mr. Whiteman was tall and slender, and may once have had a pleasing person but for the fact that popular prejudice favours the presence of a nose on a man's face, and he had none. In its place there was a curiously repellent confusion of mangled cartilage and scarred skin, like an ill-dug grave, the result, I doubt not, of a severe venereal infection. He was finely dressed in an old fashioned way which suggested a gentleman fallen on hard times on account of his own debauchery. Mrs. Hackett announced that he was there to protect her.

Mr. Melville received our unwelcome guests with stiff formality. Mrs. Hackett opened the conversation with a great show of polite and decorous manners which was so grotesque that we were almost minded to laugh at her. However, as she proceeded, the burden of her mission was made abundantly and gravely clear, namely that unless I returned immediately with them to Blackheath the most dire consequences would follow. She said that Mr. Melville would be entirely disgraced and might never practise law again, that he would be prosecuted or forced into exile, there to live out a life of shameful penury, and that moreover I should be also disgraced and friendless. Mr. Moreby, said Mrs. Hackett, had many friends in high places who could bring this about.

Mr. Melville replied stoutly that he thought foul scorn to her threats and that, on the contrary, he would ensure that Mr. Moreby might himself be disgraced unless he consented to an immediate annulment of the marriage which he understood to have been unconsummated. At this point Mr. Whiteman stepped forward.

You might ask, dearest cousin, how, having no nose, this Mr. Whiteman smelled. My answer to you is this: very foul indeed. He exuded an odour of decay similar to that of my husband's servants, like that of a three days' dead cat in a damp cellar. Mr. Melville recoiled somewhat at his advance, but more from natural repulsion than fear.

Mr. Whiteman bowed, and when he spoke it was in a low, almost whispering, but very gentlemanly voice:

"In the event, sir, of your refusal to comply with Mr. Moreby's wishes, I am commanded by this young lady's lawful husband, as his second, to issue a challenge on his behalf and to demand satisfaction on the field of honour."

"And I accept," replied my Melville instantly.

Conceive of my horror! I begged my lover to rescind his acceptance. I said that this was nothing but a trap and that he would be betrayed, but my Melville would hear nothing. No doubt he saw it as a way of expiating the scandal that must inevitably come from his elopement with a married woman.

I saw Mrs. Hackett smirk and knew that the provocation to a duel had been their intention from the very first. I shouted at her to leave the room instantly which, having dropped me a mocking curtsey, she did. Mr. Whiteman, however, remained behind to conclude, despite my protestations, the arrangements for the duel.

It was decided therefore that Mr. Melville and Mr. Moreby should meet at dawn the following morning at the duelling ground in Putney Fields. These negotiations concluded, Mr. Whiteman bowed again and took his leave. In the silence that followed I realised that I could not succeed in persuading Mr. Melville to abandon the course upon which he was resolved. I therefore pleaded with him to take all the precautions that he could: to find a good second and a skilled man of medicine who might attend him should he be wounded. To all this Melville agreed, but when I suggested that I myself might attend the duel he forbade me in the most forceful terms.

I bowed my head in acceptance of my fate, but said that I was not to be left alone here at the Gray's Inn Chambers lest some of Moreby's ruffians come in Melville's absence to carry me away. After much debate (and a further and most passionate amorous exchange) Melville and I resolved that I should disguise myself as a boy and take myself to lodge with Mrs. Miller, the aunt of my faithful servant Jane, a laundress and a very respectable woman. There, I should hope to evade capture by Mr. Moreby's minions for a while.

So, shortly before nightfall, having cut my hair and put on a boy's clothes, borrowed from the son of one of Melville's colleagues, I slipped out of the chambers in Gray's Inn and made my way to Mrs. Miller's at Gallows Lane in the City. I knew the way, for my Jane, of whose present whereabouts I have — alas! – no notion, had taken me there several times. There I was received kindly into her humble rooms.

The following morning I rose before dawn, for I was determined, despite Mr. Melville's explicit instructions, to witness the duel between my true lover and my husband. Still dressed as a boy, I found a livery stables from which I hired a nag to take me to Putney Fields. In the half-light of dawn it was some time before I could locate the duelling ground. The combatants had not yet arrived so that I was able to choose at leisure a suitable tree where I could tether my horse and behind which, unobserved, I might spy upon the proceedings.

Presently Mr. Moreby's carriage arrived accompanied by an outrider whom I saw to be Mr. Whiteman. From the carriage stepped Mr. Moreby in a long, dark blue cloak, followed, to my great amazement and disgust, by Mrs. Hackett. I saw the three pace about the duelling ground in deep consultation. Would that I might have heard what they were plotting!

Shortly afterwards there came three riders onto the scene, they being Melville, his second, a Captain Lucas, and a surgeon in black. A case of duelling pistols was produced from Mr. Moreby's carriage and Melville was invited to choose his weapon. After a brief consultation the two antagonists took their places back to back in the middle of the duelling ground. Captain Lucas gave the signal and the two men began to pace away from each other. One, two, three, four . . . eight, nine, ten – only ten paces before they turned! Mr. Moreby did so a few seconds before Melville, and fired. My Melville had barely turned around before he was shot and he fell before he had time to pull his own trigger.

I let out an involuntary cry and the tears started from my eyes. I saw the surgeon run over to Mr. Melville with a grave look on his face. Captain Lucas seemed in despair. Melville lay cradled in the Captain's arms, a great flower of blood blossoming on his white shirt about his chest. I came out of hiding to see if there were any hope for my love, and at that moment Mr. Whiteman saw me. He pointed me out to my husband who commanded Whiteman to get on his horse. Mrs. Hackett smiled and did her mock curtsey at me once more. I ran to the tree and untethered my nag, but Mr. Whiteman was already galloping towards me.

My poor horse was not made for the chase and Mr. Whiteman began rapidly to gain ground on me as I fled from him. My only hope was to make for the village of Putney which was happily not far distant. As I came into the main street I saw several village boys playing in the dust of the road. I halted my horse and cried out to them that there was a terrible man with no nose pursuing me. Scattering some coins among them, I begged them to render me assistance. Just then Mr. Whiteman came galloping into the village, whereupon the boys responded to his presence with that natural animosity against deformity that distinguishes the ill-bred. I felt no shame at being, for once, its beneficiary.

These bumpkins immediately began to pelt him with clods of earth and horse turds which they found on the road so that Mr. Whiteman was toppled from his mount. A chambermaid then emptied a pot full of night soil onto him from an upper window. I meanwhile accosted a young cobbler's apprentice who was leaning idly against his master's shop window and surveying the scene. I offered him half a guinea to ride my nag back to the livery stables while I made a long and weary journey on foot to the City and Mrs. Miller's, trusting that I would thus throw my pursuers off the scent.

When I finally arrived back in Gallows Lane I was too exhausted to feel any apprehension or grief but immediately fell into a deep sleep from which I have but lately woken. I will entrust this letter to the faithful Mrs. Miller, but I cannot stay here long, lest I imperil her, for I doubt not that I will be found out by Moreby. I will endeavour to take a Post Chaise into the country, to you, cousin, but I have no very lively hopes of success, and therefore I write to you. I dare not send a message directly to my father, for I know that Moreby's spies and creatures will intercept it. You, my dearest Catherine, are my only hope. Come at once, I implore you.

I have just looked into the street and have seen Mr. Whiteman there. Pray God that he has not seen me.

He has, for a note has this very minute been delivered to me by Mrs. Miller. It is in my husband's own hand. These are his words:

> Your Melville is mortally wounded and has but a short time to live. If you wish to hear his dying words, then you must give yourself up to Mr. Whiteman and he will deliver you to the young coxcomb for a final interview. If you do not obey, then you will see him no more this side of the grave. Choose wisely. Moreby

What must I do? Is this another trick of his? I am in agony. I must fly at once.

In direst haste, your most unhappy and desperate cousin,

Anna

▼ From: *The London Intelligencer*, October 11th, 1803:

TRAGIC & HORRIBLE DISCLOSURES IN HOB'S LANE

THE DENIZENS of Deptford, we are informed, were the witness to a most extraordinary and tragic scene on the night of Friday last, the 7th of October. Mr. Oliver Whitby, a respectable wine merchant of Cheapside in the City of London, hearing that his daughter Anna was in desperate danger at the hands of her husband Mr. Thomas Moreby, architect of Blackheath, summoned a constable and, with a considerable and motley gathering of London's citizenry who attached themselves voluntarily to them, went to the house of a Mrs. Hackett in Hob's Lane, Deptford. There, Mr. Whitby had been informed, his daughter was being held captive by Mr. Moreby, and in peril of her life.

We are apprised that Mrs. Hackett's house is a most notorious bawdy house and no fit place for a young lady to be, either with or against her will.

Mr. Whitby, the constable, and the posse of concerned citizens carrying blazing links and torches, arrived in Hob's Lane close on midnight. They were joined there by the Reverend Elias Bacon, the elderly Rector of All Hallows, Blackheath, and Mr. Melville, a gentleman who, we understand, has entertained warm feelings for Mrs. Moreby and has been severely wounded by her husband in a duel. Previous reports that he had been slain proved, mercifully, to have been incorrect.

The constable hammered upon the door of Mrs. Hackett's, demanding entrance, and was rewarded for his pains by the emptying of a chamber pot upon his head from an upper window, accompanied by a burst of raucous laughter from some of Mrs. Hackett's female charges. This so enraged the mob – as we may call them – that they exerted their collective strength to break down the door.

Having thus forcibly achieved entrance, the crowd ran amok through the house and many of them, it is regretful to announce, made free not only with its contents, but with the female inhabitants, some of whom were entertaining gentlemen at the time. (These gentlemen were turned unceremoniously into the street, many of them in their night shifts, having had their clothes, and in some cases, their most intimate parts, singed and scarified by the torches of the rabble.) But there were a sober few who accompanied the constable, Mr. Whitby, Mr. Bacon and Mr. Melville to conduct a more methodical search of the premises.

On venturing below to the capacious cellarage belonging to Mrs. Hackett's bordello, the constable and his companions broke in upon a most horrific and astonishing scene.

In a large vaulted space, illumined by many lighted candles of black beeswax, stood seven persons – four male, three female – dressed in robes of purple silk beneath which, it was later discovered, they were naked. In their midst stood a tall man in black whose features, partly obscured by a cowl, were dabbled with blood, while below him upon a stone slab, as upon an altar, lay the hideously mutilated corpse of a young woman of barely nineteen summers. This proved to be the above mentioned Anna Moreby, the unhappy wife of her slaughterer. It was more than evident that a ceremony of unspeakable blasphemy and horror had been in progress.

Mr. Moreby was forced to his knees but remained tranquil and insolent in the confusion. The same could not be said of his acolytes, as we may call them, who, stripped of their robes by the baser elements among the constable's posse, stood shivering and naked in their shame. The *Intelligencer* may disclose exclusively to its readers that some of the most eminent and noble names in England were represented in this infamous galère. Persons hitherto known for the elegance of their manners and the superiority of their breeding were now revealed as base and degraded idolaters, fornicators and worse. Our sapient readers will know whom we mean by the Marquess of M****, Lady Cecilia F***** and Lord Charles P***** amongst others. Some were beaten senseless by the avenging mob, others somehow contrived their escape; not one, however, has evaded the censure and repugnance of all respectable men and women.

To return to the chief actor of this dreadful scene. Though reproached bitterly by the grieving father of his victim, Mr. Moreby retained his defiance, claiming that his master would deliver him.

The constable wished Mr. Moreby to be given up to the law, but the mob would have none of it. They seized him and, their torches still blazing, bore him to the church of All Hallows nearby where, under instruction from Mr. Bacon and Mr. Whitby, he was cast deep into a vaulted subterranean chamber in the undercroft, and there, crying out blasphemously to his Demon Deities, he was immured by the eager hands of the assembled mob. Even after his everlasting imprisonment had been

finally secured his dreadful screams could still be heard. Some of the crowd proceeded on from All Hallows to burn down Mr. Moreby's house in Blackheath which they succeeded in raising to the ground.

It only remained for the father of the victim, Mr. Whitby, accompanied by her adorer Mr. Melville, and a woman believed to be her cousin, a Miss Catherine Orlebar, to carry the mangled corpse of the unhappy Mrs. Moreby away to be decently buried at a future date.

One further item may be added to this singularly horrific budget of news. Several witnesses to the event noted that the cellar of Mrs. Hackett's bawdy house where the blasphemous ceremonies had been taking place became infested by a great number of fleas which, we are informed by a man well known as a virtuoso of Natural Science, the Reverend Mr. Whiteman, were singularly vicious and of a size greater than ever previously recorded.

News

WORLD-WIDE PANIC SPREAD BY RADIO DRAMA

NATION AROUSED BY WAR 'HORRORS'

MANY FLEE HOMES TO AVOID 'GAS ATTACK'

LAST NIGHT THOUSANDS OF WIRELESS LISTENERS IN THE UNITED STATES OF AMERICA SUFFERED A CASE OF "MASS HYSTERIA" WHEN A BROADCAST OF A DRAMATISATION OF MR. H. G. WELLS'S FANTASY, 'THE WAR OF THE WORLDS', LED PEOPLE TO BELIEVE THAT MARTIANS HAD INVADED THE EAST COAST OF THE UNITED STATES AND WERE SPREADING DEATH AND DESTRUCTION IN NEW JERSEY AND NEW YORK.

The 'New York Times' reports "The broadcast disrupted households, interrupted religious services, created traffic jams and clogged communications systems." The broadcast was made by the distinguished American actor and director Mr. Orson Welles, who as the radio character "The Shadow" used to give "the creeps" to countless young listeners.

According to 'The New York Times', at least a score of adults required medical treatment for shock and hysteria.

Thousands of persons called the Police, newspapers and radio stations in cities in both the United States and in Canada, seeking advice on protective measures against the raids.

The wireless programme was produced by Mr. Welles and the Mercury Theatre, and was broadcast by the Columbia Broadcasting System on its coast-to-coast network, from 8 to 9 o'clock. The simulation of a regular programme was so well presented that listeners apparently failed to take note of warnings at the beginning and repeated at intervals to emphasise the fictional nature of the piece, which began with Mr. Welles describing the series of which the play was a part.

The 'New York Times' reported: "News bulletins and scene broadcasts followed, reporting, with the technique in which the radio had reported actual events, the landing of a 'meteor' near Princeton N. J., 'killing' 1,500 persons, and the discovery that the 'meteor' was a 'metal cylinder' containing strange creatures from Mars armed with 'death rays' to open hostilities against the inhabitants of the earth. Despite the fantastic nature of the reported 'occurrences', the programme, coming after the recent war scare in Europe and a period in which the radio frequently had interrupted regularly scheduled programmes to report developments in the Czechoslovak situation, caused fright and panic throughout the area of the broadcast."

CALLERS TELEPHONE FOR ADVICE

Many people started telephoning the authorities, seeking to verify the reports, or, already in a state of terror, requesting information on how they could follow the broadcaster's advice and flee from the city, and whether they would be safer in the cellar or on the roof, and how they could safeguard their children. Many of these questions have been worrying our own residents, as well as those of Paris, during the tense days before the Munich Agreement.

So many newspapers – the 'News Chronicle' included – found it advisable to check on the reports, despite their fantastic content, that The Associated Press sent out the following at 8:48 P.M. Eastern Standard Time (1:48 P.M. in Great Britain): "Note to Editors: Queries to newspapers from radio listeners throughout the United States tonight, regarding a reported meteor fall which killed a number of New Jerseyites, are the result of a studio dramatization. The A.P."

The Federal Communication Commission in Washington, D.C. has begun an investigation. Chairman Mr. Frank P. McNinch said, "The usual practice of the commission is not to investigate broadcasts unless formal demands for an inquiry are made, but the commission has the power to initiate proceedings where the public interest seems to warrant official action. Any broadcast that creates such general panic and fear, as this one is reported to have done, is, to say the least, regrettable."

PANIC SPREADS TO GREAT BRITAIN

Mr H. G. Wells, 72, the author of the book 'The War of the Worlds' which was the subject of Mr. Welles's broadcast, spoke this morning from his home in Hannover Terrace, Regent's Park, W.1. "I have to admit to some surprise at the widespread panic that has apparently resulted from Mr. Welles's adaptation of my little tale," he told the 'News Chronicle'. "I must thank Mr. Welles for bringing one of my more obscure titles to the attention of the reading public."

Mr. Wells pointed out that it was not only Americans who were susceptible to such fantastical thoughts of being invaded by otherworldly creatures, and he made mention of the odd sightings in Hob's Lane, London, as reported in this newspaper on numerous occasions. "There is more going on in the hidden, underground places than we perhaps realise," he said. "I myself have often imagined a foul smell emanating from the abandoned Underground excavations at Hobbs End Station, or heard tappings and bangings that came from nowhere and everywhere, or thought I caught a glimpse of some disfigured, dwarfish character scuttling back into the shadows whence he came. Luckily for me, I can put down my imaginings upon the page and exorcise them from my head – at least for a while."

Mr. Wells admitted he had spent time about Hob's Lane, investigating the legends in the hope of finding material for a new story. "I have a great fascination with the grand Protestant churches of England, and have whiled away many a happy hour discovering new buildings. It was whilst studying the rebuilt Church of All Hallows at Blackheath that I became aware of the architect Thomas Moreby, who built All Hallows. He was an apprentice of the great Hawksmoor. He lived nearby with his young wife Anna, until her untimely death at the age of nineteen and his own incarceration at the hands of a furious mob in an undercrypt of his own church."

Mr Wells conceded that he had loosely based the lead character in his novel 'The Island of Dr. Moreau' on the architect. Moreby became known as the "Zombie King", for he believed a body could rise after death if "expos'd to pure humours".

THE HOB'S LANE GHOST

"I wonder if even I could do justice to so far-fetched a story!" Mr. Wells said. "However, it was whilst I was at All Hallows that I heard about the Hob's Lane Ghost from a helpful cleric, the Revd. Mr. Bacon, who told me his family had served in that very church for many years."

The Revd. Ernest Bacon told the 'News Chronicle' that the ill-conceived Central Line Underground extension to Hobbs End actually extended under his church, and that he had been much concerned about the disruption to the fabric of the underparts of the building caused by the drilling. He was much relieved when the project was brought to a halt. "However, I fear the activity has disturbed something which ought not to have been awakened," he said, but when questioned further, would say no more.

Mr. Wells said, "Indeed, I will not deny that some small part of 'The War of the Worlds' was conceived whilst in the vicinity of Hob's Lane. However, like Dr. Johnson, I too have an abhorrence of the common flea, and to my surprise, have often found a strange abundance of the creatures in that particular area of London, which makes visiting it less of a pleasure."

MORE SIGHTINGS

Following the publication of our First Edition, our News Desk received a number of telephone calls from worried London residents, reporting a sudden rash of sightings of the Hob's Lane Ghost. It has been described variously as being dwarf-like, an apeman, or a horned demon.

Mrs. Enid Parker, whose family have lived in Hob's Lane for more than a hundred years, said, "I hear it at night, and I see its shadow on the wall: a great horned demon, with a stench like the very armpit of Hell."

Mrs. Amanda Grooty, whose grandson Timothy is a detective in New Jersey, U.S.A., said he had telegraphed her that morning to assure her that he was well, and that the reports of Martian invasion were a hoax. "He asked me if our own ghost had been playing up, and I told him I was quite used to the foul smells and all the strange noises in the attic," she said. "I didn't want him to worry about me, not when the Martians might be landing in America."

P.C. Peter Ellis claimed . . .

CONT on Page 6

THIRD CHILD MISSING IN HAUNTED LANE

**Exclusive
By James Fullalove,
Investigative
Reporter**

A THIRD LONDON child has disappeared from home, leaving no trace. Patricia Groome, aged nine, was last seen by her mother Mrs Dolores Groome, playing in the front garden of the family home near Hobbs Lane yesterday afternoon.

Her distraught parents told this reporter, "We just want our little girl home for Christmas – no matter what it takes."

Mrs Groome, 29, tried to hold back her tears as she said, "I just went out to tell her to come in for her tea, and I saw she was gone. She had been playing with her doll Betsy – I found the perambulator, which was lying on its side, and Betsy had fallen out onto the flowerbed. When I picked the doll up I saw the face had some strange markings, almost as if something had been gnawing at it.

"Patricia's red mittens were also lying on the ground – I knitted them myself from an old jumper. It was so cold, but she'd been cooped up all day and she would insist on going out. She's a sensible girl for all she's only seven. She knows never to leave the front garden alone. I know she would never have run away by herself. The first things I did was to check with the neighbours, but no one had seen Patricia, not since she'd come back from Sunday School, not even Mrs Chilcott, and she normally knows everything that happens around here.

"Edward and I want our little ray of sunshine home. I keep thinking I hear her on the stairs, or scratching at the walls, but when I turn around of course there's nothing there. The house is so empty without her!"

Mr Edward Groome, 31, a banker in the City of London, was one of the locals who formed a task force to try to find John Temple, the first child to disappear from the environs of Hobbs Lane. He told me, "My aunt never wanted me to stay in this area – although my family has always lived around here. She has always been sure there is something evil living here – she believes wholeheartedly in the spirit world, and after that business at Hobbs End Underground Station, and the 'five-million-year-old apeman skulls' the Government claimed were just a hoax, I am beginning to wonder if perhaps she was right."

Mr Groome said the first policeman on the scene, PC Ellis, was the first person to suggest someone – or something – was targeting the children of the Hobbs Lane area, but Inspector Patrick Calvin, who is heading the hunt for the missing youngsters, was quick to say the Police had not yet proved any link between the three children.

Run Away?

Nine-year-old John Temple disappeared on the way home from school on Saturday, July 18. Eleven-year-old Louise Pritchett vanished from her back garden on Wednesday October 22. He said, "The children obviously knew each other as they all attend Hobbs End Endowed School in Ladysmith Crescent, but they are different ages and otherwise have nothing in common. It is known that there was some familial upset at the Temple home, and we still believe young John ran away of his own accord. He may be trying to reach his grandparents in Scotland. And Louise Pritchett had talked to her best friend at school about working on a farm, so it is very likely she too has run away by herself.

"We shall most likely find young Patricia curled up in someone's shed any minute now. We are following up all leads at this time, and I appeal for anyone with any information to come forward, either in person to Deptford Police Station, or to telephone confidentially."

I tracked down Mrs Amelia Temple – Mr Fred Temple no longer lives in the marital home – and she told me none of John's grandparents have heard a word from their grandson since the day he failed to come home from school.

"I know PC Ellis thinks he's just run away on account of his dad belting him one, but it's not like it was the first time," Mrs Temple said. "And anyway, Mr Temple's gone now, so I just want my John to know it's safe for him to come home now. I know he'll be that upset that his dog Rover's gone and drowned himself because he was driven mad by flea bites, but we'll get him another."

Mr and Mrs Jeremiah Pritchett were unwilling to talk to this newspaper, but a close neighbour, Mrs Chilcott, claimed to have seen a small, dwarfish fellow sneaking down the lane just before Mrs Groome raised the alarm. She told me she and her husband have lived in the area all their lives, and they had seen plenty of strange happenings. "That dwarfish hunched creature, he's often around," she claimed. "My mam always told me Hobbs Lane was named for Old Hob, the Devil – she told me she'd even seen him herself, with his great long horns and huge staring eyes. We've all heard the noises, scratchings and dreadful sounds – sort of tapping and knocking. Like some person wanting to come in, only there wasn't nobody

there. In the floors it come. And in the walls – we could hear it too. And things would move, all by themselves, in rooms that had nobody in them. I told that nice Professor all about it. It's a fact: chairs and tables and ornaments – even the beds was moved about!"

Mrs Chilcott said her neighbours had tried everything to stop the strange visitations: "They had the police in, and a parson even. Didn't do no good. I remember one night Earnshaw run into us – the neighbours was called Earnshaw – running in yelling like a maniac. They'd seen something. We're always seeing queer things around here. The Police ought to be doing something about it, not letting decent, law-abiding folks get stolen from their own front gardens."

Mrs Groome later told the Police the Chilcotts were always claiming to be seeing strange things, just like their parents had before them.

Strange Reputation

The area around Hobbs Lane has a reputation for strange goings-on that dates back centuries.

This reporter has seen for himself archives kept at Westminster Abbey which describe in gruesome detail similar happenings to those described so colourfully by Mrs Chilcott.

One archivist translated for me: "In the winter of the year 1341 the Abbot of Westminster did strive against an outbreak of evil at Hobes Lane in the village of Blachehedfeld. Imps and demons did appear. Foul noises sent by the Devil . . ."

There have been further reports of similar ghostly activities, in 1762, and again in 1927, when the Central Line extension to Hobbs End was being constructed.

Continued on Page 5

Pilots tell of horned demon in the sky

Evening News Reporter

Scores of people on the ground and in the air last night reported a vision of a 'horned demon' emblazoned across the night sky.

Police officers at Blackheath Police Station took dozens of phone calls from spectators concerned about the strange visitation.

Eye witnesses also described an odd magnetic effect which caused objects to rise and fly about.

A Delta Airlines pilot flying a Douglas DC-9 aeroplane en route to Croydon Airport from the Continent radioed the Control Tower after seeing the image lighting up the night sky.

The Croydon Airport weather observatory told the Evening News: "I can confirm that several pilots coming into Croydon Airport reported seeing odd mirages which we believe to be caused by atmospheric conditions combined with unusual cloud formations. No further action is being taken."

Huge glowing eyes and great horns

All of the eye witnesses described an almost insectoid head with huge glowing eyes and great horns, and several also spoke of a foul smell that appeared to be seeping up from the sewers in the area around Hobbs Lane.

The Metropolitan Water Authority have sent a team of engineers to the site to investigate.

This is not the first time Hobbs Lane has been the centre of mysterious disturbances. In 1958 a British rocket expert was called in to investigate an unexploded bomb, after archaeologists unearthed the skeletons of what were at first believed to be five-million-year-old ape-men.

At the time there were reports of visitors from outer space, insect-like creatures, rather more than two feet high, with tripod legs and stick-like forelimbs hunched like those of a mantis, each face a mockery of the human, with pointed proboscis below two complex eyes. Above that triangular mask sprouted antennae shaped like horns.

The Home Office report blamed hallucinations on the gas leaks set off by the explosion of the German bomb which had lain undiscovered until the development of the Hobbs End Underground Station, part of the intended Central Line expansion, later cancelled due to financial constraints.

To: Dr. Charles Barton, Curator, St. Pancras Old Church
From: Simon Wesley, Histological Epidemiology, Hospital of Tropical Diseases & Medicine, NW1
Subject: Thomas Moreby

Dear Dr. Barton,

I was given your email by a mutual friend who informs me that you are currently writing a biography of the architect Thomas Moreby. I wonder if you are able to shed some light on rumours that in addition to designing churches for Hawksmoor he belonged to some kind of secret theosophical society?

This information is not for general use but merely to answer the query of a friend.

Best wishes,
Simon

To: Simon Wesley, Histological Epidemiology, Hospital of Tropical Diseases & Medicine, NW1
From: Dr. Charles Barton, Curator, St. Pancras Old Church
Subject: Thomas Moreby

Dear Simon,

Thank you for your enquiry. I must say, you're not the first person to ask questions about Moreby. Just this week I had a series of emails on the same subject from a government department, no less! I had no idea that my little biography would excite such interest.

You must understand that there was a fashion for so-called Hellfire Clubs during the time when Moreby was working, and as he was a man of Pagan beliefs (something you could only get away with if you were high-born, as Moreby was) he created his own society for like-minded gentlemen.

The society he founded was known as The Well of Seven, but very little is written down about it. There are some exchanges of letters on the subject, but as the formation of such societies was illegal, the terminology he used was hardly explicit. Still, one gets the distinct feeling that the activities he was involved in were pretty dreadful.

We do know that The Well of Seven met in Pentonville at dawn on the seventh day of each month. The group consisted of physicians and architects who shared certain common beliefs about the resurrection of the soul after death.

If you need any more information, please don't hesitate to get in touch. I'm always here.

Best,
Dr. Charles Barton

To: Dr. Charles Barton, Curator, St. Pancras Old Church
From: Simon Wesley, Histological Epidemiology, Hospital of Tropical Diseases & Medicine, NW1
Subject: Thomas Moreby

Dear Dr. Barton,

Thanks for your swift reply. I know that upon his demise Thomas Moreby was interred in the secret crypt he himself designed at All Hallows Church, Blackheath, but you don't happen to know where his disciples were buried, do you? It crosses my mind that they may themselves have been the subjects of his attempts to prove the existence of life after death.

Best wishes,
Simon

To: Simon Wesley, Histological Epidemiology, Hospital of Tropical Diseases & Medicine, NW1
From: Dr. Charles Barton, Curator, St. Pancras Old Church
Subject: Thomas Moreby

Dear Simon,

I can certainly help you with this one. Even though the Midland Railway cut away a great chunk of our land away for its sidings, we still have many famous corpses in our little churchyard. Sir John Soane, the architect of the Bank of England, has his tomb here (Charles Dickens makes reference to it in *A Tale of Two Cities*). The shape of the tomb inspired Scott's design for the traditional red telephone box. And I'm sure you know that Mary Shelley was romanced by Percy Bysshe Shelley on the same spot.

Mary Shelley used to come here because her mother had been laid to rest in these grounds. The couple romanced each other on the gravestones. Then there's the Hardy Tree, an old ash tree beset by great gravestones, laid end on against the trunk like a rising tide of stone, so that the wood has grown over them, nature engulfing the remains of man as it were. Most of the graves – some 8,000 of them – were relocated to Highgate and Kensal Green. The young Thomas Hardy helped to clear them, hence the tree's name.

Unusually, the members of the Well of Seven were not interred with their families when they died, but were buried together, under Moreby's explicit instructions, in our churchyard right here at St. Pancras Old Church. There's not much of the original monument left to see, just a worn marble circle with seven stone markers running around the edge, one for each of the coffins placed there. It can be visited whenever you like.

I hope this helps to answer your friend's query.

Best wishes,
Charles

To:	Prof. Margaret Winn, UCH London
From:	Simon Wesley, Histological Epidemiology, Hospital of Tropical Diseases & Medicine, NW1
Subject:	All Hallows Church, Blackheath

Dear Margaret,

I've now been through this material confirming the activities of the so-called "Well of Seven" – intriguing stuff. There are several points raised in the documents that strike me as being significant.

The fragment from Boswell's *Life of Dr. Johnson* that refers to the site of Hob's Lane obviously suggests a long-standing connection with the Devil (which in historical terms may simply denote death or illness), but from an epidemiological point of view the piece from *The Gentleman's Magazine* suggesting that there was the sound of "a great groaning" in the ground instantly made me think of water-borne disease. The area around Deptford is riddled with passages, cellars and sluices, and the sound of rushing water. The streets of ancient London followed the lines of hedgerows and underground rivers. The lowlands were poor areas largely because they were damp. Water and "miasma" (fog) brought sickness, and early deaths created superstitions; that's why ghost stories were more associated with, say, the poor East End and South of the city than London's prosperous North.

Setting aside any thoughts of supernatural agents (I'm a man of science, after all) the idea of rejuvenating the body through ritual cannibalism is far from new, but it's the connection with plague-carrying fleas that alarms me most, for what you suddenly find here is that men may have knowingly directed the path of the pathogen. That anyone would set out to do this in a quest for eternal life – well, words fail me, but I can't help thinking that you may have stumbled upon London's darkest secret, in which case it would be in the interest of the government to keep it buried.

A friend of mine says he can figure out the identities of the ceremony's attendees from the *Intelligencer* article if you want, but it's a bit out of my field of expertise, I'm afraid. I'll be happy to put you in touch with him.

Why, exactly, do you want to know about all this?

Simon

From: Josef Koczak, Associate Professor of Molecular Biology, University of Illinois—Chicago Circle
To: Jillian Christensen
Subject: Of hasty departures and other cloak-&-dagger bullshit
Date: 27 April

- -

Dear Jilly,

Again, I'm sorry for making such an abrupt departure during dinner this evening. When someone like New World Pharmaceuticals holds the strings to your research grants, you don't really get the option to say, "Sounds intriguing, but can we reschedule?"

Not to forget: These are people who have convinced the government they should hold patents on tissue samples taken from research subjects who, when they went into the hospital, had no idea that their own bodies were going to be patented by an $85 billion corporation.

Before you ask again: Yes, sometimes it DOES feel like I've made a deal with the Devil.

I'm sorry, too, that I couldn't say more when I called from O'Hare. This was not a conversation to have at any airport unless you want an eavesdropper to pick the wrong two words out of the air and next thing you know you're in a room waiting for a couple of pleasant gentlemen from the FBI.

So, I'm sorry all around. At the moment I'm still hours from touching down at Heathrow, but I'll hit "send" on this as soon as I get there, and maybe you'll have forgiven me by breakfast.

Those wrong two words, BTW, are "bubonic" and "plague."

Long story short: Someone along the food chain at New World has learned of the disinterment of two dozen or so bodies from a 17th-century plague pit at a church called All Hallows. They've been moved temporarily into a crypt beneath the church. NW needs someone to swoop in before the bodies are inaccessible again, and retrieve samples that are likely to yield intact DNA. There's apparently a very narrow window of opportunity for this, and they're not keen on going through proper channels, since those wheels grind very slowly. The whole site is due for demolition any day now, by the sound of it, a casualty of this New Festival of Britain debacle-in-the-making they've got going, that's meant to be some sort of consolation prize for the way they choked on the Olympics. I'm rooting for them, actually, although the whole thing makes me think of whenever Microsoft tries to be cool: They're way too late, and it's really lame.

Why me for this? Good question. Presumably, one person making a round trip is better than, say, sending in a local contact to violate the dead, then make a handoff to some transatlantic courier, etc etc. They know, obviously, that I was the one who got those morgue samples out of Mexico City a couple of years ago, during that peculiar outbreak during El Dia de los Muertos. I still have that temperature-controlled canister that looks like shaving cream. And it's no secret that the plague is something of a hobby of mine.

Be honest, now: Wouldn't you still prefer that out of me to a fantasy football league?

There's a longstanding mystery about the bubonic plague that no one's managed to solve yet: Why were the outbreaks in medieval Europe so much more devastating than others observed in comparatively modern times? One of the chief contrasts is an outbreak in Bombay in 1904. This was still decades before antibiotics. Even discounting cultural and genetic differences, fatality rates should've been comparable to those of medieval times. But it's not even close. The medieval plague was at minimum ten times more deadly than what we find in Bombay and other outbreaks where antibiotics aren't a factor.

There was even speculation that the cause behind what's gone down in history as the Black Death wasn't actually bubonic plague . . . that we've been laboring under a massively mistaken assumption all this time. Or that it was at least some variant strain that has hopefully gone extinct, but would show up as detectably different if the DNA were sequenced.

The National Academy of Sciences put that theory to bed once and for all a couple of years ago, after the sequencing of DNA extracted from teeth and bones pulled out of London's East Smithfield cemetery. Today it's right in the middle of everything, across from the Tower of London, but in the mid-1300s, it was built outside the city walls, specifically for a plague outbreak that they feared would be coming over from the Continent. So in East Smithfield it was the plague, the whole plague, and nothing but the plague.

What the NAS determined was that the same microbe associated with modern-day bubonic plague, a nasty little critter called Yersinia pestis, which likes to take up residence inside fleas, which in turn hitch a free ride on rats, was right smack in the thick of it in medieval London, too. Then and now, as near as they've found, it's the same DNA sequence. So no surprises there.

But that also means we're no closer to solving the mystery about what was different about the medieval plague. And there WAS something different about it. Not just in the fatality rates, either. In modern outbreaks, plague seems to spread only as fast as the rats carrying the infected fleas can get around. But the epidemiology of the Black Death indicates a much more rapid person-to-person spread. Medieval reports also described its victims as emitting a deathly stench. You don't see that today. Fascinating stuff.

Be honest, now: Wouldn't you still prefer this out of me to hitting strip clubs on the weekend?

So who knows what will come out of All Hallows. Probably nothing. I'm not aware of anyone still clinging to the theory that the Black Death and bubonic plague aren't one and the same. But you have to investigate when the opportunity arises.

I must admit, though, that I can't put my finger on what New World's angle in this even is. If there were some breakthrough in baldness or erectile dysfunction waiting, I could understand . . . but plague? Nobody worries about the plague these days.

The reason they've given me is that, if something genetically different were found in a new batch of DNA samples, they want to be the first sitting on a vaccine and cure if there's ever a modern outbreak equivalent to the medieval scourges. OK, so Big Pharma likes a good longshot now and then.

But I'd be lying if I said the thought of them HOPING to find something different, then trying to patent it, and/or weaponize it, didn't scare the feces out of me.

Maybe that's just late-night-over-the-Atlantic talk. I'm tired, I'm still cranky because I missed dessert, and most of all I miss you already.

Love,
Josef

▼ [Text message recovered from cell phone of Josef Koczak, 2:14pm, 28 April.]

PA342q:

Will pick you up to run you to AH @ midnight. Site lights go off then, per regulations. Arrangements made with site foreman, so access should be no problem. Will handle him if there is. Have been requested to furnish electric torch & cordless bonesaw. If further needs, respond by 5:00pm.

▼ [Transcript of text message exchange between Josef Koczak and Neil Stoddard, Professor of Evolutionary Biology at Tufts University, between 11:12pm and 11:46pm GMT, 28 April.]

Koczak:
Are you busy? Catch you at a bad time?

Stoddard:
No, you're my rescuer. Mind numbingly godawful end of semester faculty dinner.

Koczak:
Wanted to get your reaction to a crazy theory I'm playing around with. No way to test it, much less prove it. Just mental exercise.

Stoddard:
Ah. Peer-reviewed journals LOVE those. Shoot.

Koczak:
Do you think it's possible for a morphic field to cause radical deviations in the way a disease pandemic develops? Same disease, same microbe, same DNA, but very different virulence & behavior in different eras & locales.

Stoddard:
Is this really a conversation you want to have by text? Can it wait until I'm free to talk?

Koczak:
Humor me. In London now, can't say why. Expect meeting soon, will be busy for foreseeable time afterward.

Stoddard:
& bored right this instant?

Koczak:
Busted.

Stoddard:
Any disease in particular?

Koczak:

Bubonic plague. Medieval vs modern. Has to be more than DNA. I keep coming back to that oddly defeatist statement by director of Chimpanzee Genome Project, when genome published in 2005. See that?

Stoddard:

No.

Koczak:

At start 4 years earlier, they fully expected it to reveal why chimps are so different from us. When they finally get to compare to our DNA, it's a headscratcher. Said this alone doesn't explain our differences.

Stoddard:

So morphic fields with plague? Had enuff wine to say oh why not. Some kind of epigenetic inheritance maybe? No changes in plague genes, just gene expression. Parent microbes spawn generations of offspring with much more aggressive relationship to infected hosts? Those strains burn out, later outbreaks revert to less aggressive norm?

Koczak:

My thinking too. But still doesn't explain why parent microbes would pass on more aggressive tendencies in the first place.

Stoddard:

Ah! Causality too! Back then they just blamed that part on the Devil.

Koczak:

U = anus.

Stoddard:

Sorry. Couldn't resist. & will deny this conversation ever took place if anyone asks.

Koczak:

Our little secret. But anything that kills off ~2/3 of continent's population, then centuries later downshifts to 3% mortality rate, hard not to wonder how that happens. Interesting to speculate malign hostility at the core of it.

Stoddard:

I fear you left science behind 2 or 3 turns ago.

Koczak:

It gets worse. Would you believe I'm headed to church for midnight mass?

From: Josef Koczak
To: Rashmi Bajwa, Assistant Director of Research and Development, New
World Pharmaceutical Group
Subject: All Hallows
Date: 29 April

Here's a thought: Next time, how about expending a little more effort to
research the situation so you're not sending someone into a goddamn HOT
ZONE instead of an archaeological site.

I did manage to acquire some samples a few hours ago, but only barely, and not
as many as I would've liked. Some molars and bone fragments, and while I wasn't
expecting this as an option, hair and soft tissue. For their age, the remains are in
a surprisingly good state of preservation. I'm assuming that the conditions of
their burial approximated what's been found many times with peat bogs. They
had that look, like tea-stained leather.

I've at least got no problems with your man on the ground here . . . your PI or
whatever he is. I don't think he said one word more than he had to, but he did
facilitate things well with the site foreman, and he'd prepared an accurate map
that got me into the church through an unlocked side entrance, then down below,
and finally to a corridor leading to the crypt itself. Crypt may be overstating it. It's
really just a glorified root cellar, although the atmosphere is dreadful.

It's no mystery where the OLD bodies came from. What I'd like to know is the
story behind the FRESH one.

Yes. There was a dead woman down there, on the floor and propped against a
wall. I didn't even notice her right away, just the smell of recent decay, which I
didn't think could be attributed to the disinterred bodies. I guessed a rat or two
had gotten down below and died. I practically stumbled over her before I realized
she was there.

Cause of death wasn't obvious (I wish it were), but she was enveloped in a cloud
of fleas the likes of which I'd never seen before and hope to never see again:
large, a vivid red-brown color, and the infestation was so bad it made her appear
to twitch. Maybe you've seen the way horses twitch their hide to shake off a
horsefly? Like that.

That's when I left. These things were highly active. I think I sustained a few bites,
but fortunately I did get the vaccination before leaving Chicago, and I've started a
regimen of streptomycin, so I'm not worried, but I cannot stress enough how
unacceptable a situation like this is.

One more thing of note: When I was leaving the site, I saw someone else on the way in, another woman looking highly unsure of herself and wobbling along on heels. As it was coming up on 1:30am, I can't imagine her business there was any more official than mine, but the point is, this location appears to be drawing some very curious attention.

Will let you know when I'm in transit to return stateside.

From: Josef Koczak
To: Jillian Christensen
Subject: All this technology and we still can't connect
Date: 1 May

Dear Jilly,

Where are you, love? Eight or nine calls, and nothing but voice mail. I'm trying to figure where you'd be now. It's what, seven hours earlier there in Chicago? Or six? I knew this yesterday. Up too late, too long, too much reading.

I've been wanting to tell you I won't be coming home as soon as I thought I would. Just a couple more days. I'm thinking it might be a good idea for me to stay here in my hotel for now. Just to make sure of something. Don't worry.

Just need to talk now, is all. I've never had much use for concepts like good or evil. You and I are good, of course. That's all that seemed to matter. But if there is evil, beyond merely a value judgment, I've been to a place that's absorbed it, or been permeated with it by design. I've felt something that is deeply, palpably wrong. This place they sent me to, they did so without seeming to have any clue of its background, which isn't hard to find even from a hotel room.

I'm just venting. Who would it have mattered to even if they'd done their homework? They could've given me the full rundown and I would've only regarded it as a quaint old bagful of superstition and quackery.

But then you get there, and you feel it. You feel it and sense it, and you tell yourself it's just your imagination, and before long you pray it's just your imagination, and then you catch yourself and realize: Why are you even praying, when you've always maintained there's nothing listening?

So I've been thinking a lot about fields lately: energy fields, electromagnetic fields, morphic fields, quantum fields, information fields. I wonder if somewhere tangled up in them is the answer to what we call evil, and all its manifest works, and we could find it if only we'd start by admitting it's there, and perhaps vulnerable to the warping influence of staggeringly corrupted minds. As such, I would think it prefers not being found.

I've also been thinking some about psychoactive substances, and those controlled studies in which test subjects report a significant overlap in visual hallucinations: the same shapes and geographic patterns, and even more interesting, the same faces sometimes, like harlequins and hybrid forms.

I've got a recurring one to tell you about. No psychoactives involved, but I've had a bit of fever lately, and the ugly bastard keeps showing up in my sleep. Is it a man dreaming he's a flea, or a flea dreaming it's a man? If I describe it, maybe you can sketch it. You're so good at that.

I just hope I don't have any trouble getting out of here once I'm a little more rested. I see on the television that there's been some trouble spreading in the streets, and you know how once a thing like that gets started, the mob is quick to join in. Loot first, ask questions later.

It's starting to look like the old Sex Pistols song, "Anarchon in the U.K."

Typo. Hah. I intended to write "Anarchy in the U.K." I almost corrected it, but let's leave it. I wonder where it came from. Wonder what it means.

Love you more,
Josef

London, April 30

THE GOVERNMENT has ignored its own public safety regulations to steamroller its plans to build its New Festival of Britain park over a seventeenth century plague pit.

Hard News can reveal the Home Secretary's decision to rush through the demolition of the Grade II listed Church of All Hallows in Blackheath has angered MPs, professionals and locals, who are calling for a radical rethink in the siting of the three-week event.

There have been demands for the entire area to be cordoned off after one contractor working on the demolition – which is being carried out under unique conditions of secrecy – claimed hundreds of corpses have already been exhumed and reburied in a hidden location.

Archeologists, historians, clerics, doctors and locals are banding together to fight the decision to knock down the eighteenth century church, much of which was designed by Thomas Moreby, who was apprenticed to black magician Nicholas Hawksmoor, himself a disciple of Sir Christopher Wren. *Hard News* has seen proof that Thomas Moreby, known as "the Zombie King", built a hidden crypt, using certain "magical" formulae, where he intended to bring the dead back to life.

Massive security now surrounds the church following yesterday's *Hard News* exposé of the plot by the so-called Resurrectionists to bring Princess Di (the People's Princess) back to life. This was revealed in a tip-off by a worried insider – JCB operator Marek Schwarinski – who has since left the country, according to his former bosses.

Health advisor and local historian Professor Margaret Winn, 57, has been researching All Hallows for the London Archeological Society. She told me, "I have recently discovered that one Oliver Whitby, the Justice of the Rolls at Lincoln's Inn Fields, built and maintained a number of burial sites around London, the first of which was constructed here at Blackheath in 1642. In his will he left instructions that it be used for plague victims. The dead were buried outside the city walls, and once the official sites – known as the 'Dead Grounds' – at Priory Hospital of the Blessed Virgin Mary without Bishopgate (or St Mary Spital, as it became known), Charterhouse and St Botolph's were full, plague victims were brought here.

"Although it had long been theorised that Blackheath got its name from its use as a plague pit, this is the first actual evidence of that."

Prof. Winn has uncovered even more strange facts about the mysterious Church of All Hallows.

"It is obviously sheer coincidence," she said, "but my research into this church also turned up the fascinating fact that a Miss Anne Whitby, most probably a direct descendent of that same Mr Whitby, married the architect Thomas Moreby in the church he built on Wednesday, September 7, 1803 – sadly, she died not long after, and from what I can see, so did he. He, of course, was interred in the same secret crypt from which he intended to reanimate his own body.

Hobbs End connection

"The Church of All Hallows has had an unsavoury reputation for most of its life," Professor Winn added, "with locals convinced the unfinished Central Line extension to Hobbs End has brought even more evil beings to the area.

"I don't believe in spirits, but I do believe in science. There has been plenty of proof that the Bubonic bacillus, which came to London via cotton bales transported from the Netherlands and spread primarily by fleas, does not necessarily die but can lay dormant for many, many years, centuries, even, and that is a risk I do not think the government should be taking.

"The Home Secretary is playing Russian Roulette with people's lives."

Prof. Winn may not believe in the Hobbs End Ghost that terrified Londoners in the 1950s, when hundreds of people claimed to have seen a great horned devil in the night sky – the outbreak of mass hallucination was later put down to mass hysteria caused by inhalation of gas after a massive leak – but locals are not so sure.

Mrs Joan Akuma, 79, of Ladysmith Crescent, Greenwich, is one of the many local residents who have tried to stop the construction.

"They tried to make me leave my house," she told *Hard News*, "but I told them no way was I leaving my home: I have lived here since I came to Britain from the Gambia in 1972, and I have raised a family and taught piano to hundreds of local children: this is my home. I have written to the Home Secretary, but he just sends more lawyers' letters.

"I am beginning to think maybe I should go to my son

Steven in Catford – that church has always been an evil place, but now I hear things in my own home, things in the attic, scratchings on the walls."

Mrs Akuma, a pillar of the local Baptist Church, claims the Hobbs End Ghost has been haunting her attic. "My son Steven did it up beautiful for me, with wooden walls and electric lights, but now I don't dare go up there. That nice Sergeant Calvin said there was nothing wrong – he said it was probably birds roosting in the eaves. But I know birds and it's not birds, but big evil.

"At first I thought it was the local kids – they're all going to the bad round here, no jobs, all playing truant all the time – just look at the mess they've made of that old Tube station at the end of the road, the one Transport for London use as a depot now. They've sprayed graffiti all over it.

"But that's just human badness, isn't it? The police keep checking my house and there's never anyone there. You don't see souls – souls are invisible – but they're not all good, are they? That church has always had an evil reputation. Mysterious forces are abroad. It's the centre of everything that's wrong."

Abandoned London Under Ground

Hard News has discovered that the Hobbs End portion of the Central Line is far from being the only abandoned part of the London Underground system. A Tube enthusiast, Peter Venaron, 23, told us: "My dad used to talk about the closed-down stations – when he was a boy he used to go down there and explore – London Underground as it was then used to run tours and everything. On the Piccadilly line alone there are nine dead stations, most at very deep level – I guess most people know about Aldwych, but you've also got Brompton Road, Down Street, Holloway Road, Hounslow West, Osterly Park & Spring Grove, Park Royal & Twyford Abbey, Strand and York Road, between Kings Cross and Caledonian Road – and that's just one line!

"If I wanted to hide away from the reanimated corpse of Princess Di, that's where I'd go. Or if I was the Hobbs End Ghost – so maybe they're not the safest places to be after all!"

The Home Office has refused to comment on the allegations that they are risking public safety, but

(continued on page 26)

A PLAGUE

by *Hard News* staff reporter

LONDONERS are bombarding local council pest control offices with demands for flea-powder!

Local residents in Blackheath and Greenwich have all reported a huge increase in the number of fleas around, and many people are claiming the insects are not just infesting household pets but are jumping onto humans as well.

Pest Controller Alan Frutelup of Rentokill maintains that whilst fleas are a common problem, especially in homes with cats or dog, it is rare for fleas in this country to transmit disease. "The primary concern is the distress that flea bites cause to people and pets," he said.

"There are many species of flea. Most are 2–3 mm long, and red or brown in colour, although recently we have been receiving reports of much bigger insects, some as long as 5 mm or even bigger. Adult fleas feed on the blood of mammals and birds, which they get by piercing the skin. However, flea larvae can live in carpets and material like bedding, feeding on organic matter like wool or cotton, so it is important to maintain high levels of hygiene. Flea cocoons can remain dormant for two years or more, and they can be awakened by the vibration of footsteps – we often see apparently empty homes, until people move in and their noise wakes the fleas up."

Mr Frutelup explained that fleas have evolved to feed on different animals. Cat and dog fleas will bite humans when handling pets or pet bedding, but the most common place for flea bites are the feet and lower legs,

OF FLEAS

from the fleas living on carpets and pet bedding who will jump up and bite people as they come close. The human flea is rare in this country, except for farms, where human fleas are found on pigs. Human fleas will bite anywhere on the body and cause great itching.

Flea bites are marked by a tiny dark spot surrounded by a reddened area, but the swelling is not pronounced, unlike mosquito bites. A single flea will often bite two or three times in the same area in search of blood, and although the bite is often felt immediately, it does not particularly hurt until the itching starts, a result of the body producing histamine to combat the bite. Consult your local pharmacist for advice and treatment.

If you have pets, you should:

- Vacuum thoroughly, especially the area where pets sleep. Take care when emptying the vacuum cleaner (fleas will still be alive).
- Shake or beat rugs and pet bedding outdoors.
- Wash pet bedding weekly, ideally at above 60°C.
- Take care when moving pet bedding to avoid spreading flea eggs.
- Consider placing pet beds on wooden floors, not carpets.
- And call in the professionals to deal with the problem.

Local council pest controllers reported a backlog of up to six weeks, and urged people to practise good hygiene themselves whilst waiting for their appointments.

Next week: Collect Tokens to win your own Pest Controller, only with *Hard News*!

MEMO

To: Commissioner's Office
From: Borough Command, Greenwich
Date: 02-05
Subject: Radio transcript

As requested   full transcript of radio dispatch: subsidiary CAD suite   G Division. Greenwich Police Station, NFOB excavation site.

Morning shift, 01-05.

* * * * * * * * * * * * * * * * *

07:18h

BERTELLI *(Ch.Insp. 2897 Ray Bertelli)*: S022 to Golf Control? *(Dead air)* S022 to Golf Control, receiving, over?

NOVEMBER GOLF 03 *(Civilian Radio Operator Uma Bhupathi)*: S022, receiving.

BERTELLI: Ahhh . . . finished your shift change then? It's only taken you 20 fucking minutes!

NOVEMBER GOLF 03: I'm sorry, I didn't get . . .

BERTELLI: Just keep your fucking carrot-crunching monkeys off my plot, yeah?

NOVEMBER GOLF 03: Could you repeat . . .?

BERTELLI: No I fucking couldn't. *(Background noise – discordant gunfire)* This is Chief Inspector Bertelli, Green Team, Heavy Weapons. We're at NFOB, and as you may have noticed, we've got something of a situation. The last thing we need is fucking plod getting in the way.

NOVEMBER GOLF 03: Sorry if there's been a blue-on-blue, sir, but Golf Division have a patrol-and-contain role at the excavation site . . .

BERTELLI: And a fucking marvellous job they've been doing. Benson, don't try to arrest the fucker, shoot it . . .

NOVEMBER GOLF 01 *(PS 1293 Don Maybury)*: Golf Control to S022, receiving, over?

BERTELLI: Receiving, go ahead.

NOVEMBER GOLF 01: Is there a problem at the site, over?

BERTELLI: No, everything's just tickety-boo! (*Background noise – discordant gunfire*) For fuck's sake, Benson . . .

NOVEMBER GOLF 01: Golf to S022, over?

BERTELLI: Which chimpanzee working for monkey nuts am I talking to now?

NOVEMBER GOLF 01: This is CAD Room Manager, Sergeant Don Maybury, over.

BERTELLI: What can I do for you, sergeant?

NOVEMBER GOLF 01: We're assuming you have Trojan units at the excavation site?

BERTELLI: You're assuming, are you?

NOVEMBER GOLF 01: Do you mind telling us how many?

BERTELLI: Five at the last count. We may be calling for more.

NOVEMBER GOLF 01: It seems a little unreasonable not to have informed us you were coming, over?

BERTELLI: Fuck me sideways, Maybury. Does this mean you've been sidelined by your own chain of command? Or have the previous woodentops in your office not been updating the log. Neither would be a surprise from what I'm fucking seeing here.

COOPER (*Insp. 8720 Jeanette Cooper*): November Golf from Five-three?

NOVEMBER GOLF 03: Inspector Cooper?

COOPER: What the hell's going on, Uma?

NOVEMBER GOLF 03: Where are you, ma-am?

COOPER: Where I'm supposed to be. At the MobComm unit, which has been left wide open by the way. Not only that, there's no sign of Inspector Makewaite for a debrief, or any other members of 5 Relief, including Sergeant Calvin.

NOVEMBER GOLF 03: Ma-am, can you come into the nick, over?

COOPER: Hardly. The rest of 1 Relief are now showing, and we haven't got a vehicle between us. We've also got S022 running all over the place – as uncooperative as ever. Their OIC's just told me to fuck off. We've got shots fired . . . have these blokes got XXX fever, or what? We've even got military units being deployed around the excavation site.

NOVEMBER GOLF 03: The Special Response Battalion have been on stand-by for several days, ma-am.

COOPER: I'm perfectly aware of that, Uma. But why've they suddenly been activated?

NOVEMBER GOLF 03: I'm afraid it's the blind leading the blind, ma-am. We walked into a hell of a mess here this morning. All I can tell you is it kicked off during the last shift. Someone's sent an e-mail and it's hit the fan. Meanwhile there's a big protest gathering . . .

COOPER: I can see that, Uma. Where are 5 Relief?

NOVEMBER GOLF 03: Inspector Makewaite, Sergeant Calvin, PC Gatewood and PC Mackintosh are all off the grid, ma-am. PCs Fletcher, Barkworth and Stopford were last reported at University Hospital. No update on their progress. Though I'm led to believe there's a developing incident at the hospital, which Lewisham are dealing with, over.

– –

07:30h

BERTELLI: S022 to Golf Control, over?

NOVEMBER GOLF 03: Go ahead, S022.

BERTELLI: This is Bertelli again. I need to speak to the CAD Room Manager, over?

NOVEMBER GOLF 03: Sergeant Maybury's on the phone at the moment, sir.

BERTELLI: Ordering his breakfast, no doubt. Look, we've moved in as part of an operation response. Things are on a need-to-know basis, which is pissing us off as much as you. We seem to have got things under control here for the time-being. But several officers have sustained injuries, so we need ambulances ASAP.

NOVEMBER GOLF 03: Roger that, sir.

BERTELLI: S022 to Golf Control.

NOVEMBER GOLF 03: Go ahead, sir.

BERTELLI: There's one other thing . . . who'm I talking to, by the way?

NOVEMBER GOLF 03: I'm Radio Operator Uma Bhupathi, sir.

BERTELLI: Civi?

NOVEMBER GOLF 03: That's correct, sir.

BERTELLI: You've no actual bobbies in the suite, Uma?

NOVEMBER GOLF 03: PC Prendergast didn't report this morning, sir. And Sergeant Maybury's still on the phone . . .

BERTELLI: And that's it?

NOVEMBER GOLF 03: Greenwich CAD's next door, but they're down in numbers too.

COOPER: November Golf from Five-three?

BERTELLI: Never mind, our own Control's on the fucking blink as well – seems like every fucker in the job's gone sick this morning. Listen very carefully, Uma. This is so fucking important you'll have to post your resignation if you fuck it up, you get me?

NOVEMBER GOLF 03: Affirmative, sir.

BERTELLI: Call 6669. It's Counter-Terrorist Command at New Scotland Yard. Tell them you need Biohazard Casevac at Blackheath Road, over.

NOVEMBER GOLF 03: Could you repeat that, sir . . .?

COOPER: November Golf from Five-three, receiving?

BERTELLI: No I couldn't, for Christ's sake! Look . . . we've got some hazardous materials down here which need moving, and quickly. *(Background noise – discordant shouting)* Jesus Christ, Benson . . . get these fucking sightseers shifted. What? I don't give a fuck what they're protesting about. This area is not safe. SO22 to Golf Control? Receive that?

NOVEMBER GOLF 03: Affirmative.

BERTELLI: I've got something else for you too. Forget what I said earlier. Get some units back to All Hallows church. We've got idiots coming out of the woodwork down here. Anarchists, church people. Some stupid Goth bitch seems to be stirring it all up.

COOPER: November Golf from Five-three?

NOVEMBER GOLF 03: Go ahead, ma-am.

COOPER: Uma, I've been trying to get through for the last five minutes.

NOVEMBER GOLF 03: Apologies ma-am, we're very under-strength.

COOPER: Join the club. Listen, without vehicles we're as much use as a chocolate fireguard. So I'm authorising everyone to use their own. Can you make a note of that?

NOVEMBER GOLF 03: Affirmative, ma-am.

COOPER: Any calls, put them through to me or to Sergeant Oggleby at MobComm. Seeing as SO22 don't want us near the site, we're going to trace all the bodies missing from the last shift. 8276 and 3987 are already *en route* to University Hospital.

NOVEMBER GOLF 03: SO22 have changed their request, ma-am. They'd like 1 Relief to provide support, over.

COOPER: Received, Uma. The way those trigger-happy prats were behaving half-an-hour ago, we're not going near them. And you can put that on paper, if you want. Besides, they've got the army, haven't they, over.

OGGLEBY *(PS 9738* Ian Oggleby*)*: Five-two to November Golf, receiving?

NOVEMBER GOLF 03: Go ahead, Sergeant Oggleby.

OGGLEBY: It's 07:40h, Uma, and I'm registering an official complaint about the unhygienic condition the MobComm unit was left in by 5 Relief. Not only were the premises insecure, but the walls, floor, desk, the ref's armchair, the office computer – both the VDU and the keyboard, the tea-making area, can you believe that!, and even the medicine cabinet – even the fucking medicine cabinet, I ask you! – are stained with blood and what look like other body fluids. The previous shift's paperwork is also in disarray. I can find no trace of an incident log or diary. This is an absolute disgrace, and nobody should expect to turn in for work, even in a time of crisis like this, and have to operate under such conditions. Am I clear, November Golf?

NOVEMBER GOLF 03: Clear, sergeant. I'll pass it on.

COOPER: Five-three to November Golf.

NOVEMBER GOLF 03: Go ahead, ma-am.

COOPER: I take it you've tried to raise Mr. Makewaite's Supervision Car, over? *(Dead air)* November Golf from Five-three, receiving over?

NOVEMBER GOLF 03: Apologies ma-am, we're being flooded with 999 calls.

COOPER: November Golf is designated for excavation matters during day-shift. Bounce them over to Greenwich.

NOVEMBER GOLF 03: I'm trying, ma-am. But Greenwich are inundated too. I think we're getting their overspill.

COOPER: Contact Force, tell them you need extra capacity, over.

NOVEMBER GOLF 03: I haven't time to sort that yet, ma-am.

COOPER: Are you on your own there, Uma?

NOVEMBER GOLF 03: I'm expecting PC Prendergast at some point, ma-am, but Sergeant Maybury's had to leave the office to deal with a personal matter, over. *(Dead air)*

COOPER: Do you want to run that by me again?

NOVEMBER GOLF 03: His little boy's been attacked by a dog and taken to hospital by his wife. Sergeant Maybury's gone to meet them there. Apparently it's quite bad.

COOPER: How the bloody hell can we expect the general public to respect these curfews if our own officers' kids aren't doing it?

NOVEMBER GOLF 03: As I understand it, ma-am, the dog actually came into the house. Managed to smash its way through the French windows while the little boy was watching Donald Duck.

COOPER: When is Sergeant Maybury expected back, over?

NOVEMBER GOLF 03: Couldn't tell you that, ma-am.

COOPER: Right . . . I'm on my way in. But listen . . . there's a copy of the Idiot Guide on IntraNet. You won't have clearance, but my sign-on is Zentropia256. It gives response procedures for all major incidents. Open it up, Uma. Have it ready for me when I get in.

NOVEMBER GOLF 03: Received, ma-am.

- -

07:45h

COOPER: November Golf from Five-three?

NOVEMBER GOLF 03: Go ahead, ma-am.

COOPER: Just out of interest, what was Mr. Makewaite's last reported position, over?

NOVEMBER GOLF 03: South end of Eliot Park, ma-am. That was at 05:07h.

COOPER: I take it all these unofficial absences have been noted?

NOVEMBER GOLF 03: Affirmative, ma-am. Chief Superintendent Kay's well aware of the situation, over.

COOPER: Aware of the situation but doing nothing? I see.

NOVEMBER GOLF 03: She and the rest of the borough commanders are attending a crisis meeting at New Scotland Yard. It's being chaired by the Assistant Commissioner.

COOPER: Great, so that's 32 of them fiddling while Rome burns.

NOVEMBER GOLF 03: Didn't receive that, ma-am.

COOPER: Forget it, Uma. Are Borough Command aware how undermanned we are?

NOVEMBER GOLF 03: That's affirmative, ma-am. Sergeant Maybury put that message through at 07:02h. The reply he got was "hold the fort".

COOPER: Roger that. ETA ten minutes.

COSGROVE *(PC 7001 Keith Cosgrove)*: November Golf from 7001.

NOVEMBER GOLF 03: Go ahead, Keith.

COSGROVE: I've found the Supervision Car. It's abandoned but intact on the east side of the Ravensbourne, over. Croxley Court. Under the arches where the DLR passes over.

NOVEMBER GOLF 03: Any sign of Inspector Makewaite, Keith?

COSGROVE: That's negative, over. A lot of blood inside, I have to say.

NOVEMBER GOLF 03: Five-three from November Golf.

COOPER: Go ahead, Uma.

NOVEMBER GOLF 03: 7001's located the Supervision Car, ma-am. On Croxley Court. No trace of Mr. Makewaite.

COOPER: Received. I'm diverting over there. Tell 7001 to stay with it. *(Dead air)* November Golf, did you receive, over?

NOVEMBER GOLF 03: Received, ma-am. Apologies. Every phone's ringing in here. There's a request for Fire Brigade turnout on the Brookmarsh Industrial Estate, over.

COOPER: In that case turn them out.

NOVEMBER GOLF 03: I've tried, ma-am. But I'm getting no reply. *(Dead air)* Ma-am . . . I've just received an e-mail that Lewisham High Street Fire Station is under attack.

COOPER: Can you confirm, Uma? You say Lewisham and Greenwich Fire Station is under attack?

NOVEMBER GOLF 03: Affirmative, ma-am. No further details.

COOPER: Tell 8276 and 3987 to divert from the hospital. You may need to use the other channel. They'll be across the border by now.

NOVEMBER GOLF 03: Received ma-am.

COOPER: And tell Sergeant Oggleby to commence foot patrol at All Hallows Church. He's to leave the MobComm and secure it. He can tell SO22 he's all we've got at present, over.

NOVEMBER GOLF 03: Five-two from November Golf, receiving?

OGGLEBY: Go ahead, Uma.

NOVEMBER GOLF 03: Sarge, a message from Inspector Cooper. Can you close up the office and go for a walk, over?

OGGLEBY: November Golf from Five-two . . . could you

ask Inspector Cooper to explain her thinking? I'm a bit busy.

NOVEMBER GOLF 03: We're very short staffed, sarge. She wants someone on the ground at the excavation site so we can observe what's happening with regard to S022 and the demonstrators, over.

OGGLEBY: And while I'm observing S022, who as a rule don't like being observed, who's going to deal with this shit-pile of paperwork?

NOVEMBER GOLF 03: I'm relaying a message from Inspector Cooper, sergeant. That's all I can tell you, over.

COOPER: November Golf from Five-three?

NOVEMBER GOLF 03: Go ahead, ma-am.

COOPER: Put me on talk-through with Sergeant Oggleby, Uma. *(Static dissonance)* Five-two from Five-three?

OGGLEBY: Receiving ma-am, go ahead.

COOPER: What's the problem, Eric? I've asked you to patrol the perimeter of the excavation site. That's what we're attached to Golf Division for, over.

OGGLEBY: The admin trail doesn't stop just because there are public order issues, ma-am. 5 Relief have left the job half-done. Calvin's shift report is about the only thing that's been completed and, frankly, it makes bizarre reading . . .

COOPER: Eric, please do as I ask you. Secure the MobComm.

OGGLEBY: That's easier said than done, ma-am. The lock on this door doesn't function any more . . .

COOPER: And then liaise with S022.

OGGLEBY: Ma-am, I don't think you understand. I have a shit-pile of paperwork that needs . . .

COOPER: Eric, I don't give a fuck about your shit-pile of paperwork. The wheel's coming off and you're hiding in the office. That won't look too good if I put it in my report, will it? Received, over?

OGGLEBY: Received, ma-am. Though what good I'll be on the plot when PSUs and military support are already in attendance, I don't know . . . over and out!

08:00h

COOPER: November-Golf from Five-three. Did you manage to access the Major Incident Guide?

NOVEMBER GOLF 03: Affirmative, ma-am. Just now. I'm not sure any of the contingencies cover what's actually happening today.

COOPER: There's no updated info at all?

NOVEMBER GOLF 03: There's been one upload in the last hour. Crisis management in the event of . . . *(Dead air)*

COOPER: November-Golf from Five-three?

NOVEMBER GOLF 03: Receiving, ma-am.

COOPER: You were saying you had new contingency details?

NOVEMBER GOLF 03: That's affirmative, ma-am.

COOPER: A full schematic?

NOVEMBER GOLF 03: Negative, ma-am. It just says . . . "Run away screaming".

COOPER: November Golf . . . is this some kind of joke?

NOVEMBER GOLF 03: No ma-am, I swear. That's what it says: "Extreme Incident First Phase Response Measures — Run Away Screaming".

COOPER: You haven't got the wrong page and found some prat's bloody stupid observation? *(Dead air)* November Golf from Five-three? Uma, can you respond, please?

NOVEMBER GOLF 03: Apologies, ma-am. I've just had a call from Chief Superintendent Howell at Major Incident Command. He wants to know if November Golf is suitably equipped to provide an Incident Control Point. I've to call him straight back.

COOPER: Patch him through to Borough Command. Chatsworth should be there even if Kay's at the Yard.

NOVEMBER GOLF 03: Superintendent Chatworth's gone India 99, ma-am. He wants a bird's eye view of the situation.

COOPER: And at the same time to be as far from it as possible, I see. Try him on Channel 6.

NOVEMBER GOLF 03: Already tried, ma-am. I don't think he's airborne yet. And apparently he hasn't got a PR with him.

COOPER: Christ in a cartoon! Tell Howell he'll have to wait.

NOVEMBER GOLF 03: I can't tell him that, ma-am. And there's no one more senior here. I don't know how long Sergeant Maybury's going to be. Or Tom Prendergast. You said you were coming in to assist, but there's no sign of . . .

COOPER: Uma, pull yourself together, over.

NOVEMBER GOLF 03: It's easy to say that, ma-am. You're not here.

COOPER: Miss Bhupathi . . . just follow your orders. You can't do more than that.

NOVEMBER GOLF 03: Which orders, ma-am . . . "Run away screaming"?

COOPER: Hold the fort! Over and out!

BERTELLI: Bertelli to November Golf.

NOVEMBER GOLF 03: Go ahead, sir.

BERTELLI: *(Background noise: discordant shouting)* I thought you were sending me ambulances and extra manpower?

NOVEMBER GOLF 03: I'm trying sir, but we haven't got anyone available.

BERTELLI: *(Background noise: engines rumbling)* Let me put this on the line for you, darling. We've got hundreds of fucking demonstrators here now. Not only that, we've got demolition crew . . . who actually think they're going to start work today. Has no one read that fucking report I sent through this morning . . . about what we saw when we first arrived? About the XXX orders we had to execute?

NOVEMBER GOLF 03: Some kind of report went in sir . . . there's a big meeting . . .

BERTELLI: A big meeting's no fucking good to us, Uma. There's several hundred people here now, in more danger than they could ever imagine. Now get someone at the Big House to shake their fucking arse!

NOVEMBER GOLF 03: November Golf to Inspector Cooper, receiving, over?

COOPER: Five-three receiving.

NOVEMBER GOLF 03: We have a serious public order situation at the excavation site. S022 want Borough support and ambulance turn-out ASAP.

COOPER: Who's that ignorant bastard acting as OIC?

NOVEMBER GOLF 03: Chief Inspector Bertelli, ma-am.

COOPER: Patch me through, over.

NOVEMBER GOLF 03: *(Static dissonance)* Go ahead, ma-am.

COOPER: Inspector Cooper to Chief Inspector Bertelli? *(Dead air)* Inspector Cooper to S022, receiving, over? *(Dead air)* Five-three to November Golf?

NOVEMBER GOLF 03: Ma-am?

COOPER: Until he can be bothered answering his radio, he can whistle for his assistance. Not that we've got much to give him. What's the situ with the ambulances, over?

NOVEMBER GOLF 03: No units available from Lewisham, over.

COOPER: There's a subsidiary station on Amersham Road, Uma.

NOVEMBER GOLF 03: I've tried that number as well, ma-am. But it seems to be permanently engaged.

NOVEMBER GOLF 03: They have a radio too. The call-sign is Foxtrot Zulu 911. Try them on Channel 9, over.

- -

08:15h

NOVEMBER GOLF 03: Foxtrot Zulu 911 from November Golf, receiving? *(Dead air)* Foxtrot Zulu . . .

FOXTROT ZULU *(Unidentified respondent)*: Mmmmmffff . . . receiving. Zulu November yaaannkee . . . one . . . M-I-C . . . K-E-Y . . . M-O-U . . .

NOVEMBER GOLF 03: This is Golf Control at Greenwich police station, special designation for NFOB excavation site. We have a major public order situation on Blackheath Road. Require immediate ambulance support, over.

FOXTROT ZULU: Wilco . . . K-E-Y . . . M-O-U-S-E . . .

NOVEMBER GOLF 03: Who'm I speaking to, over?

FOXTROT ZULU: M-I-C . . . K-E-Y . . .

COOPER: November Golf from Five-three, receiving?

NOVEMBER GOLF 03: Receiving, ma-am.

COOPER: Any luck with Amersham Road?

NOVEMBER GOLF 03: Erm . . . negative at the moment, ma-am.

COOPER: Keep trying, Uma. In the meantime, 7001 and myself are at the Supervision Car. Keith was quite correct. There's an awful lot of blood here. Inside and out. We're securing the scene. Also there are some lock-ups under the railway arches, and a door next to them has been forced open. There's a stair leading down into some kind of underground vault. 7001 has an idea it connects with the tunnels that link the old York Road and Hobbs End Tube Stations. Received?

NOVEMBER GOLF 03: Received, erm . . . ma-am. Any reported incidents from Hither Green, over?

COOPER: Not to me, Uma. Anything at your end, over?

NOVEMBER GOLF 03: Negative, ma-am.

COOPER: Well . . . good. I take it you're concerned about your mother and sister?

NOVEMBER GOLF 03: I'm sure they'll be fine.

COOPER: If they followed the recommendations of the National Security Act, they should have sorted themselves out a panic room, over.

NOVEMBER GOLF 03: Yes, ma-am. "All citizens are responsible for their own safety once inside their own home". They have a panic room, I understand . . . of sorts. Over.

COOPER: Don't worry about it, Uma. I'm sure they'll be fine. Nothing reported at Hither Green as yet. But once we've sorted this lot, I'll get someone over there. In the meantime, 7001 and myself are going to see if Inspector Makewaite found his way down into the tube tunnels. Find Eric Oggleby wherever he's having a cup of tea, and tell him I want him in the CAD suite with you until either Sergeant Maybury or Tom Prendergast gets in, over.

NOVEMBER GOLF 03: Ma-am . . .

COOPER: In the meantime, put me and Keith on talk-through. I don't know how well these digital handsets work underground, but now's a good a time to find out.

NOVEMBER GOLF 03: Received, ma-am.

(Static dissonance)

COOPER: Five-three . . . November Golf?

NOVEMBER GOLF 03: Go ahead, ma-am.

COOPER: We've descended . . . two levels and come to a junction . . . going to split up here . . . still receiving us, over?

NOVEMBER GOLF 03: You're breaking a little, ma-am, but I can hear you.

COOPER: Copy that.

NOVEMBER GOLF 03: Five-two from November Golf.

OGGLEBY: Go ahead, Uma.

NOVEMBER GOLF 03: Message from Inspector Cooper, sergeant. Can you come into Greenwich and assist in CAD until Sergeant Maybury returns, over?

OGGLEBY: I think Inspector Cooper needs to decide which jobs need prioritising, over.

NOVEMBER GOLF 03: Are you still at Blackheath Road, over?

OGGLEBY: Erm . . . that's negative, Uma. I'm indoors at present. A local resident, Mrs. Wilberforce – quite elderly and infirm. She lives on Devonshire Drive and she's finding the uproar a little disconcerting. Two sugars, please, my love. Yeah, I'm just doing the old reassurance bit, over.

NOVEMBER GOLF 03: ETA to Greenwich, sergeant?

OGGLEBY: Is there a patrol that can pick me up?

NOVEMBER GOLF 03: That's negative at present.

OGGLEBY: What's Inspector Cooper actually doing?

NOVEMBER GOLF 03: Trying to find Inspector Makewaite, over.

OGGLEBY: Good luck to her on that one. Tell her to check a few married women's bedrooms. That'd be a start. ETA 25 minutes . . . while it seems I have to walk, over.

- -

08:30h

COOPER: Five-three to 7001. Receiving me . . . Keith?

COSGROVE: Loud and clear . . . ma-am.

COOPER: Where . . . are you?

COSGROVE: Not sure. Mesh fences . . . fuck me!

COOPER: What's . . . the problem?

COSGROVE: I think there are rats . . . yeah, there are rats down here, ma-am. I can hear them . . . moving in the walls.

COOPER: Where . . . are you?

COSGROVE: . . . track-bed, over.

COOPER: I'm down the next . . . Like a rabbit warren . . . down here. I can't see . . . you.

COSGROVE: My torch isn't doing . . . so well, ma-am.

COOPER: . . . check the batteries before you . . . on duty?

COSGROVE: Didn't think I'd need it on earlies . . . over.

COOPER: . . . if they run out of juice . . . your arse in the dark.

COSGROVE: Nothing like learning on the job . . . eh, ma-am?

COOPER: See if you can find your way . . . to the platforms. I'll meet . . . there.

OGGLEBY: Five-two to November Golf?

NOVEMBER GOLF 03: Sergeant Oggleby?

OGGLEBY: *(Background noise: traffic, shouting)* Yes, Uma. I've found Inspector Makewaite, over. He was on the corner of Deptford Broadway and Brookmill Road, in a confused and dishevelled state. Not totally surprising given what's going on. He's also displaying injuries to his hands and face.

NOVEMBER GOLF 03: Does he know what happened to 5 Relief, over?

OGGLEBY: Negative at present. He's not making a lot of sense. Not that these chinless wonders from

Bramshill ever do. Listen Uma, I'm not asking for transport back to the nick now, I'm *requiring* it. I certainly can't walk his lordship back in this condition, over.

NOVEMBER GOLF 03: Is there no place of safety he can be removed to in the vicinity?

OGGLEBY: *(Background noise: traffic, shouting)* Hardly love, it's like a war zone round here. People running everywhere. What's going on?

NOVEMBER GOLF 03: Sounds if the protest at the site has turned violent, sergeant. It's not very clear, but we have no units to respond, over.

OGGLEBY: In that case call me a cab. Charge it to Borough Command, over.

NOVEMBER GOLF 03: Can I just confirm, sergeant . . . you want me to call you a cab, over?

OGGLEBY: Alternatively, call Cooper and tell her she can come and pick us up herself. She was the one looking for Makewaite in the first place, wasn't she?

NOVEMBER GOLF 03: Inspector Cooper keeps breaking. I think it's because she's underground, over.

OGGLEBY: How convenient . . . hang on, whoooaaa . . . no you don't!

NOVEMBER GOLF 03: Five-two from November Golf? *(Dead air)* Five-two, receiving? *(Dead air)* Five-two from November Golf.

COSGROVE: 7001 to Five-three, over?

COOPER: Go ahead . . . Keith.

COSGROVE: Reached end of tunnel . . . sealed up. Heading back now . . . your position . . . hopefully.

COOPER: Can you see . . . anything yet?

COSGROVE: It's tricky . . . light's virtually gone. Hang on. When was this station . . . last operational, ma-am?

COOPER: Couldn't . . . tell you, why?

COSGROVE: We've got film posters here . . . Trevor Howard and Celia Johnson . . .

COOPER: . . . should give you a clue. Where are you . . . now?

COSGROVE: Hard to say. Wait . . . is that your light? It winked on . . . off . . . assume you passed an entrance?

COOPER: Affirmative . . . leads through to . . . platform.

COSGROVE: In that case, I'm on . . . other platform.

COOPER: Stay where you are . . . coming through. Uh . . .

COSGROVE: 7001 to Inspector Cooper . . . all right, ma-am?

COOPER: Supermarket trolley. How . . . hell did that end up down here?

COSGROVE: Fucking tea-laves . . . get everywhere.

COOPER: Yeah . . . that may mean this entrance to the station . . . open before the Supervision Car got dumped . . . may be unrelated, over.

COSGROVE: Ma-am . . . don't understand why Inspector Makewaite would have come down . . . here anyway.

COOPER: Hold up . . . shut up, Keith. Just listen.

COSGROVE: What am . . . listening for, ma-am?

COOPER: Thought . . . heard something . . . a rumbling noise. Nearby. I can just about see you now. That torch of yours . . . as much good as a . . . candle.

COSGROVE: That's why I'm staying away from . . . platform edge . . . any trains still run through here?

COOPER: Only . . . the London Necropolis Railway . . . sometimes known as the "Dead Body Train".

COSGROVE: That's a joke . . . assuming?

COOPER: Not at all. Heavy bombing during . . . war created massive fatalities. Corpses . . . loaded onto a special train to be transported across the river to . . . mortuary at . . . Royal London Hospital for ID . . . and final disposal at Brookwood Cemetery. There's one ran through . . . East End as well.

COSGROVE: So why . . . it still be running now?

COOPER: . . . just a ghost story, Keith. Relax.

COSGROVE: Hell of a time for ghost stories . . . hang about . . . think I hear something . . .

--- --- --- --- --- --- --- --- --- --- --- --- --- --- --- --- ---

08:45h

OGGLEBY: Five-two to November Golf?

NOVEMBER GOLF 03: Sergeant Oggleby?

OGGLEBY: *(Background noise: loud traffic)* Chasing Inspector Makewaite on foot, Uma. Assistance required. Heading south along Brookmill Road. *(Dead air)* Five-two to November Golf. Still in pursuit. Turning right down Strickland Street, heading south. Any back-up appreciated, over.

BERTELLI: *(Background noise: discordant gunfire, screaming)* SO22 to November Golf . . . , where's my fucking ambulances? Where's my Biohazard Casevac? Not that there's much need for it now.

NOVEMBER GOLF 03: The request has been passed on, sir,

BERTELLI: *(Background noise: discordant gunfire, screaming)* Tell them to get a fucking move on! We've got a fucking disaster unfolding here. Multiple casualties, both civi and police! This whole district should be put under quarantine. Get onto Force and tell them we have a "Category A" situation at Blackheath Road. At least eighteen unofficial XXX orders have been cleanly executed. But we need extra men right now. We also need heavy plant to build barricades. One more thing – put it out via Force that only clean head-shots appear to be effective. Tompkins, there's another one over there! Headshots, I said. Are you fucking listening . . .

COSGROVE: 7001 to Five-three . . . can still hear it, ma-am. Sounds like . . . dunno what it sounds like . . .

COOPER: Stop moving around . . . listen.

COSGROVE: Sounds like . . . someone's crying, ma-am.

COOPER: Your side of the track-bed . . .?

COSGROVE: Do you want to cross over . . . ma-am?

COOPER: Negative . . . acoustics in here . . . deceptive.

COSGROVE: Sounds like . . . coming from the north end.

COOPER: Proceed . . . caution, Keith. Silent approach . . . over.

OGGLEBY: *(Background noise: loud traffic)* Five-two to November Golf. Is anyone actually coming, Uma? Makewaite's crossing roads like it doesn't matter. He's just caused a cab to swerve and mount the pavement at the junction of St. John's and Bold. Get Traffic support to deal with it, over.

NOVEMBER GOLF 03: Sergeant Oggleby . . . I'm afraid you're on your own at present. I've no one available.

OGGLEBY: This is going on fucking paper, let me tell you. Turning east along Lewisham Way. Wait up . . . assault in progress on Lewisham Way. Three male youths attacking an elderly female. *(Background noise: shouting)* You little shitehawks! . . . AP is down in a collapsed state, apparently severely injured. About to render first-aid. *(Background noise: unidentified male voice: "Stupid twat . . . she's infected!")* Stay where you are, you little . . . Uma, you receiving this, over?

NOVEMBER GOLF 03: Affirmative, sergeant. I'm sorry . . .

OGGLEBY: *(Background noise: traffic)* Don't be sorry, just get an ambulance to the junction of Lewisham Way and Loampit Hill. AP still in a collapsed state. Hang fire . . . she's coming round, over. No sign of the youths responsible now . . .

COSGROVE: Five-three . . . from 7001?

COOPER: I said silent approach . . . Keith.

COSGROVE: Appreciate that, ma-am, but . . . just found what looks like a half-eaten rat . . . over.

OGGLEBY: Five-two to November Golf?

NOVEMBER GOLF 03: Receiving, sergeant.

OGGLEBY: Lady from a house nearby has put a blanket over the AP. She seems to be conscious but she's incoherent. You've got to get an ambulance here ASAP. I'm still looking for Makewaite . . . wait, I see him. Standing on the footbridge over the railway cutting. Looks like he's going to jump off, over.

COOPER: November Golf . . . from Five-three?

NOVEMBER GOLF 03: Receiving, ma-am. You're very faint.

COOPER: Anyone available . . . provide back-up at Hobbs End Tube?

NOVEMBER GOLF 03: That's negative, ma-am. No one available anywhere.

COOPER: Five-three to 7001 . . . is that half-eaten rat as in . . . freshly half-eaten . . .?

COSGROVE: Pretty fresh, ma-am. Still bleeding . . . over.

COOPER: . . . still hear that crying sound . . . Keith? Because I think . . . I can.

COSGROVE: Could be crying, ma-am . . . could also be chuckling, over.

OGGLEBY: November Golf from Five-two?

NOVEMBER GOLF 03: Sergeant Oggleby?

OGGLEDY: Makewalte's still stationary in the middle of the footbridge. Well done getting me some back-up.

NOVEMBER GOLF 03: Apologies for that, sergeant, but we're pulled out . . .

OGGLEBY: Negative, Uma. I mean well done for real. There's another unit approaching the bridge from the other side.

NOVEMBER GOLF 03: Nothing to do with us, sergeant.

OGGLEBY: Doesn't matter. We've got him cornered. I'm going up and talking to him.

COSGROVE: Five-three from 7001? Your torch . . . on the blink as well, ma-am . . . can hardly see you . . .

COOPER: Place is thick with dust. Probably . . . reverberations from our conversation . . . bringing it down. What's that . . . smell . . .?

COSGROVE: Don't know, but it's fucking rotten . . . ma-am . . . can see someone . . . in front of me. Crouching . . . at the end of the platform.

COOPER: Yeah . . . see him. Keith hang fire . . . coming over . . .

COSGROVE: Wouldn't advise it . . . Oh, Jesus Christ . . . Jesus God Almighty!

COOPER: Keith . . .!

OGGLEBY: Five-two to November Golf. Makewaite's being compliant again. No ID on the support unit. He's coming over the bridge towards us now. Looks like a dog man . . . without his dog.

NOVEMBER GOLF 03: Sergeant Oggleby, be careful . . .

OGGLEBY: Stand by, November Golf. Detaining Makewaite under the Mental Health Act. It's the only thing I can do to ensure he doesn't . . . wait . . . don't . . .

NOVEMBER GOLF 03: Sergeant Oggleby, receiving?

OGGLEBY: Immediate assistance, Uma . . . something badly wrong with these two . . .

NOVEMBER GOLF 03: Five-two receiving? *(Dead air)* Five-two receiving, over?

OGGLEBY: Uma . . . Jesus Christ, get some support . . . for fuck's saaaa . . .

COSGROVE: Oh my God, ma-am. Oh my . . . Christing God!

COOPER: Keith . . . get away from there!

COSGROVE: It's a woman . . . just stood up and turned around. She's been burned . . . head to foot . . . like fucking fried bacon.

COOPER: Keith, backtrack . . . get away.

COSGROVE: God in Heaven, ma-am . . . it's Charlotte Gatewood from 5 Relief!

COOPER: Keith . . . November Golf from Five-three, urgent message!

NOVEMBER GOLF 03: Ma-am, I can't . . . I can barely . . .

COOPER: Require immediate assistance . . . Hobbs End Tube Station. Oh my God . . . oh my God in Heaven . . .

NOVEMBER GOLF 03: Ma-am. You're breaking badly.

COOPER: Jesus, she just clawed his eyes out. Just . . . clawed them right out. Now . . . ripping at his . . . *(Background noise: gunfire)* . . . she's ripped out his . . . gullet!

NOVEMBER GOLF 03: Jeanette, run for it, run please
. . .

COOPER: No effect . . . soever.

NOVEMBER GOLF 03: Inspector Cooper, run for your
life.

BERTELLI: SO22 to November Golf.

NOVEMBER GOLF 03: Thank God, sir . . .

BERTELLI: You alright, Uma? Sound as if you're having
as rough a time of it as we are . . .

NOVEMBER GOLF 03: Sir, all our patrols are in trouble.
We desperately need back-up . . .

BERTELLI: One thing at a time, Uma. We seem to be
getting on top of this situation again. That's "we"
as in SO22 and, to a lesser extent, the SRB. This
message needs to go out on all channels *(Background
noise: gunfire)* Benson, staff the bugger if you've
run out of slugs! Cave his fucking bonce in! I don't
give a fuck if he's wearing a paramedic's uniform.
He's not a paramedic any more. You still there, Uma?

NOVEMBER GOLF 03: Sir . . . you're not listening to
me . . .

BERTELLI: No Uma, you're not listening to me. This is
it, where we are . . . Ground Zero! You get that? This
is where it's all spreading from . . . so this is more
important than anything else. Now take note of this
message. As from this moment, the following roads are
closed: Lewisham Road, Blackheath Hill, Greenwich
South Street, Greenwich High Road and New Cross Way.
You understand that, Uma? They are closed to all
members of the public and any security services
acting without authorisation. This area is now an
official control zone, and heavily armed units will
be patrolling it, under orders to XXX any intruders.
You understand that, Uma?

NOVEMBER GOLF 03: Sir, I don't understand. You've
taken this decision unilaterally?

BERTELLI: That's correct. As no message has come down
from God in the last two hours, Man has taken it on
himself to save the world. Now you get that message
to the Press Office. Have them contact all local radio
and television outlets, over.

NOVEMBER GOLF 03: All attempts to contact the media have failed, sir.

BERTELLI: All of them? What about the BMC? They were here half-an-hour ago.

NOVEMBER GOLF 03: No one at BMC is replying now, sir.

BERTELLI: They're still transmitting, aren't they?

NOVEMBER GOLF 03: For most of the day they've been transmitting Disney cartoons on a loop, over.

BERTELLI: Try the satellite companies.

NOVEMBER GOLF 03: I've had a report that all satellite transmissions are being disrupted . . . they think their signals are being jammed.

BERTELLI: This is fucked!

NOVEMBER GOLF 03: Sir, can you spare a couple of your men to visit Taunton Road in Hither Green, over?

BERTELLI: What the fuck do you not understand about we've got a job to do here first? Keep trying the Press Office, and if they can't do their fucking job, you'll have to do to it for them. Pick the telephone up and speak to someone for Hail Mary's sake! *(Background noise: unidentified howling)* Tomkins! There's another one coming . . . I thought you'd cleared that . . .

- -

09:15h

COOPER: November Golf . . . Five-three?

NOVEMBER GOLF 03: That you, ma-am? I can hardly hear you.

COOPER: I've got . . . whisper, Uma. You don't understand . . . can't talk aloud.

NOVEMBER GOLF 03: What's your location, over?

COOPER: Don't know. I lost my torch. Amateurish of me . . . suppose. Got my gun though. For all the good that is . . . I'm somewhere in the guts of this old station. Can't find my way out . . . lost.

NOVEMBER GOLF 03: Surely you remember the way you came in?

COOPER: Got turned around . . . down here in the tunnels.

NOVEMBER GOLF 03: Ma-am, sorry about this, but I need your permission to send someone to check on 14, Taunton . . .

COOPER: Shhhh . . . no contact, Uma . . . no contact.

BAINBRIDGE (*PC 9722 Andy Bainbridge*): 9722 to November Golf, receiving?

NOVEMBER GOLF 03: Receiving? That you, Andy?

BAINBRIDGE: Affirmative, Uma. *En route* back from Lewisham. I'm driving and I've got 3987 with me.

NOVEMBER GOLF 03: Don't go anywhere near the excavation site. Come to the nick, but make your way over Burnt Ash, if you can, and take Lee Road. Head for Greenwich via Shooters Hill.

BAINBRIDGE: Problems, Uma?

NOVEMBER GOLF 03: NFOB site's become a riot zone.

BAINBRIDGE: You should see it round the hospital.

NOVEMBER GOLF 03: What's causing all this, Andy?

BAINBRIDGE: No one's briefed you yet?

NOVEMBER GOLF 03: In the special contingency measures there was some reference to . . . it just sounded crazy.

BAINBRIDGE: Crazy doesn't come close to covering it.

NOVEMBER GOLF 03: What's your ETA, over?

BAINBRIDGE: Christ knows. I'm nowhere near the excavation site, and I'm seeing crashed cars, people wandering dazed. Other people running . . .

NOVEMBER GOLF 03: Listen, Andy . . . before you get back here, can you divert to Taunton Road. My mum and my sister live at number 14. Pick them up, please. Bring them here, if you can. Or better still just take them somewhere, anywhere away from all this.

COOPER: November Golf from Five-three? Uma, are you there?

NOVEMBER GOLF 03: Ma-am?

COOPER: Uma . . . I think . . . think I've shaken her off . . . can still hear her. I'm making my way along

. . . service passage . . . so dark down here. I'm literally groping my way along . . .

NOVEMBER GOLF 03: Ma-am . . . you're breaking badly. You need to stop whispering and speak up . . .

COOPER: I know when . . . she gets close . . . I can smell her. Can you believe that? It's . . . so dark. But . . . can literally smell her. Burned meat. It's sickening. Uma . . . she killed Keith Cosgrove. Now she's . . . hunting me.

NOVEMBER GOLF 03: I know that, ma-am.

COOPER: I don't know whether she can smell me . . . or hear me. I seriously doubt she can . . . see me. Glimpsed her in . . . gun-flashes. Eyes like tarnished baubles in a face as . . . black as tar. No bottom jaw. Entire lower abdomen burned away . . . just a cavity under exposed ribs. Shred of charred innards hanging out. Like a martyr chained to a stake. Hehehe . . . don't know why I thought . . . that. Hardly right for . . . this situation. Oh my God . . . can hear her again. Blundering along the passage . . . behind me. She just keeps following, Uma . . .

BAINBRIDGE: 9722 to November Golf, over?

NOVEMBER GOLF 03: Receiving, Andy?

BAINBRIDGE: You crying, Uma?

NOVEMBER GOLF 03: Just had a fright. Bad things are happening, Andy. Even next door. I'll be all right. Go ahead.

BAINBRIDGE: Have a full medical kit for when we arrive at the nick, over. 3987 got badly assaulted at the hospital. By a woman with one arm, would you believe. She bit four of his fingers off. He's bleeding copiously. I've tried to fix him, but my first aid knowledge has its limits, you know what I mean. Not only that, he's crawling with bugs. Little red bastards. Christ knows what they actually are. What were you saying about diverting over?

NOVEMBER GOLF 03: Negative. Forget it, over.

BAINBRIDGE: You mentioned Taunton Road?

NOVEMBER GOLF 03: Negative. Cancel that.

BAINBRIDGE: Roger . . . Christ, I'm feeling rough. Eh . . . what the . . . hang on . . .

NOVEMBER GOLF 03: Andy what's the matter?

BAINBRIDGE: It's Tony . . . he's screwing around with the steering wheel, Tony, what're you . . .

NOVEMBER GOLF 03: 9722 from November Golf? *(Dead air)* 9722 from November Golf, receiving, over? *(Dead air)*

- -

09:30h

NOVEMBER GOLF 03: November Golf to Five-three, receiving?

COOPER: Receiving, Uma. Go . . . ahead.

NOVEMBER GOLF 03: Ma-am, have you got yourself out of there, yet? We have full-scale emergencies all over the division. I've just . . . wait, I'm just reading an e-mail which states . . . which states that a police officer has just been thrown from the footbridge over the overland railway between Lewisham Station and Blackheath . . . apparently by two other police officers!

COOPER: It's . . . good day for extreme action, I think . . .

NOVEMBER GOLF 03: Ma-am, no confirmation on this, but I have reason to believe it may be Sergeant Oggleby, over.

COOPER: If it's any consolation . . . he got it quicker than PC Cosgrove . . .

NOVEMBER GOLF 03: Apparently not, ma-am. We've just had an update . . . though run over by a train and severed at the waist, the police officer thrown from the bridge is . . . "is crawling along the railway siding, dragging strings of what look like internal organs behind him". They're saying he's not dead, ma-am.

COOPER: Shhh! No contact, Uma.

NOVEMBER GOLF 03: But I think he is . . .

COOPER: Shhhh! She's . . . hunting me. I can hear her . . . blundering up and down these . . . passages . . . hear that crunching sound? That's the impacts of her feet. They're totally carbonised . . . just cinders. And she's . . . walking around. Can you

believe it? What chance for us? Bobbies I know . . .
call in sick with . . . stubbed toes. Hehehehe!

NOVEMBER GOLF 03: Ma-am, just lie low. I'll get help
to you when I can. All units from November Golf . . .
urgent message. A young family in Hither Green
requires immediate police assistance. Any unit to
respond, over? Any unit to respond? *(Dead air)* Please
. . . any unit to respond?

MAYBURY: Affirmative, November Golf.

NOVEMBER GOLF 03: Sergeant Maybury, is that you? You
finished at the hospital, over?

MAYBURY: Affirmative, November Golf.

NOVEMBER GOLF 03: You don't mind . . . I know it's
not very professional of me, but please divert. Call
at 14, Taunton Road, Hither Green. It's my mum's
house. She improvised a panic room in the cellar. She
and my sister will probably be hiding in there by now.
It'll be locked. But there's a spare key under the
clock on the mantelpiece. Get them to a place of
safety, will you?

MAYBURY: Affirmative, November Golf.

NOVEMBER GOLF 03: You won't believe what's been
happening here. One of the Greenwich patrols came up
and attacked the radio operators next door. I don't
know what the outcome was. I've had to bar the door.

MAYBURY: Affirmative, November Golf.

NOVEMBER GOLF 03: Sergeant Maybury? How's your little
boy?

MAYBURY: Affirmative, November Golf.

NOVEMBER GOLF 03: Who . . . what are . . . don't you
dare! Don't you dare go to Taunton Road! Do you hear
me! Don't you lay one finger on them. Don't you dare
. . . don't you dare . . .

MAYBURY: Affirmative, November Golf.

COOPER: November Golf from Five-three. Uma . . . can't
find my mobile phone. Must've dropped it . . . along
with the torch. How stupid am I? . . . so deep under
London. But I . . . think I've found a disused tunnel.
Must've been bricked up at one time . . . bricks have
been knocked through . . . you know, I think it's the
old line which the Necropolis Train used to . . . run

along. Goes north under the river . . . links with
the rest of the network. Realise what that . . .
means, Uma? Don't know whether . . . ever officially
called the "Dead Body line", eh? But how appropriate?
They can use it . . . spread out across London and no
one will . . . notice.

BERTELLI: November Golf from S022? *(Dead air)*
November Golf, receiving? *(Dead air)*.

COOPER: Uma . . . me again . . . think I've shaken her
off. Knocked a few bricks . . . through into . . .
Dead Body tunnel. But I didn't go that way. I carried
on across . . . track-bed. I've passed through some
kind of ventilation shaft . . . think I must now be
in the vicinity of York Road Station . . . can sense
that I've foxed her. How hard can that be . . . her
brain got flambód. Hehehe. Can't smell anything now
. . . can't hear her. *(Dead air)* Uma, I've found an
old spiral stair . . . steel gate across it. Totally
blind down here . . . but . . . can feel the gate.
Right . . . in front of me . . . fastened with chains,
covered . . . rust and cobwebs. I'm ignoring it . . .
can't risk trying to force it . . . make too much
noise. Uma . . . why the hell, I mean it's ridiculous
. . . why the hell are old tube stations . . . always
littered with yesterday's papers? Heheheh . . . if I
had . . . cigarette lighter, could perhaps read . . .
what would I see? . . . VE Day? Coronation? Beatles
at Wembley? History's not too good, Uma, but . . .
doubt any of those . . . days will go down in history
the way this one . . . eh? *(Dead air)* You're very
quiet, Uma . . . doesn't matter. I don't suppose you
. . . afford to speak loudly either, over?

BERTELLI: November Golf, this is Bertelli. *(Dead air)*
November Golf from Chief Inspector Bertelli,
receiving? *(Dead air)* I don't know where you are, but
you may be interested to know that a member of the
public has reported a massive RTA on Lee Road.
Multiple casualties. Sounds like a vehicle has just
ploughed along a crowded pavement before hitting a
bus stop. Latest report is that there are two police
officers in the car. Both look to have sustained
serious injuries. We have no one to spare, Uma. You
lot will have to deal, over.

COOPER: Uma . . . I think I've located a way out at
last . . . maintenance ladder. It goes straight up a
circular shaft. Possibly . . . fire-exit of some sort.

It can't be safe after so long, but . . . got no
choice. Wherever it comes out . . . may be sealed off
. . . something built on top of it . . . could finish
up in . . . foundations of a house. But they do say
. . . fortune favours the brave. Sorry I'm still
whispering by the way. I haven't heard anything . . .
PC Gatewood for quite some time . . . daren't speak
any louder. I'm sure I'm alone . . . but I imagine
suddenly snapping a light on . . . finding completely
surrounded by those . . . better to not . . . think
about it, eh? I'm sure . . . be back in the nick soon.
Tell Eric to put the kettle on. He's . . . good at
that. *(Dead air)*

- -

09:45h

COOPER: It's as I feared, Uma. I've reached the top
of this ladder. It was a bit rickety, but it held.
Must have climbed 50 feet easily. Anyway, it ends in
some kind of crawlspace. The ceiling's so low I have
to crouch and there's brickwork to either side – very
old brickwork. Damp, covered with mould. The floor is
. . . I don't know, just debris. Rotted masonry, dirt.
It's difficult to crawl along without making a noise.
Do you hear that, Uma? *(Dead air)* Will that be echoing
through the tunnels below? Will that bring them after
me?

BERTELLI: SO22 to November Golf? *(Dead air)* SO22 to
November Golf . . . we've pretty well secured this
area around the church and the excavation site. But
we still need that Biohazard Casevac. That needs
prioritising, over.

COOPER: Uma . . . a development! There's an aperture
on my left. I obviously can't see it, but the bricks
are just not there any more. In fact, they're strewing
this crawlspace. It's like they've been pushed
through from the other side. It's just a void in
there, pitch-black. It smells terribly. Not the smell
of before. Not scorched flesh. This is different –
odious, revolting, a reek of decay. God alone know
what's in there. I can't go that way. I must continue
along this passage, Ouch . . . I'm hurting myself.
These broken bricks under my knees. I must go faster.
Even though there's intact brickwork again to my left
and right, I have a horror of that aperture behind

me, as if something's climbing out. That can't be. I hear nothing. But my God, Uma . . . wait, I see light! Uma . . . I can confirm that I see a light. There's a corner just ahead. This is difficult - scraping me, gouging my skin. This passage was never designed for a human to crawl along. But I'm round it now. The light is glinting down from above.

- -

10:00h

COOPER: I'm not sure what I'm seeing here, Uma. It's like gazing up from an alley between two factories. A horizontal space, tight . . . so tight I can't turn my shoulders. But I can stand, and I can climb. Uma, I'm exhausted, I'm filthy, I'm cut all over and bleeding. But I can't stay down here. I'm going to have to climb. *(Dead air)*

- -

10:15h

BERTELLI: SO22 to November Golf. Don't know whether you've managed to open a media channel or not, yet. But if you have, pass this on - heavily armed police units proceeding from building to building inside the control zone, searching all premises. Anyone we find, so long as they're co-operative, will be escorted to the perimeter. If they aren't co-operative it could have very serious consequences. *(Dead air)* November Golf, I understand there are problems at Greenwich Police Station, but if you could acknowledge receipt? *(Dead air)* Fuck you, November Golf. Will continue reporting until otherwise instructed, over.

COOPER: Uma . . . I've made it. It wasn't as hard as I feared. There were joists jammed across, the brickwork had rotted, creating hand and foot holds. Would you believe it, I've emerged in the attic of a house. There's nobody here, I'm sure. But from the turret window I see All Hallows church. There was a riot there earlier, but it seems quieter now. I can hear voices outside, however.

BERTELLI: SO22 to November Golf? Has everyone now abandoned their post in the radio suite? *(Dead air)*

Sincerely hope not, as you appear to be our last link with the outside world, over.

COOPER: Seems I'm in one of the houses on Ladysmith Crescent. I'm going downstairs. I'm hurt, Uma. I can barely walk straight. But I'm not going off sick on a day like this. I can still get to the CAD room. I can help you . . . God, that fresh air . . .

BERTELLI: SO22 to November Golf. We're on Ladysmith . . . Benson, one's just stepped out that fucking door! Take it down. (*Background noise: gunfire*). SO22 to November Golf? This head-shot malarkey actually works. If you get nothing else to the outside world, get that. We've just mopped another of the bastards up. We haven't got endless ammo of course, so get us some help. We'll hold the fort in the meantime. They don't call us the fucking glory boys for nothing.

(Dead air)

✳ ✳ ✳ ✳ ✳ ✳ ✳ ✳ ✳ ✳ ✳ ✳ ✳ ✳ ✳ ✳ ✳ ✳

Final message received at station November Golf 03 10:19h. Memo ends.

✳ ✳ ✳ ✳ ✳ ✳ ✳ ✳ ✳ ✳ ✳ ✳ ✳ ✳ ✳ ✳ ✳ ✳

Thank you for reading the information about our research and agreeing to take part, please read and sign this form.

Centre number: *2*

Patient study identification number: 13

Title of project: *All Hallows*

Name of researcher: *Prof. M.T. Déesharné*

Research team: *University Hospital, Lewisham*

CONSENT FOR RESEARCH INVOLVING NEW SAMPLES OF HUMAN BIOLOGICAL MATERIAL

Deceased adults

Consent can be given by the adult prior to death or may be given by someone after death. There is a hierarchy as to who can give such consent and this is set out in the draft code of practice on consent at paragraph 53.

Deceased children

Consent can be given by the child prior to death if able to take such a decision; it is good practice to involve those with parental responsibility in this process. Otherwise consent must be given by someone with parental responsibility. Consideration should be given to the views of an older child if they were known prior to death.

As the Act creates an offence of using human tissue without appropriate consent, it is now more important than ever to ensure that the consent attached to any tissue stored or used in research is documented and tracked with the tissue; and that use of the tissue is only within the terms of that consent.

Please initial boxes

1. I have read the attached information sheet on this project, dated ___May 1___ (version ___#2.5___), and have been given a copy to keep. I have been able to ask questions about the project and I understand why the research is being done and any risks involved.

S.J.

2. I agree to give a sample of tissue for this project. I understand how the sample will be collected, that giving a sample for this research is not voluntary and that I am not free to withdraw my approval for use of the sample at any time without giving a reason and without my medical treatment or legal rights being affected.

S.J.

3. I give permission for someone from the research team to look at my medical records to get information on *Bite Marks*. I understand that the information will be kept confidential. *S.J.*

4. I understand that I will not benefit financially if this research leads to the development of a new treatment or medical test for HRV. *S.J.*

5. I know how to contact the research team if I need to and how to get information about the results of the research before my eventual death. *S.J.*

6. Should, for any reason, my body be reanimated after death, then I hereby absolve the research team of any negligence and agree that they can use my remains (either whole or truncated) for any future research project as they see fit. *S.J.*

7. Consent for storage and use in possible future research projects

I agree that the sample I have given and the information gathered about me can be stored by *Prof. M.T. Déesharné* at *New World Pharmaceutical Group* for possible use in future projects, as described in the attached information sheet[11]. I understand that some of these projects may be carried out by researchers other than *University Hospital* who ran the first project, including researchers working for commercial and / or government companies. *S.J.*

8. Consent for genetic research[12]

(a) For genetic tests of known clinical and / or predictive value: I give permission for tests to be carried out on the samples I give, as part of this project. I have received written information about this test and I understand what the result could mean to me and / or members of my family if I do not comply. *S.J.*

I want / do not want (delete as applicable) to be told the result of the tests. I understand that I cannot change my mind about this later.

S.J.

(b) For other genetic research:
I understand that the project / future research using the sample I give may include genetic research aimed at understanding the genetic influences on "The Death" but that the results of these investigations are unlikely to have any implications for me personally as by then it will be too late.

S.J.

SUSAN JENKINS   May 1   Susan Jenkins
Name of patient   Date   Signature
(BLOCK CAPITALS)

Dr. James Lancaster   May 1   S. Lancaster
Name of person taking consent   Date   Signature
(if different from researcher)

Prof. M.T. Déesharné   May 1   M.T. Déesharné
Name of researcher   Date   Signature

Thank you for agreeing to participate in this research. Your next of kin will be notified.

To: Prof. Margaret Winn, UCH London
From: Simon Wesley, Histological Epidemiology, Hospital of Tropical
             Diseases & Medicine, NW1
Subject: All Hallows Church, Blackheath

Margaret—

I need to speak to you urgently, but nobody knows where you are. I've tried your mobile and your direct line and just keep getting your voicemail. It's really important you call me the second you get this.

I've been doing some more digging and I think I've found documented proof that Moreby experimented on his colleagues with their full consent. According to one report they made a human sacrifice – picked up some poor woman on the embankment, took her to a "low dwelling in Pentonville", raped her and cut off her breasts and hands. At least, I think that's what they did; the original document is couched in such convoluted language.

It's hard to tell at this distance how much of what I've found is true, but I think Moreby allowed himself and the other members of his society to be deliberately impregnated by the toxic bites of plague fleas in order to provide they could live on after death.

If that's the case, it would mean that All Hallows Church isn't the only site risking danger from excavation – the spot where all seven members of his inner circle are buried is just behind St. Pancras Station, one of the busiest crossing points in the world.

As far as I know there are no current plans to dig up the graveyard at St. Pancras Old Church, but we still need to talk.

Simon

cant believe we got wi fi coming in from somewhere so can work on my laptop but its cool its all cool again now just sooooo fucked up man.

South London overrun, crazies everywhere. Like the bank crisis riots all over again, but waaay worse. South London though. Bet the streets don't look much different to how they normally looked. Even if they smash the place up they could only do about a hundred and fifty quids worth of damage I reckon ha ha but how is it even possible this happened? Fuckers in government never listen to the people never let us have our say, that's why the old riots happened you don't have to be a rocket scientist or nothing to work that one out.

Cant believe they got a chocolate machine down here, one of the old ones and it STILL doesn't work they never do. We took the front off but the chocolate inside was fucked, all crumbly and white. Got some supplies from Pret but nothing sweet because Tabby grabbed most of it and she doesn't eat sweet things – thanks for thinking of us Tabs – gonna turn this off and recharge because the battery is low. I might try recording stuff on my mobile later but that uses up power faster than making calls not that we got anyone to call

---

Okay we have the power. Real power from a generator that was down here in a service bay at the other end of the platform. Stone's old man taught him all this mechanical shit when they had a boatyard so hes gonna be our resident mr fix-it.

Don't know how long this place has been empty but my guess is longer than I originally thought 25 – 30 years.

Kaz found an old map of the London underground and this station is still open on it but theres no date. It was called York Road station and was between Kings Cross and Caledonian Road station on the Piccadilly line.

If I write it clears my head so let me get the facts down first.

Theres five of us, Kaz Stone Tabby Mercia and me – Kane to my mates but my mates are all dead because they were in town when things kicked off and the others – well maybe theyre alive again who knows? Do you know how mad that sounds to write down? The first thing we did when we got down here was we banned the Z word. The Z word has no place in our new society says Stone whos got this mad idea that if we stay down here long enough we can repopulate the world like in that film with Will Smith.

None of us knew each other before we came in here how weird is that? Id like to pretend we were brought together in a big fight fending off the Zs but no, we all happened to be queuing in the same branch of Pret A Manger when the Zs found us. One minute Im standing in line with a tuna baguette and a can of yoga bunny detox drink and the next theres hundreds of dead people shambling up the road from the station, a great wall of bleached bloody faces, and we knew we were in trouble.

Its weird with everything that's going on, some parts of town are like photos I've seen of the blitz nothing but smashed windows and burned out buildings and then you get these untouched pockets where the houses look normal and the shops are open and people are trying to pretend theres nothing wrong. Some woman told me there are housewives queuing up outside the butchers in islington like it's a normal shopping day, but just down the road the flats round the old arsenal football ground are on fire.

We saw the Zs coming and ran, didn't pay for our food just grabbed as much as we could carry and ran up Ladysmith Crescent. Ahead on the right was the old tube station. They used the ground floor as a Transport for London works depot. The place was wide open but there was no one about. We went inside and barred the door, waiting for the Zs to fuck off away from the building but they didn't they just kept coming.

We went up to the first floor and watched them and the crowd behind got deeper and deeper like they were pouring in from all the surrounding hoods. Stone said "why do they all just follow each other? Theyre not exactly using their brains are they". Stone's a posh twunt and keeps acting like he's expecting daddy to come down from east finchley and sort it any minute now. I told him theyve just got herd instinct they see one bunch of Zs crowding round a building and they all do it theres no logical reason for it. Then Stone starts on about "well if I was a Z I would get myself a bit more organised", and I say "you wouldn't be able to you daft Sauron youd be dead, wouldn't you".

He said, "What's a Sauron?"

I said "It's the giant red throbbing hole in Lord of the Rings. A massive arsehole". That shut him up.

It got dark and we took bedding from the work team cupboards and tried to sleep on the office floor but I could hear the crowd outside bumping and moaning and sometimes terrible screams like they were tearing into each other as well as the living. I wouldn't let anyone put the lights on in case it attracted more of them. From tomorrow were gonna move down onto the platforms below where we cant hear them.

We're all the same age the 5 of us all first year students of art and design at St Martins College across the road. Or we were at any rate – don't know whats gonna happen now that the country's overrun with dead people. Mercia doesn't speak much English, I think she's Macedonian or something. We couldn't go back there because the place has too many windows and we'd have had no way of making them all secure. 4,500 students in there and hundreds of teachers and we have no way of knowing how many of them are still alive. Heres a good safe place though. Two platforms tunnels, control room staff room toilet and lockable front doors. There's a staff fridge that works and its full of food for the tube crews. Medical supplies consisting of a thermometer iodine and bandages nothing else. Theres a washing facility just a tap but it has hot water so we can hold out here as long as we want which is cush. Gotta go someones starte

---

Well that was fun. Only our second day and our resident blonde vegan airhead Tabby used the upstairs shower and get this, fucking opened the window to clear the steam, then left the room. About 2 mins later the first of the Zs had figured out how to climb the drainpipe but luckily she was as fat as a hog and got stuck halfway through the small square window. We heard her squealing and came upstairs and Kaz swung a tubeworkers pickaxe right at her face. The sharp end went through her mouth and out the back of her head, soft and easy, so then we couldnt get her out the window because the pickaxe handle was holding her in, so Kaz cut her head off with a hacksaw, then freed his pickaxe. He did it as if he was carving the sunday fucking roast dead casual.

The girls were screaming and screaming so we sent them downstairs and told them to set up a proper camp on one of the platforms. Kaz cleared up the mess and washed the bathroom clean again and locked the window. When I looked out I saw them, the Zs, about 30 deep all the way around the building just milling about. Seriously fucking creepy man

Food situation. Apart from the Pret stuff weve got eggs bacon sausages peas (frozen and tinned) lots of stay-fresh sandwich packs thatll last until like 2035 or something and a lot of canned drinks mostly the fizzy sugary American shit junkfood stores always try and shove on you. Water in big plastic cooler bottles four beers saving those

Youd think as first year art students wed be able to agree on something but no. Everyone wants something different. Weve agreed on one thing though and thats we don't know how long we're gonna be down here. Already the traditional order of the world has started to exert itself here. We make the girls cook and prepare the camp while we go around the building checking its security. Hey the girls chose it that way round so not my bad OK. The sleeping bags are lined up along the southbound platform. I lay in mine listening to the tube mice foraging up the line and turned to Stone to see if he was still awake.

"yeah Im awake" he says "whats wrong?" Hes a hopeless posho but hes got more of a clear head now and has stayed calm so far. Kaz has just kind of gone away into himself and doesn't talk since he killed the fat bird he just sits reading through a load of books he found upstairs in one of the lockers.

"the tunnels" I say. I raise my head and look down into the dark mouth of the southbound tunnel leading to Kings Cross. "I know the station's been shut for years but we have to check and make sure they can't get through. The first big wave of Zs we saw was coming up from King's Cross which means they could be down into the tube system by now looking for victims.

What if they came pouring out of that?" and I point to the great gaping black hole with the faint sound of wind coming through it, a distant rustling dry and strange like trapped pigeons or the pages of a newspaper turning and turning.

"Don't fucking do that to me man," says Stone "you are totally creeping me out."

"Then we have to go and look" I tell him.

Weve got some stuff that can be used as weapons mostly workmans tools and equipment but we decide not to take anything into the tunnel except torches because of the weight. I figure if we see something it will be easier to run if we're not carrying. "what do you fancy north or south?" I ask.

"better go south first." Stones not thrilled either way and neither am I. The others are all spark out in their sleeping bags so we walk to the end of the platform and drop down onto the line. "stay away from the live rail," I tell him, "cause some sections of the track may still be working."

"do you really think theyd go down into the underground?" Stone asks "cause they wouldn't smell food down there would they? The underground doesn't smell of anything."

"they would if there were living people hiding out down there, be like ready meals for them," I said.

"but we're in a kind of siding though, we must be otherwise youd see York Road station from the train every time you went north. That's got to protect us a bit."

"I don't know man. Theres no fuckin rules about this. Ive seen every zombie film ever made and they all make the same mistake." I walk beside him into the dark. The tunnels smell like they always did, copper wire and dust and still dead air.
"whats that?"

"them things are like animals and you cant predict animals. You can train them a bit but they do whatever the others do or whatever they feel. And theyll turn on you for no reason just cause everyone else does. Don't think they scare as easily as animals though."
"why do you think that is?"

"cause there's so many of them and fewer and fewer of us."

Thats a depressing thought. We carry on walking until we get to a split in the tunnels.
"this must be where the old Central Line extension joined to the Piccadilly so its got to be the left fork."

We take the left branch and head into it. By now the breeze has fallen

away. Theres nothing here but dark and silence and stillness. Even our own footsteps are hard to hear.
I raise the torch and the beam hits a solid grey break of concrete blocks that goes all the way to the walls and the ceiling.

"do you think killing that Z in the bathroom has fucked Kaz up?" Stone asks. "hes hardly spoken a word since it happened."

"how do you think youd feel?" I say. "the biggest thing Ive ever killed is a mouse and it was a really small one."

Stone laughs. The wall is sealed good and solid so we start heading back. "What are we going to do? I mean in the long term. We cant stay in the station forever."

"weve got enough supplies here to last for at least a couple of weeks if we're careful. I guess the Zs will move on soon when they realise they cant get any living food here. Maybe they can still smell us. I don't know. We just have to wait them out. You got any better ideas tell me."

"I got a signal on my mobile earlier. Tried to get hold of my parents but there was no answer. There was no answer from anyone on the vodaphone network. O2 seems to be OK. No broadcasts no news no government help. I bet the politicians are all in that bunker in store street off tottenham court road."

"don't think about it," I tell him, pulling him back up onto the platform. The others are still asleep. Students can sleep through anything even the apocalypse. "maybe we should take Kaz's advice and stay here to repopulate the world."

Stone snorts poshly. "well Mercia's a bit of all right. Fabulous tits. The other one is a bit annoying. I don't see how shes going to be a vegan down here for much longer."

"Three blokes and two girls looks like we'll have to share. We'll check the other tunnel in the morning, I'm knackered."

I look at Kaz and the two girls dug into their bags asleep. Mercia has curls of long dark hair like ebony wood shavings over her face. She looks like any student after a big night out, dead to the world. Tabby has taken off her makeup and looks like a child again. It would be a shame to lose that innocence but theres no innocence left in the world now.
I get in my sleeping bag and write this up.

Me and Stone and Zac opened the beers a couple hours ago and talked about how we're gonna repopulate the world with just Mercia and Tabby and I said it could be tricky cause one of us will have to share. Zac said no we wouldn't cause it turns out hes gay and has a boyfriend in peckham -- I should say "had" a boyfriend as peckham is now just a fucking huge no-go zone full of smashed up shops and chowing Zs. He said it was just a shag and they were going to break up anyway.

So I get Mercia and Stone gets Tabby who he fancies – so the plan for world repopulation is on. Sweet.

Its raining now. Im listening to water dripping somewhere above us. That's all I can hear and its calming me down because it sounds so ordinary like just another day.

I remember one of the night of the living dead remakes where the Zs moved really fast and it was all splintering doors and boards nailed across windows and screaming and running to cars. This isn't like that its – I don't know almost calm. We lock the station doors and go down the dusty spiral staircase into the tube. There's a gate at the bottom, but Stone manages to break the rusty lock that holds the chains and now we spend most of our time on the platform or in the office. Theres a lift from the booking hall that works but nobody wants to use it just in case the power goes off. There's a main entrance to the station that consists of an old fashioned trellis then a pair of double doors with three locks top middle and bottom so its very secure. Theres a fire exit too with a London bar that hasn't been opened in years and is rusted into place. The windows are all covered from the inside except upstairs and they cant be accessed anymore because me and Stone kicked the drainpipe away from the wall.

From the first floor window we look down and watch the Zs hanging around like herds of grazing cows not doing much at all just standing in the rain but I know theyre getting hungry and desperate. The lines are not so deep around the station now but theres still too many of them to make a run for it and anyway we're not sure where would be safe.

"Higher ground" says Stone, "like the old forts and castles." But I have a problem with that. The high ground is occupied by rich people and theyre going to be guarding their property with guns and dogs. No way are they going to let a bunch of uninfected students in.

Me and Stone are going to check out the upline in a few minutes to make sure that its blocked off too although I guess it is as we havent seen or heard anyone coming down the rails but its best not to wait until something bad happens. Its getting hard to tell the days from the nights now. Theres some kind of drama going on so I have to

---

That's all we needed – a girl fight. Tabby has been complaining about having to prepare the meals because she doesn't like to touch meat products. She seems to think shes not trapped here at all but at some kind of fucking sleepover and she keeps going on about her compromised ideals.

She and Mercia just had a big war. Mercia told her to grow the fuck up and made her cry. She said that in Macedonia the women are expected to look after their men and Tabby told her that in Macedonia child brides could be bought for husbands and were made to wear tall tin hats for the first year of their marriage so theyre basically savages. Nice one coming from a liberal vegan. So Mercia decked her and we had to pull them apart.

Ive changed my mind about repopulating the world. Stone and me are going up the line now.

I think we got complacent yes I think that was the problem my bad my bad I know fuck though fuck.

We set off into the tunnel with torches just like last time but there was more wind and some distant sounds running water and something else. I said "theres got to be other lines coming in if the tunnel ahead is closed cause theres too much air in this part."

Stone didn't answer just kept walking. Hes a good guy under the middle class bollocks and we understand each other. We get to the end of the tunnel – about the same distance that we went in the other direction – and found the same thing: concrete blocks to the roof and walls, proper sealed off but there was still a draught.

Kaz had given us a map so I dug it out and held it under the torch. If there was another tunnel connecting to the Piccadilly it wasnt marked.

"I don't like this," Stone said and neither did I. I could definitely hear water rushing somewhere now, and felt strong cold air. When I shone the torch straight ahead the beam faded into infinite brown dark. Only the odd fluttering moth was caught in its beam.

"I cant see where its coming from" said Stone. But by that time I had already found it. A grey metal door torn off its hinges. One of those that led to a ladder with iron rungs set in the wall just a sewage overflow thats all.

I was just telling Stone that when out of the door this poor thing with no lower jaw and burned black all over jumps on him crazed with anger and hunger and fear and it slams Stone over on his back with a terrible noise in its throat and the smell – man Ill never forget that stench – but this time I had something with me. dont even know why I brought the fire-axe but I did and swung it into the Zs back where it stuck fast. I was able to pull the Z off Stone by lifting the axe handle which had split its spine in half and thought I must have killed it instantly because its limbs fell and it suddenly became heavy – and I thought so much for having to shoot them in the head.

I pulled Stone out from underneath but he was really losing it so I dragged him out of the tunnel and just kept pulling. When I turned around and ran the torch back over the ground in front of the overflow the body had disappeared. I think it might have been a woman, but it was hard to tell.

They make very little sound when they move about and Stone had been crying out so it must have just got up and crawled off.

When I turned back the fucking thing fell on top of Stone and me. How it had got up behind Stone so fast I still dont know but it did. Stone screamed and I dragged at him trying to pull him away but the Z wasn't having it so I kicked out and kicked hard and when it fell I stamped on its head until there was nothing left except stuff that looked and smelled like the brown meat inside a big month-old crab.

It took me the best part of an hour to get Stone back and I remember he kept saying "I'm not cut it didnt break my skin no teeth it couldn't bite me Im not cut."

Stone was right. When I got him back me and Mercia washed him down and we didn't find any obvious tears in his skin but he didn't look well wasn't feeling right so we put him to bed and I got into my sleeping bag to write it up. Tired sick and tired of this fucked up life going to sleep now

---

We are all drifting

Weird couple of days all of us arguing Stone really sick Zak keeps trying to talk to me about something he says is really important. Zs still outside the doors of the station just standing there in the rain black rain but I cant be doing with it going back to sleep

---

Mercia says the station is haunted and she has to get out before something terrible happens. Well this is a new fucking twist. I know shes eastern European but I'm trying not to stereotype her. Says she hears running water getting closer and a weird knocking noise at night. Says running water means death is coming. Cheerful thought. She only hears the knocking at certain times. "Yeah," said Tabby, "only when theres nobody else around you just need the attention" and then they start fighting again.

I looked for Zak to back me up a little – Stone is slick with sweat and out of it – and instead the little douchebag says "I think she may be right."

I ask him what the hell hes talking about and he says "I've been trying to tell you for days."

So I say "Tell me now."

He takes out a book with a brown cover thats hanging in pieces and opens it. "one of the managers here was interested in the background of the station. There are other books that help to explain things but take a look at this."

▼ [Pages from *Abandoned Underground Stations of London* by D.F. Gray, published by Transport Guides Press, 1938]

YORK ROAD STATION

This underground station was opened on York Road in 1906 and closed in 1932. It is one of only two in the London system whose elevators descend directly to the platforms and not to a separate tunnel on the floor above. The other is Hobbs End, Deptford, with which it shared the same designer.

When the station was closed, concrete blocks were placed over its locking frames, which effectively sealed its platforms from the rest of the subway system. Latterly the building has been used by Transport for London.

THE MYTH OF THE PENTON

Like its sister station, Hobbs End, the York Road station existed in a very poor area, and services were reduced after the General Strike. There was much talk at the time about the station being haunted. Many members of the public stopped using the station during hours of darkness because they believed that the spirits of the dead had become trapped in the tunnels.

This belief stems from several old myths and superstitions, the principle one being that the area of Pentonville, which the station borders, was the site of human sacrifice in pre-Roman times. The hill was a perfect spot from which to witness dawn over London, and so dawn became the time to make a sacrifice.

The word "Pentonville,, can be interpreted as "Hill of the Head,,. Many Celts believed that the soul resided behind the eyes, and at Pentonville they built a sacred mound in which they buried the heads of opponents. This is the mound that was known as the Penton, hence Pentonville, town of the sacrificial mound. It is also in the diocese of St. Pancras, a saint who was himself beheaded. This, incidentally, is why we have a head on coins of the realm.

St. Pancras Church as we know it was founded in the 3rd Century, but it is built on a much earlier temple to Mithras, and the area has deep connections with the occult. The return of the area's oldest god could be regarded as an incarnation of the great god Pan himself, Jack-in-the-Green, the basis for the myth of Robin Hood and London's oldest and most enduring legend.

THE HORNED ONE

In the Middle Ages, St. Pancras was part of the great forest of Middlesex. The last remaining piece of that is Caenwood – what we now call Kenwood – in Hampstead. Where there is water, there are villages, crops and fertility rites. In 1550 a fable resurfaced about the Pindar of Wakefield. The pindar warns that no-one may trespass upon his land, is challenged and acquits himself by winning a sword fight. He appears in folk songs and his story forms the basis for part of the Robin Hood legend, where he becomes a man named George a Green, and his challenger is Little John.

A "pindar,, was a man who kept the village's stray cattle in a pen, or pinfold. The pindar's story went back to Paleolithic times, because he was based on a pagan British god, the lord of the forest beasts, the animal-headed "Horned One,,. This character reappears throughout our history as Herne the Hunter, and represents the fertile male power of nature.

Throughout the 1920s strange noises – mainly consisting of a loud knocking – were heard in the walls of the station and in buildings above the tube line at seasonal intervals, roughly corresponding to changes in the weather. The situation became so serious that the police were brought in to investigate, but they found nothing. Members of staff and the public were easily frightened by such things; it must be remembered that an entire generation of males had been lost in the First World War, and superstition was rife even in urban areas, but especially among the poor.

"I think this is what she's talking about," said Zak, stabbing at the shredded book with his forefinger, "she says she hears a heavy regular knocking in the walls after we're asleep."

"Let me get this right," I said, lifting him up by his raggy sweater. "We are running out of food and may lose our electricity at any minute. One of us is sick but we dont know why. We're trapped in an abandoned tube station with a HORDE OF FUCKING FLESH-EATING ZOMBIES SURROUNDING THE BUILDING and there may be no-one left in the rest of the world for all we know, and now you want us to start playing SCOOBY FUCKING DOO?"

The girls stared at me in silence. Even Stone shut his mouth.

"Im just saying that it's a weird coincidence thats all," said Zak, retreating into a grubby corner as I dropped him.

I wish I had a fucking gun

Okay. I've got my cool back now. I'm sitting here calmly, typing. I'm breathing slower. I'm even taking the time to punctuate. It was just a coping mechanism, I know that. Zak has to cope with this fucked up situation, we're all handling it in different ways. Tabby has joined Mercia in her belief that there's something inside the station walls, but then I get the feeling that she'd believe anything. She's kind of gullible and talks about how the Zs could be "turned" with the power of healing crystals. If she's like this now I can't imagine what she'll be like when she's forty. Barking.

There's rainwater coming into the tunnel through the roof, not a lot, just enough to leave an icy trickle on the back of your neck. Fucking great.

This is bad. Stone is really sick. Something happened back in the tunnel, I don't know what, but I think he may be dying. He has a really bad fever, he shits himself all the time and is pouring sweat. He won't let us examine him and just burrows deeper into his sleeping bag, but we're going to have to open it soon because it stinks. It looks like the symptoms they were giving out on the news before we ended up in here but the girls say his skin wasn't torn. I don't understand it.

We have no medication in here. I need to get to Boots at King's Cross but I don't have a vehicle – hell, I can't even drive, none of us can except Stone and he can't move. Went up to the first floor and looked down – most of the Zs have dispersed now but I could see a bunch crouched in a circle further down the road by the wall, it looked like they were eating from a big bulging pile of red stuff like car tyres. I think it was people. They were eating people.

I'd have to get past them, then to the chemist by the station, then all the way back. And I don't even know what I'd get, general antibiotics maybe, if there's anything left in the place and it hasn't been ransacked. I don't know what to do.

I don't know what to do.

I heard it. I swear to god I heard the knocking noise that Mercia and Lady fucking Gaga keep going on about. I went into the passage that connects to the circular staircase – it's the one place in the building where the girls will let me smoke and I'm down to my last pack as it is – and I'm leaning against the wall thinking about how I really don't know how we're going to get out of here, and how Stone is going to be dead in the next twenty four hours if I don't get to a chemist, and how I really don't want to have sex with either of the girls now because I've got to know them too well and don't fancy either of them anymore so we won't be repopulating the world together after all.

And I'm thinking and smoking and the bang was so loud I thought the tiles had come in and I bounced away from the wall. Then it came again, hard and loud and sharp, right behind the tiles where I was standing. And it kept happening at regular intervals of a few seconds.

I ran and got Zak and Mercia but by then it had stopped. But I heard it.

I heard him.

The Horned One.

He's in the wall. He's trying to get through. The world has gone to Hell and he's trying to come back into His domain.

I believe in the Devil

I sat with Stone last night. His face was the colour of old newspapers and there was a thick foamy yellow coat on his tongue. I made him drink some water but he wouldn't eat anything. He had a few lucid minutes earlier and asked me what was happening outside. I told him it had quietened down, but we hadn't seen anyone who looked normal ie. alive. No point lying to him now. I don't think he's going to make it.

He insists that the Z in the tunnel didn't try to bite him and I believe him, but what was it then? He started feeling sick as we came back out of the tunnel. I was with him all the way but I'm fine. It doesn't make sense.

He asked me what will happen and I said "What do you think? The food will run out and we'll have to make a run for it and we'll be killed. I wish it could be like the movies where they go off to an unspoiled island and start again but this is London for fuck's sake, there's nothing unspoiled. Everything is spoiled."

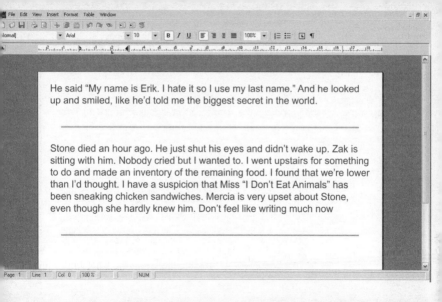

He said "My name is Erik. I hate it so I use my last name." And he looked up and smiled, like he'd told me the biggest secret in the world.

Stone died an hour ago. He just shut his eyes and didn't wake up. Zak is sitting with him. Nobody cried but I wanted to. I went upstairs for something to do and made an inventory of the remaining food. I found that we're lower than I'd thought. I have a suspicion that Miss "I Don't Eat Animals" has been sneaking chicken sandwiches. Mercia is very upset about Stone, even though she hardly knew him. Don't feel like writing much now

Calm stay calm stay calm deep breath keep talking this is better calm. I'm using my mobile to record this cause it's all I got left now.

Zak and I were sitting with Stone. Zak said, "Can you see something moving?"

And I'm like "what are you talking about?"

And Zak says "Under the sleeping bag cover". And he points down at Stone's blue sleeping bag and sure enough the nylon is lifting and falling. And Zak goes "Do you think that's his hands? Are they still moving? Is he still alive?"

And I'm like "No man, take a look at his face he's as dead as Madonna's career he's fucking brown bread."

And Zak goes "Do you think I should open it?" and I tell him "Hey, do what you want man but if you're asking me whether I would, I wouldn't."

So he reaches over and grabs the end of the zipper and starts to pull it slowly down. And he keeps pulling until he gets to the moving part.

Fleas. Hundreds and hundreds of fucking fleas infesting him, hopping out of Stone's rotted stomach. We both screamed and jumped up. Bubonic plague, Black Death, that's all I could think: plague fleas. My laptop went flying down onto the track and we ran, we left the platform as fast as we could.

Me and Zac stripped and showered with the last of the water – it's cold now, the hot stopped yesterday – and we examined each other's skin, making sure we had no flea-bites on our bodies. I think we're fine.

We're going to leave the tube station tomorrow. We have no choice now. We argued about which direction to head in but it has to be North to high ground. There's nothing below but narrow streets and shadows too many blind corners.

Tomorrow then.

Nothing to pack – we just open the doors and watch our backs. I think we can make it. For the first time in days, I think it's the right move.

It's nearly midnight and the noise in the walls has started again – it's incredible, much louder this time and maintaining a steady rhythm, a loud hollow boom and boom and boom about every 10–15 seconds.

Some of the tiles have shaken right off the passage wall. This is not imagination it's real and way more scary than the fucked up shit that's happening outside. Mercia has her hands over her ears and Tabby is wailing like a wounded cat which is appropriate given her name. Zac is coming with me to check out the passage aga

Okay, I want to record this noise.

[sound of loud booming]

Isn't that something? Isn't that fucked up? Can you hear that?

Listen Listen

I guess the sound gets magnified down here. Curved passage walls. There's tiles coming down all the way along now, more every second. It's like something is forcing its way through.

Fuck! It's coming through – shit! Water, a fuck of a lot of filthy black water – stinks – nearly fell over – can't – wait – the noise is from – coffins? COFFINS? What the fuck? One two three – Tabby just got washed down the steps – six, seven of them, really old coffins, some are smashed open and—

Fuck fuck fuck
Fleas – millions of red fleas . . .

It's over, man – Mercia's gone, covered in the things, bright red fleas the colour of blood all over her face – I can still hear her screaming – can't see Zak – water's rushing out too fast for me to reach the stairs – can't hold on any longer – can't keep on my feet for much . . .

[At this point Kane's voice is drowned out by rushing water and the sound of splintering wood.]

Margaret,

I know you're not there now. I think you may be dead. Or worse. But I can't stop writing this. I need to "talk" to you because there's no one else. There's no one else who might understand. Since I last wrote the world has descended into madness.

And it gets even stranger. You asked about Thomas Moreby. He was buried at All Hallows, but the members of The Well of Seven were buried in St. Pancras Old Church. We have reason to believe that they deliberately injected themselves with plague bacillus in some kind of occult ritual, and died of its effects.

I thought, if Moreby was the cause of the plague surfacing in South London, what might happen if The Well of Seven was excavated?

They were called The Well of Seven because they met beside a well connected to an underground river – the Fleet. You probably know that there are many wells along the path of this river, including Sadler's *Wells*, Clerken*well* and Bride*well*. There's a ghost-map under London, a city inverted. Basements, tunnels, railways, ducts, security bases, crypts, wells, tubes of all kinds. And connecting them, a hidden roadmap created by the rivers of London. The one where The Well of Seven met is the same well that they were buried in. From there the Fleet river connects to other tributaries that run right under the city, all the way to Hobbs End underground station in Deptford.

Naturally the thought occurred to me that the corpses had been dug up for some reason and the bacillus had been released, possibly with seven times the strength. I'd been hiding out at the house, obediently following the government messages to stay indoors, but my curiosity finally got the better of me.

Scientific curiosity. I knew it would be the death of me.

So I went over to the St. Pancras churchyard to take a look. It's a strange place – tall black iron railings surrounding the entrance, each spear topped with a gold-painted *fleur-de-lis*. I had an illustration from a book to guide me. The gate was shut so I had to climb over the wall. When I got inside I found something unexpected.

The ground hadn't been disturbed at all. There was no excavation of any kind.

I walked around the marble circle and its surrounding seven stones, and as I did so the heels of my boots sank into the soft grass. It has been raining for days.

Suddenly I had a terrible thought. I remembered something: the water table has always risen and fallen sharply in this part of London.

What if the rain had caused the Fleet to go into one of its periodic floods? What if it had softened the soil from the *bottom* of the well upwards and washed the infected bodies out into the Fleet?

Where might they be now . . .?

LA PETITE PARISIENNE: MAY DAY

We all knew this May Day was going to be bigger than usual, what with the collapse of the euro and the riots. There was talk of banning the traditional marches, though eventually it was decided to let them go ahead, the theory being that suppressing them altogether could lead to even more unrest. At least with a *manif*, the police know in advance where the marchers are going to be, so they can control crowd movements. But the mood is usually more festive than political; it's a national holiday, all the shops are shut, and everyone buys small bunches of lucky *muguet des bois* – lily of the valley – to pin to their lapels. It was sunny and warm, pleasant weather to be outside on the streets.

Isabelle, who works for French *Vogue*, had invited me to a party thrown by her ex, who has a balcony overlooking the parade route, just up the road from la Place de la Bastille. This was the first time I'd seen Jean-Jacques' flat, which is done up in that concrete brutalist style that always seems to me as though the decorators have gone home before they've finished painting. Pride of place was given to a huge scarlet and grey abstract which looks as if someone has blown their brains out against the wall; it made me feel uneasy, but several people knew the artist personally, and admired it, so I kept quiet. When I think about what happened later, I keep seeing this painting in my head. It was a bad omen.

I knew some of the people there; a brilliant jewellery designer called Gilles, and Louise, a freelance stylist, and Jerome, who's married to the daughter of the Minister for Culture. I also recognised the philosopher Paul Lellouche (and you have to remember this is *France*, where philosophers regularly appear on TV chat shows) who's always being featured on the pages of *Paris Match* with his lovely actress wife, the one who's had so many facelifts her mouth no longer moves when she talks. She wasn't present because (and you could see Lellouche enjoyed telling us this) she was off somewhere, fearlessly posing naked for an *Elle* photo-shoot.

Anyway we clinked champagne glasses, said the French equivalent of "Up the workers!" and watched from the balcony as the demonstrators marched past with their banners and drums and megaphones and loudspeakers blaring out from the backs of vans. It was exciting and colourful, and some of the banners were beautifully designed, but after twenty minutes it started getting samey so we lost interest and went back into the flat, where we drank more champagne and chain-smoked.

Jean-Jacques said it would probably take all afternoon for them to go past. At some point, though, I recall thinking the sound the demonstrators were making had changed, that it wasn't so much chanting and singing any more as shouting, counterpointed by breaking glass and distant sirens, but I just assumed they'd been drinking too much, and didn't think too much of it. So it wasn't until we heard screaming that we all rushed back outside to see what was happening.

"Merde!" said Lellouche, "The cops are being really heavy-handed."

Last time we'd looked, it had all been so orderly and cheerful, but now the demonstrators, instead of ambling down the boulevard in an orderly fashion, had broken up into scattered clumps. Some were obviously trying to pick a fight; others were attempting to get as far away from the troublemakers as possible, but police vans and cordons were making it hard for them to escape the danger zone. Earlier on, the police had been discreet, blending in with the marchers, but now there were two rows of them in full riot gear on each side of the street, as far as the eye could see. Where had they all come from?

As we watched, trying to make sense of what was happening, we saw a demonstrator hurl himself headfirst at the riot shields, so violently that he left a streak of pale red on the plastic; the impact didn't knock him out, but he was clearly concussed because he staggered around in a wide circle before, incredibly, launching himself directly at the shield again. Further down the line, another marcher sank his teeth into a policeman's arm and clung there like a Pit Bull, refusing to let go even when other policemen started clubbing him with their batons. I was glad we were five floors up.

Pierre, who recently shot a *Vogue* feature on economy-chic, was already clicking away with his camera and Jean-Jacques got out a camcorder and started to film the action. By now, the rioters were throwing not just cans and bottles, but café chairs and tables, even bicycles and a pushchair. "Mon dieu," someone said, "It's like '68 all over again. They'll be tearing up pavements next." The words were barely out of his mouth when someone lobbed a chunk of concrete at the police. It bounced harmlessly off the shields, but the policeman bearing the brunt of the impact was knocked off balance. Before his colleagues could close ranks around him, the rioters had scrambled through the breach and the fallen man disappeared under a scrum of punches and kicks. I was thankful he was wearing protective clothing, but didn't say so out loud because I didn't want anyone thinking I was on the side of the Fascist pigs. Someone shouted, "Yay! Storm the Bastille!" in my ear.

It was then that a piteous shriek went up from behind us and we whipped round, expecting to see cops breaking down the door. But no: someone had realised we were out of cigarettes. We started scrabbling around desperately, but there wasn't even enough tobacco for a small roll-up. This wouldn't do at all. Jean-Jacques offered to pop down to the nearest tabac; it would be quite safe, he assured us, because it lay in the opposite direction from the Boulevard Beaumarchais, where all the fighting was. We sorted out the money and he jotted down our orders and slipped out, and we rushed back to the balcony to see what was happening. The police, or maybe it was demonstrators, hard to tell any more, were letting off different coloured smoke bombs, so the running battles downstairs took on a carnival air with people scampering hither and thither through streams of red and blue smoke.

The police were drafting in reinforcements and started forcing people into the backs of vans, and clubbing anyone who resisted. But the demonstrators were giving as good as they got, flinging themselves at the police like lemmings, scrambling to their feet even after being beaten to the ground, staggering around with blood all over their faces and screaming. It was horrible, and once again I was glad we were five floors up, but all the same I was now starting to worry about how I'd get home; it was only fifteen minutes' walk away, but I didn't fancy having to cross the boulevard while all this was still going on.

At some point someone asked if Jean-Jacques was back, and we realised he wasn't. Isabelle started hyperventilating, and eventually Jerome and Ron (author of *An American Idiot in Paris*) went out to search for him. It was another twenty minutes before they came back, supporting Jean-Jacques between them. There was blood running down his face and he didn't seem to know where he was. "The flics beat him up," said Rob. They sat him down and Isabelle started examining his head wound, but after a while she said, "We need to get him to a hospital," and there was a lot of milling and babbling, and I just tried not to get in the way. But at one point someone moved aside and for a few seconds I had a clear view of Jean-Jacques, who was wearing his hair in a ponytail, which was odd because I didn't remember it being like that earlier. But there was a horrible moment (I'm ashamed of it now) when I despised him for being unfashionable before I saw it was actually a flap of his scalp hanging down with the hair still attached, and there was something showing which reminded me of the abstract painting on his wall, so then I felt sick and had to go and sit down and put my head between my knees.

Monday, May 6th

Colin – sorry about last week – I realise I strayed
into hard news territory, and that's maybe not what
people want to read about right now. And I know you have
nice photos of it, but I'm afraid I never got the chance to
ask Gilles about his jewellery because Jean–Jacques bit his
arm, and he got sick, and then a few hours later he started
getting violent and we had to shut both of them in the
kitchen, so I decided I was just getting in the way and time
for me to go home. Which was easier said than done:
everyone was going crazy in the street, and there were
running battles and everything, so a bunch of people from
the party ended up coming back to my place, because it
was close by. And they're still here! If you honestly don't
think there's much danger of us getting sued, I'll try to
squeeze a bit more gossip in. In any case I changed the
names, just to be on the safe side.

LA PETITE PARISIENNE: THE WALL

The air smells like fatty bacon. We've started praying for rain, or at least for a
breeze to clear some of the toxic fug away. It's like living in the giant kitchen of
the world's worst greasy spoon cafe. We're having to breathe through our
mouths; whenever you forget and inhale through your nose the stench makes
you gag. I've actually seen people vomiting in the street.

What few tourists realise is that there's another side to Paris. There's the
romantic side, everyone's imaginations fed by movies that weren't even shot
on location but on Hollywood backlots. That's the Eiffel Tower, Arc de Triomphe,
Notre Dame and all the other famous monuments and museums, as well as
the cafés where Jean-Paul Sartre or Jean Cocteau or Ernest Hemingway drank
and smoked, and the boulevards where famous artists once strolled, and the
shops selling mini-macaroons in jewel colours.

But the Paris everyone loves so much is a theme park; no-one who isn't rich or powerful can afford to live here, and the less wealthy have been pushed outside the twenty *arrondissements* (arranged in the form of a spiral, or *escargot* – look at the map!) and across the *Périphérique* ring road. Somehow, modern Paris has managed to banish all its worst poverty and social problems to the suburbs, where the lower classes won't spoil the view for visitors, who can then coo to each other about how lovely and unspoiled the city is.

There are nice suburbs, sure, where young couples can bring up families, but there are also vast and desolate tracts of public housing, where the police have to tread carefully, where lone travellers wander at their peril, where even at the best of times the cityscape is strewn with the burnt-out shells of stolen cars. And no-one who lives in central Paris ever gives it a second thought – until the hotspots flare up into riots which threaten to spill over and spoil everyone's dinner. It happened in 2005, and it happened again last year. Which was when the authorities erected The Wall under the feeble pretext of keeping pedestrians off the *Périphérique*. It's not really a wall, of course, more like high concertinas of razor wire on either side of the road, with easily secured checkpoints on the site of each of the old city gates. They call it the MDT – the *Mur de Thiers* – after the fortifications erected in 1844.

The wire is electrified. It was supposed to be a secret, but it isn't a secret any more, because for the past week, people have been walking into it and sticking there, entangled in the barbs, gently grilling. It takes about a day for them to be cooked all the way through, and even then some of them continue to twitch. It's like being trapped in the middle of a giant smoking kebab. Though I daresay some of the old-school *bourgeoisie* would have preferred a simile more nationalistically French, such as *cassoulet*.

The government still thinks the danger is coming from the other side of The Wall. They're convinced Paris is under siege from rampaging gangs of alienated zonards being manipulated by anarchist foreign masterminds. They've slapped us with curfews, quarantines, shoot-on-sight martial law and emergency health measures, but to no avail – what they don't seem to realise is that the danger isn't coming from the other side of The Wall, it's already in here with us. It's no longer us versus them. It's just us.

Terrestrial TV is choc-a-bloc with emergency programming, with commentators and politicians and health officials locked in endless debate. Do we have the right to pronounce death sentences without formal arrest and trial? Do zombies have rights like the rest of us? Are they even human? What is a human anyway? And ought we even to call them *zombis* (the French spell it without the "e") – a word which is etymological anathema to L'Académie Française because they think it's imported English (actually it isn't – I looked it up and it appears to be of West African origin). Among the proposed alternatives are *morts-vivants*, *abrutis* and *assommés*, but the media seem finally to have settled on *revenants* (which literally means "returners" but has often been used to mean ghosts) as suitably descriptive without being either alarmist or politically incorrect.

It's quite hard to winkle out the truth from the barrage of misinformation. There's a paranoid faction still convinced it's a biological attack by terrorists. City Hall is blaming pollution. But the consensus is that it's some sort of virus, spread from London via the Channel Tunnel. Like Mad Cow Disease, it infects the brain. Anti-British fervour is running so high that on the couple of occasions I've ventured outside to stock up on supplies, I pretended to be American. But mostly I just let Jerome or Louise nip down to Franprix, which is only a couple of doors away.

It's cramped with four of us in the flat, but I'm quite relieved I don't have to face this situation on my own. Once Jerome had confirmed that his wife and kids were safely holed up in Languedoc, he relaxed and made absolutely no attempt to get back to their empty apartment in the 15th; he's very charming and attentive, and he's been doing most of the cooking, and manages to concoct fantastic meals out of practically nothing. Louise lives up in the 18th, north of Sacre Coeur, but she can't get hold of her neighbour on the phone and doesn't fancy going back on her own to find out what's going on. Lellouche, of course, refuses to lift a finger to help, but just expects everyone to wait on him hand and foot. He appears to have forgotten all about his lovely actress wife and keeps disappearing into the bedroom – *my* bedroom – with Louise; if I were her, I would tell him to get lost, but she seems quite happy for him to paw her. Flattered, even. She says he's a Great Man, with appetites to match, and shouldn't be expected to adhere to the same moral standards as the rest of us.

I tried to get through to Isabelle to find out what happened with Jean-Jacques and Gilles, but her phone was turned off. I suppose she could just have forgotten to charge it, but after seeing the reports on TV, the worst may have happened. In any case, I'm not about to go back to the Boulevard Beaumarchais to find out; I'm sure she wouldn't either, if our positions were reversed. But none of us are going outside any more than we need to; not just because of the walking dead – honestly, there doesn't seem to be *that* many of them – but because at the slightest hint of eccentric behaviour, you're liable to get a bullet through the brain

Thursday, May 9th

Colin – I'm sorry you thought that was too political. I was just writing about what was going on. So I'll do my best to keep this "lighthearted and fashion-orientated", as requested.

LA PETITE PARISIENNE: WHAT THE WELL-DRESSED ZOMBIE IS WEARING

It's that time of the year – Victory Day swiftly followed by Ascension Day, both bank holidays, which means everyone heads for the hills and Paris is like a ghost town. If this were the wild west, you would see tumbleweed blowing along the streets. This year, though, it literally *is* a ghost town.

Paris is the centre of the fashion world, so it comes as no surprise that the city's walking dead are more stylishly turned out than elsewhere. I have only to glance out of my window and, sooner or later, you can see a bunch of them shambling down the Rue Saint Antoine, which is part of the main east-west axis linking the Arc de Triomphe to Bastille and beyond. It's the main route for the Bastille Day parade, though I doubt that will be going ahead in any recognisable way this year, unless it's a march past by the army of the dead.

I haven't spotted any Chanel suits on dead people, but this is probably the wrong side of town for that; I bet the wide avenues off the Champs Elysées are brimming with expensive *haute couture* on the hoof. Here, on the edge of Le Marais, the look tends to be more cutting-edge, with an occasional hint of camp. Ripped fabric is a recurring theme, of course, and you can't always tell if the torn material is a result of street fighting, or if it was an integral part of the original design. I've been seeing a lot of skinny jeans, and sequins in unexpected places, and decorative skull motifs and T-shirts sporting such ironically amusing slogans as NOUS SOMMES TOUS DES INDÉSIRABLES (We are all undesirables) or A BAS LA SOCIÉTÉ DE CONSOMMATION (Down with the consumer society) and, of course, splotches of scarlet. Lots of splotches of scarlet.

Hair and make-up, meanwhile, have undergone a radical rethink. French women are world-renowned for their impeccable grooming, but you'd never guess it to look at some of them now. No-one seems to be bothering much with foundation and powder any more; instead, complexions range from pale to grey to greenish-yellow, with the skin sometimes flaking off or striped in livid scratches or covered in a sort of light stippling of, I don't know, mould. Hair-dos have undergone a sort of punk metamorphosis, ranging from the just-got-up bedhead all the way to wild and crazy Mullets, Mohawks and Triceratops, none of these piliferous configurations intentional but the chance product of sickness, death and ultraviolent confrontation. Instead of gel, the hair is sculpted into place with an impasto of blood, spit and brains. It will be interesting to see what effect, if any, this will have on next season's catwalks.

LA PETITE PARISIENNE: SHOPPING

On Monday we were joined by Jerome's friend Rachid, who says he was making some sort of delivery when he got trapped on the wrong side of the *Périphérique* and couldn't get home. Which now makes five of us squeezed into my flat; as you can imagine, the sleeping arrangements are quite interesting!

According to Rachid, there are problems in the suburbs too, but the prefecture has simply abandoned them, saying the seat of central government needs to be protected at all costs if France is ever to recover from this crisis. Rachid says that, where he comes from, the residents of houses too easily accessible from the street were all having to seek refuge in the HLMs – the rent-controlled high-rise housing blocks – where the prison-like layout and sheer height of the constructions were helping to fend off the revenants. In fact, says Rachid, the despised "rabble" that politicians in the past expressed a desire to see hosed off the streets like so much dogshit are proving more adept at keeping danger at bay than the pampered *bourgeoisie* in the city centre, who expect the police to do it for them.

Most of the shops are closed now. Rachid comes and goes quite easily, and sometimes Jerome goes with him. They've obviously found some way of getting into BHV, the department store up the road, because they came back laden with backpacks full of batteries, torches, padlocks, binoculars, wirecutters and wrenches – Rachid said we'll probably need them, and that very same evening we lost the electricity, so we're all grateful for his prescience. He carries a metal rod he says was part of a tripod, and it's clear he's prepared to use it; once when he came back in from one of his expeditions, I caught him wiping something that looked like blood and hair off the end before Jerome distracted me. On purpose, I think.

Rachid also took a good look through my wardrobe, which made me think that, despite all that's going on, he was maybe interested in fashion – his own sweatshirt, I've noticed, is Amerigo Rogas, and he's wearing Naudin trainers. But the next time he came back from BHV he handed me and Louise large carrier bags and smiled quite charmingly and said, "Cadeaux." I was thrilled till I looked inside the bag and found a rather ugly padded shellsuit and some horrible clumpy shoes. "I can't possibly wear these," I told him, but he just said that we would probably have to move soon, and that I shouldn't expect him to come to my rescue if I tripped over my Natacha von Brauns while trying to run away from the bloodthirsty revenants. He tugged at the shellsuit sleeve and pointed out that it was composed of several layers of slippery fabric. "Harder for zombies to take a bite out of your arm while you're wearing this," he said, and he has a point, even though Lellouche sneered and remarked that the shoes would make us look like feminists, and that it was surely worth suffering so long as we looked beautiful.

I started thinking about what Rachid had said about people having to help themselves. Up till now I've been thinking the police, or the army, will just kill all the revenants, and everything will get back to normal. But now I'm not so sure. We're seeing more dead people than live ones on the street outside, and I guess every time someone dies or gets bitten, they just add to the numbers. My flat is pretty safe, I think – they can't get into this building unless someone actually leaves both downstairs doors wedged open, which I don't think even my stupid neighbours are stupid enough to do – but Rachid reckons it's going to get increasingly difficult to go outside to forage for supplies and if we don't watch out we'll just end up trapped.

The television is no longer working, and it's hard to get anything useful from the radio; most of the stations seem to be churning out Johnny Hallyday or Claude François in an attempt to soothe the populace. But Jerome said he'd been talking to one of the soldiers stationed outside the Hotel de Ville, and that both the National Assembly and the Senate were already being moved to the Palais de Justice on the Île de la Cité in the middle of the river. There was also a steady stream of traffic ferrying artwork from the Louvre across the Pont Neuf, as well as smaller columns from Orsay and the Pompidou. They're expecting a siege, said Jerome.

So the government is preparing to abandon the rest of the city to its fate. I asked what good would it do, being surrounded by water, if the revenants were already dead and therefore couldn't drown. Surely they'd just swim over. Or they wouldn't even have to swim – they could walk along the bottom of the Seine.

"Ramparts!" said Lellouche. "The Île de la Cité is a fortress; the only way the revenants could get into it from the river is if three or four of them were to stand on each other's heads like acrobats, and in case you hadn't noticed, physical co-ordination isn't their strongest suit. They'll have to knock out the steps leading up from the promenades at water level, of course, but with an army at your disposal that's easily done."

Thursday, May 16th

Colin - wi-fi connection here is better than from my flat, so fingers crossed I can keep supplying copy.
I can't BELIEVE the readers still want lifestyle pieces.
Are you kidding? Anyhow, I've tried to work a bit of that in.

LA PETITE PARISIENNE: ISLAND IN THE STREAM

The Montparnasse Tower has gone, all 59 floors of it. An Air France 747, presumably taking its cue from 9/11, flew straight into it; for three hours it blazed brightly before collapsing (I'm ashamed to say to some cheering) into a storm of dust. But why? We could only speculate. Perhaps the pilot had found himself the last living soul on a plane full of the living dead. Or perhaps, suggested Lellouche, "He was simply a man of impeccable taste." From the top of the south tower of Notre Dame, Lellouche points out that, to the north, there is another cloud of smoke rising from the place where Les Halles shopping centre ought to be. He has even expressed the idea that the zombie wars could turn out to be a useful way for people of good taste to rid us of all the architectural blemishes on the face of the city. And I'm not sure he was joking. "Next up, the Pompidou Centre," he said, "and the Opéra Bastille. Though I have to say I'll miss those excellent acoustics. The old place at Garnier is so pretty, but really, the sightlines are abysmal."

There are other plumes of smoke too, the biggest ones rising up from Belleville in the east, Montmartre in the north, and somewhere just beyond the Panthéon in the south. The air is so choked that even when the weather is clear, you can no longer see the Grand Arche de la Défense in the west. Two thousand years of steady expansion, Lellouche is fond of telling anyone who'll listen, and in only a matter of weeks, Paris has been knocked back to Roman times. I started wondering about history; I guess the view from the South Tower is not unlike the one Quasimodo might have had in the Middle Ages, except, of course, he wouldn't have had binoculars, and this would have been four centuries before Baron Haussman drove his mighty boulevards through the mediaeval streets in an attempt to make the troublesome lower classes easier to manage. Well, the laugh's on Baron Haussman now, because those broad avenues, designed to facilitate the urban displacement of troops, have now become perfect thoroughfares for the shambling armies of the dead.

We can see them from the top of Notre Dame. They seem aimless, until they get downwind of the island, scent the humanity here and start shuffling towards it. You can hear them too – it's a sort of constant grumbling in a soundscape oddly devoid of the usual rumble of traffic with its intermittent chorus of sirens and dogs. The dogs. I wonder how many are left. I myself have tasted escalope of Pomeranian; Jerome made a good job of it, but it was a little too rich for my taste.

I hated having to leave the flat, but the journey was less of an ordeal than we'd been expecting; we just nipped across the Pont Marie to the Ile Saint Louis, and then across the Pont Saint Louis to where we are now, and the only revenants we saw were too far away to be much of a threat, though I was glad I was wearing those ugly shoes, because they're a lot easier to run in than cha-cha heels. We feel safer here, and we're certainly at the centre of things now. Quotas were imposed quite early, tollgates erected, roadblocks on all the bridges. To be allowed to cross over you have to be rich or well-connected, or already a resident (which amounts to the same thing, given that rents here are sky-high); luckily Jerome and Rachid were able to pull a few strings between them. Apparently, some people try to avoid the checkpoints by jumping into the river and swimming over, but it always ends badly; the lucky ones are immediately swept away or pulled under by the current; the less fortunate discover there are things under the water, things with fingers that fasten around their ankles or gouge their bellies as they swim, and the last thing they'd feel through the cold water would be the warmth of their own blood and guts draining away.

The government and its hangers-on have set up shop in the Palais de Justice; the army has taken over the Prefecture de Police, where it maintains an uneasy truce with the *gendarmerie*, the Nationale and their various SWAT teams. I've heard they spend most of their time bickering over whose jurisdiction is whose. Most of the refugees have bedded down in the Hotel Dieu hospital. A few have forced their way into private flats, and there's not a lot the occupants can do.

Meanwhile, Rachid – who, thanks to his delivery service seems to have friends everywhere – has commandeered a couple of rooms off Notre Dame's Galerie des Chimères, the high walkway which connects the two towers. There's a WC (which, amazingly, is still working) and a hotplate, but no bathroom; the rooms are for the use of cathedral employees whose job is to keep an eye on the tourists climbing the tower, and who can't be expected to run up and down 255 steps each time they need to go to the toilet. It's one hell of a view from up here, and an even more spectacular panorama if you can be bothered to climb the extra 132 steps to the top of the towers, though I swear one day soon Lellouche will have a heart attack on the stairs. Just one of the drawbacks of a 40 Gitanes-a-day habit, though I guess he'll have to give that up soon enough, when his supplies run out.

It's crowded as it is, with the five of us packed into the two rooms, but I guess that if and when the revenants ever do make it over to the island, there'll be a lot more people wanting to take refuge up here. It would be an easy position to defend – no more than one at a time on those winding stairs, the slippery treads evidently designed for the daintiest of mediaeval feet. You could block incomers indefinitely, though of course there would be problems when the food ran out. As it is we keep our stash of (strictly rationed) dried fruit and tinned tuna, and bottles of wine and whisky in a locked cupboard. The other cupboard is Rachid's, and he never opens it when I'm there. I wonder what's so important it warrants four industrial-strength padlocks. Guns? Pornography? The Mona Lisa? (No, I know for a fact that the Mona Lisa is currently in residence in the Palais de Justice, along with the rest of the VIPs.)

Much to Jerome's disapproval, Rachid has been teaching me slang from the *banlieue*.

We can see them crowding the quaysides, obviously getting a whiff of *eau de vivant* (especially now no-one can spare the water to wash) and the part of their brain left functioning training their faces in the same direction, like meerkats. Every so often one jumps, or falls (it's hard to tell which) into the river with a dull splash. So now the waters around the island are seething with writhing corpses, all trying to wade or float or swim over to this all-you-can-eat buffet in the middle of the stream. The handful which manage to scramble ashore immediately get snarled in the razor wire; they seem insensible to having their flesh stripped off, but the wire slows them down enough to give the sharpshooters time to take aim. If you ask me, they seem to enjoy their work a little too much.

But most of the revenants who fall into the water get trapped in the mud of the riverbed until the gases in their bodies expand and they float back to the surface, twisting and turning awkwardly while their flesh sloughs off in spongy grey strips. The stench is quite ghastly – even worse than the frying bacon smell from the fence. Most people on the island now go around with scarves draped across the lower half of their faces; I've seen every sort of scarf, from

Hermès silk to keffiyeh cotton and being French, of course, they manage to make it look like the height of chic, though when I do it, it always looks as if I've wrapped a table napkin around my head.

I do wonder, though, what will happen when there are so many rotting corpses and skeletons piled up on the riverbed that the others will simply be able to use them as a sort of sunken causeway to walk across the surface of the water, like an army of Jesuses, all risen rotting from the dead. Someone told me the Seine is eight metres deep, which is around what? 26 feet? That's quite a depth to fill, and we'll either die of starvation or go insane and kill ourselves long before it gets to that point. But even so, I lie awake at night worrying about it.

Monday, May 20th

Colin – something terrible has happened. Even more terrible than everything else, I mean – you'll see what I mean when you read this. The Internet is down, but some of the phone networks are still functioning, so I'll try and get through to a copytaker.

PS: Louise has threatened to get in touch with you; I don't think she'll manage it, but if by any chance she does, please don't take anything she says seriously. She's gone a bit soft in the head and is babbling all sorts of nonsense. Take anything she says with a pinch of salt, especially if it's about me. None of what she says is true.

LA PETITE PARISIENNE: A MOVEABLE FEAST

Jerome is dead. Since Jean-Jacques' party we'd grown quite close, and now I feel as though the bottom has fallen out of my world. Though, of course, the bottom probably fell out weeks earlier, whenever this thing started, before I or anyone else was even aware of it. I tried to get a message to his father-in-law over in the Palais de Justice, thinking he could maybe contact Jerome's wife in Languedoc, but security is so tight I couldn't even get past the first line of soldiers, one of whom gave me a hanky to blow my nose on after I burst into tears, and who kindly but firmly explained they were under orders not to allow any contact at all between us regular folk and the important people under protection inside. And that if we were to try and force our way past, we would be shot. The soldiers are all dressed in camouflage uniform; I'm not sure why because it doesn't really help them blend in with anything on the Ile de la Cité, and I'm not sure why I'm telling you this except it did start out as a lifestyle and fashion blog. Yesterday I saw three soldiers adjusting the angle of each other's berets.

OK, so this is how it happened. We were all getting fed up with tinned tuna and fricasseed spaniel, so Jerome and Rachid decided to mount an expedition back across the river to Franprix, where they thought they might be able to turn up some Foie Gras or Confit de Canard. Anything to inject a little *joie de vivre* into our mealtimes. They weren't keen on me going along, but I talked them into it, mainly by reminding them I knew the *quartier* better than they did, which is true; I wanted to pick up a few things from my flat – basic stuff I'd forgotten, like nail-clippers and a sewing kit and some pearl earrings my mother had given me for my 21st birthday.

Access to the remaining bridges was tightly controlled, but Rachid, as ever, worked his magic and after some intense negotiation we hitched a ride in the back of a VBL – an armoured patrol vehicle – which took us back over the Pont Marie. I found myself squashed between Rachid and Jerome, which wasn't entirely unpleasant. Most of the revenants seemed to be massed on the quay, gazing with blank and hungry faces at the Ile Saint Louis; they didn't take much notice of the VBL as we passed, even when it ploughed through them, which felt like really bad turbulence on an aeroplane. The driver dropped us off at the point where Rue de Rivoli turns into Rue Saint Antoine. "You're on your own," he said. "If you get into trouble, don't expect us to come to the rescue." I didn't dare look too closely at what was wrapped around the front wheels.

I'm not sure that I was fully aware of the seriousness of the situation, even then. Up to that point, the whole thing had all felt like some sort of disaster movie or shoot-em-up computer game I'd been watching from a series of high windows. But now here I was at street level, clutching a sharpened metal rod that had once been part of a bedside lamp. "Remember," Jerome reminded me. "If one of them comes near you, don't wait for it to attack, and don't let it get within biting distance – smash it in the mouth as hard as you can, and as many times as you can, till it goes down. If you smash all its teeth it won't be able to bite you. But it can still scratch and tear, so stick that sharp bit in its eye." And then what? I asked. "And then you run like hell."

My eyes were smarting with the smoke, which seemed much thicker here than on the islands. It was almost as deserted as Paris in August. Had the living just upped sticks and headed out of town, the way they do every summer? I wondered what had happened to the corpses. Had they *all* got up and walked away? Were they all now crowding the quays by the river?

The front of Franprix had been totally smashed in and the whole place, including the stockroom, cleaned out. But I knew that only a couple of doors away there was a small shop selling jars of pâté; I'd never bought anything there because it was too expensive, but the shutters were still intact, so Jerome and Rachid went to work on the locks. I told them I was going to nip up to my flat; I could see the doorway to my building from where we were, and everything looked just the way we'd left it. "Be quick," said Jerome. "You've got my number on speed-dial?" I nodded and left them to their jemmying.

I had to use my keys to open both the front door and the security door at the foot of the stairs, which I thought was a good sign. It didn't look as if anyone or anything had got in since we'd been there. I knocked on Mia and Yannick's door as I passed, but was quite relieved there was no reply as I didn't really want them tagging along with us. The building seemed empty, so I suppose I got a little over-confident, and I didn't lock my front door behind me. I know I should have done; I'm still kicking myself over that.

The gas was still working. I calculated I just had time to grab a cup of proper coffee before I went down again so I lit the stove and put the water on and started rounding up the bits and pieces I wanted to take back with me: tweezers, paracetemol, anti-perspirant, sticking-plaster, Miss Dior, Durex, and sundry toiletries, such as conditioner, that I'd forgotten to grab the last time. Not that there were a lot of hair-washing opportunities. But you never knew. As an afterthought, I threw in a pair of my sexiest Natacha von Brauns. Because you never knew, even in a zombie apocalypse, when you might need to turn on the charm to get what you wanted.

It was while I was hesitating over whether to pack my Armani leather jacket – after all, it was *leather*, which would offer some protection – when I heard the sound of my front door opening, followed by a sort of animal growling, so I grabbed my metal lamp-stand and tiptoed back to the open doorway and peered round it. It was Jerome! Relief flooded through me, until he turned round and I saw there was blood around his mouth and a strange blank look in his eyes. Jerome had turned into a revenant!

"Where's Rachid?" I demanded, but the only answer was a low rattle from the back of his throat. Had he killed Rachid? He advanced on me, drooling, so I did what he'd told me earlier and smashed his teeth in, again and again, till he staggered back, and then I hit him over the head again and again till he went down on his knees and then I jabbed the sharp end as hard as I could into his eye, several times, till he stopped moving. Then I grabbed my backpack and legged it out of the flat and down the stairs and out into the street, just in time to see Rachid emerging from the pâté shop with a full rucksack. "Where's Jerome?" he asked, and I burst into tears and told him what had happened.

Getting back on to the island was harder than getting off it. There was no way of getting past the hordes of revenants on the quays, so Rachid ingratiated himself with the guards manning the entrance to the Métro – this time I caught sight of him slipping something into one the men's pockets – and we walked for about 20 minutes through the tunnel to Châtelet, which is blocked off and swarming with military because it's a major transport hub, and then changed lines for the short hop under the Seine back to Cité. On the way, I asked Rachid a question that had been bugging me for days. If, as I'd seen, he could talk or barter his way past all these checkpoints, how come he'd found himself trapped on the wrong side of the *Périphérique*? Surely he would have been able to get home if he'd wanted? In answer, he took my hand and squeezed it.

I should explain that the trains are no longer running, but all the exit grilles are locked and the entrances heavily manned. The tunnel was a bit grim and dirty, but we had our torches, and it felt safer than trying to negotiate the streets at ground level. We ran into a few other people down there, but no revenants, thank goodness. But when we got back to Cité, even Rachid had trouble persuading the soldiers at Cité to let us back up; they made us strip off (which as you can imagine was extremely unpleasant) and examined us all over for bites or other injuries before allowing us to get dressed and ushering us roughly through the cordon back to the east side of the island. Rachid was furious; he exchanged angry words with them and told them they couldn't expect him to help them out again. There was nearly a fight, till I pulled him away.

There's talk of flooding Le Marais, turning the whole *quartier* back into the swamp it used to be before the land was reclaimed. I cried to think of all those chi-chi boutiques and *pieds-à-terres* and hyper-trendy gay bars, all flooded with corpse-water. But then I cry very easily these days.

Thursday, May 23rd

Colin — writing this on a typewriter we borrowed from
the offices of the Hotel-Dieu. All but one of the
networks are down; the last is reserved for army and
police, and you're liable to get shot if anyone catches
you using it. I'm giving this to a soldier whose squad
is due to head north this afternoon. Rachid tried his
usual methods of persuasion, and the guy swore he'd
make sure it was faxed or sent with the courier
through the tunnel. But I've got no way of ensuring
that he'll do as he promised.

In answer to your question, how should I know if it's
possible for someone to transform into a zombie that
quickly? I'm not an expert. Maybe he'd got bitten
earlier and hadn't told anyone? Now you mention it, he
had been coughing quite a lot. But I quite understand
why you edited that part out. And no, I really don't
think you can expect me to remember all the little
details — it was very traumatic, and I'm still in shock
and prefer not to think about it.

We're hearing Chinese Whispers about what's happening
on your side of the Channel, and I'm wondering if the
website is still online. But I'm going to keep writing —
it's a good way of keeping calm. Frankly, if I didn't
have this I'd probably think about ending it all, like
so many are doing around here. For a while, it became
quite fashionable to jump off the South Tower. Louise
was one of the trend-setters there. She'd been quiet
lately — Jerome's death hit her even harder than it hit
me, and she'd got it into her head that it was my fault
— but even so I had no idea she felt the situation was
so hopeless.

I saw her using Rachid's wire-cutters on the safety wiring, but before I had a chance to ask what she was doing, she was clambering out on to the back of a horned gargoyle and shrieking at me to stay away from her. I said, "Louise! NO!" But too late, she was already tumbling sideways off her perch. I peered over the balustrade to the concrete 150 feet below, where she'd morphed into a black aphid dissolving into an expanding aura of red. After a shocked moment or two, to my astonishment, she raised her head and start to haul her broken body on its elbows back towards the cathedral, but hadn't gone more than a couple of inches before a shot rang out and what remained of her head disintegrated. Two soldiers sauntered over, wrapped the smashed body in plastic sheeting and dragged it over to the stump of the Pont au Double; they heaved it over the rail into the water, where it joined the other decomposing corpses.

So many people were jumping from the Galerie that the Place du Parvis, viewed from above, was starting to resemble a field of scarlet poppies. The army got fed up with having to finish off the jumpers, and finally turfed us out of our nook and stopped anyone else going up. While we were packing up to go, Rachid allowed me to see the contents of his cupboard; I couldn't understand why I hadn't guessed earlier. His popularity with the troops, the way he was able to sneak us past checkpoints — it all finally made sense. Stacked behind the padlocks were hundreds of small packets, each one carefully wrapped in cooking-foil. "Francs won't be much use to us," he said as I helped him transfer the packets into our backpacks. "This is our currency now."

Lellouche, who's drunk most of the time now, refused to
move at first. But one of the soldiers, who obviously
didn't recognise him from the telly, waved a gun in his
face, so he had no choice but to cram two of the bottles
under his jacket and follow us down. He dropped one of
the bottles on the stairs. The fumes made my eyes water,
but even so the smell was better than Notre Dame
itself, which stinks like a brothel ever since the
priests started eking out their stock of votive candles
with scented ones from the perfume shop up the road.
The Bishop tried at first to preserve the cathedral as
a place of worship, but with the Hotel-Dieu packed to
bursting point and the west end of the island out of
bounds to everyone but the army and government, he had
no choice but to start admitting refugees, and soon the
whole place was echoing with weeping and organ music.
Greasy smoke curled up from small cooking fires; I just
hoped whatever was giving off that greasy smell was
dog. Rachid and I decided we needed some fresh air;
Lellouche pecked me on both cheeks before squatting
down next to a marble Madonna, lighting a cigarette
and refusing to budge. "I raise my glass to you," he
mumbled. "La belle dame sans merci!" We left him there,
talking to the statue, with his last bottle of whisky
and his last packet of Gitanes.

Things are falling apart. After we left Notre Dame,
there was some sort of panic over on the Ile Saint-
Louis and a mob rushed the bridge between the islands.
The Nationale tried to hold them back, but of course
they wouldn't be stopped and there was shooting, and
then they mined the bridge, which left survivors on
the other side at the mercy of whatever was going on
over there. The screaming was awful. Rachid made me
come away; he said we couldn't help them, and we should

concentrate on looking after ourselves, because no-one
else was going to do it for us. But I already knew that.

And I don't really like to think about this, but just in
case something happens to me, I should probably make
sure I've left some sort of testimony about what's been
going on. There'll be official records of course, but
you know they'll be economical with the truth. So when
I've finished writing this, I'm going to roll it up and
put it into something watertight, like a Tupperware
container, and hide it somewhere down in the crypt
After all, those stones have been there since Roman
times, so there's no reason why a manuscript in a
watertight receptacle shouldn't be around for another
couple of millennia.

ETA: I wrote that before Rachid outlined his plan.
We already walked from St Paul to Cité through the
Métro tunnel, but what I never realised is that there's
yet another Paris, an underground city hardly anyone
knows about. It's a labyrinth of interlinked caves,
catacombs and sewers large enough to walk through
(though you have to wear boots and cover your nose). I'm
told there are caverns where they grow mushrooms on
an industrial scale, and vast underground reservoirs,
and nuclear war shelters stocked with enough non-
perishable food to feed an army for decades. There's
even a secret cinema club.

Apparently, the Germans came down here towards the end
of the Second World War – they mined the city and were
ready to blow it to bits rather than relinquish it to
the Allies – but so did the French Resistance, which
used the tunnels to move around the city undetected.
Since then, it's been a hang-out for secret societies,

underground artists and the homeless, some of whom have suddenly found themselves very popular as guides since they know the network like the back of their hands.

So that's where we're going — underground, greasing palms with Rachid's packets as we go. Maybe we'll even be able to get out of Paris that way, though I'm not sure there's anywhere left to go. In any case, there's a whole new world for us to explore.

Don't think that we can't see the irony — we the living trapped beneath the cold, dark earth, while the dead roam unchecked in the open-air necropolis over our heads.

But maybe one day we can take it back from them.

British Army Field Manual
Volume 1 Part 10
Countering Infected Insurgency

ARMY

Army Code 52013
May

FOREWORD

This manual is a short guide to Infected insurgency, and the principles and approaches needed to counter it. It has been written to complement allied and joint doctrine and the authors have been careful to insure that the principles and framework that are explained in Part A are entirely coherent with those in UK joint doctrine and that of our principal allies, in particular USA, Canada and Australia. For maximum effect Part A should be read as a single continuous narrative while Part B can be read in its constituent chapters.

There will always be times when our nation's security is threatened and our backs are against the wall. There will be times when fear and unrest are everywhere and it seems impossible that we will win back the happy way of life we once knew. There are times when the odds are against us, when it seems that all is lost.

These are the times when we SHINE

These are the times when people like YOU prove just what it is that makes this country of ours great.

In this manual we will look at the important work undertaken by the National Peacetime Reserves, what sort of duties they perform and general advice about how recruits can help deal with those infected with the Human Reanimation Virus (HRV).

Most importantly, we look at how YOU can be a vital part. How YOU can be the hero of our times.

Given the Infected insurgency's constant adaptation, things will change and this publication will have to adjust accordingly. The authors will track developments in order to keep it relevant and take account of emerging views. In this respect your views and insights are important. Comments on this publication are encouraged and should be sent to OPERATIONNEWORDER@NFP.MOD.UK

Son, I'm writing this down so you know. That's important, however hard this may be to read at times, actually knowing.

My dad went off to fight too, you see. He went off to the Middle East and we never saw him again.

I spent most of my young life wondering what was so important in the desert that he had to go and die for it. What was so much more important than me and mum.

I know now, because I've done the same thing. Sometimes you have to ignore your own feelings and do a thing because it needs to be done. It doesn't make me love you any less. In fact, if it wasn't for you I might not even have done it. This may seem stupid to you because I don't even know you yet. Your a shape on a scanner screen. A bulge. Your a heartbeat I can hear through the skin of your mother's belly.

But your the most amazing thing I have ever known.

I love you so much.

One day you'll get this, you'll understand how something can be so important it changes everything. Just knowing your there I make different decisions. I don't want you growing up into the world as its become. I want something better.

Your mother doesn't get that. Your mother doesn't get a lot of things. I guess that's why you and I wouldn't have spent as much time together as I would have liked even if I hadn't joined up. Some people just don't match. Its not her fault, I suppose, its just who she is.

And who I am can't be with her.

This is what she doesn't get: being a parent means making sacrifices.

This is mine.

I hope you understand.

PART A

- **How Did This Happen?** The honest answer is: we simply don't know. But of course we are working hard to find out. Thanks to the work of the New World Pharmaceutical Group, the UK has been at the forefront of disease research and you can rest assured that a cure to HRV will not be long in coming. In the meantime we must let ourselves be guided by facts rather than panic. While the localised effects of HRV may seem terrifying – and certain irresponsible people in the media do little but fan the flames with their biased reporting – the truth is this: outside of a few serious outbreaks, the authorities are fast gaining control over the situation. With your help, we will soon see things returning to normal.

- **How Can I Help?** We need volunteers to join the National Peacetime Reserves. We need people willing to support their communities and the country in general. We need those who are willing to help provide security and support to medical and research teams. In short, we need YOU!

- **What Qualifications Do I Need?** We're not interested in your academic history or employment background. The qualities we're looking for are not so easily defined. We want the best this country has to offer. We want the brave and resourceful. People with a strong practical sense and plenty of determination. This is not just a chance to help your country, this is a chance to redefine yourself as the very best you can be. This is a how you find out what you are capable of and who you really are.

The news was bad everywhere you looked. People talking like it was the end of the world. Course you can't believe half of what you read these days, there's nothing the TV and papers used to like more than putting the wind up people. I figured things must be bad in the cities – especially London, where it all started – but that didn't mean the whole country was done for. People just needed to get up off their arses and do something about it.

I picked up a field manual about the National Peacetime Reserves. That decided it. It was a chance for me to help out, stand up like my old man and make sure you still had a decent world to grow up into.

The book explained all about it, about how you signed up, what training they'd give you, what work needed to be done. Reading it, I suddenly felt like I'd found my place. I was about to do something, the very first thing, that would define me as who I was. I hope you find that one day. Its a great feeling. Knowing your where you should be.

To be honest, I've always coasted through life. Had no time for school and no interest in a career. None of it seemed to be for me. It was stuff you saw other people doing while you stood back and got older.

I'm sure your mother will have said I was a waster. She liked telling me often enough.

It wasn't laziness. Well, alright, it wasn't just laziness . . . If someone could have showed me something to do with my life that actually made sense, that suited me, that seemed worthwhile, I'd have done it. Nobody ever had.

Then I found out about you and I knew things had to change.

Soon after, all this kicked off and, stupid as it sounds, the timing couldn't have been better. I had something important to do.

I'm happier now than ever before. Just goes to show: find what your good at and then get on and do it.

There, my first piece of fatherly advice.

- **How Do I Sign Up?**   We have set up recruitment centres all over the country. Please check the list at the back of this manual to find the office closest to you. Be aware that the location of these offices is subject to change depending on the current situation. We suggest you check our website: www.army.mod.uk/npr for the latest news with regard operational offices. You can also find us on Facebook (www.facebook.com/pages/NPR) and follow the #NPR hashtag on Twitter.

Once you've decided that you want to join us you need only call in at your closest recruitment centre. Our highly-skilled recruitment team will then assess your suitability to see if you're what we need. Make no mistake, not everyone can join the National Peacetime Reserves. If you haven't got what it takes, then I'm afraid we have no room for you. Only the best need apply.

- **What Happens Next?**   Assuming you're successful in your application you will be categorised according to your skill set and offered an initial posting in the field. Obviously, we work with you very carefully to decide where you might best be placed within our ranks. Our recruitment team has a lot of experience in allocating people where they can flourish. From technical roles such as IT or engineering to more social-orientated placements (do you have what it takes to lead others for example?). We will find the best place for you.

- **I'm Already Qualified in a Particular Field.**   In that case we will probably give you a posting that reflects that. Do bear in mind, however, that we have a lot of positions to fill and a lot of diverse skill areas to address. If we are unable to match you with your first choice of posting then you must accept that, in this state of national emergency, the importance of serving the overall needs of the community outweighs all other considerations.

The back of the manual said my closest recruitment centre was on the Thorpe Wright Industrial Estate. Half of that place had closed down within a year of it opening and it made sense for them to take over the empty space for something worthwhile. How many discount furniture places do you need, eh? You'd think DFS had forgotten we were in the middle of a bloody recession.

Heading over there, if I'd had any doubt that I was doing the right thing then the state of town would have convinced me. The streets were packed with traffic, people trying to get out into the country. First sign of trouble and they were loading up the car and buggering off for the hills. Pathetic.

I must admit I've never actually seen one yet. You know, a zombie (that still sounds stupid to me, probably be just another word to you growing up). You'd think there were hordes of them marching down the street with the way everyone was behaving.

I'd seen plenty on the TV of course, but that never sinks in does it? With the way the news is these days, all those spinning CGI graphics and people shouting in studios . . . it just looks like special effects. None of it feels like something you'd see in your own street.

The recruitment place was empty, just a bored-looking bloke sat behind a cheap desk. I'd been expecting something a bit more polished, I'll admit. The manual had made it sound a lot more flash.

Never believe everything you read in manual's. That's your second piece of fatherly advice.

I walked up to the desk. Up close I could see the bloke only had one leg. That's probably why he was stuck here, waiting for recruits that never showed up. You'd have thought he'd be pleased to see me wouldn't you? Yeah, you'd have thought that.

"I'm here for the assessment," I told him.

"You've passed," he said, "welcome to the fucking army, son."

- **Do I Need to Bring Anything?** No. Should you be lucky enough to be selected for recruitment everything you need is provided. From a durable, comfortable uniform to all the equipment you will need in the field. We have the tools to build a better future, we just need people like you to use them.

- **What About Training?** Of course we don't just send you out unprepared, you will receive extensive military training in a variety of practical fields. This is not just a chance to sharpen your skills, it's a chance to gain new ones!

Education within the British Army has always been second to none, with many recruits acquiring superb qualifications in a variety of subjects. We offer a wide range of language courses and IT training, as well as apprenticeship posts in engineering and communications.

How would you like to learn to drive a range of different vehicles? From military transport to artillery deployment.

We also give you the physical training you need. Tone up your body strength and learn the fighting skills a British Army recruit can employ if necessary.

The British Army is not just about fighting, we use a variety of techniques, body and mind, to improve the world in which we live.

The one-legged soldier handed me a piece of paper with my name, date of birth and address on it. He'd rubber-stamped it but the ink was dry so you couldn't really see it. I don't think it mattered. Nobody wanted to see it anyway.

"That it?" I asked.

"What more do you want?" he replied, "a fucking medal?"

(I've just realised your mother would have a fit if she saw you reading this with swearwords in it. Not that she has the cleanest mouth on her, mind. You want to hear the stuff she comes out with on a Friday night when she's the wrong side of a case of Bacardi Breezers. Or rather you don't. Anyway, don't let her see it, alright?)

"If this is all I need," I told him, "then that's fine. Where do I get my uniform and everything?"

He nodded towards the door. "Next building along."

I decided it was best to leave our conversation at that. As I'm being honest with you about all this I'll admit I can have a temper on me too and this bloke was getting it working a treat. I didn't want my first act as a member of the National Peacetime Reserves to be slapping the recruitment officer. I had a feeling that, however relaxed things looked, they'd soon get serious if I lost my rag.

The next building along had once been a car showroom but now it had a laminated printout stuck to the window with Blu-tack that said STORES.

I could see through the window that things were not in a good way. It looked like the back room in a charity shop, piles of clothes and junk waiting to be organised. An old man was stood in the doorway dressed in a badly-fitting uniform that looked like it had last seen daylight worn against the Nazis.

"Just signed up?" he asked, lighting a fag.

"Yeah."

"Well help yourself to anything that fits. Mind though, you'll have a job finding one of everything, stocks are low."

"There's mountains of stuff," I said.

"Most of its jackets from the Falklands, but they've mildew on 'em so I wouldn't bother unless you want to stink like a junkies mattress."

- **Will I Live in Barracks?** Yes. Even though you may be stationed close to home, it's important that the men of the National Peacetime Reserves are able to respond immediately to any emergency. In order to achieve that they must be stationed together as a unit.

Besides, the army is not just a job, it's a family and it's important that you get to know the men you're serving with. The bond between recruits is like no other. Your fellow cadet is your brother. He is your support and your confidante, he is the man who will always be there for you, the man who has your back. As much as you come to depend on him know also that he depends on you.

Some find such close living quarters difficult to begin with but many find it one of the most rewarding parts of army life.

Obviously, in this state of emergency, facilities might not be up to the standard we would normally be able to maintain in our dedicated, modern-design, training facilities. However, we are strictly requisitioning areas that meet the needs of our men. If you're willing to work hard then it's only fair we're there to ensure your reasonable comfort. You will have your own bed, storage area and personal space. Cooking facilities will be of a high standard: we have always maintained the importance of regular, tasty, nutritious meals. All specific dietary requirements – be they medical or religious – will be catered for.

Obviously, full toilet and bathroom facilities will also be allocated and scaled according to the size of the unit. Naturally, all fittings will be made to adhere to the latest health and safety regulations. The British Army has spent hundreds of years looking after its men, that tradition still continues today, whatever the difficulties we currently face.

The old bloke had been right about the jackets. Some twonk had stored them in the damp and the whole lot had white mould growing on them. I found most of what I needed though, and by the time I'd finished, looking at myself in the reflection of one of the windows, I was half-approaching a proper soldier. It felt good. You feel powerful in a uniform. It gives you confidence. You walk differently in it.

I think it was that that stopped me caring about the state of the barracks. I'm not an idiot (whatever your mother's told you!). I was getting the idea by now that things were not all they were cracked up to be. Still, the state of the place was something else. Rows of rickety camp beds in a small building that had been a mechanic's workshop. You could tell by the oil-stains on the concrete floor and the stink of petrol that hung over the B.O. and stale smoke. It was a dump.

"Not a new recruit!" shouted a weedy-looking Welsh guy. His real name was Bryan but of course everyone called him Taff.

"Yeah," I admitted, "I get the idea you don't have many."

"You got that right."

They gathered around, six men in all. I recognised some of them, always the way in a small town: you know everyone's face if not their name. As well as Taff there was Danny, a body-builder type who ran his own gym and fancied himself the hard man; Joe, a quiet lad who ran an accountancy firm until the balloon went up; Evan, a manager at Burger King who once threw me out of the place for being drunk (not my proudest moment, thankfully he didn't remember); Barry, who hardly ever said a word, just sat scratching his beard and staring into space, and Lewis who was the youngest of all of us, fresh out of school and eager to beat something up. Not the sort of professional mob you might hope for, but a decent bunch of lads all things considered.

- **What Would Be My Initial Duties?** Obviously, in this time of national emergency we'll need your help from the first. Your duties will be simple while your training progresses. You will work in crowd control and basic logistics, helping us escort people and services to where they need to be.

Your unit will also help organise a safety cordon around the area, maintaining the perimeter of your designated detail and ensuring that Infected insurgents are not allowed to enter. This may not be the most glamorous of duties and will involve a lot of standing-around. However, it is obviously one of the most important tasks as we look to mop up the dwindling number of Infected in the wild. The Infected are slow-moving and often fairly docile, it is a perfectly simple task to dispose of them safely (see HANDLING THE INFECTED).

You will also be expected to assist the staff at your local DISPOSAL CENTRE. Unfortunately, the vital work at these centres has been frequently disturbed by the anti-social and misguided demonstrations of the vocal minority. It must be remembered that the safe disposal of the Infected is the only sure way to bring this outbreak to a close. The naïve and ill-informed response of the demonstrators does them little credit and it is an unfortunate fact that their behaviour is as counter-productive to national safety as the Infected insurgents themselves. Therefore it is important that members of the National Peacetime Reserves are able to keep a cool head but retain authority when dealing with such situations. The centre staff must be allowed to carry out their duties unmolested.

The British Army has become an extra emergency service and our duties are varied. We expect our recruits to be the sort of people who can adapt on the move, not only would they be willing to follow the directions of their commanding officer, but they would also show initiative in dealing with hostile situations.

I'm writing this as I go, son, usually in the evenings, so you'll have to forgive the way things shift about. I look at the first few pages and they seem funny to me now. Not that I've changed my mind that what I'm doing is important, I wouldn't be here unless I still believed that, but now that I have some idea of how the reserves are run I can't help but laugh at the sound of the idiot that started writing this! He thought he was King of the Bloody World.

Never mind. I've been here a couple of weeks now and its OK. The lads are good company (except for Barry, who's a bit of a twat if I'm honest).

Mainly we've been organising the cordons around the town. To begin with I thought the six of us would have to handle it on our own (which would have seen us spread a bit thin!) but Sergeant Lowe (the bloke with the one leg) explained that we have to organise conscripted teams of council workers to do it. He sorts out the perimeter on the map, we then dump everyone where they need to be and keep working a tour around them to check everything's fine and nobody's buggered off for the afternoon. Obviously, there a right mix, from road sweepers to librarians. Some of 'em are knocking on too, but they all pull their weight. They've been issued with mobiles and they call us if there's a sighting. Which so far there hasn't been. Two weeks and still nothing more exciting than a false alarm with a scarecrow. Taff blew the fucker up with a grenade.

It'll come of course, we all know that. Whether the news is exaggerating or not things have completely fallen down in the capital and some of the other big cities aren't far behind. The "dwindling number" of infected that my manual goes on about is bullshit, the disease is spreading and unless we pull our fingers out they'll be on our doorstep soon enough.

- **Will I Be Given Permission to Visit Family and Friends?** Of course! The National Peacetime Reserves isn't a prison! Obviously, the amount of time allowable will be restricted; everyone in your unit will want to take advantage of the opportunity of catching up with their loved ones and, particularly in the case of units with limited numbers, we must always ensure that operational efficacy is maintained. Still, we appreciate how important it is for recruits to be able to spend time with their friends and family, after all these are the very people you signed up to protect. We will also endeavour to show extra sensitivity in the case of those with special circumstances. Sometimes emergencies crop up and its only natural you would want to rally around at such a time.[1]

---

[1] During this time of national emergency home visits may not always be possible.

They actually nuked London! That was the point where the "It'll be alright, the media just likes to make a big panic out of it" discussions stopped. The lads and I just sat listening to the news, none of us knowing what to say.

Still its quiet out here, the cordons are in place and we haven't seen anything.

The mood has turned bad though. Everyones on edge. There was a panic in town when a couple of lads beat an epileptic to death because they thought he was "turning" when he had a fit. Fucking ridiculous. Shows how scared everyone's become.

I went to see your mother today. We're not supposed to be allowed home visits due to the state of emergency but the Sarge allowed it as its not as if we're rushed off our feet (or "foot" in his case).

She didn't really want to see me. No surprise there. I just wanted to make sure you were alright.

Your nearly with us. Doctors say she could go into labour at any time. I just hope it happens soon, before anything kicks off here. We're OK for now, the hospital is busy what with people panicking and being stupid, but its fine. After half of the town buggered off at the first sign of panic, amenities aren't exactly spread thin.

If they come though, the infected, then who knows how things will change?

I'm not going to worry about it. After all, we know your alright don't we? Here I am talking to you!

The cordons are fine, we're doing everything we need to keep ourselves safe.

Any day now I'll get to meet you properly!

- **What If I Need to Return Home Immediately?** Obviously, we would always do our best to ensure you were able to take compassionate leave. However, you must understand that your duty lies foremost to your country. You can do your family and friends the most good by helping us deal with these current problems. What benefits them the most, your presence with them now or the healthy future we're fighting to restore?

We appreciate that decisions of this nature are never easy and we are happy to provide professional counselling and advice in your time of need. The British Army has always worked hard to ensure its recruits are happy and healthy in both body and mind.

- **Counselling Wouldn't Help Me.** You'd be surprised. Seeking help through counselling and discussion therapy is not a sign of weakness. Far from it. It's a wise person who knows when they need to address the issues they're facing and seeks help from a professional.

- **My Family Can't Manage Without Me.** No, they can't, they need you right here ensuring that health and safety is restored to the country as soon as possible. You're fighting for them and supporting them every day you're here. It's something for which they will always be proud.

So Barry's mums dead then.
It was no great surprise to find out he was living with her before he signed up. Here's another piece of fatherly advice: move out before you hit forty otherwise everyone will laugh at you. Hell, with your mother I'd move out once you can walk!
Sorry, I shouldn't say that sort of thing. Only joking.
Barry's pretty gutted about it, mind. Her carer contacted the Sarge and passed the message on. Seems the silly old cow decided to go wandering in the night and ended up going for a burton down the stairs. No way to go.

Here we are in the middle of a national emergency, monsters wandering the country, and this silly old mare ends up dying by falling down some stairs. Life's ridiculous son, I'll tell you that, its absolutely mental.

Of course he wants to go home, but the Sarge won't have it. He's got a point, its not as if he can put her back together is it? Sobs done, sad but there you go. The authorities will have her up to the Disposal Centre and that's that, flip of a switch and shes ashes. Take no risks, see? Barry may be missing her now, but I bet even he'd agree that the last thing he'd want was for her to get back up again.

It was hard going though, sitting in barracks with him wailing every five minutes, We tried to be supportive but after a few hours of it you want your sleep and your not so much in the mood for offering a shoulder to cry on. Eventually Danny put our point across.

"Stop fucking crying!" he told him, then shoved him in the food store over night so we might get some peace.

It was a lot quieter, but the porky bastard had eaten all the biscuits come the morning.

PART B

The Myths   There is a lot of ill-educated discussion with regards the Infected. It is understandable that imaginations get carried away in this sort of situation, but it is important we hold on to the facts.

While we are still exploring HRV there are a number of things we can say with conviction:

1.   **The Infected are no longer the people they once were.** This may be difficult to grasp for those that knew the carrier prior to contracting the virus, but it is scientific fact. These things are no more human than a flu virus. HRV animates the dead cells sufficiently for it to become mobile and therefore re-infect. There is nothing supernatural about this. The media's preoccupation with over dressing the situation using colourful theories and speculations is predictably rooted in the urge to sell papers not science. We are approaching the matter in as clinical and practical way possible. The Infected must be gathered and disposed of so that the virus can be eradicated.

2.   **The Infected are not cannibals.** For a start, the term cannibal would be wholly inaccurate as the Infected are no longer human (as explained above). That aside, the Infected wish no more than to pass on the virus and, because HRV is not airborne, they must do this via blood or saliva. The footage we have all seen of the Infected attacking and biting people is simply their automatic attempt to re-infect. Discussion of the Infected eating corpses, indulging in organised attacks or exhibiting signs of extreme hunger are not only inaccurate they are extremely unhelpful. The last thing we need in this current situation is for people to become more scared than they need to be. The best way to progress through the current situation is through facts, not scare-mongering. Don't panic! It's not as bad as it seems.

Well, thats it. They're here and everything we've been told is a crock of shit.
   We got the call from one of the south-eastern perimeter guards mid-morning. They'd seen some infected approaching and wanted assistance. Which was all well and good until the phones started ringing all over.

It hadn't occurred to anybody that they might approach from all sides at once had it? And the eight of us (including the Sarge and Old Patrick, the Quartermaster) couldn't even begin to cope.

I'd been heading south-east with Joe, responding to the initial call. When we got there the old bird on duty was pointing towards the windmill farm where we could see three figures making their way towards us. They weren't bloody scarecrows this time. I know what the field manual says about them not being human, but when you come up against one that goes right out of your head.

These things were not just mobile flu viruses.

The one in the lead was a fat girl, dress hanging off one shoulder, great wobbling mass of purple flesh. She looked like a bruised jelly. Following on behind her were a pair of blokes who were so decomposed it was hard to tell anything about them. One of them was missing his left foot. He wasn't letting it slow him down though. He'd got the hang of limping along on his stump, a crusty black thing like a hammered wooden tent peg, encrusted with grit and lumps of bloodied dirt.

"You want to get down there and shoot them," said the perimeter guard, a grumpy old sow who worked in Town and Country planning. "There's no need to wait until they're on top of us is there?"

By then the walkie-talkie was going like the clappers with the Sarge taking calls from all around the town.

"Jesus," said Joe, "First sign of 'em and the plan's down the shitter already."

"Don't tell me your surprised," I told him.

We headed down to sort the three of them out.

- **Handling the Infected.** It is always best to leave contact with Infected insurgents to those specifically trained for it. The workers at the DISPOSAL CENTRES have all been trained in safe and hygienic handling and will be wearing the correct protective suits and gauntlets.

Of course, sometimes this may not be possible and you will have to deal with Infected personally. In this situation you should be perfectly safe as long as you observe some basic safety considerations:

1. Do not touch the Infected directly. Always use something that allows you to maintain your distance, a broom perhaps or any long pole.

2. Cover up any open wound.

3. Keep your mouth closed and take care not to swallow any fluids the Infected may emit. If you do accidentally swallow anything then encourage vomiting and seek the assistance of your closest medical professional.

4. Be aware that it will try and scratch you or bite you. It's prime intention is to break the skin so it can pass on the virus. Therefore keep yourself as covered as possible and maintain your distance.

5. Do not goad or "play" with the Infected. Simply dispose of it as quickly and simply as possible. The longer your exposure to the Infected, the more the chances of becoming infected yourself increase.

6. Use the minimum force required. The Infected can be fragile, so be aware that yanking or shoving may result in their physical break up, further spreading the chance of contamination.

7. Keep calm. A panicking person is one who makes mistakes. Careful handling of the Infected is perfectly safe.

"I'll take the fat girl, you can have Sarge," said Joe.
It took me a minute to figure out he meant the zombie with the missing foot. I was pleased Joe was keeping it together enough to crack a joke — however unfunny.
"What about the other one?"
"Depends who finishes first," he said.

What with the state of the rest of the supplies, you might imagine we'd been issued with broom handles for weapons, but luckily we did have firearms. According to the Sarge they were older than Old Patrick, but they worked well enough. Even better if someone had trained us how to use one properly. We'd been allowed ten rounds each (thats what they call bullets in the army) back at the barracks. A couple of minutes and a row of old water bottles — that was my experience. I had managed to hit two of the bottles.

Joe raised his gun and pressed the trigger. He blew a piece off the fat girls thigh. A target that big, and he only caught the edge of it.

"Careful," I told him, "we don't want chunks of the stuff all over the place, we'll have to pick it up."

"The sights are out," he said. Someone plays Call of Duty a couple of times and they think they know everything about a gun.

"Yeah right," I laughed and lined up my own shot.

Looking back on it, with what came later, I can't believe we were still laughing. I suppose at that point we didn't know how bad things could be. When stuff is too big for you to get your head around you just switch off. You shrug and have a laugh because the alternative is beyond you.

I took my shot and missed completely. Checking on Joe, he hadn't noticed and was still trying to shoot the girl in the head.

"They'll be on top of us in a minute," I told him.

"Probably manage to hit the fucker then," he replied.

We took our next shots.

- **How to Neutralise the Infected.** Infected insurgents are easily neutralised. The science behind it is incredibly simple. HRV utilises the human body to become mobile. The human body is reliant on the controlling influence of the brain for motor function. Therefore, if one removes the brain's connection to the rest of the body – or at least damages it significantly – then basic bodily functions will no longer be possible and the Infected body is safely neutralised.

This can be achieved in a number of effective ways, but bear in mind the following points:

1. Removing the head from the spinal column is the cleanest and most certain method, though clearly it will require both a suitable tool for the job and a practical angle with which to use that tool. Due to the previously mentioned malleability of the Infected, it may be possible to remove the head simply by swinging a suitably bladed instrument at their neck when facing them directly. However, for increased efficacy we suggest you rely on this method only when the Infected is at a perpendicular angle so as to be sure that your blow will strike cleanly.

2. Be aware of contamination risk. While striking the skull with a heavy object – say a brick or sledgehammer – will certainly have the desired effect, it will also cause considerable splatter. Every droplet of blood or brain tissue may be sufficient to spread the infection were it to enter the bloodstream, so the more this is minimised the better. Spare a moment to consider whether there is a neater method available to you. If you are armed, then clearly a bullet may be used at a safe distance where the spread of cranial fluids is less of a concern. At close quarters perhaps a long thin object may be inserted in its eye? If so, then insert the object at a shallow depth and then "stir" in order to maximise cerebral damage.

Joe finally managed to hit his target in the head. There was an eruption of wet hair and the pitter patter of lumps of meat raining down on the grass. The thing pole-axed and we were down to two.

My second shot hit Sarge Zombie in the mouth, which was pretty good considering he was thin and loping from one side to the other 'cos of that stupid foot. It didn't stop it though. If there's one thing the manual tells the truth about its the fact that you've got to get them in the brain.

I took a third shot while Joe went for the last of them, still a few feet behind the others or it would have been on top of us already.

I finally got my shot in and the thing went down fast, that stump of a leg coming straight up in the air like a salute. There was a bright blue lump of chewing gum on it, I noticed, all pulled into gooey strands. Its strange how much information you pick up when your in that situation. I guess its adrenaline. Your brain's on overload and sees every detail in case its important.

"If you've finished?" asked Joe, taking another shot as his first had missed. He took out a chunk to the right side of its skull and we both assumed that would be enough, there was a whopping great crescent on one side of its head, half the brain gone for sure. It kept walking though, so I tried to get the other half. Like Joe, my shot was a bit wide and blew a hole on the left side of its head. The thing stood still for a moment, a strange antennae of nose and skull poking up to where its eyes had been. Finally it fell over.

"Not so bad," said Joe after a moment.

"My heroes," said the Town and Country planner. "Now are you going to clear this mess up or am I going to have to stand here breathing virus fumes?"

- **How to Dispose of the Infected.** Once Infected insurgents have been neutralised it is important that the remains are safely disposed of. Just because the virus is no longer able to animate the body doesn't mean that it has been rendered inert, the remains are still a potential contaminant and must, therefore, be disposed of responsibly.

Obviously, the preferred method would be for the remains to be securely transported to your closest DISPOSAL CENTRE. If you are unsure where this is or it is simply impractical to get there, then there are several recommended options (note: ALWAYS check with your commanding officer before dealing with Infected remains as it is possible there are standing orders in your area that relate to cadaver disposal).

1. Burning the remains is the most approved method. Suggestions that the smoke could carry the infection are, once again, the product of press speculation and have no basis in scientific fact. Tests show that if the body is subjected to sufficient heat, then the infection is effectively eradicated. It is important, obviously, that all the parts of the cadaver are collected together and then the incineration is carefully supervised. Given the potential danger of leaving portions unburned, it's important that the fire is continually fed until all the remains are reduced to ash.

2. Burial is also possible, though tests are inconclusive as to how long it takes for the infected flesh to decay to the point of being virally inert. It's important therefore that the remains be buried at sufficient depth as to ensure containment. This may well be impractical unless you have access to heavy plant machinery.

3. Chemical erosion. Possibly this is beyond the capabilities and resources of most units, but there are several industrial chemicals that are capable of destroying the infected flesh.[2]

---

[2] The handling of such chemicals is extremely dangerous. As above, speak with your commanding officer about what facilities are open to you and what the preferences are for your unit.

So Joe and I are trying to gather up the mess while the walkie-talkie is roaring away.

"We havent time for this." Joe was complaining, "they could be breaking through the cordon."

Which of course they were.

"You can't leave it like that," the Town and Country Planner moaned, but in the end we kicked as much of it into a pile as we could and left her with a bottle of paraffin and some matches.

"Sort it out love," I told her, "we've got to get moving."

She shouted her considerable lungs out about that, but we saw a plume of smoke in the rear-view mirror on our way back into town, so she obviously managed.

"We can't hold them!" Sarge was shouting on the walkie-talkie. "There's hundreds of the fuckers and eight of us. We're pissing into the wind."

"So what do you want us to do?" Joe was asking, but I was already driving to your mother's house and to hell with orders. I wasn't going to leave you high and dry were I?

Except you weren't bloody there were you? One of the neighbours told me that your mother had gone into labour a couple of hours earlier. The silly bitch never did have much consideration for others.

The Sarge was talking about instigating "Emergency Protocols", whatever the hell they were, and demanding that we all return to base immediately.

I was torn, mate, I've got to say, but if you were in hospital then there was sod-all I could do for you there, my best bet was to do as I was told and try and protect the town.

- **Emergency Protocols.** In the unlikely event that the Infected are present in your district to such a number that maintaining a cordon becomes impossible, your commanding officer will instigate "Emergency Protocols".

Put simply, this is a series of contingencies specifically designed to make the town as safe as possible given the circumstances.

1. Martial Law is declared. Your commanding officer has final authority within the district.

2. A curfew is instigated. If Infected insurgents are on the streets then the simplest method of safeguarding against them is to ensure the populace are locked within their homes. The Infected are not intelligent; as long as simple precautions are taken residents can live safely in their homes for many days. Should you be asked for advice, refer civilians to leaflet 40GR HOW DO I PROTECT MY HOME AGAINST THE INFECTED?, it is full of useful tips to guarantee the security of most homes and is freely available in all post offices and libraries.[3]

3. Organise a clean-up procedure. The numbers of Infected insurgents are clearly finite. While it may seem catastrophic that they have infiltrated your town it should be possible, using a methodical sweep of the district, to drastically reduce their numbers to the point that they no longer represent a major threat.

4. Guard all essential amenities. It is vital that water and services should continue to function within your district, so prepare to safeguard these facilities. Your local hospital or medical centre will also be a vital hub during the oncoming days and it is essential that clear lines of communication are maintained at all times.

---

[3] If your closest post office or library has been closed down, then it is also available from selected branches of Tesco or Tesco Express.

So I managed to pull a duty at the hospital didn't I? Couldn't be better! Your upstairs, giving your mother grief (can't say I blame you wanting to stay inside, warm and safe, given what's going on out here). I'm down in the foyer, writing this up and keeping an eye out for the Infected.

The Sarge has split the rest of them into two teams: Barry, Evan and Lewis running a loud-hailer to get everyone to stay in their homes, Taff, Joe and Danny patrolling the streets, killing as many of the things as they can get their hands on (literally in Danny's case, so Taff tells me on the walkie-talkie — the silly sod's become so convinced he's invincible he's running down the street in a boiler suit, welding mask and boxing gloves, smacking everything in sight, I suppose it saves rounds).

Were still acting like this is no big deal. And I'm thinking about that, sat here while civilians mill about fussing over their usual ailments. Were so arrogant, we don't think anything can really get us. Whatever you see on the TV that's not REAL, that's not YOU. Even with most of the capital gone up in a fucking mushroom cloud, these idiots are buzzing around acting like life will be back to normal soon enough.

"No worse than the war," one old git says to me, sat in the doorway in his wheelchair. "They bombed us then too."

"They didn't bomb us," I try and explain, "we did it ourselves. The city was so knackered there was no other option but wipe most of it out."

He just shrugs. "Never did like London," he says after a bit, "whole place was up it itself."

He wheels himself off to go and find a bed bath.

Its mad, son, just mad.

But then, upstairs, maybe even right now, your coming into the world and that changes everything.

You'll take care of it won't you? Yeah . . . my son will shake the world by the scruff of its neck and make his mark. My son's going to be special!

Hang on . . . someone upstairs says there are infected on their way, they've seen them through the window.

Back to work!

• **Dealing with the Infected in Quantity.** It goes without saying that the safest method of dealing with the Infected is to never allow them to gather en masse. They are slow and dumb, and it should always be possible to keep ahead of the pack as long as you keep your wits about you.

If the situation is unavoidable, however, there are a number of options open to you:

1. Pick the clearest route and stick to it. Before you become entirely surrounded, find the option with the least obstruction and use it as fast as you can.

2. Keep a zone of personal space around you at all times. You may find that your rifle[4] is more use to you being swung either side as you are running, rather than being fired. You can beat back a number of the Infected this way rather than relying on the need to shoot them one at a time.

3. Remember: the Infected are soft and easily broken. The Infected decompose at a faster rate than normal cadavers, which means their physical tissue is extremely pliable. You will be surprised how easy it is to fight your way through a herd of them. Always remember to minimise your exposure to contaminated matter. If you have to force your way through a crowd then ensure as much of you is covered as possible and keep your mouth closed at all times.

4. Are there any wounded in your party? If so then be aware that, once contaminated, there is nothing you can do for them. While it may seem callous, the very moment someone is infected they have become your enemy and you should treat them as such. However, if someone has been recently infected and still in control of their own actions, suggest that they run in an opposite direction to the rest of the party in order to split the attention of the Infected. If you yourself have become infected then this is a wonderful opportunity for you to help the rest of your comrades. Can you draw a section of the Infected away? Or maybe just slow them down for long enough that the main party can escape. Be a hero! Show them what you're made of!

5. Current research suggests that the Infected are very sensitive to loud noise. While tests are ongoing in this area, there has certainly been convincing evidence that extended, high-pitched sounds can disorientate the Infected. Try singing or screaming, it may just create enough of a distraction for you to slip away.

6. There have been numerous rumours about the effects of smearing yourself with infected matter. The main thrust of the argument is that if you smell like the Infected, then they will ignore you. Ignoring the, by no means certain, notion that the Infected can smell, there is very little evidence for this being effective. It seems, like so many of the myths repeated by unreliable media, to hail from the cinema rather than the laboratory. Spreading infected matter on yourself is only likely to cause infection. It is not recommended.

7. If all else fails, is there somewhere you can barricade yourself while you wait for back-up from the rest of your unit? While "painting yourself into a corner" is not ideal, sometimes it's the only viable course of action. Perhaps there is a cupboard or storage area close by? Maybe you could even climb to higher ground and avoid the reach of the Infected that way. Sometimes it's best to accept that there's nothing left to do but ensure your own survival and act accordingly. Get safe and then get help.

---

[4] If you have not been issued with a rifle then refer to the section USEFUL WEAPONS FOUND AROUND THE HOME for further suggestions.

(Excuse the writing, its pretty dark in here and I can't really see what I'm doing.)
We just don't learn do we? I saw the infected making for the main entrance and made a pretty good effort as far as barricading the doors went. Considering the tools (and people) I had to work with, I think its amazing they held as long as they did. Still, I didn't think about the rear did I? It was the perimeter cordon all over again, they were

coming from all sides. How could I defend the entire building on my own? I tried, son, honestly I did. I tried as hard as I could.

In the end though there were just too many of them. I found myself stuck in one of the wards, the beds piled up against the doors, while a handful of us hoped we could keep them out until reinforcements arrived.

Only there wasn't to be any reinforcements was there? I heard Danny dying over the walkie-talkie, the reckless bastard had got himself infected tearing the heads off the infected using his hands. He'll be a right nasty bastard now, presuming he's come back. I think Taff got it too, I could hear him shouting his head off, shooting at them. Then there was nothing.

There's just too many of them son, too many. Sometimes you have to accept there are fights you can't win. I think the Sarge got that. I heard him on the radio - he was telling all of us to find our loved ones and keep them safe. He didn't say anything else. I've a feeling he may have topped himself. Well, its not like he could have run for his life is it?

I took his advice though. Eventually anyway. It took me an hour or so to be able to get up to the maternity ward, 'cos of all the barricades and the infected being everywhere.

I was too late for your mother of course. She was lying there, spread out over the bed - nothing but blood and shattered bone from the chest up. If it weren't for the clipboard at the foot of the bed, I wouldn't have known it was her.

I felt sorry for her. Of course I did. I know we hadn't seen eye to eye for months, but I'd loved her once, you know? They'd had most of her legs away too, the meat anyway, the bones were intact, bowed out and pipe-cleaner thin. Like an ostrich's legs. But the belly was intact. Like they knew.

And I got to see it! I was there for the birth! Just like every proud father should be.

Obviously, this wasn't quite what I had in mind. But I got to thinking about it – watching you chew your way out, those beautiful little purple fingers of yours tugging you free – maybe this is for the best. Cos I wanted you to have a secure future didn't I? I wanted you to be able to grow strong and make your own way in the world. Having seen how unstoppable the infected are, I think your on the right side. You've joined the winning team.

I've just heard you scratching at the door! You know its your old dad on the other side don't you? Your old man.

Most babies take weeks to get around, look at you! Motoring along under your own steam already.

You make me so proud.

BRITISH EMBASSY

Smolenskaya Naberezhnaya 10, Moscow 121099. Tel: (495) 956 7200.

```
RR FCO
FM MOSCO
TO ROUTINE FCO
UNRESTRICTED
FM MOSCOW
TO ROUTINE FCO
TEL NO 1 OF 10 MAY

CHANGING ALL COMMS TO TELEX AS PER FCO INSTRUCTIONS.

HEAD OF COMMS
PP SIR EDWARD CARTLEDGE
```

BRITISH EMBASSY

Smolenskaya Naberezhnaya 10, Moscow 121099. Tel: (495) 956 7200.

OO FCO
FM MOSCO
TO IMMEDIATE FCO
CONFIDENTIAL
FM MOSCOW
TO IMMEDIATE FCO
TEL NO 34 OF 13 MAY

WITH REGARDS TO LAST NIGHT'S FIRE AT THE S P BOTKIN HOSPITAL.
ITAR-TASS AND RIA ARE HOLDING WITH THE OFFICIAL LINE THAT THE
CAUSE OF THE DEVASTATION WAS AN ELECTRICAL FAULT. HOWEVER,
ALTHOUGH BOTH THE PRESIDENT AND PRIME MINISTER PUTIN ARE
INSISTENT THAT RUSSIA HAS NOT BEEN AFFECTED BY THE RECENT
PROBLEMS WITH THE DEAD, THE AREA AROUND THE HOSPITAL WAS
CLEARED OF LOCAL OBSERVERS BY BOTH THE ARMY AND POLICE.

THERE ARE ALSO UNOFFICIAL REPORTS COMING FROM THOSE WORKING
WITHIN THE HOSPITAL THAT THERE WERE "PROBLEMS" IN BOTH THE
MORGUE AND THE INFECTIOUS DISEASES WING WHERE MANY OF THOSE
SUFFERING WITH THIS RECENT EPIDEMIC OF FLU AND WINTER VOMITING
WERE BEING TREATED. SOME PATIENTS WERE PRESENTING VERY UNUSUAL
SYMPTOMS.

OUR VIEW IS THAT RUSSIA HAS NOT BEEN UNAFFECTED AND THAT THE
FIRE WAS STARTED INTENTIONALLY TO DESTROY THE DEAD WHO WERE
RISING. HAVE REQUESTED MEETING WITH THE FOREIGN MINISTER TO
DISCUSS BUT AS YET NO RESPONSE.

WEATHER REPORTS STATE THAT THE CURRENT LATE FREEZE HERE WILL
SOON BE OVER AND TEMPERATURES ARE SET TO RISE ABOVE FREEZING
BY THE END OF THE WEEK.

HEAD OF COMMS
PP SIR EDWARD CARTLEDGE

BRITISH EMBASSY

Smolenskaya Naberezhnaya 10, Moscow 121099. Tel: (495) 956 7200.

The following consists of unedited material received from Moscow

```
OO FCO
FM MOSCO
TO IMMEDIATE FCO
RESTRICTED
FM MOSCOW
TO IMMEDIATE FCO
TEL NO 18 OF 15 MAY

LENIN'S TOMB HAS BEEN CLOSED FROM PUBLIC VISITATION DUE TO AN
ELDERLY WOMAN FROM MINSK CLAIMING THAT SHE SAW THE DEAD
LEADER'S FINGER TWITCHING. THE BODY HAS NOT BEEN REMOVED AND
IS BEHIND BULLET-PROOF GLASS BUT THERE IS A HEAVY ARMED GUARD
PRESENCE NOW IN RED SQUARE

THERE HAS BEEN SOME DISGRUNTLED NOISE FROM THE ELDERLY AND
STUDENTS AT THE MAUSOLEUM BEING CLOSED, SOME CLAIMING THAT
IT'S THEIR RIGHT AS CITIZENS TO HAVE ACCESS TO LENIN.

THE AIRPORTS REMAIN CLOSED AND THE INTERNET SHUT DOWN. VERY
LITTLE INFORMATION IS COMING THROUGH TO THE GENERAL PUBLIC
ABOUT THE REST OF THE WORLD.

FLU EPIDEMIC APPARENTLY SPREADING. THE PUBLIC ENCOURAGED TO GO
TO WORK AND STAY AT HOME BUT NOT SOCIALISE OR GATHER IN LARGE
GROUPS TO AVOID UNNECESSARY SPREADING OF THE DISEASE.

ONCE AGAIN, A REQUEST HAS BEEN PLACED FOR IMMEDIATE
REPATRIATION OF REMAINING BRITISH EMBASSY STAFF.

HEAD OF COMMS
PP SIR EDWARD CARTLEDGE
```

BRITISH EMBASSY

Smolenskaya Naberezhnaya 10, Moscow 121099. Tel: (495) 956 7200.

The following consists of unedited material received from Moscow

RR FCO
FM MOSCO
TO ROUTINE FCO
RESTRICTED
FM MOSCOW
TO ROUTINE FCO
TEL NO 1 OF 17 MAY

THE SUDDEN SHARP AND STEADY RISE IN TEMPERATURE THAT STARTED
ON 15 MAY HAS LED TO A QUICK THAW. MOST OF THE CITY IS NOW
CLEAR OF SNOW AND ICE. DESPITE MY WARNINGS TO THE RUSSIAN
FOREIGN MINISTER, VERY FEW PRECAUTIONS HAVE BEEN MADE TO
SECURE CEMETERIES AND GRAVEYARDS WITHIN THE CITY. HE IS
CONTINUING WITH PRIME MINISTER PUTIN'S ASSERTIONS THAT THIS IS
NO MORE THAN A NEW-STRAIN FLU EPIDEMIC. HE DID ADD THAT THEY
NOW BELIEVE THE FLU ORIGINATED IN EITHER THE UK OR AMERICA AND
ARE NOW CONSIDERING CUTTING DIPLOMATIC RELATIONS WITH BOTH
COUNTRIES.

I FEEL THAT THIS IS SIMPLY A MEASURE TO FURTHER LIMIT
INFORMATION.

EXTERNAL SOURCES CLAIM THAT THE DEAD HAVE STARTED TO RISE FROM
SHALLOWER GRAVES IN THE COUNTRYSIDE, INCLUDING THE BAY OF JOYS
RIVER RESORT. THE MINISTER FOR INTERNAL AFFAIRS HAS FAILED TO
RETURN FROM HIS DACHA BREAK IN THAT AREA AND AGAIN THERE HAVE
BEEN REPORTS OF GUNFIRE AND A HEAVY ARMY PRESENCE IN THE AREA.

HEAD OF COMMS
PP SIR EDWARD CARTLEDGE

BRITISH EMBASSY

Smolenskaya Naberezhnaya 10, Moscow 121099. Tel: (495) 956 7200.

The following consists of unedited material received from Moscow

OO FCO
FM MOSCO
TO IMMEDIATE FCO
RESTRICTED
FM MOSCOW
TO IMMEDIATE FCO
TEL NO 34 OF 18 MAY

REPORTS OF EARLIER NOW CONFIRMED. ALL ROUTES IN AND OUT OF THE
CITY ARE NOW CHECK-POINTED AND GUARDED. CURFEWS ARE BEING
PLACED ON ALL CITIZENS THE DETAILS OF WHICH WILL BE ANNOUNCED
ON THE RADIO LATER.

WE ARE STILL OFFICIALLY ACCORDED DIPLOMATIC PRIVILEGES BUT
HAVE BEEN REFUSED PERMISSION TO LEAVE UNTIL THE EPIDEMIC IS
OVER.

THERE IS A HEAVY ARMY PRESENCE ON THE STREETS AS WELL AS
AMBULANCES AND UNMARKED VEHICLES WHICH PROBABLY HOLD THE
INFECTIOUS DISEASES TEAMS.

EMBASSY STAFF HAVE SEEN THE DEAD ON THE STREETS. NOT MANY BUT
EMERGING. SOLDIERS ARE SIMPLY CALLING THEM "THE INFECTED".

THE ONLY CONCLUSION THAT CAN BE DRAWN IS THAT PRIME MINISTER
PUTIN HAS SOMEHOW CONVINCED HIMSELF AND HIS MINISTERS THAT THE
FLU IS WHAT IS CAUSING THEIR CURRENT CRISIS AND IT IS NOT IN
ANY WAY RELATED TO EVENTS OUTSIDE OF THIS COUNTRY.

I ADVISE THE ACTING PM TO CONTACT HIM IMMEDIATELY AND PRESS
THE WIDER SITUATION UPON HIM.

HEAD OF COMMS
PP SIR EDWARD CARTLEDGE

BRITISH EMBASSY

Smolenskaya Naberezhnaya 10, Moscow 121099. Tel: (495) 956 7200.

The following consists of unedited material received from Moscow

PP FCO
FM MOSCO
TO PRIORITY FCO
SECRET
FM MOSCOW
TO PRIORITY FCO
TEL NO 8 OF 20 MAY

THE SITUATION HERE IS BECOMING CRITICAL. THIS MORNING A LARGE
GROUP OF STUDENTS CARRYING YOUNG SOCIALIST FLAGS MARCHED
THROUGH THE CITY, ENDING IN RED SQUARE AND DEMANDING THAT THE
AUTHORITIES BE HONEST WITH THE NATION ABOUT THE DEAD
SITUATION. TIM HETTON, THE TIMES CORRESPONDENT, INTERVIEWED
ONE OF THEIR LEADERS WHO SAID THAT THEY HAD BEEN LISTENING TO
PIRATE RADIO BROADCASTS AND KNOW THAT WHAT IS STARTING HERE IS
A GLOBAL PHENOMENON.

ONE STUDENT WAS SPEAKING LIVE ON THE NEWS WHEN THE TV SIGNAL
CEASED.

THE MILITARY ARE NOW IN ALL THE TV STATION BUILDINGS ACROSS
THE CITY AND HAVE TAKEN CONTROL OF ITAR-TASS AND RIA. IGNORE
ALL BULLETINS FROM THEM AS THEY CAN NO LONGER BE SEEN AS
RELIABLE INFORMATION SOURCES.

HEAD OF COMMS
PP SIR EDWARD CARTLEDGE

BRITISH EMBASSY

Smolenskaya Naberezhnaya 10, Moscow 121099. Tel: (495) 956 7200.

The following consists of unedited material received from Moscow

```
ZZ FCO
FM MOSCO
TO FLASH  FCO
TOP SECRET
FM MOSCOW
TO FLASH FCO
TEL NO 12 OF 20 MAY
```

CONFIRMATION OF TELEX 11 OF TODAY. RED SQUARE MASSACRE OF
STUDENTS GUNNED DOWN BY ARMY. CASUALTY NUMBERS UNKNOWN BUT
FIGURES PRESUMED SOMEWHERE IN THE REGION OF A HUNDRED.

THERE HAS BEEN ONE TELEVISION BROADCAST SINCE ALL STATIONS
WENT OFF AIR. PRIME MINISTER PUTIN ADDRESSED THE NATION AND
DECLARED A STATE OF EMERGENCY FROM "INTERNAL TERRORISTS" AND
THE FLU EPIDEMIC.

HEAD OF COMMS
PP SIR EDWARD CARTLEDGE

BRITISH EMBASSY

Smolenskaya Naberezhnaya 10, Moscow 121099. Tel: (495) 956 7200.

The following consists of unedited material received from Moscow

OO FCO
FM MOSCO
TO IMMEDIATE FCO
RESTRICTED
FM MOSCOW
TO IMMEDIATE FCO
TEL NO 14 OF 20 MAY

AS PER INTERIM GOVERNMENT'S INSTRUCTIONS I HAVE REQUESTED
INFORMATION CONFIRMING THAT THE BODIES OF THE MASSACRED
STUDENTS HAVE BEEN DESTROYED.

I HAVE NOW MADE THIS REQUEST THREE TIMES BUT HAVE YET TO
RECEIVE AN ANSWER. I HAVE ALSO SENT A COMPLAINT THAT AS THE
BRITISH AMBASSADOR TO RUSSIA I SHOULD BE AFFORDED THE COURTESY
OF MEETINGS AND RESPONSES.

HEAD OF COMMS
PP SIR EDWARD CARTLEDGE

BRITISH EMBASSY

Smolenskaya Naberezhnaya 10, Moscow 121099. Tel: (495) 956 7200.

The following consists of unedited material received from Moscow

```
PP FCO
FM MOSCO
TO PRIORITY FCO
SECRET
FM MOSCOW
TO PRIORITY FCO
TEL NO 1 OF 21 MAY
```

ALARMING DEVELOPMENTS. TIM HETTON, TIMES CORRESPONDENT,
ARRIVED THIRTY MINUTES AGO AT THE EMBASSY WITH FOLLOWING
INFORMATION.

PRIME MINISTER PUTIN AND MINISTERS HAVE SERIOUSLY MISJUDGED
THE SITUATION. THE DEAD STUDENT PROTESTERS WERE NOT DESTROYED
BUT STORED. THEY ROSE UP IN THE NIGHT AND ATTACKED THE ARMY
UNIT POSITIONED IN RED SQUARE.

WHILE THIS ATTACK WAS TAKING PLACE THE DEAD BEGAN TO RISE IN
NOVODEVICHY CEMETERY WHERE NEARLY 30,000 PEOPLE ARE BURIED.
TIM HETTON HAD GONE THERE ON A TIP AFTER A REPORT OF SMALL
SEISMIC ACTIVITY IN THE AREA. HE STATES THAT SOME OF THE
RISING DEAD ATTACKED GUARDS WHILE OTHERS DUG OUT SOME OF THE
REMAINING DEAD.

TWO OF THE GRAVES EMPTIED WERE THOSE OF KRUSCHEV AND BORIS
YELTSIN. HETTON LEFT DURING THE FIGHTING. BY HIS REPORTS HE
WAS LUCKY TO GET OUT ALIVE.

LARGEST CONCERN FROM THIS REPORT IS THE APPARENT CO-ORDINATION
OF EVENTS. THE DISTRACTION BY THE DEAD STUDENTS AT RED SQUARE
ALLOWED THE DEAD AT THE CEMETERY TO RISE AND OVER-RUN THE
SOLDIERS.

ARE THE DEAD WORKING TOGETHER, AND IF SO, WHO IS LEADING THEM?

HEAD OF COMMS
PP EDWARD CARTLEDGE

BRITISH EMBASSY

Smolenskaya Naberezhnaya 10, Moscow 121099. Tel: (495) 956 7200

The following consists of unedited material received from Moscow

OO FCO
FM MOSCO
TO IMMEDIATE FCO
CONFIDENTIAL
FM MOSCOW
TO IMMEDIATE FCO
TEL NO 2 OF 22 MAY

I HAVE PLACED THE EMBASSY IN LOCK DOWN. IT'S CLEAR ALL
DIPLOMATIC RELATIONS HAVE BROKEN DOWN DESPITE OUR BEST EFFORTS
TO MAINTAIN THEM.

THE NECROPOLIS IN THE KREMLIN WALL WAS BURNED LAST NIGHT WHICH
AT LEAST IS A SIGN THAT THE PRIME MINISTER AND PRESIDENT HAVE
REALISED THE THREAT THE DEAD POSE.

I ONCE AGAIN URGE THE ACTING PM TO APPLY PRESSURE FOR
IMMEDIATE REPATRIATION OF ALL EMBASSY STAFF.

HEAD OF COMMS
PP SIR EDWARD CARTLEDGE

BRITISH EMBASSY

Smolenskaya Naberezhnaya 10, Moscow 121099. Tel: (495) 956 7200.

The following consists of unedited material received from Moscow

ZZ FCO
FM MOSCO
TO FLASH FCO
SECRET
FM MOSCOW
TO FLASH FCO
TEL NO 5 OF 22 MAY

DR ROBERTS IS CONCERNED ABOUT TIM HETTON. THE REPORTER LOOKS
PALE AND HASN'T EATEN SINCE HE ARRIVED. HE HAS SCRATCHES ON
HIS LEFT ARM THAT HE INSISTS WERE CAUSED RUNNING THROUGH TREES
WHEN GETTING AWAY FROM THE SITUATION AT NOVODEVICHY CEMETERY.

THE DOCTOR IS RUNNING SOME MORE BLOOD TESTS AND WE WILL KEEP
AN EYE ON HIM FOR FURTHER CHANGES. REQUEST INSTRUCTIONS OF HOW
TO PROCEED SHOULD HE BE INFECTED.

HEAD OF COMMS
PP SIR EDWARD CARTLEDGE

BRITISH EMBASSY

Smolenskaya Naberezhnaya 10, Moscow 121099. Tel: (495) 956 7200.

The following consists of unedited material received from Moscow

PP FCO
FM MOSCO
TO PRIORITY FCO
SECRET
FM MOSCOW
TO PRIORITY FCO
TEL NO 1 OF 24 MAY

CITY WIDE POWER OUTAGE OF YESTERDAY APPEARS TO HAVE BEEN
REPAIRED BUT WE NOW HAVE THE GENERATOR ON STANDBY, ALTHOUGH
OUR GASOLINE RESERVES ARE LOW AND WE HAVE BEEN UNABLE TO
ACQUIRE ANY IN THE CITY. MANY PERSONNEL ARE ALSO RELUCTANT TO
LEAVE THE EMBASSY BUILDING AND I FEEL UNABLE TO COMMAND THEM
TO DO SO GIVEN THE RISKS TO THEIR LIVES ON THE STREETS. MAJOR
HEPBURN, THE MILITARY ATTACHE, AND HEAD OF CHANCERY STEPHEN
MORRIS HAVE BOTH GONE OUT HOWEVER AND REPORT THAT THE CITY IS
IN A GENERAL STATE OF CHAOS AND PANIC. THERE ARE ALSO FEWER
SOLDIERS PRESENT THAN EXPECTED.

PRIME MINISTER PUTIN CONTINUES TO MAKE DAILY ADDRESSES ON THE
TELEVISION BUT HAS NOT BEEN SEEN IN PERSON FOR A WEEK. THERE
ARE RUMOURS THAT HE'S FLED THE COUNTRY WHICH ARE NOT HELPING
WITH THE CIVIL UNREST.

HUGE CALL FOR CHANGE OF LEADERSHIP. MUCH TALK OF THE SAFETY O
THE OLD REGIME.

HEAD OF COMMS
PP SIR EDWARD CARTLEDGE

BRITISH EMBASSY

Smolenskaya Naberezhnaya 10, Moscow 121099. Tel: (495) 956 7200.

The following consists of unedited material received from Moscow

```
ZZ FCO
FM MOSCO
TO FLASH FCO
TOP SECRET
FM MOSCOW
TO FLASH FCO
TEL NO 2 OF 24 MAY
```

MAJOR HEPBURN AND STEPHEN MORRIS BOTH REPORTED THAT THE DEAD,
ALTHOUGH STILL ATTACKING THE LIVING, ARE, IN SOME CASES,
STARTING TO BECOME SENTIENT. THERE ARE SLOGANS ON WALLS ACROSS
THE CITY THAT CAN BE TRANSLATED AS 'WE ARE ALL EQUAL IN THE
EYES OF DEATH'. IN OTHER AREAS LENIN'S SLOGAN 'PEACE LAND
BREED' IS APPEARING WITH MORE FREQUENCY. THERE HAVE BEEN NO
ATTEMPTS TO CLEAN THESE AWAY WHICH SUGGESTS THAT THE CURRENT
REGIME IS PERHAPS LOSING ITS HOLD ON THE ARMY.

PEOPLE ARE DISOBEYING THE CURFEW AND GATHERING AT STATUES OF
LENIN AND AT THE LENIN LIBRARY AS ACCESS TO THE RED SQUARE AND
THE MAUSOLEUM IS CURRENTLY CLOSED OFF. DISTURBINGLY, THERE ARE
REPORTS OF BOTH THE LIVING AND THE DEAD GATHERING IN THESE
LOCATIONS.

I CANNOT STRESS ENOUGH THE IMPORTANCE OF SECURING IMMEDIATE
REPATRIATION FOR EMBASSY STAFF. WE HAVE HAD STONES AND PETROL
BOMBS THROWN AT THE GATES.

HEAD OF COMMS
PP SIR EDWARD CARTLEDGE

BRITISH EMBASSY

Smolenskaya Naberezhnaya 10, Moscow 121099. Tel: (495) 956 7200

The following consists of unedited material received from Moscow

PP FCO
FM MOSCO
TO PRIORITY FCO
SECRET
FM MOSCOW
TO PRIORITY FCO
TEL NO 13 OF 24 MAY

WORST FEARS REALISED. TIM HETTON IS INFECTED. HE HAD BEEN
ISOLATED AND RUNNING A FEVER BUT AN HOUR AGO HE ATTACKED THE
SECURITY OFFICER WHO WAS GUARDING HIS ROOM. THE OFFICER
MANAGED TO CONTAIN MR HETTON IN HIS ROOM BUT DID SUSTAIN A
BITE. DR ROBERTS HAS SEDATED THE SECURITY OFFICER AND WE HAVE
LOCKED HIM IN A SEPARATE ROOM TO TIM HETTON.

ADVISE COURSE OF ACTION.

HEAD OF COMMS
PP SIR EDWARD CARTLEDGE

BRITISH EMBASSY

Smolenskaya Naberezhnaya 10, Moscow 121099. Tel: (495) 956 7200.

The following consists of unedited material received from Moscow

ZZ FCO
FM MOSCO
TO FLASH FCO
SECRET
FM MOSCOW
TO FLASH FCO
TEL NO 19 OF 24 MAY

HUGE AMOUNT OF ACTIVITY IN THE STREETS. FIREWORKS GOING OFF
SOMEWHERE IN THE CITY FROM THE DIRECTION OF GORKY PARK. MAJOR
HEPBURN AND TWO OTHERS WENT OUT THROUGH THE BACK GATE TO
INVESTIGATE. MANY OF THE SOLDIERS HAVE FLED.

LENIN'S MAUSOLEUM HAS BEEN OPENED. WHEN HE EMERGED THE LAST OF
THE SOLDIERS PUT DOWN THEIR GUNS. BOTH THE LIVING AND THE DEAD
ARE IN THE STREETS CARRYING 'PEACE LAND BREED' SIGNS.

SIR EDWARD CARTLEDGE AND THE HEAD OF CHANCERY HAVE TAKEN THE
OFFICIAL CAR AND HEADED TO THE KREMLIN TO TRY AND VERIFY
RUMOURS THAT PUTIN HAS ALREADY FLED RUSSIA AND TO SEE WHO, IF
ANYONE, IS LEFT IN CHARGE.

WE WILL CONTINUE WITH KEEPING THE TWO INFECTED MEN IN
ISOLATION AS PER INSTRUCTIONS.

BRIAN CARTER
HEAD OF COMMS

BRITISH EMBASSY

Smolenskaya Naberezhnaya 10, Moscow 121099. Tel: (495) 956 7200.

ZZ FCO
FM MOSCO
TO FLASH FCO
TOP SECRET
FM MOSCOW
TO FLASH FCO
TEL NO 1 OF 25 MAY

LADY CARTLEDGE IS GETTING SICK. SHE'S BEEN RUNNING A FEVER AND
IS STARTING TO BEHAVE ERRATICALLY. DR ROBERTS IS CONVINCED SHE
IS INFECTED DESPITE NOT HAVING BEEN OUT OF THE EMBASSY SINCE
THE CURRENT SITUATION BEGAN.

THIS BRINGS UP A DELICATE ISSUE.

A FEW WEEKS AGO RUMOURS OF AN AFFAIR BETWEEN LADY CARTLEDGE
AND TIM HETTON CIRCULATED THROUGH THE EMBASSY. MOST PEOPLE
BELIEVED IT TO BE SIMPLY IDLE GOSSIP, HOWEVER, IF IT WERE TRUE
THEN IT COULD GO SOME WAY TO EXPLAINING HOW SHE MIGHT NOW BE
INFECTED. SHE HAS NO CUTS OR WOUNDS ON HER SKIN - MAJOR
HEPBURN INSISTED THAT DR ROBERTS CHECKED HER. SEVERAL OTHERS
AGREED AND THIS WAS DONE PRIVATELY. IF SHE WAS ENGAGED IN A
SITUATION WITH TIM HETTON WHEN HE RETURNED TO THE EMBASSY THEN
THE DOCTOR BELIEVES SHE COULD HAVE BECOME INFECTED THROUGH AN
INTIMATE ACT AND EXCHANGE OF BODILY FLUID.

OF COURSE THIS RAISES THE QUESTION OF WHETHER LADY AND SIR
CARTLEDGE HAVE HAD PHYSICAL RELATIONS SINCE THAT TIME. IF SO,
HE TOO COULD BE INFECTED.

WE HAVE PLACED LADY CARTLEDGE IN A ROOM NEXT TO THOSE OF TIM
HETTON AND PETER BROWN, THE SECURITY OFFICER, AND ARE WATCHING
HER FOR MORE CHANGE.

SIR CARTLEDGE AND THE HEAD OF CHANCERY HAVE THUS FAR FAILED TO
RETURN.

BRIAN CARTER
HEAD OF COMMS

BRITISH EMBASSY

Smolenskaya Naberezhnaya 10, Moscow 121099. Tel: (495) 956 7200.

The following consists of unedited material received from Moscow

```
ZZ FCO
FM MOSCO
TO FLASH FCO
SECRET
FM MOSCOW
TO FLASH FCO
TEL NO 2 OF 28 MAY
```

STILL NO RETURN OF THE AMBASSADOR.

LENIN IS NOW IN CONTROL OF THE TV AND RADIO NETWORKS. THERE
WAS A BRIEF PUBLIC BROADCAST TODAY WHERE HE STOOD SIDE BY SIDE
WITH THE LIVING RUSSIAN PRESIDENT AND THEY DECLARED THAT THE
LIVING AND THE DEAD WOULD WORK SIDE BY SIDE AS EQUALS TO
CREATE A NEW KIND OF SOVIET UNION. BORIS YELTSIN IS TO BE
LENIN'S PRIME MINISTER.

AS IN THE PUTIN ADMINISTRATION, MEDVEDEV IS LIKELY TO BE
NOTHING MORE THAN A PUPPET PRESIDENT. IF HE SURVIVES.

PRIME MINISTER YELTSIN HAS DECLARED THAT TODAY WILL BE A DAY
OF SOBOTNIK - LIKE THOSE OF THE OLD DAYS OF THE SOVIET REGIME
WHERE EVERY CITIZEN WILL WORK FOR THE STATE FOR NO PAY. IN
THIS CASE THE LIVING AND THE DEAD MUST GO TO THE CEMETERIES
AND GRAVEYARDS AND DIG UP THOSE TRAPPED IN THE EARTH.

AS YOU CAN IMAGINE THIS IS A VERY ALARMING DEVELOPMENT FOR ALL
OF US.

LENIN THEN WENT ON, THROUGH A SPOKESPERSON, TO EXTOL THE
VIRTUES OF COMMUNISM FOR TEN MINUTES. HE FINISHED WITH HIS
SLOGAN 'PEACE LAND BREED'.

WE DON'T KNOW WHETHER HE MEANS THE LAST WORD TO APPLY TO THE
LIVING OR THE DEAD.

BRIAN CARTER
HEAD OF COMMS

BRITISH EMBASSY

Smolenskaya Naberezhnaya 10, Moscow 121099. Tel: (495) 956 7200.

ZZ FCO
FM MOSCO
TO FLASH FCO
TOP SECRET
FM MOSCOW
TO FLASH FCO
TEL NO 19 OF 30 MAY

MAJOR HEPBURN TOOK CONTROL OF THE LIMITED EMBASSY WEAPONRY
TODAY AND SHOT THE INFECTED WE HAD LOCKED AWAY. IT HAS BEEN
SOMETHING OF A RELIEF. ON TOP OF THE NOISE COMING FROM THE
STREETS AT NIGHT, THE UNNATURAL SOUNDS FROM WITHIN WERE TOO
MUCH FOR OUR STRAINED NERVES.

THERE WAS HOWEVER SOME DISAGREEMENT ABOUT SHOOTING LADY
CARTLEDGE AS SHE WAS STILL CONSCIOUS AND IN CONTROL OF HER
FACULTIES. SHE BEGGED FOR HER LIFE BEFORE HE SHOT HER AND THAT
WAS HEARD BY SEVERAL JUNIOR STAFF MEMBERS. MORALE IS NOT GOOD.

NO ONE HAS BEEN OUT FOR DAYS. IT ISN'T SAFE. FROM WHAT WE CAN
SEE THERE ARE FEWER LIVING OUT AND ABOUT AND, IF THEY ARE,
THEY ARE UNDER GUARD FROM THE DEAD DOING TASKS THAT REQUIRE
LIVING HANDS.

MAJOR HEPBURN HAS KEPT THE GUNS.

BRIAN CARTER
HEAD OF COMMS

BRITISH EMBASSY

Smolenskaya Naberezhnaya 10, Moscow 121099. Tel: (495) 956 7200.

```
ZZ FCO
FM MOSCO
TO FLASH FCO
TOP SECRET
FM MOSCOW
TO FLASH FCO
TEL NO 20 OF 30 MAY
```

PLEASE RESPOND TO PREVIOUS FIVE COMMUNIQUES.

THE SITUATION IS NO LONGER MANAGEABLE. THE DEAD HAVE GATHERED
OUTSIDE THE GATES MAKING IT IMPOSSIBLE TO LEAVE THE COMPOUND.

OUR COMMISSARY FOOD STOCKS ARE LOW.

THERE HAS BEEN A LOT OF ARGUING AMONGST THE PERSONNEL. THE
MAJOR IS DETERMINED TO SEND SOME PEOPLE OUT TO SCAVENGE FOR
WEAPONS AND VITAL NECESSITIES, BUT NO ONE WILL VOLUNTEER. I
FEAR THAT HE WILL SOON RESORT TO INTERNAL VIOLENCE TO GAIN HIS
OWN ENDS.

EARLIER TODAY HE SHOT AT SOME OF THE DEAD THROUGH THE GATES.
NOT ONLY DID THIS WASTE AMMUNITION IT MERELY CAUSED MORE TO
GATHER.

PLEASE RESPOND AND ADVISE.

BRIAN CARTER
HEAD OF COMMS

BRITISH EMBASSY

Smolenskaya Naberezhnaya 10, Moscow 121099. Tel: (495) 956 7200

The following consists of unedited material received from Moscow

ZZ FCO
FM MOSCO
TO FLASH FCO
TOP SECRET
FM MOSCOW
TO FLASH FCO
TEL NO 2 OF 2 JUNE

TOP PRIORITY INTERIM GOVERNMENT

DEVELOPMENTS.

SIR EDWARD AND THE HEAD OF CHANCERY RETURNED. THEY WERE AT THE
GATES WITH THE OTHERS WAVING THEIR LENINIST PLACARDS OF 'PEACE
LAND BREED'. AT LEAST I THINK THAT'S WHAT THEY SAID. THE WORDS
WERE SCRAWLED BADLY.

THE FIRST SECRETARY, ANGELA DOBSON, WANTED TO LET THEM IN. THE
MAJOR SHOT HER.

I'VE LOCKED MYSELF INSIDE THE COMMS ROOM. NO ONE CAN GET IN OR
OUT WITHOUT ME LETTING THEM IN. I CAN HEAR GUNFIRE AND - AND
OTHER NOISES - COMING FROM WITHIN THE BUILDING.

I CANNOT STRESS THE URGENCY FOR SOME KIND OF MILITARY
RESPONSE.

BRIAN CARTER
HEAD OF COMMS

BRITISH EMBASSY

Smolenskaya Naberezhnaya 10, Moscow 121099. Tel: (495) 956 7200.

ZZ FCO
FM MOSCO
TO FLASH FCO
TOP SECRET
FM MOSCOW
TO FLASH FCO
TEL NO 7 OF 4 JUNE

TOP PRIORITY INTERIM GOVERNMENT

BEEN LOCKED IN FOR NEARLY TWO DAYS. NO FOOD. NO WATER LEFT.

NOISES OUTSIDE HAVE FADED TO NOTHING.

I'M GOING TO HAVE TO GO OUT.

PLEASE ANSWER YOU BASTARDS AND TELL ME WHAT'S GOING ON.

BRIAN CARTER
HEAD OF COMMS

BRITISH EMBASSY

Smolenskaya Naberezhnaya 10, Moscow 121099. Tel: (495) 956 7200.

The following consists of unedited material received from Moscow

ZZZZZZZZZZZZZZZZZ
FFFFFFF CCCCCCCCCC 00000000000

PEACE LAND BLOOD PEACE LAND BLOOD PEACE LAND BLOOD

BLOODBLOODBLOODBLOODBLOODBLOODBLOODBLOODBLOODBLOODBLOODBL
OODBLOODBLOODBLOODBLOODBLOODBLOODBLOODBLOODBLOODBLOODBLO

New World Pharmaceuticals Group

YOUR WORLD IN OUR HANDS

Orientation

a) Preliminary Information

(To be issued to all members of research teams upon arrival)

Thank you for agreeing to take part in this research project. While we appreciate that every effort is currently being made by the UK government to combat the plague that has threatened to overwhelm these shores (and indeed much of the rest of the world) over the past few days, we also realise that many researchers, doctors, technicians and other highly trained individuals who have managed to survive thus far may well be unable to contribute to official programmes due partly to their remote location and of course because of the breakdown of the usual transport routes. Many consider Wales to be remote from England in more ways than one, but at last this is something that we consider we can use to our advantage.

The plague began in London and, because of population factors and the reasons stated above, it has taken longer for Wales to be affected and therefore there are more healthy individuals per capita in this part of the country at this moment than elsewhere. It therefore seemed reasonable to contact and rescue as many of you as possible and take you somewhere safe where your knowledge and experience may be put to its best use in determining the course, outcome, prognosis and management of what has been termed "The Death" or the "Lazarus virus". We appreciate that some of you may feel the text messages you were sent gave you an unreasonably short time in which to decide whether or not you wished to be brought here. We also hope you will appreciate our refusal to allow the accompaniment of any family members – our unit is self-sufficient, but only for a limited number of individuals, and it was considered wasteful to bring extraneous members of the general public. That is also why the majority of the invitations were issued to those of you whom we understand are either unmarried or have lost your family in the recent events. We would also hasten to add that you are free to leave if you so wish, although we would ask that you allow us notice of one week as our helicopter can only make a limited number of trips owing to the current fuel shortages. We sincerely hope, however, that you will prefer to stay with us to work towards a way of treating the condition.

We appreciate that as you have just arrived you may have a number of questions and hope that this orientation document, and the FAQ list below, will answer most of your queries. Any other points may be raised at the regular feedback and review sessions you will be required to attend, details of which will be posted around the complex in due course.

b) Location

You are on Ramsey Island, which lies one mile off the Pembrokeshire coast, close to the St David's peninsula at the northernmost aspect of St Brides' Bay. Pre-Death it was a nature reserve owned by the RSPB. Its isolated nature (at four hundred feet the cliffs overlooking the sea are amongst the highest in Wales) coupled with its proximity to the mainland have made it the ideal location for us to erect the pre-fabricated units that comprise our research complex. The units are durable and hard-wearing but, because of the sometimes extreme weather conditions that can occur in this part of the world, we insist that any storm damage be reported immediately to the officer on duty.

c) About Us

We are a team of researchers and businessmen who have severed our ties with the pharmaceutical companies with whom we have enjoyed long and fruitful relationships for many years so that we might come together to serve the common good. Because of our links with investors and equipment suppliers it has been possible to put this project together very quickly indeed, and we hope that you will soon start to feel a part of our "New World". The New World Pharmaceutical Group has a number of aims which are listed below, but our overall brief is to provide the public with the treatment it so desperately needs by a means that is both acceptable to everyone, and affordable by all.

d) Your Role

Each of you will be involved in a research programme tailored to play to your specific strengths and areas of expertise, the details of which will be explained to you in due course. Please record all your findings, observations and thoughts in the log books we have provided, ensuring that every entry is signed and dated and that completed pages are handed back at each feedback session. Any questions should be directed to your group supervisors or, if it is a security matter, to one of the officers on duty. Because of security issues we are sure you will understand that communication with the outside world is not permitted unless sanctioned through official channels. We hope it goes without saying that we expect all residents within the complex to behave in a civilised manner, and would like to take this opportunity to remind you that as this is such a vitally important project, anyone considered to be harming, delaying or sabotaging the progress of experiments will be dealt with extremely harshly.

e) And Finally

Good luck! Remember, it's not just us or Great Britain who are counting on you, but the rest of the world as well.

Clare Fremont's Diary — Entry One

My name is Dr Clare Fremont and I don't
even know why I'm writing this. I suppose it's
because I want there to be some record of
me being here other than the paperwork I'm
supposed to complete and hand in. So I'm
writing on toilet paper and concealing the
sheets in a space I've made between the two
sheets of compressed plywood that constitute
the back of the wardrobe they've given me.
    Before I came here, before all of this, I
had been a Consultant Cardiologist at
Carmarthen General Hospital for nearly two
years after qualifying from the West Wales
medical training rotation. Now I feel less like
a doctor and more like a prison inmate.
I've only been here long enough to read the
hastily typed document they handed us on our
arrival here, and to attend the meeting
where we were allocated our research
laboratories. Our sleeping quarters are next
door to where we work and while it hasn't
been explicitly mentioned, I think the intention
is that we work, sleep and most of all don't
fraternise with other specialties, except at the
special meetings arranged for us. Why that
should be I have no idea. Perhaps I will bring

it up at the next meeting which is later this evening. It's strange the things you remember when you're under stress but all I can think of at the moment is a Monty Python sketch set during the second world war about a joke that was so funny it could kill you, and how the only safe way to use it against the Germans was for a separate team of translators to work on each word. I don't know what it is they're so worried about, but then I don't even know what they want with a psychiatrist. We can't get off this island, or communicate with anyone, and they've told us that every precaution is going to be taken with what they term the "experimental material". Apparently the first batch of test subjects will arrive tomorrow. I am already more scared than I have ever been in my entire life.

Graham Harman's Dictation – Tape 1

I have no idea what the date is and there are no calendars here so that's a bit pointless for a start isn't it? Anyway, seeing as we are supposed to keep some sort of record and I'm not bloody writing everything down because no one other than me can read my handwriting anyway, I've been given these tapes to dictate on. I've no idea whose job it's going to be to type them up, but I suppose I'm going to have to spell any word longer than two syllables for some untrained temp to get wrong anyway, but that's for someone else to worry about.

My name is Graham Harman BSc, MBBS, MD, FRCS, consultant general surgeon from Swansea. My experiences to date with the disease we have all been brought together to research have been fairly limited, which ironically is probably why I'm still alive. I was on leave when the outbreak occurred and returned to find the department in a state of chaos and my operating lists overbooked with nothing but emergency amputation cases. Some kind of accident had occurred in the intensive care unit and it had been closed by the police. There were so many severely ill cases that my entire 28 bedded surgical ward had been converted into a makeshift ICU and the minimal ward round I was able to make confirmed that the end-of-the-bed prognosis for most of them was hopeless. I had just finished going round when I got the text message inviting me here. I returned to the department to ask my secretary if she knew anything about it only for her to attack me. I was able to herd her into my office with the aid of a fire extinguisher and lock her in before a large explosion in the burns unit made me realise that something catastrophic was taking place. The helicopter was exactly where the text message had said it would be and as I had no family ties or other commitments, save the girl I had left locked in my office, I decided to take the company up on its kind offer.

Exactly what I'm supposed to do, I'm not sure. I've been told that I will be provided with "test subjects". If they're anything like the patients I left behind in Swansea they'd better have a bloody secure intensive care setup – the strength of some of them was astounding. I saw one girl who was missing her left arm lift someone bodily into the air with the other. A recent bilateral lower limb amputation seemed to have little effect on a man who was able to skitter across the floor on his stumps in pursuit of what I can only call a victim.

I don't think there's a surgical cure to this. There may be surgical "solutions" (can you put that in inverted commas please?) but not a cure.

Clare Fremont's Diary — Entry Two

So they want a physician who specialises in
pharmacology to look at the effects of
certain drugs on victims of the disease. I
told them my specialist training was in
cardiology, but they told me the
pharmacologist they had selected had made
it here but was now no longer in a fit state
to do research work. I dread to think
what that means.

The second meeting also gave me more of a
chance to meet the other team members. They
have recruited a histopathologist called Eric
Tremlett, who specialises in abnormal brain
structure, and James Staniforth, a
haematologist who will be checking on blood
specimens. Alison Treadwell is a psychiatrist who
for all I know may be here in case the rest of
us go mental. We also have an anaesthetist,
Richard Patterson, who looks very young, and
Graham Harman who I understand is a
surgeon, although what his specialist interest is
I cannot say. They all seem quite nice, apart
I have to say from Mr Harman who has sat
at the back of both meetings and said very
little. When I asked him what they wanted him
to do here he all but ignored me and I intend
to give him a wide berth.

Graham Harman's Dictation – Tape 2

I've met most of the team now and if anything they all seem more shell-shocked than I am. The pathologist seems a decent enough chap and actually knows his stuff – I had a word with him afterwards and he has a few theories about what might be happening. I even remembered some of the CNS (*central nervous system – ed*) anatomy from my days in the dissecting rooms at the Royal College. The haematologist seems all right, if a bit quiet. There's a physician as well. Very pretty, but we're bound not to get on and I can't imagine we'll be having much interaction anyway.

Dick Patterson's an anaesthetist – I know him from before. Odd to refer to our lives of less than a week ago as "before" but that's already what it feels like. The plan is for us to work together to see if there's any way this condition can be treated by surgical debridement or reconstruction, or by any other method I can think of. Of course the first thing he needs to do is work out how to gas the damn things (it's difficult to think of them as people anymore – they behave more like animals). I will formally state now that I have no intention of going near any of those infected monsters unless they are completely and utterly knocked out.

Anaesthesia of Test Subjects

Notes by Dick Patterson FRCA – Anaesthetist

The intention of anaesthesia in all test cases was to produce the recognised "Anaesthetic Triad" of paralysis, unconsciousness and analgesia. For human test subjects recognised drugs delivered by accepted means in appropriate doses were used as per normal anaesthetic protocol. Anaesthetising zombie specimens immediately presented itself as our first challenge as it quickly became apparent that such protocols were at best useless and at worst dangerous. Initial attempts to administer intravenous Propofol were met with abject failure. The junior doctor selected to perform the procedure became specimen ZS 31 within the first ten minutes of contact with the test specimen and parts of her were later used in experiment MN 3/5. Analgesia was not so much of a concern as it had been observed in preliminary experiments P1 through P5 that zombies were insensitive to pain ranging from piercing the skin with a 16-gauge needle through crush injuries of fingers right up to limb amputation. For the purposes of scientific objectivity a series of similar control experiments were proposed on human test subjects but the lack of availability meant that it was not possible to carry out all of these tests.

Unconsciousness was desirable if not absolutely necessary and it was not until one of the veterinarian anaesthetists suggested a technique be employed similar to that used to anaesthetise horses and other equine breeds using a barometric chamber and a large quantity of ketamine that loss of consciousness was achieved. It should also be noted at this point that the more recently dead required smaller doses than those who had succumbed for some time.

Muscle paralysis was in many cases noted to be unnecessary, the requirement again being proportionate to the length of time dead, with the recently deceased treated with suxamethonium, the dose decreased in proportion with the length of time following the terminal heartbeat.

Graham Harman's Dictation – Tape 3

The first few experiments to anaesthetise undead subjects have met with disaster. I'm not going to say any more and I'm sure Dick will mention anything pertinent in his report. What I wasn't expecting was for us to be provided with living human subjects as well. I have no idea who they are or where they have been obtained from, but that's not important – it has been made clear to us that the only way to study the condition scientifically is to have a group of appropriately age-sex matched controls and to this end I suppose they are right. We have also been informed today that if we no longer wish to participate in the research we can be returned to the mainland where we will be dropped off by helicopter at the nearest peninsula. Alison Treadwell has gone, saying she would rather die than experiment on normal human beings. Everyone else has stayed but they look understandably uneasy. Someone mentioned the Nazis, but this is a very different situation. The human subjects they have locked up downstairs seem close to death anyway, so if they contribute to science then that hasn't made their lives utterly worthless. Has it?

Clare Fremont's Diary — Entry 3

I don't even know why I've stayed. I should
have gone with Alison. Maybe we would have
stood something of a chance if we'd left
together. I hardly knew her but now I fear
for her, being left somewhere on the Welsh
coast. The Death getting worse by the minute,
those creatures roaming the countryside,
chasing and tearing apart anyone they come
across. And what about me? I hate myself
for staying, and I hate myself for being so
scared that my fear outweighed my revulsion
at what they're expecting me to do. But we
all know the score now — participate in the
experiments or be thrown off the island to
fend for ourselves. I've never fended for
myself in my life.

James Staniforth is the haematologist and
apparently he's the one they want results from
first. They've asked him to research the bite.
Apparently it leads to a strange
configuration of the blood cells — how they
know that I have no idea, but that's why
they want him to do it. He argued, first that
he wasn't trained to look at wound
pathology, and second that for that he
would need a range of samples from fresh bite

wounds to ones that had been allowed to fester for days, and where were they supposed to get those from? I'm already hating the tinny sound of the voice that comes through the black box in the conference room, the one set high up on the wall so we can't turn it off. Anyway, the voice said that Staniforth was the best they could get under the circumstances, and that he needn't worry about subjects. There were plenty that could be rounded up from the mainland and besides, hadn't Dr Patterson and Mr Harman ended up with a couple of fresh specimens during their experiments today? The meeting was adjourned in silence, pending Dr Staniforth's report. I went back to my room where I'm writing this. I don't know what to do. I feel so lost. I need someone. Anyone.

The Bite – Summary of Histological Examination

Notes compiled by James Staniforth, who emphasises that this should be the work of a pathologist rather than a haematologist and that therefore his observations may not be as reliable as a trained expert.

1   Initial break of skin.
2   Traditional acute inflammatory response – blood vessel dilatation, leakage of plasma proteins, margination migration and emigration of neutrophils.
3   Pronounced foreign body reaction including granuloma formation at site of injury.
4   Macrophages altered.
5   Macrophages migrate away from the wound and begin a process of autodigestion by beginning to attack healthy tissue.
6   Later, altered macrophages invade nervous system and shortly after death of individual cause alteration to brain tissue that is currently being researched by Dr Tremlett.

Conclusions from the above:

The bite itself is not the cause of death, but rather a specific foreign particle that is transmitted in it. This is then ingested by the patient's own macrophage cells which then become altered to attack the host. The process appears to need vast quantities of protein to fuel it, hence the ravenous appetite of the affected individual. With all the effects upon the central nervous system it is not surprising that an affected individual suffers disorientation accompanied by hunger which only increases once death has occurred.

Graham Harman's Dictation – Tape 4

Everyone is working on their individual projects now. There's some co-ordination from whoever is communicating with us from the conference room, but I very much suspect we are being left to come up with ideas ourselves. We are the experts after all, so that approach is very sensible. Dick and I have tried a number of different things and I'll be summarising our experiences when I'm required to present my report. I never imagined we would get through so many specimens, though. Thank heavens the security team here seem to double up as refuse collectors!

The only other item of note is that I've started seeing Dr Fremont, for want of a better turn of phrase. It passes the time and relieves the tension and, to be honest, she seems to get more out of it than I do – I suspect she needs the security more than the contact but as long as we both get something out of it I see no reason not to continue. It's hard to believe we've been here for three weeks now. At the meeting this evening I was berated for not keeping up with the paperwork, hence this tape. I've been so busy I haven't had much time to maintain my records, but the Powers That Be will be getting a summary of my findings in due course. What I will say is that my work so far ties in with what Eric Tremlett has discovered about the neuropathology of the disease.

Neurohistopathology

Notes compiled by Dr E Tremlett, formerly Department of Histopathology, Morriston Hospital, Swansea

The following table summarises observations made in the alteration of the histology of the brain and central nervous system (CNS) in infected specimens at various time stages following the terminal heartbeat (TH). Comparisons are with normal human nervous tissue. It should be mentioned at this point that proper fixation of brain tissue takes at least a week. As this was not possible the formalin-hydrogen peroxide technique of Lagerloef and Torgersrud (1934) was employed and this should be taken into account when interpreting these results.

Days Post TH	Histological Changes
0	Typical post mortem appearance
1-4	Generalised cerebral atrophy
4-7	Profusion of microglial cells and selective phagocytosis of neurones
7-9	Mutation of microglial cell nuclei
9-10	Fusion of microglia with oligodendrocytes to form an entirely new kind of neurogenic cell, which leads to the genesis of specialised atypical neurones I have dubbed Tremlett cells
11	Tremlett cells undergo mitosis and migration around surviving network of ependymal and other glial cells to form new brain tissue
12	Establishment and organisation of Tremlett cells to form new cerebral cortex

The key stage appears to be the mutation of the microglia. One suspects this is virally mediated, possibly via a reverse transcriptase enzyme. Any attempt to halt the progress of the disease by therapeutic means will need to be directed at this step in the cycle, as once it has been completed the genesis of new altered brain tissue seems rapid and irreversible. Also of great interest is the ability of these new neurones to divide and replicate themselves. It is ironic that something that researchers pre-Death had been searching for for years to treat spinal cord injuries and neurodegenerative disorders should be the cause, however indirect, of so much death and despair.

As microglial alteration seems to be a key event one wonders if this is limited to the central nervous system or whether the effects are more widespread to include other body systems? Could these be the key cells in the sequence of events that occur post death?

Clare Fremont's Diary — Entry ?5 ?6

It's been a while since I've last written and the previous entries have got stuck together from the rain that's leaking through the ceiling and dripping down the back of the wardrobe. We've got a big meeting coming up where we all have to present what we've found so far. I hope they're okay with my theories. I'm not going to specifically mention that I haven't actually used any test subjects — the mere thought of experimenting on someone, living or "dead", just repels me too much. Some of the bite victims have been brought to me and I've given them antibiotics but after a few doses I haven't seen them anymore, and I don't think it's because they've got better. Some of the others are lucky — they've just had to look at slides in the lab to try and work out what's going on. Graham never tells me what he's been doing but sometimes his surgical scrubs are in a terrible state when he comes to see me. Maybe that's why he likes doing it in the shower so much.

What the hell am I doing? I shouldn't be here. I'm starting to feel I'd be better off out there taking my chances. I probably wouldn't last long but at least this horrible pain I have in my heart would go away.

Summary of Discussion at Treatment Management Meeting

Present:

Mr G Harman	Consultant Surgeon
Dr E Tremlett	Consultant Neuropathologist
Dr J Staniforth	Consultant Haematologist
Dr R Patterson	Consultant Anaesthetist
Dr C Fremont	Consultant Physician

The broad outcome of the meeting was that strategies for treatment of The Death may be divided into two broad categories:

a) Chemotherapeutic intervention. This would include:
   i) The use of drugs to eradicate the condition. This would of course be the best case scenario. Results so far suggest this would only be possible if the condition is caught at an early enough stage.
   ii) Drugs to combat and limit the progress of the disease. From the valuable work done by the neuropathology and haematology departments some form of immunosuppressant regimen may be appropriate here but no research programme has yet been put into action.
   iii) Drugs to palliate symptoms and ensure a dignified death.
   iv) Drugs to prevent reactivation post terminal heartbeat.

b) Surgical intervention – ideally only to be employed in the most extreme cases. Options include amputation, transplant and surgical reconstruction where indicated. Surgical destruction of the central nervous system of affected individuals was also mentioned but not discussed in any detail.

Unfortunately until an appropriate pharmacological regimen can be developed the only viable treatment available for affected individuals at the moment is option (b). Despite the reservations expressed by a number of individuals present at the meeting further research in this area has been sanctioned by our controlling body and apparently the necessary equipment and experimental material is already being assembled. It was noted that Mr Harman has yet to present any kind of formal report regarding his work so far and it was emphasised that unless some form of report was imminent his position at the facility would need to be reviewed.

Surgical Management of Infected Cases – Mr G Harman

The following surgical options have been considered and attempted, with observations and rates of success detailed below:

1 Debridement

An approach was taken similar to the technique used to surgically treat Fournier's Scrotal Gangrene (a rapid life-threatening condition that begins with the rotting of the skin of the external genitalia and then rapidly spreads to the rest of the body). The site of infection was subjected to surgical resection of the soft tissues and these were "cut back" until healthy bleeding tissue could be observed. Necrotic resected tissue was disposed of. Results were unsuccessful – no matter how far back tissue was cleared within hours signs of infection returned. A repeat procedure on the same specimen was similarly unsuccessful and a third procedure deemed foolhardy and rather pointless.

2 Amputation

Initially advocated as the treatment of choice for bites to the distal aspects of the upper or lower limbs. As with tissue debridement the minimum amputation thought necessary was initially performed with the intention of resected necrotic material and preserving as much viable tissue as possible. To this end treatment for a bite to the foot initially took the form of the Lisfranc forefoot amputation. When this was unsuccessful a Symes trans-ankle amputation was attempted, swiftly followed by a below knee, a through knee, an above knee and finally a hind-quarter amputation. The translumbar hemicorporectomy was not considered owing to the absence of urological expertise to perform the urinary diversion and ileal conduit, and the extremely poor state of the subject by this time.

Upper limb amputations were similarly unsatisfactory. On the basis of my experiences with lower limb disease, for a bite to the hand or wrist I immediately proceeded to a below-elbow amputation with the intention of constructing Krukenberg claws, in which the remaining segments of radius and ulna are split apart from one another and covered in skin to create what the textbooks term "lobster claws". The first test subject was a failure and became frankly dangerous as it quickly learned to use these claws as a weapon against research staff. Subject was despatched by method (4) below. Other subjects were treated with above elbow and forequarter amputation (removal of shoulder girdle including scapula and clavicle and all structures of the arm). The distance between the site of infection and the level of amputation does seem to make a difference to the time to recurrence of the condition but only by a matter of hours.

3 Transplantation

I have yet to identify appropriate test subjects for this extremely experimental approach. I also understand that research in this area has not yet been authorised by those who can provide me with them.

4 Despatch

Destruction of the central nervous system, and in particular the brain, is a rapid and effective method of palliation rather than cure, rendering the subject immobile, lifeless and consequently no longer a threat to others. Blunt or penetrating trauma to the cranium is equally successful but the brain tissue must be sufficiently damaged for immobilisation to occur.

Test specimens were subjected to craniotomy and then to ablation of selected areas of the brain tissue by injection of phenol. While ablation of higher centres produced a sluggish, poorly responsive subject, it was the ablation of the brainstem (pons and medulla oblongata) that eventually produced the desired effect although ablation of the diencephalons of the midbrain has almost as good an outcome.

Clare Fremont's Diary — Entry ??

I've no idea what number entry this is as
when I returned from the meeting tonight I
found that my previous diary pages had been
taken from their hiding place. Why am I
writing this then? Because if I wasn't I'd
probably be writing on my skin with a knife,
that's why. I don't know why I'm here. I
don't know why I'm doing the research. I
don't know why I'm seeing Graham Harman.
I don't know why I'm not just walking down
to where they keep the results of some of the
experiments, opening the door and letting them
wipe the slate clean on this terrible fucking
place.

Maybe I should.

Graham Harman's Dictation – Tape 5

That stupid woman! I had my suspicions that she was getting to be unstable, but I had no idea she would be so stupid as to endanger the rest of us. According to the remaining security guards she must have made her way from that little room of hers to the conference chamber and smashed the communications system before heading down to where they've been keeping the specimens. Even I haven't been down there – why the hell should I want to? She managed to knock out the guards on duty with some chloroform containing compound she must have been working on to subdue the victims of The Death.

And then she opened the gates to the cells.

She must have survived only because they're so slow moving. I have seen dead specimens move very rapidly, but the ones in there have been subjected to so many of my experiments over the last few days that even the living ones have so few limbs left, if any, that they can barely manage a crawl. In fact, I very much suspect it was the attacking of the remaining living specimens by the dead that gave her the chance to get away.

The amount of damage that woman has caused! I have no idea how many of the team have been killed or injured, but we ended up with more dead than can be accommodated in the cells, and so the excess have been despatched by method (4) in my presentation notes. Only a few of us are left alive now, and in the absence of any communication with the Powers That Be I have suggested that we do things my way or we are going to end up like the things we have chained-up downstairs.

One good thing has come of all of this. In view of what she has done and her somewhat miraculous survival, I now have in Clare a suitable specimen for some experiments I have been entertaining thoughts of for some time now.

Graham Harman's Dictation – Tape 8

Tremlett dead, Staniforth dead. Security non-existent. The last of the guards tried to leave in the helicopter, but the ones that can still walk were too quick for them and tore them to pieces before they could make it across the compound. Thank heavens there are heavy locks on the doors to the research area, and that our employers / captors intended us to work around the clock – there's enough canned food and water here to keep me going for at least a year, although I suspect my work will be finished rather sooner than that.

From what I can ascertain, I am the only living human being left on the island. The only totally living human being. Clare cannot be thought of now as entirely alive as so much of her has been replaced by dead tissue. But I'm getting ahead of myself. I'm going to find a fresh cassette so I can document everything on one tape.

Graham Harman's Dictation – Tape 9

Voices identified as "Mr G Harman" (GH) and "Subject" (CF)

GH: After a successful peri and postoperative course I felt it would be most useful to record any pertinent observations regarding the outcome of the surgery via audio tape in the absence of video recording equipment. The specimen is a healthy intelligent thirty year old living woman who, following some preliminary experiments, has been shown to exhibit considerable resistance to the condition know as "The Death". Because of this, over the last few months, she has undergone a number of transplantation procedures of tissues and organs from specimens of the recently dead in an attempt to determine whether or not her immunity can be transmitted to already infected tissue. The procedures so far have included: amputation of right upper limb above the elbow and replacement by the arm of a zombie specimen of similar sex and age. This was met with some success, with the necrotic tissue exhibiting some evidence of healing and revitalisation when perfused with the subject's blood. This then led me to attempt similar procedures with the left lower limb, followed by transplantation of a zombie kidney. The internal organ seemed to take better than the limbs, which despite early signs of promise are now deteriorating and will need to be replaced. Encouraged by the successful renal result, however, I have subsequently removed the subject's liver and replaced it with zombie hepatic tissue and that also has been functioning nicely. This has led to what I consider to be my most successful experiment yet, where it would appear that I have been able to successfully transplant the heart of one of the dead specimens downstairs into this young woman. She still lives and, forty-eight hours later her vital signs appear to be stabilising.

I should point out here that for the entire duration of these experiments the subject has been kept anaesthetised and is entirely unaware of what has become of her. There are several reasons why I have done this. Firstly, and most important, any movement on the part of the subject may have severely compromised the success of the project by disrupting the delicate anastomoses I have performed. Also, any unnecessary movement could have damaged tissue that is already in a compromised state.

Now, however, having performed all the tests I can on an unaware subject, the time has come for me to bring her to consciousness so I can perform a far more thorough neurological examination, including that of the higher centres. In view of the fact that the subject may exhibit some confusion and possibly distress at her current state, I felt it would be easier to keep an audio record of events rather than try to note everything down.

I am now injecting the reversal agent to bring about consciousness in the specimen. Interestingly I have selected a vein in the arm I transplanted and have had no problem in establishing venous access. The drug has entered her system and now it is just a matter of time before she wakes up.

After a few moments of dead air a very faint moaning can be heard.

GH: Excellent! The drug has circulated through her zombie cephalic vein, through her zombie basilic vein and via her own superior vena cava to her zombie heart, the transplanted pulmonary arteries of which will have carried the drug to her own human lungs for oxygenation and then back to the zombie heart to be pumped through her own aorta to the rest of her body. I was aware that her circulation was working, but I had no idea how efficiently. This is very interesting indeed.

During this part of the dictation there have been increasingly loud groans over the top of what has been said.

GH: Clare? Clare, can you hear me? (She has just turned her head in my direction, which means she can localise my voice.) Clare, you've been asleep for a while, but it's all been to the good. You've been helping medical science.

A very loud groan after this.

GH: That's right Clare – you're still alive. Isn't that wonderful? Now don't try to struggle too much – those straps are merely to prevent you from hurting yourself. I wouldn't want you falling off the table and spoiling all my delicate work, now would I? First of all I need to check if you have managed to regenerate the nerves in the dead tissue I have transplanted onto you. I'm going to start with your right arm and your right index finger. Do you understand? Nod if you do. Oh well, maybe you can't nod yet. Anyway, just tell me when you can feel the needle going into your fingertip.

There is a pause, and then a scream.

GH: Excellent! Pain localisation to the zombie limb and functioning vocal cords! You should have told me, Clare. Now I shall proceed to test pain and temperature localisation over the rest of her body.

CF: Please . . . please . . . stop.

GH: Now you know I can't do that. I need to record these observations for the good of mankind. And the organs and limbs I've replaced appear to be working well. Not normally of course, but well! It's a tremendous step forward in dealing with the condition. Perhaps we are not meant to combat it, but live with it!

CF: What . . . what do you . . . mean?

GH: You're the first zombie-human hybrid, Clare! A living person capable of reanimating the dead tissue I've grafted onto you. Now please – keep still. I need to check your responses to pain.

There is a sound of tearing leather and a wrench of metal.

GH: Please, Clare, get back on the couch and replace the straps. I don't want to damage you – you're all I have to show for my work here.

CF: Graham . . . put the gun . . . down.

GH: If you don't get back on the bench I will have to kill you.

There is a pause here as if there is a struggle to form words, or perhaps it is merely a pause for thought – or realisation.

CF: You can't . . . kill me, Graham. I'm . . . already dead.

This dialogue accompanied by the sound of movement and clattering objects.

GH: Now we both know that's not true. Parts of you are alive and parts of you are from dead donors, but you have revitalised them and given them new life.

CF: No, Graham . . . you've got it the wrong way around. You see . . . I actually died during one of those interminable operations of yours . . . or at least I assume I must have. God knows what you were thinking when . . . when you decided to perform those procedures on me . . . but they've proved nothing . . . nothing other than it's possible for . . . for the dead to receive transplants from . . . others . . . of our kind. But I have to admit . . . your surgery was good. Very good . . . indeed. In fact . . . your notes may come in . . . extremely useful . . . when I get back to the mainland and we can begin to organise society again . . . I can already hear *him* calling to me . . .

Another, much louder crash.

CF: A society free from the living . . . and dedicated only to the dead. A society that's going to need just as much, if not more . . . medical care, than the old one . . . the one that we have attacked, overrun and superseded. One day this place may even be turned into a shrine . . . a place of historic interest to our New Society. We may even put a plaque here   "On this site the first experiments into improving the healthcare of the New Order were performed", it might say. I don't think we'll mention your name though. It'll be buried somewhere in all these records of course – the ones I'm going to take with me. The Textbook of New Zombie Medicine has to start somewhere, doesn't it? And as for you . . .

There is a loud crash followed by a gasp, followed by nothing at all.

DIARY OF DR CLARE FREMONT

DAY 1 OF A NEW ERA

IT'S JUST BEGUN.

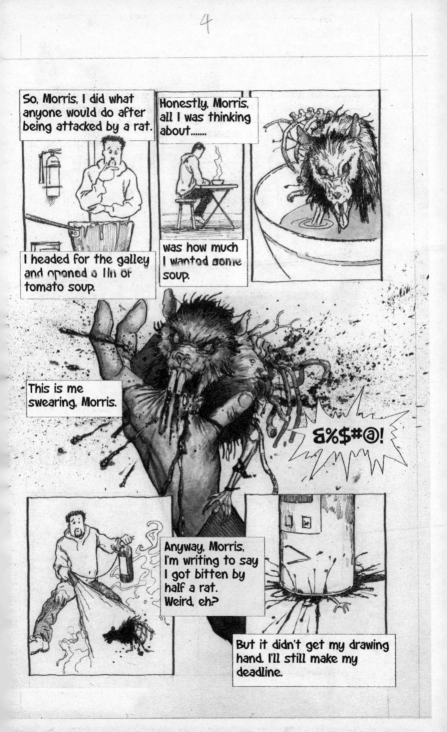

zOmBEY

CITY-TV

"It's CityPulse News, with your host, Gord Martineau. Tonight: Breakdown at the border.

"Hundreds of cars remain stopped at the U.S./Canadian border in Niagara Falls, Ontario, due to a United States ban on all international travel. Our own Peter Kim reports live from the scene."

"Thanks Gord. Authorities here are suspiciously quiet over what transpired early this morning. We're getting mixed reports of threats to the U.S.A. from an outbreak of HRV, or Human Reanimation Virus, that has afflicted a growing number of locations in the United Kingdom, leading to the devastation in London, England. Witnesses claim that at approximately 8:00 A.M. Eastern Standard Time, a team of U.S. soldiers appeared at the border and halted all traffic crossing in both directions. They then ushered the three transport trucks you see behind me to cross the laneways, thereby blocking any vehicular access to or from the United States. Commuters have been trapped here for hours, waiting to cross, and tempers are running high. There have also been unsubstantiated reports of gunfire originating from U.S. soldiers, but so far no official statement by the U.S. Press Secretary has been made. CityPulse News has approached the Department of Homeland Security but our calls have not yet been returned.

"Gord, the scene here continues to be chaotic, and the June heat has only enflamed the tensions of the stranded motorists – wait, do you see that? Can you get a close-up on the barricade? Something is happening. Some commotion. I'm not sure what it is I'm seeing . . ."

[Bulletin on City*Pulse* News, CITY-TV, Toronto, Canada, June 10]

From: garyspender <spider98@rogers.net>
To: petercaleb <Day4Night@sympatico.net>
Sent: Mon, Jun 10, 9:31 pm
Subject: zOmBEY

___

Hey Peter I finally figured out what we should do. It came to me while my mom was watching all the messed up news about shutting down the border. Have you seen those trucks? They're like big blank walls! Do you get where I'm going with this? Do you? I know what you're thinking: "It's dangerous. Those trucks are there for a reason." What's the reason? No way is it to protect us – the Americans don't give a shit about us. They probably think WE'RE the one's that caused this panic. Gave them Mad Cow or something. They just want to keep us out, and I have absolutely no plans for going in. Get this: those trucks got me thinking about Banksey and what he did at the West Bank. Hell, people will let you do whatever you want if you just act like you're supposed to be doing it. So, I whipped this together. Pretty awesome, right? Like right out of Fairey! Fucking zOmBEY! This would TOTALLY make us!

You're probably all like what the hell is he talking about? This. We get this picture blown up to poster size at Kinko's like usual, then we get Martin and Darlene and drive to Niagara Falls. We sneak up to the border and Martin and Darlene film us while we put this up. Then, we come home, stick it on YouTube, and we're gods!

I've already started talking about it on Twitter to generate some buzz. You should, too. Tomorrow, we go make the posters and get the wheat glue, then we go tomorrow night. I told my mom I'm staying at your place so she wouldn't panic, so make sure you don't say anything stupid. If she finds out where we're going, I'll never be able to leave the house again.

I'm telling you, bro. We might end up famous.

<attachment:zombey.jpg>

spider98

Something big coming tomorrow night
9:45 PM June 10th from Tweetbot

Retweet everyone you know: tomorrow night BIG NEWS
10:50 PM June 10th from Tweetbot

The Spider Strikes tomorrow night!
11:30 PM June 10th from Tweetbot

I will be incommunicado tomorrow to get ready for the
big unveiling
11:38 PM June 10th from Tweetbot

@deadsea All good things
11:45 PM June 10th from Tweetbot in reply to DeadSea

@JMont Let's just say #Banksy's a nothing
11:48 PM June 10th from Tweetbot in reply to JMont

Checklist? Check! Waiting for a lift from @Day4Night and
we'll get this going
8:38 PM June 11th from Tweetbot

I appreciate it when my mom's so wrapped up in the
news she doesn't even listen to me.
8:39 PM June 11th from Tweetbot

@JMont Is it irresponsible she let me out? LOL
8:42 PM June 11th from Tweetbot

"Are you nervous" @Day4Night asked. AS IF!!! This is going to be the greatest thing ever!
8:44 PM June 11th from Tweetbot

Stopped for coffee. Gotta stay awake.
9:38 PM June 11th from Tweetbot

Checked everything in trunk is okay. Don't tell @Day4Night but I'm starting to get nervous.
9:45 PM June 11th from Tweetbot

Never wanted to go to #London anyhow.
9:49 PM June 11th from Tweetbot

@deadsea Yeah, me neither.
9:49 PM June 11th from Tweetbot in reply to DeadSea

I can't tell you that @deadsea2, but I can tell you who's with me: @Day4Night, @MartinLG, and @karmaKat
10:05 PM June 11th from Tweetbot

Whole thing will be recorded by @MartinLG and put on YouTube ASAP. It's going to be great! If I don't die :-)
10:05 PM June 11th from Tweetbot

Okay, I'll give you a hint. It has something to do with #niagarafalls
10:06 PM June 11th from Tweetbot

We're getting close now, so I'll give you another hint. #rainbowbridge !
10:08 PM June 11th from Tweetbot

@deadsea Close, but you'll never guess what.
10:08 PM June 11th from Tweetbot

@deadsea Nope!
10:08 PM June 11th from Tweetbot

@deadsea HAHAH Guess again!
10:09 PM June 11th from Tweetbot

Every time I've been to #niagarafalls it's been wall-to-wall people. This time it's D-E-A-D
10:26 PM June 11th from Tweetbot

LOL @karmaKat didn't like that joke. Sorry @karmaKat
10:26 PM June 11th from Tweetbot

There are like almost no cars around. Just some cops cruising by. Only people walking round are homeless.
10:26 PM June 11th from Tweetbot

Bums never give a crap about world events. Probably don't even know what's going on.
10:27 PM June 11th from Tweetbot

Are all homeless guys this creepy? . . .
twitpik.com/6poksle
10:29 PM June 11th from Tweetbot

Change that rain slicker, please! It's too old for you. And another thing:
10:29 PM June 11th from Tweetbot

Don't get too close! LOL
10:29 PM June 11th from Tweetbot

Got told to put down the Twitter. Think @Day4Night is getting scared.
10:30 PM June 11th from Tweetbot

Driving in #niagarafalls is impossible. Too many cops around. We're going to park the car on Clifton Hill.
10:44 PM June 11th from Tweetbot

We're pretty close to the border, and it's night.
10:45 PM June 11th from Tweetbot

That why everyone else is nervous? I feel weirdly calm.

10:47 PM June 11th from Tweetbot

@Orphan_Tears Watch the news tomorrow morning. I bet it'll be the first story!

10:51 PM June 11th from Tweetbot in reply to OrphanTears

Just realized: we don't have enough flashlights.

10:53 PM June 11th from Tweetbot

Stupid. Only two. We'll make it work.

10:53 PM June 11th from Tweetbot

Okay. We got everything. It's heavy to carry, but we can do it. Fame, here I come!

11:03 PM June 11th from Tweetbot

Here WE come! (oops!)

11:04 PM June 11th from Tweetbot

At the border now. Me and @Day4Night split off. The others need to setup first.

11:27 PM June 11th from Tweetbot

Think @karmaKat is afraid she'll catch something if she gets too close.

11:27 PM June 11th from Tweetbot

Probably too late. Already been too close. To @MartinLG that is! XOXO LOL

11:27 PM June 11th from Tweetbot

What's that smell? Is it the Falls? I don't remember what it's supposed to smell like.

11:33 PM June 11th from Tweetbot

Smells . . . weird.

11:33 PM June 11th from Tweetbot

Walking to the #USAborder wasn't hard at all. There was like no one guarding the Canadian side of the bridge. Just pylons.
11:35 PM June 11th from Tweetbot

Guess guards need their Tim's like everyone else! LOL
11:36 PM June 11th from Tweetbot

twitpik.com/6rsitk
11:38 PM June 11th from Tweetbot

That's the #USAborder. You can tell because of the massive trucks parked in front of the booths.
11:39 PM June 11th from Tweetbot

Like a giant canvas, those things. Calling to me.
11:39 PM June 11th from Tweetbot

Oh yeah. And because of all the abandoned cars. If you think it looks creepy you should be here.
11:39 PM June 11th from Tweetbot

Why would you leave your car at the border and walk away? People are crazy.
11:42 PM June 11th from Tweetbot

Passed a #CityPulse news van. Do they already know?
11:50 PM June 11th from Tweetbot

That would be sweet. No one inside, though.
11:51 PM June 11th from Tweetbot

My hands are shaking. Did Banksy feel like this on the West Bank?
11:59 PM June 11th from Tweetbot

Now @Day4Night 's mocking me LOL Like I can't hear his teeth chattering.
12:02 AM June 12th from Tweetbot

It's not that cold.
12:02 AM June 12th from Tweetbot

@FRenn Oh yeah! You're starting to get it!
12:07 AM June 12th from Tweetbot in reply to FRenn

Everybody: I'm not afraid of no stupid #HRV Quit asking about it!
12:08 AM June 12th from Tweetbot

@MartinLG @karmaKat Are you guys ready or are you going to make out all night?
12:12 AM June 12th from Tweetbot

@MartinLG @karmaKat Yep. Whenever you are.
12:15 AM June 12th from Tweetbot in reply to MartinLG

Gotta go everyone. Be cool!
12:18 AM June 12th from Tweetbot

Border Surveillance footage - Camera CBSA1213 - via CSIS

Camera location: Facing United States of America entry point: Rainbow Bridge
Footage quality: Poor; Forensic enhancement performed to retrieve data.

Timecode: 00:23:11

Two unidentified subjects approach U.S. barricade, worming their way between cars. Both have their arms full of unidentified equipment. Subjects appear nervous. Facial recognition cannot be performed: not enough data to extrapolate identity. Subjects approach barricade, lights of United States border cast them in shadow. Faint sound of the items being dropped. Shushing. Subjects appear to glue a large poster to the side of first truck. Footage compromised from this point with artifacts. When image resolves again, third individual appears to be standing on edge of frame. Sound of gravel crunching recorded, but subjects seem unaware. Continue posting sign. Third individual approaches unnoticed and without caution. Once within reach, individual reaches out toward subjects.

Recording terminates: timecode: 00:31:02

spider98

Srry was gone so long.
12:57 AM June 12th from Tweetbot

Hope @karmaKat and @MartinLG got the footage!
12:57 AM June 12th from Tweetbot

Me and @Day4Night almost got caught. Had to dump
our equipment and bolt. Hope the camera worked!
12:57 AM June 12th from Tweetbot

Once a uniform shows up, even if it's border guard, you
run!
12:58 AM June 12th from Tweetbot

You should have seen me bolt! I dropped all my gear so
fast.
12:58 AM June 12th from Tweetbot

I'm at the car now, hiding behind it. No one else is here yet.
1:06 AM June 12th from Tweetbot

@Orphan_Tears I don't know. @Day4Night was right
behind me.
1:06 AM June 12th from Tweetbot in reply to OrphanTears

@Orphan_Tears No, I didn't look. I'm sure he got away,
though.
1:06 AM June 12th from Tweetbot in reply to OrphanTears

@Day4Night **Are you okay? Where are you?**
1:09 AM June 12th from Tweetbot direct message to Day4Night

Cops really swarming around now. I'm staying calm.
1:10 AM June 12th from Tweetbot

They're like sharks, moving through the streets like the scent of blood is in the air.
1:10 AM June 12th from Tweetbot

It was worth it, though. Check it out!
1:10 AM June 12th from Tweetbot

twitpik.com/6ppiux
1:10 AM June 12th from Tweetbot

twitpik.com/6prdis
1:10 AM June 12th from Tweetbot

We didn't get both posters completely up, but we got one.
1:11 AM June 12th from Tweetbot

Can't wait to watch the news tomorrow.
1:11 AM June 12th from Tweetbot

@JMont **It's like OBEY, but with zombies!**
1:12 AM June 12th from Tweetbot in reply to JMont

@JMont **Screw you! Like you'd know art!**
1:12 AM June 12th from Tweetbot in reply to JMont

#zOmBEY **! Everyone say it with me!**
1:12 AM June 12th from Tweetbot

#zOmBEY **!!**
1:13 AM June 12th from Tweetbot

#zOmBEY !!!
1:13 AM June 12th from Tweetbot

LOL
1:13 AM June 12th from Tweetbot

Still here. @MartinLG and @karmaKat arrived finally.
1:22 AM June 12th from Tweetbot

Out of breath.
1:22 AM June 12th from Tweetbot

They don't know where @Day4Night is. They didn't look.
They've been hiding from the cops.
1:22 AM June 12th from Tweetbot

Problem: @Day4Night has the car keys!!
1:22 AM June 12th from Tweetbot

We're stuck until he makes it back too :-(
1:22 AM June 12th from Tweetbot

Thought about breaking into the car but it's a bad idea.
1:23 AM June 12th from Tweetbot

There's a crapload of O.P.P. out here.
1:23 AM June 12th from Tweetbot

And we look weird, @MartinLG with a camera and me
with my wheat-pasted arms.
1:23 AM June 12th from Tweetbot

All it will do is call attention to us. But we can't wait
outside anymore.
1:23 AM June 12th from Tweetbot

Car's parked in front of some old store or something.
Lights are off. @karmaKat thinks it's empty.
1:23 AM June 12th from Tweetbot

Me and @Day4Night looked in window. Can't see anything. It's covered in fingerprints and something else . . .

1:23 AM June 12th from Tweetbot

Holy shit was that gunfire?

1:24 AM June 12th from Tweetbot

#zOmBEY !

1:24 AM June 12th from Tweetbot

Still wired! Want to start screaming but @karmaKat 's already freaked.

1:24 AM June 12th from Tweetbot

See? HA! . . twitpik.com/6udiss

1:24 AM June 12th from Tweetbot

@Day4Night We couldn't stay outside. @MartinLG forced the door of the place. We'll wait in here.

1:26 AM June 12th from Tweetbot direct message to Day4Night

@FRenn It was closed. Everything around here is closed cause of the #TheDeath quarantine.

1:28 AM June 12th from Tweetbot in reply to FRenn

@FRenn Dunno. I guess they figure the bridge is the best transmission point for the virus.

1:28 AM June 12th from Tweetbot in reply to FRenn

Hey everybody: I told you IM NOT AFRAID OF THE VIRUS

1:28 AM June 12th from Tweetbot

I'm not hurt, and I haven't touched anybody hurt. I feel fine.

1:28 AM June 12th from Tweetbot

@MartinLG and @karmaKat are fine, but they aren't happy.

1:28 AM June 12th from Tweetbot

I'm sure @Day4Night 's fine too.
1:28 AM June 12th from Tweetbot

@Day4Night Seriously, dude, where are you?
1:28 AM June 12th from Tweetbot direct message to Day4Night

@Orphan_Tears Did the news say anything about anyone getting caught?
1:29 AM June 12th from Tweetbot in reply to OrphanTears

Just checked the trending on #TheDeath Not really sure what to believe.
1:30 AM June 12th from Tweetbot

Things are getting nuts out here. Lots of yelling. We need to hide better.
1:30 AM June 12th from Tweetbot

Think @karmaKat is imagining things. I can't hear anything.
1:30 AM June 12th from Tweetbot

We're going in. If signal dies it's reception. Don't worry.
1:34 AM June 12th from Tweetbot

@Day4Night Come in by the alley door. Hope you're okay bud. Call me!
1:34 AM June 12th from Tweetbot

twitpik.com/7bsiek
1:36 AM June 12th from Tweetbot

Just our luck. I think it's one of those stupid wax museums. Like about criminals or movies or something.
1:36 AM June 12th from Tweetbot

Why would anyone leave these wax things here anyway?
1:36 AM June 12th from Tweetbot

Bums or cops moving around outside but they can't see us in here. Just in case I'm going to turn off my flashlight.

1:36 AM June 12th from Tweetbot

First statue in, and already @karmaKat wants to leave. LOL

1:37 AM June 12th from Tweetbot

It's a good thing museums put up signs with the exhibits so we can tell who's who

1:37 AM June 12th from Tweetbot

"Im-Ho-Tep/Mummy (1932); Boris Karloff"

1:37 AM June 12th from Tweetbot

Hey, you know what? I saw this movie with my mom.

1:37 AM June 12th from Tweetbot

It's that guy that played Frankenstein all wrapped in bandages.

1:37 AM June 12th from Tweetbot

Not a bad movie, but the remake was better.

1:38 AM June 12th from Tweetbot

Am I the only one creeped out by wax statues?

1:40 AM June 12th from Tweetbot

Besides @karmaKat I mean

1:40 AM June 12th from Tweetbot

Uh oh. Sirens louder. I think I saw a shadow across the front window. We gotta go deeper inside.

1:42 AM June 12th from Tweetbot

We took a vote. @karmaKat lost. We go in.

1:43 AM June 12th from Tweetbot

She is NOT happy with @MartinLG She hasn't said it, but she blames me for getting us in here.
1:46 AM June 12th from Tweetbot

You don't get trapped anywhere until you give up, I say.
1:46 AM June 12th from Tweetbot

I told her: we only stay until @Day4Night gets back. We can't leave him.
1:46 AM June 12th from Tweetbot

@Blindside She can go on her own if she wants. Who's stopping her?
1:46 AM June 12th from Tweetbot in reply to BlindSide

Weird a deserted museum is still full of exhibits. Probably got locked out for not paying rent.
1:47 AM June 12th from Tweetbot

This place is dusty. Cobwebs on half the statues. And they're all gruesome.
1:48 AM June 12th from Tweetbot

I don't want to say it in front of @karmaKat , but these things definitely creep me out.
1:48 AM June 12th from Tweetbot

Do you think it's worse when they look familiar? Like I can almost recognize the actors?
1:48 AM June 12th from Tweetbot

I think it's worse when you almost recognize them. There's a display here of witches being burned.
1:48 AM June 12th from Tweetbot

You can see where the bulbs of the exhibit were too close to the figures. The witches' faces are melted.
1:48 AM June 12th from Tweetbot

It's like their features have been smeared off. I can't keep the flashlight on them too long.

1:48 AM June 12th from Tweetbot

In the dark, even with these guys, it messes you up.

1:48 AM June 12th from Tweetbot

Now that we're deep enough inside the museum that we can't hear the outside, @karmaKat wants to stop and plan.

1:49 AM June 12th from Tweetbot

What the hell are we going to plan?

1:49 AM June 12th from Tweetbot

Okay, that was a waste of time. Just a bunch of arguing. What the hell are we supposed to do?

1:52 AM June 12th from Tweetbot

Obviously we're not leaving until @Day4Night arrives. No amount of crying will change that.

1:52 AM June 12th from Tweetbot

I'm alone right now. Needed my space. They wanted to talk. It's cool. Get to check out another exhibit.

1:56 AM June 12th from Tweetbot

Probably talking about me anyhow.

1:56 AM June 12th from Tweetbot

Some movie about someone with curly hair melting. Or maybe it's the lights again melting stuff.

1:56 AM June 12th from Tweetbot

Can't find the description so I don't know which movie it comes from

1:56 AM June 12th from Tweetbot

I can hear murmuring from somewhere. Crying? WTF??

1:56 AM June 12th from Tweetbot

@Blindside I'm starting to wonder. How afraid should I be? I mean, no one is dead, so we're okay, right?
1:57 AM June 12th from Tweetbot in reply to Blindside

Felt my stomach growl. I wonder how long those two want to be alone. I hope @MartinLG got her to chill the hell out.
1:57 AM June 12th from Tweetbot

Think I have to kill @karmaKat soon. She read the #TheDeath trending and now is convinced we need to check each other for scratches.
1:59 AM June 12th from Tweetbot

I'll take off mine if she takes off hers.
2:00 AM June 12th from Tweetbot

#zOmBEY your new master!!
2:00 AM June 12th from Tweetbot

LOL
2:00 AM June 12th from Tweetbot

Okay. Now I'm really wishing there were more lights in here. We just have the flashlights.
2:01 AM June 12th from Tweetbot

If you wave them wrong, the wax dummies look like they're moving. Totally freaked me for a second.
2:01 AM June 12th from Tweetbot

@JMont SCREW YOU! So it freaked me. You'd be a bit freaked too
2:02 AM June 12th from Tweetbot in reply to JMont

I'm starting to come down from the adrenaline. That can make you shake, right?
2:02 AM June 12th from Tweetbot

Heard knocking. @MartinLG thought it was @Day4Night
but I don't know. I still haven't heard from him.
2:02 AM June 12th from Tweetbot

They think we should leave. @MartinLG and @karmaKat
Where are they going to go?
2:02 AM June 12th from Tweetbot

They have no good answer. It isn't like there's a bus
from here to Toronto anymore.
2:03 AM June 12th from Tweetbot

I wish @MartinLG would grow a spine and stand up to
her. I can tell he agrees with me.
2:03 AM June 12th from Tweetbot

They've finally shut up about it, at least. Now they're
just hugging each other around the flashlight.
2:05 AM June 12th from Tweetbot

You know, I remember when @MartinLG wasn't such a
suck.
2:05 AM June 12th from Tweetbot

It's not easy being an artist. It took #Banksy and
#ShepardFairey years before they were noticed
2:06 AM June 12th from Tweetbot

And I bet their team backed them up
2:06 AM June 12th from Tweetbot

You'd think after
2:06 AM June 12th from Tweetbot

Sorry I th
2:06 AM June 12th from Tweetbot

Motherfucker!
2:08 AM June 12th from Tweetbot

I'm going to kill that bitch!

2:08 AM June 12th from Tweetbot

Never lend your shit to anyone cause they'll screw you.

2:08 AM June 12th from Tweetbot

Darlene was being a wimp, so I let her hold the flashlight while we walked.

2:09 AM June 12th from Tweetbot

Everything was cool for a bit, then she flipped the hell out and scratched the crap out of Martin, then ran off screaming and balling.

2:09 AM June 12th from Tweetbot

Martin took off after her. WITH the other flashlight.

2:09 AM June 12th from Tweetbot

I yelled at him to stop and tripped in the dark headfirst.

2:09 AM June 12th from Tweetbot

Did I black out? I was dizzy and they were gone when my head came back on.

2:09 AM June 12th from Tweetbot

Have to use my phone as a light now.

2:10 AM June 12th from Tweetbot

What did i trip over?

2:10 AM June 12th from Tweetbot

Shit. Is THIS what that bitch freaked out over?

2:10 AM June 12th from Tweetbot

Are you ready for this?

2:10 AM June 12th from Tweetbot

Ready?

2:10 AM June 12th from Tweetbot

It's a hand. A WAX hand.
2:10 AM June 12th from Tweetbot

Motherfucker.
2:10 AM June 12th from Tweetbot

Now I'm stuck here alone and have no idea what
direction I came and I don't have my fucking flashlight.
2:11 AM June 12th from Tweetbot

Damn it all.
2:11 AM June 12th from Tweetbot

I don't even know which statue lost the hand.
2:11 AM June 12th from Tweetbot

This place is really messing with me. Where is
@Day4Night ???
2:11 AM June 12th from Tweetbot

I wonder if they caught him.
2:12 AM June 12th from Tweetbot

Sirens outside are still nuts. What the hell happened?
2:12 AM June 12th from Tweetbot

@deadsea What?? This morning? How many? Did anyone
die?
2:12 AM June 12th from Tweetbot in reply to DeadSea

Does anyone know if anybody died at the #USAborder ?
2:12 AM June 12th from Tweetbot

Shit. And then nothing?
2:12 AM June 12th from Tweetbot

Have they said anything? What's the hash tag?
2:12 AM June 12th from Tweetbot

Checked but no one seems to know.
2:12 AM June 12th from Tweetbot

Shit.
2:12 AM June 12th from Tweetbot

Border Surveillance footage - Camera CBSA1213 -
via CSIS

Camera location: Facing United States of America
entry point: Rainbow Bridge
Footage quality: Poor. Forensic enhancement
performed to retrieve data.

Timecode: 02:12:23

Three individuals wandering between abandoned
cars. Facial recognition software unable to
confirm location of subjects in footage. Multiple
false positives generated. Footage quality
severely compromised and little is useful. Sound
recording suggests commotion on non-visible side
of border wall. Yelling or crying. Impossible to
determine origin of individuals and whether in
state of ingress versus egress. Impossible to
confirm whether barrier has been breached.
Further analysis recommended.

Recording terminates: timecode: 02:13:07

spider98

Okay. I'm seriously freaking out right now. I want to leave but can't.
2:13 AM June 12th from Tweetbot

I think there's som
2:13 AM June 12th from Tweetbot

I've been trying to get out of here for an hour but I can't remember where I am. I mean, I KNOW where I am, but I dont know
2:13 AM June 12th from Tweetbot

How do I get back?
2:13 AM June 12th from Tweetbot

I'm lost. I went too deep. I thought I heard someone come in, so I hid further back where there wasn't any light.
2:17 AM June 12th from Tweetbot

@FRenn No, I don't know who it was. I never saw them. Thought I heard movement though.
2:17 AM June 12th from Tweetbot in reply to FRenn

@FRenn It wasn't @Day4Night If it was, don't you think he would have told me?
2:17 AM June 12th from Tweetbot in reply to FRenn

I waited until the noise was gone but when I came out there was more darkness. I must have taken a wrong turn.

2:17 AM June 12th from Tweetbot

The only light I have is from this phone. It's not enough.

2:17 AM June 12th from Tweetbot

All the wax dummies look weird when I hold the phone up close to them. Weird and freaky. One's like the #zOmBEY poster.

2:17 AM June 12th from Tweetbot

Frankenstein, or whatever.

2:17 AM June 12th from Tweetbot

Like that's something I want to see when I'm in here.

2:18 AM June 12th from Tweetbot

Can someone Google me a map? I can't get 3G on my phone in here. Is it because we're so close to the border?

2:18 AM June 12th from Tweetbot

What if they're jamming the lines? Wait, why would they do that?

2:18 AM June 12th from Tweetbot

@Orphan_Tears I'm in some abandoned wax museum at Niagara Falls.

2:19 AM June 12th from Tweetbot in reply to OrphanTears

@JMont How would I know? The abandoned one with the Frankenstein in it! How many can there be??

2:19 AM June 12th from Tweetbot in reply to JMont

@Day4Night ? @MartinLG @karmaKat are any of you guys out there.

2:21 AM June 12th from Tweetbot

This is some messed up shit.

2:28 AM June 12th from Tweetbot

I'm starving and I'm lost in this damn museum.

2:28 AM June 12th from Tweetbot

And I don't think I'm alone.

2:28 AM June 12th from Tweetbot

I mean I know I'm not.

2:28 AM June 12th from Tweetbot

There's someone else in here. I hear him. Out there. In the darkness.

2:28 AM June 12th from Tweetbot

So I keep waiting until it's quiet before I start to move.

2:28 AM June 12th from Tweetbot

But I have no idea if he's gone, or if he's waiting too. Waiting for me.

2:28 AM June 12th from Tweetbot

I've turned the ringer off on my phone too, just in case he hears it.

2:29 AM June 12th from Tweetbot

Any word on the outside? I can't hear crap now. Christ, I'd be happy if the OPP came in right now.

2:29 AM June 12th from Tweetbot

Holy shit my heart stopped.

2:31 AM June 12th from Tweetbot

I think he's knocking shit over.

2:31 AM June 12th from Tweetbot

Hng n.

2:31 AM June 12th from Tweetbot

Is anybody still reading this?

2:32 AM June 12th from Tweetbot

Hello?

2:32 AM June 12th from Tweetbot

I can't tell if anyone is out there. I haven't seen another
tweet in half an hour.

2:32 AM June 12th from Tweetbot

No responses.

2:33 AM June 12th from Tweetbot

I really don't want to be here. This was pretty stupid.

2:33 AM June 12th from Tweetbot

I'm worried for Darlene and Martin. I hope they made it
out of here. I'm worried about Peter, too. I'm worried
about everyone I got into this mess.

2:33 AM June 12th from Tweetbot

Sorry I couldn't

2:34 AM June 12th from Tweetbot

I have no idea how to get out of here.

2:34 AM June 12th from Tweetbot

I have no idea where that other person is. If he was
dead, I'd smell him by now, right?

2:34 AM June 12th from Tweetbot

I think I'd smell him.

2:34 AM June 12th from Tweetbot

Not if he's made of wax.

2:34 AM June 12th from Tweetbot

Where'd that thought come from?

2:34 AM June 12th from Tweetbot

Can someone tell me what's going on?

2:39 AM June 12th from Tweetbot

Anyone?

2:39 AM June 12th from Tweetbot

Can anyone read this?

2:39 AM June 12th from Tweetbot

Can you call the police? Tell them I'm here? I don't want to be here anymore.

2:39 AM June 12th from Tweetbot

Anyone?

2:40 AM June 12th from Tweetbot

Okay. I'm going to try and calm down. I'll tell you a story. What do you want to know?

2:42 AM June 12th from Tweetbot

Anyone? Anything. Please, ask me anything. Just talk to me.

2:42 AM June 12th from Tweetbot

Hello?

2:43 AM June 12th from Tweetbot

Where the hell is Peter . . .

2:43 AM June 12th from Tweetbot

I first met him at summer camp in Kearny, if you can believe it.

2:44 AM June 12th from Tweetbot

What was that? About 8 years ago? We were in the same bunk house.

2:44 AM June 12th from Tweetbot

Parents liked to send kids away back then. Maybe my mom couldn't handle me on her own.

2:44 AM June 12th from Tweetbot

Newsflash: I was a handfu
2:44 AM June 12th from Tweetbot

Sorry. I thought I heard something.
2:44 AM June 12th from Tweetbot

I got there and on the first day I met Peter. Him and couple guys stole my hat and threw it in the Muskoka lake.
2:44 AM June 12th from Tweetbot

God I haven't thought about that in 4ever.
2:45 AM June 12th from Tweetbot

Bastard :-)
2:45 AM June 12th from Tweetbot

We got along soon after, though. Once those guys were gone and he saw the comics I brought.
2:45 AM June 12th from Tweetbot

Captain Americium, Spider-man
2:45 AM June 12th from Tweetbot

America
2:45 AM June 12th from Tweetbot

Tomb of Dracula.
2:45 AM June 12th from Tweetbot

We hung out all summer. Then camp was over and he was gone.
2:45 AM June 12th from Tweetbot

Didn't see him or hear from him for years. Forgot all about him really.
2:46 AM June 12th from Tweetbot

Then first day of high school, I'm walking down the hall and there he is!

2:46 AM June 12th from Tweetbot

Weird when the past appears from out of nowhere. Like a ghost.

2:46 AM June 12th from Tweetbot

It's weird to think we've been friends for only a couple of years now.

2:46 AM June 12th from Tweetbot

It feels li

2:46 AM June 12th from Tweetbot

Sorry I thought I heard shuffling again. Like the sound the mummy made in that movie. But that's stupid I

2:47 AM June 12th from Tweetbot

I don't want to be famous anymore. I don't want to be #Banksy or anyone anymore. I just want to be home.

2:48 AM June 12th from Tweetbot

What good is being famous if the world is going to hell? Who's going to remember any stupid poster when there's goddamn dead people walking around?

2:48 AM June 12th from Tweetbot

Why am I so stupid?

2:49 AM June 12th from Tweetbot

London's a mess. USA is boarded up. And like an idiot I got my friends out of their houses.

2:49 AM June 12th from Tweetbot

They aren't safe. I made them not safe.

2:49 AM June 12th from Tweetbot

How can the dead be alive again? It doesn't make any sense.
2:51 AM June 12th from Tweetbot

Is someone there? Can someone explain it to me??
2:53 AM June 12th from Tweetbot

They're probably all dead. Darlene, Martin, Peter
2:54 AM June 12th from Tweetbot

All dead.
2:54 AM June 12th from Tweetbot

But what if it's worse? What if they're dead . . . but walking around?
2:54 AM June 12th from Tweetbot

What have I done? Why didn't we stay home?
2:55 AM June 12th from Tweetbot

I'm waiting waiting but
2:55 AM June 12th from Tweetbot

No one has come in here, which means no one called the police. Probably no one is reading these tweets.
2:56 AM June 12th from Tweetbot

No one is listening.
2:56 AM June 12th from Tweetbot

I hope my mom is ok
2:56 AM June 12th from Tweetbot

Okay. I've decided. I'm getting myself out of here.
3:01 AM June 12th from Tweetbot

I've been thinking about it. This place isn't huge. I saw it from the outside. It's not tiny, but it's not huge. It's just got a lot of rooms.

3:01 AM June 12th from Tweetbot

But I have a plan.

3:01 AM June 12th from Tweetbot

These places, they're built to move as many people through as quickly as possible, right? They don't want you to linger.

3:01 AM June 12th from Tweetbot

How do they do that?

3:01 AM June 12th from Tweetbot

By laying out the place in a continuous line! Maybe not a straight line, but still a line.

3:01 AM June 12th from Tweetbot

Exit Through the Gift Shop, like the #Banksy movie!

3:01 AM June 12th from Tweetbot

This whole place has to be the same. One path from entrance to exit.

3:02 AM June 12th from Tweetbot

Whoever's in here with me, he came in the same way as me. Started knocking shit over.

3:02 AM June 12th from Tweetbot

If I go that way, even if he doesn't find me I'll probably trip over the mess he's making

3:02 AM June 12th from Tweetbot

I haven't heard him in a while, but he couldn't have got passed me.

3:02 AM June 12th from Tweetbot

So, I go in the other direction. Start feeling my way deeper into the museum.

3:02 AM June 12th from Tweetbot

Eventually, it has to lead me to the exit, right? It has HAS to. There can't be a dead end. It doesn't make any sense.

3:02 AM June 12th from Tweetbot

You know that Shepard Fairey OBEY poster came from a joke?

3:02 AM June 12th from Tweetbot

Andre the Giant has a posse.

3:02 AM June 12th from Tweetbot

Now he sells goddamn tee shirts and mugs and posters for presidents.

3:03 AM June 12th from Tweetbot

For a stupid drawing of a wrestler, and a slogan stolen from a movie.

3:03 AM June 12th from Tweetbot

How is that fair?

3:03 AM June 12th from Tweetbot

I'm listening close but I don't hear that other guy. Maybe he's gone. Maybe he found a way out.

3:04 AM June 12th from Tweetbot

Maybe he's not a guy. Maybe he's a thing. A wax dummy come to life.

3:04 AM June 12th from Tweetbot

I don't even know if he knows I'm here. He didn't say anything.

3:04 AM June 12th from Tweetbot

Okay. I'm going. Will use my phone to light anything I need to, but I need to conserve the battery. It's starting to run low.
3:06 AM June 12th from Tweetbot

If anyone can read this, pls pls pls respond.
3:06 AM June 12th from Tweetbot

Tweet me anything. Anything at all.
3:06 AM June 12th from Tweetbot

Hello?
3:06 AM June 12th from Tweetbot

Okay. Here I go. Wish me luck.
3:07 AM June 12th from Tweetbot

That did not go well.
3:52 AM June 12th from Tweetbot

I made it through a couple of rooms. Ended up in some medieval torture room.
3:52 AM June 12th from Tweetbot

Last room I wanted to be in.
3:52 AM June 12th from Tweetbot

Crazy guy with a bald head and bulging eyes hanging over me, a big axe raised like he's going to chop my head off.
3:52 AM June 12th from Tweetbot

I fell over and dropped my phone. It skidded away and for a second I didn't know if that guy was going to grab me
3:52 AM June 12th from Tweetbot

Or what was happening. My brain – my whole body fucking froze.
3:52 AM June 12th from Tweetbot

All I could do is watch the light of my phone's display blink out and I was in the black.

3:53 AM June 12th from Tweetbot

My breath wheezing so quick that I was seeing stars in the dark, but I was still paralyzed by the image of that raised axe.

3:53 AM June 12th from Tweetbot

But my eyes were stuck on where the phone had gone to.

3:53 AM June 12th from Tweetbot

I must have been standing like that for only a minute, but it felt like hours.

3:53 AM June 12th from Tweetbot

Have you ever felt that? So afraid that time actually stops?

3:53 AM June 12th from Tweetbot

Anyway, after a while, my body loosened enough that I could slowly drop myself to the ground.

3:53 AM June 12th from Tweetbot

Each inch I dropped I waited for something to happen, for someone to come through the door and grab me.

3:53 AM June 12th from Tweetbot

No one came.

3:53 AM June 12th from Tweetbot

They came for Peter. And for Darlene and Martin, but they didn't come for me.

3:53 AM June 12th from Tweetbot

Yet. But I could have sworn I heard something.

3:53 AM June 12th from Tweetbot

Like a single footstep drag. Then again. Not for long,
but there.
3:54 AM June 12th from Tweetbot

I finally pawed around on the ground until I felt the cold
plastic of the phone in my hands.
3:54 AM June 12th from Tweetbot

I didn't even stop to look, I just opened it up. The light
broke a bit of the darkness.
3:54 AM June 12th from Tweetbot

Enough to see the crazy bald man statue. I think was
another of what's his name? Karloff.
3:54 AM June 12th from Tweetbot

Still it was freaky to look at with its missing hand but
better than being able to see nothing.
3:54 AM June 12th from Tweetbot

That is, until I took a closer look.
3:54 AM June 12th from Tweetbot

Half its face was bitten off!
3:54 AM June 12th from Tweetbot

On the ground were chewed pieces of wax. One had a
footprint in it.
3:54 AM June 12th from Tweetbot

That confused me.
3:54 AM June 12th from Tweetbot

Then everything got worse.
3:55 AM June 12th from Tweetbot

Mom, I saw
3:55 AM June 12th from Tweetbot

I can't really explain
3:55 AM June 12th from Tweetbot

Everything
3:55 AM June 12th from Tweetbot

Everything went to hell.
3:55 AM June 12th from Tweetbot

I'm hiding in the dark right now for all the good it will
do me.
3:55 AM June 12th from Tweetbot

My knee is banged up. Its not bleeding, but its swollen
up so much I can't even bend it.
3:55 AM June 12th from Tweetbot

I can't walk on it. That's for sure.
3:55 AM June 12th from Tweetbot

Can anybody read this? Hello? Hello?
3:56 AM June 12th from Tweetbot

I need help. Somebody help me!
3:56 AM June 12th from Tweetbot

@Day4Night @karmaKat @MartinLG are any of you
there?
3:56 AM June 12th from Tweetbot

@deadsea @FRenn Anyone?
3:56 AM June 12th from Tweetbot

I wish I could talk to my mom right now but I can't get
any goddamn bars.
3:56 AM June 12th from Tweetbot

Saw the half eaten statue and spit out wax. Before I
could figure it out it was figured out for me

3:56 AM June 12th from Tweetbot

Another statue fell and scared the hell out of me, but
not as much as the grunting.

3:56 AM June 12th from Tweetbot

I couldn't see its face

3:56 AM June 12th from Tweetbot

Thank god I couldn't see its face

3:56 AM June 12th from Tweetbot

But I saw enough to know it was coming right for me.

3:56 AM June 12th from Tweetbot

I saw enough to know it was wearing an old rain slicker
just like that bum earlier.

3:57 AM June 12th from Tweetbot

Don't let it touch you. I remember that from the news.
Don't let it touch you.

3:57 AM June 12th from Tweetbot

Was it glowing? I thought but it couldn't have been.

3:57 AM June 12th from Tweetbot

I couldn't see its face. Its head was hanging back, like it
was looking at the sky

3:57 AM June 12th from Tweetbot

But too far back, you know?

3:57 AM June 12th from Tweetbot

Still it knew exactly where I was.

3:57 AM June 12th from Tweetbot

And then my phone went dark.

3:57 AM June 12th from Tweetbot

I ran. It was pitch blank and I ran.

3:58 AM June 12th from Tweetbot

I don't know what I was more afraid of. That thing behind me, or that I had no idea what was in front of me.

3:58 AM June 12th from Tweetbot

I've never run in nothing before. The blood in my ear pumping so loud it echoed.

3:58 AM June 12th from Tweetbot

And I had no idea if that thing was right behind me.

3:58 AM June 12th from Tweetbot

My knee hurts so bad. My god, it hurts so bad.

3:58 AM June 12th from Tweetbot

I don't know what I tripped over. I was too afraid to find out.

3:58 AM June 12th from Tweetbot

But it didn't feel like a plastic hand.

3:58 AM June 12th from Tweetbot

In the black, you barely know you're falling. You just know when you stop. And it was a long way down.

3:58 AM June 12th from Tweetbot

I fell for too long. I fell forever.

3:58 AM June 12th from Tweetbot

I wanted to scream so much but I stopped myself. I can't believe it but I did.

3:59 AM June 12th from Tweetbot

I kept hearing something coming toward me as I lay there.

3:59 AM June 12th from Tweetbot

My head was swimming, and all I heard was a dragging noise coming.

3:59 AM June 12th from Tweetbot

I turned on my phone and nearly screamed.

3:59 AM June 12th from Tweetbot

Above me, staring down at me with maniacal glee, was that face, that misshapen face I'd seen all night.

3:59 AM June 12th from Tweetbot

Karloff's face, and above his head was a shovel, underneath his foot a tombstone.

3:59 AM June 12th from Tweetbot

I was in a grave. I was in a goddamn grave waiting to be killed.

3:59 AM June 12th from Tweetbot

That should have killed me right then and there.

3:59 AM June 12th from Tweetbot

My head was still groggy, and when I started to get out of the grave my knee started screaming loud.

4:00 AM June 12th from Tweetbot

If I didn't have stars in my eyes from the fall, I did from the pain.

4:00 AM June 12th from Tweetbot

But that rumpling sound was coming, and I only had one chance.

4:00 AM June 12th from Tweetbot

I wish I knew if someone was reading this. If someone was sending help.

4:00 AM June 12th from Tweetbot

That broken-necked thing was coming toward me in the dark, and I knew I'd never out run it.

4:00 AM June 12th from Tweetbot

So I got out of the grave and I waited.
4:00 AM June 12th from Tweetbot

It took all my nerve to slow my breathing, stop thinking about the pain.
4:00 AM June 12th from Tweetbot

Adrenaline helps, I bet.
4:00 AM June 12th from Tweetbot

I kept as quiet as I could and listened to it coming down the hall toward me.
4:00 AM June 12th from Tweetbot

Listened as every step got closer.
4:00 AM June 12th from Tweetbot

The smell hit me like it hadn't before.
4:00 AM June 12th from Tweetbot

It was a little like cheese. Cheese, and old fish. And something else I can't even describe.
4:00 AM June 12th from Tweetbot

I don't know. But I heard it. Like sandpaper on cardboard. Slow and deliberate.
4:00 AM June 12th from Tweetbot

Slow and deliberate.
4:01 AM June 12th from Tweetbot

Getting closer.
4:01 AM June 12th from Tweetbot

It came so close I thought I could feel it pass by.
4:01 AM June 12th from Tweetbot

Wondered in the absolute dark if I felt its dry fingers on my skin.

4:01 AM June 12th from Tweetbot

I held out as long as I could, but I broke.

4:01 AM June 12th from Tweetbot

I screamed.

4:01 AM June 12th from Tweetbot

God, I screamed so loud.

4:01 AM June 12th from Tweetbot

I don't know if that made a difference, but I know it lunged toward me.

4:01 AM June 12th from Tweetbot

I know, because I heard it fall into that fake unearthed coffin in the ground.

4:01 AM June 12th from Tweetbot

Heard something snap like wood or maybe bone.

4:02 AM June 12th from Tweetbot

I didn't want to know.

4:02 AM June 12th from Tweetbot

Instead, I used the shovel Karloff had been holding and swung it down where I thought the thing was.

4:02 AM June 12th from Tweetbot

I hit wood sometimes and the wood shook my arms so bad I almost dropped the shovel.

4:02 AM June 12th from Tweetbot

But when I hit something else, the sound in the dark was

4:02 AM June 12th from Tweetbot

Was like nothing I'd heard
4:02 AM June 12th from Tweetbot

I don't know what kind of damage I did, but I didn't hear
it moving any more after a while.
4:02 AM June 12th from Tweetbot

I didn't hear it rumpling.
4:02 AM June 12th from Tweetbot

I didn't see anything like a glow.
4:02 AM June 12th from Tweetbot

But, for good measure, I pushed the Karloff statue over
on top of where the grave should have been.
4:02 AM June 12th from Tweetbot

Then, I crawled away, crawled as far as I could into the
dark.
4:03 AM June 12th from Tweetbot

I have no idea how long I've been writing that. My
phone's almost dead, but I don't know what else to do.
4:03 AM June 12th from Tweetbot

I've been listening as hard as I can but I haven't heard
that thing moving.
4:03 AM June 12th from Tweetbot

God, I hope it's not coming.
4:03 AM June 12th from Tweetbot

My leg.
4:03 AM June 12th from Tweetbot

My leg my leg my leg my leg
4:03 AM June 12th from Tweetbot

I can barely keep from crying.

4:03 AM June 12th from Tweetbot

Is there anyone who is getting this?

4:03 AM June 12th from Tweetbot

Mom I'm

4:03 AM June 12th from Tweetbot

My phone is flashing. My battery won't l

4:05 AM June 12th from Tweetbot

Border Surveillance footage - Camera CBSA1213 - via CSIS

Camera location: Facing United States of America entry point: Rainbow Bridge
Footage quality: Deteriorated, forensic enhancement impossible.

Time code: Missing

Unable to retrieve more than a few seconds of footage without loss of video. Light edges sky behind short-term barrier. No sound on recording, though impossible to confirm whether due to loss of microphone data or to absence of life. Sound of Falls indistinguishable from drone of static. No evidence of movement at border. Video artifacts suggest fine mist floating above ground. A bright light appears in the sky behind the border, lasting only a few seconds before going out.

Recording terminates.

spider98

I'm still alive.
5:13 AM June 12th from Tweetbot

I must have fallen asleep. I don't know how I could have, but it's morning and I can see.
5:13 AM June 12th from Tweetbot

My phone pretty much dead but I need to keep trying to get help.
5:13 AM June 12th from Tweetbot

There's just enough sunlight for me to see the shape of the room. To see where the door is.
5:13 AM June 12th from Tweetbot

I can see what's left of the exhibit. Wax legs are sticking out of the coffin.
5:14 AM June 12th from Tweetbot

I hear a scratching which terrifies me, but it's faint, whatever it is
5:14 AM June 12th from Tweetbot

And I see the door.
5:14 AM June 12th from Tweetbot

I'm going to try and stand up.
5:14 AM June 12th from Tweetbot

I don't know if I c
5:14 AM June 12th from Tweetbot

I have to get to that door. It can't be very far. I can see
the light.
5:16 AM June 12th from Tweetbot

Am I hearing that scratching or imagining it?
5:16 AM June 12th from Tweetbot

Need to get out of here. Need to go now.
5:16 AM June 12th from Tweetbot

Okay, Gary. Forget the pain
5:16 AM June 12th from Tweetbot

Forget the pain
5:16 AM June 12th from Tweetbot

Forget the pain
5:16 AM June 12th from Tweetbot

Forget the pain
5:16 AM June 12th from Tweetbot

Just go go go
5:16 AM June 12th from Tweetbot

Mom, I love
5:16 AM June 12th from Tweetbot

Peter, Darlene, Martin, I hope you're alive.
5:16 AM June 12th from Tweetbot

I'm sorry everybody.
5:16 AM June 12th from Tweetbot

I'm so sorry.
5:16 AM June 12th from Tweetbot

SOS
5:20 AM June 12th from Tweetbot

HELP
5:23 AM June 12th from Tweetbot

READ THIS READ THIS READ THIS
5:23 AM June 12th from Tweetbot

Is anybody getting this tweet?
5:25 AM June 12th from Tweetbot

Gary Spender is trapped in an abandon wax museum on
Clifton Hill, Niagara Falls, Canada!
5:27 AM June 12th from Tweetbot

Cell signal not working
5:30 AM June 12th from Tweetbot

Battery about to die
5:32 AM June 12th from Tweetbot

Im at the front door, but it's locked. I can't get out
5:43 AM June 12th from Tweetbot

Cant break the glass. I tried but I cant. I don't have any
strength.
5:45 AM June 12th from Tweetbot

Send help
5:46 AM June 12th from Tweetbot

Send help
5:46 AM June 12th from Tweetbot

Send help.

5:46 AM June 12th from Tweetbot

OMFG

5:49 AM June 12th from Tweetbot

Thank you. Whoever sent help, thank you. Thank you!

5:49 AM June 12th from Tweetbot

There's a guard outside

5:49 AM June 12th from Tweetbot

My god I didn't think Id get

5:49 AM June 12th from Tweetbot

What is he banging on the glass for?

5:49 AM June 12th from Tweetbot

He's going to br

5:50 AM June 12th from Tweetbot

CITY-TV

"We continue our coverage of the Rainbow Bridge disaster.

"U.S.A. barricades, designed to help contain the HRV outbreak, have failed. Residents of the Niagara Falls area have been warned to stay indoors and keep their doors locked. The downtown core, a popular tourist area, has been designated a danger zone. The following helicopter footage shows the streets have been overrun. There appears to be no survivors."

[Newsflash on City*Pulse* News, CITY-TV, Toronto, Canada, June 12]

BORIS KARLOFF

WAX MUSEUM

At the Corner of
Oakes Drive and Buchanan Avenue
Niagara Falls, Canada

Dr Alison McReady's journal, 19/06:

Ralph the Spook is on the top of the silo tank with his rifle and high-powered binoculars; the King of the Dead is doing a good imitation of being asleep (I think he's sulking after Ralph interrupted our conversation); I have a chance to note down what happened in the camp today, how we got here and why. Old habits die hard, I guess. I've been keeping this journal for just over a month now. It'll take more than a little diversion involving a secret agent on the run with a mad dead guy to stop me.

It started with a call from the duty officer at you-have-to-be-kidding ack emma: there was a problem at the main gate, could I come straight down. So the acting head of Displaced Persons Camp #16 (Oxford Emergency Area) got out of the nice warm cot she'd fallen into less than a couple of hours ago, pulled a raincoat over her pyjamas, and walked past the dark admin block to the main gate, where the duty officer and four squaddies were standing in front of a Range Rover.

It was lit up by floodlights, engine running, exhaust pumping a plume of vapour into the frosty air, black paint job on its left flank scarred by several high-velocity rounds and a short burst from a sub-machine gun, tinted windows crazed. The driver stood by the open door, smoking, watching the darkness beyond the yellow splash of the floodlights and the triple razor-wire fence. Tall, trim, blond, dressed in camo gear and combat boots, a pistol holstered at his hip. I recognised him before he turned to me. My very own secret agent, Mr Blond, aka Please Call Me Ralph Pronounced Rafe. Turning up cool as you please after we'd set free a certain undead royal personage and gone our separate ways. Telling me now that he was in a spot of bother: he had one person mortally wounded and another who needed treatment, was wondering if I could lend a hand.

Well, what could I do?

Once I'd been shown what he'd brought with him, I called my chief nurse, told her I was going to deal with a couple of difficult cases in the quarantine zone. I was in the middle of giving her a list of supplies I would need when Ralph drew his pistol and pushed me behind the Range Rover. I didn't have a chance to ask him what the hell. A moment later, gunfire crackled beyond the perimeter and bullets zipped through the air and kicked fragments from the concrete apron. Ralph leaned out from the cover of the Range Rover and returned fire with his pistol; a moment later the soldiers got their act together and dropped to the ground and started firing too.

Figures materialised out of the gloom. Four, six, eight of them, moving slowly and unsteadily, firing rifles from the hip. They wore ragged clothes and walked like drunks. The noise was tremendous. I saw Ralph jam a fresh magazine into his pistol and step out into the open and brace and aim and fire, saw a figure jerk backwards and collapse. He yelled at the soldiers, told them to take head-shots, fired again. A woman missing her lower jaw was struck in the chest. She took two steps backwards and Ralph shot again and matter sprayed from her head and she collapsed. He shot a man scrabbling at the outer wire and the soldiers got the idea and took down the rest.

In the echo of gunfire, Ralph turned to me and asked if I was all right. I said stupidly that they were the dead, the attackers had been *dead people*. He looked straight into my eyes and said yes, they were the dead and now they were really dead. *Firing guns!*, I said. I was having a hard time understanding what I had seen. He said they were a new kind of dead, a crowd of them had attacked him and his friends, and that was when one of them stood up behind the wire and I screamed like a silly little girl and Ralph turned and fired a single shot and the dead man dropped his rifle and fell against the razorwire and hung there.

Ralph apologised for causing me trouble, said it was a matter of national survival, and he couldn't think of anyone better qualified to help.

I said that his chat-up line sounded awfully familiar.

I'd forgotten how nice his smile was.

While he had a little talk with the soldiers, I checked the mortally wounded patient in the back of the Range Rover and made another call to my chief nurse, finishing up that list of supplies, asking her to stop by my room and pick up some warm clothes and my good hiking boots. Then I climbed into the Range Rover beside Ralph, and we drove down the main drag, past rows and rows of tents, most of them empty, to one of the huts in the quarantine area in the western quadrant. Ralph, asking questions about my work, asking how many people still lived here. I told him the camp was almost empty and would soon be shut down, explained about the new Core Optimisation Initiative that was moving displaced persons out of camps like this and into those cities that were considered relatively safe.

"Managed retreat," he said. "You're having trouble keeping your quarantine zone clear."

London was still not safe to go into after the government had detonated a nuclear device over the south of the city. I asked him if it was bad everywhere.

"Pretty much, I'm afraid," he said. And added that it was good to see me safe and well.

The mortally wounded man on the back seat groaned as we bounced over a bad pothole and pulled up in front of the hut. My chief nurse, Katherine Hughes, was waiting for us. She was Welsh, forthright and completely unflappable. She said she would stay and help me, and stared Ralph down when he tried to tell her it wouldn't be necessary.

"You should have taken him to the secure facility run by that New World Pharmaceutical Group. The one on Ramsey Island," she said, after she'd seen the wounded man.

"You were closer," Ralph said. "Also, he may have been bitten."

"We'll do what we can," Katherine said. "But it won't be what he needs."

The hut was warm and humid. The only light was from battery lanterns because the generator was switched off after midnight to save what little diesel we had left. We hadn't used the place for more than a month. People seeking serious medical help weren't sent to the DP camps any more. They went to reception areas run by NWP and if they didn't turn or die they were treated and sent on. And now the original residents of the camp were being dispatched to Oxford, twenty or so a day; soon the camp would be empty, and I'd be in Oxford too, or reassigned elsewhere.

We got the man inside, did our best to make him comfortable on a gel mattress Katherine had brought in the SmartCar we used to tootle around the camp. He was burned over more than ninety per cent of his body, with a broken femur and a shattered pelvis, several shrapnel wounds to his chest, glass cuts to his face, and a bad bite on his forearm.

Katherine giving me a look after she'd sponged off a crust of dried blood and revealed the tooth-marks. The poor man was awake, exhibiting the lucidity the recently badly-burned often possess, not yet in real pain. His name, Ralph said, was Dr Toby Maggs, a psychologist. Katherine kept up a stream of encouraging chat as we did what we could, which wasn't much more than cutting away what was left of his clothing, cleaning and bandaging his various wounds, covering him with a Mylar blanket, and giving him fluids and morphine. I tried to tell myself that even the best hospital wouldn't have been able to do any better and that if he didn't die of his wounds the infection from the bite was certain to kill him. It didn't much help.

I told Ralph that he'd been right about the bite. He said he could deal with it right away, end the poor chap's suffering and make sure he got eternal rest.

I said that he was on a high dose of morphine and that when the time came we had our own way of making sure the dead stayed dead, and explained about the slaughterhouse bolt guns we used.

Ralph raised an eyebrow, said that I'd toughened up since he'd last seen me, laughed when I asked if that was a new chat-up line.

While Katherine finished settling Dr Maggs, I changed out of my pyjamas into a sweater and jeans in the bathroom, then helped Ralph move the other person he'd brought. *The dead person.*

He was in the cavernous rear of the Range Rover, strapped to an ortho stretcher, a rigid plank of blue plastic used for people with spinal injuries. He was dressed in an orange boilersuit and a backwards restraint jacket. He appeared to have broken the long bones of his arms and legs: steel pins protruded through holes in sleeves and legs of the coveralls. Then I saw the pins ended in eyebolts and each eyebolt was padlocked to doubled lengths of steel chain that looped through slots either side of the stretcher. There were straps across his thighs and chest and his head was restrained by a strap across his forehead. He was painfully thin. Skeletal. A death's-head face, the sutures of his skull showing through a patchy stubble. He looked up at me when I looked down at him, and smiled. Baring his teeth the way the dead do before they bite. Then the worst shock of all: he spoke.

A dry voice with some kind of old-fashioned London accent. Asking me which of my parents had been a slave. I told him my father had been a Tube driver, my mother a nurse.

"And are you also a nurse, like your mother?"

"A doctor."

"Ah. I confess little liking for your profession. They have caused me much pain in the past."

"We're going to take care of you here."

"Those firearms I heard. Were they *my* people?"

Those yellow eyes. Like old ivory. That intent unblinking stare.

"You mean, were they the dead?"

I was frightened of him, but I was curious too. Trying to put everything together.

"I am their king," the dead man said, matter-of-factly. "Perhaps you will be my queen, by and by."

Ralph interrupted then, told the dead man he'd get the gag if he caused any trouble. We lifted him out and carried him in and set him upright against a wall, and I hooked him up to transfusion bags as per Ralph's instructions. He thanked me, the dead man, for the blood.

He'd been dead a very long time, according to Ralph. His name was Thomas Moreby, aka "Patient Zero", aka "the Package". He'd been an assistant to an 18th-century architect, and was a self-confessed sorcerer who believed he'd found the key to immortal life. Instead, what he had apparently discovered was the key to never-ending life in death. When he'd been accidentally revived beneath All Hallows Church in London, he and a cargo of fleas had escaped. The fleas carried bacteria; the bacteria carried a virus; the virus, transmitted by saliva and blood, killed people and brought them back to life.

During the troubles that followed, Moreby had eventually been captured somehow by security forces and transported to a heavily-guarded facility outside Manchester, where researchers had been desperately attempting to discover if his body possessed the key for curing the plague he'd set loose. They hadn't, according to Ralph, but they had found out that Moreby wasn't your usual shambling teethsnapping nailclawing flesheating walking dead.

It seemed that bacteria from the fleas had established a kind of network inside his nervous system. Also, his body harboured several variations of the virus that killed people and then resurrected them. One strain appeared to transmit memories and skills between the dead, Ralph said. And if one of the dead infected with that particular strain of virus ate the brains or part of the brains of their victim, some of the victim's memories were then copied by the virus and subsequently absorbed by the host.

"The dead who attacked us earlier hadn't been soldiers when they'd been alive. But at least one of them must have eaten part of a soldier. They knew one end of a weapon from the other. And one of them sure knew how to fire an anti-tank missile. Poor Maggs was in the vehicle behind the one that the missile hit."

Ralph was tired but alert, spooning up tuna from a can while he talked, washing it down with bottled water. Telling me the convoy had been taking Moreby from Manchester to a safer location when it had been hit. Either it was bad luck – a random strike by a roving gang of the new kind of dead – or Moreby was telling the truth when he claimed to have got word out to his "followers".

Ralph said, "I wouldn't put it past him. He's a cunning so and so." (The Spook and I have shared some very tense moments in the past few weeks, but I've never yet heard him swear.) "The memory-transfer virus got out, after all. And it's been spreading fast. The scientists tracked it by mapping victims whose brains were eaten. Brains and nothing else."

It wasn't a nice idea. The ordinary walking dead were bad enough. *Smart* walking dead armed with guns and missiles, capable of making and carrying out plans, raised the game to a new level. He left me to think about that while he went outside to check the perimeter. I tried to ignore the yellow stare of the dead man fastened to the upright stretcher and checked on Katherine and poor Dr Maggs.

The morphine had taken hold. Maggs was awake but soporific. Feeling no pain. If he was lucky, systemic organ collapse would kill him before the pain kicked in, or before the virus did its work. His face was covered in big blisters. His arms and legs were swelling with fluid. His unburned forehead gleamed with sweat. Like all bad burns cases he was having problems regulating the core temperature of his body. Katherine was holding his right thumb, the only part of his hands that hadn't been burned. He was talking to her. His voice was hoarse – he'd breathed in smoke or superheated air. She was smiling at him and telling him he was doing really well, and he was staring at her and trying to explain something about the dead. The politics of the dead. Why they were not democrats. Why they followed strong leaders – something about virus load and memes. "The King rules through the heart, not the head. His blood is royal because it carries the strongest strains of virus. That carries the strongest memes. Darwinian competition for ideas. In the blood."

Katherine told him that he shouldn't get excited and glanced up at me. From her look I knew Dr Maggs didn't have long.

I went to fetch another bag of saline and the dead man called to me, saying that the good doctor was right about one thing. Kings were kings because it was in their blood.

I said something about his blood being diluted by common ordinary blood. He said that it would be transmuted in his body as ordinary wine was transmuted to the blood of the upstart Redeemer during Holy Communion.

"I have much in common with the so-called Saviour," he said. "We both died and were born again. We both suffered at the hand of torturers. Our followers venerate and drink our blood in holy rituals. We are both called 'King' by mocking unbelievers who do not know they speak the truth."

He spoke very seriously. I supposed he was mad. It did not seem unlikely. Why should the living dead be in any way sane? Especially one who claimed to be nearly 300 years old.

He asked me if I believed in the Holy Scriptures. I said that I was an agnostic who tended towards unbelief, these days. He said, "We are all part of *my* Master's plan. Would you like to be part of *my* plan, child?"

I asked if he'd planned his escape.

"We all have plans. Ask your friend Ralph about his plans. Ask him about the plans of the Colonials."

"Can you really spread ideas through your blood?"

"And with a kiss too," he said, his accent suddenly changing to cockney. *Wiv ah kees.* Saying, *Ow baht a nice leetle kees, gurl?*

His tongue was shockingly pink and alive, waggling between his black lips.

Then he looked past me and said in his normal voice, "You look very serious, Ralph. Bad news, I hope."

Ralph ignored him. We went outside into the semi-darkness. It was four in the morning and everything was as quiet as the tomb. Ralph said he'd been on the radio. Said some bad guys were coming. Said the brand-new lieutenant on the gate had probably called in the incident, even though he had ordered him not to. Said that he hated to cut and run, but he had to move on.

I asked him if the bad guys were more of the dead, or Americans.

"He told you, did he?" Ralph said.

"He told me to ask you about your plans. And mentioned that the 'Colonials', as he called them, had plans too. What plans? What Americans?"

Ralph looked straight at me and said he trusted me, and if I came with him he'd explain everything. Said that it would be the most enormous favour, because I might be able to talk with Moreby and get more information out of him.

"I think he likes you. And it would really be a great help. Especially if we can find out how he communicates with his followers. Some of the scientists suspect some kind of telepathy. No one really knows. Knew."

I told him I had a camp to run.

"I'll only be borrowing you until my friends come. We work together well, you and I. Especially around royalty."

"This is different."

"Also, I need someone to pump more blood into our friend. The scientists drained him and I would like him a bit livelier, in case I have to let him go."

"Is that your plan?"

"It's plan B. Plan A, I get him to a safe place. And that's all I can tell you for now."

He said he'd give me a couple of minutes to think about it. But he knew that I didn't need more than ten seconds to decide. Knew that I wanted to know what happened next.

Attachment #1

To: G. Harman, New World Pharmaceutical Group,
Ramsey Island
Re: Population Variation and Change in Viral
and Bacterial Load in the Resurrected Dead
R. Hopkin, F. Gibbons, H.H. Chou, T.R. Maggs

ABSTRACT
Viral load (units per ml) and variation in the
Human Reanimation Virus (popularly known as the
"The Death", "Beltane plague" or "Lazarus virus")
was measured in a sample of 12 deceased,
resurrected subjects over a period of 21 days
following injection of 10 ml samples of whole
blood taken from Patient Zero. Viral load
increased rapidly and reached a plateau 10 - 14
days after exposure. Variation in strains of HRV
as measured by shotgun DNA sequencing showed
significant differences between individuals. In
11 cases strain variation in the viral load
rapidly reduced until only the primary strain and
a low level (>0.002 units per ml) of the so-
called meme-transfer (mtHRV) strain could be
detected. In one case the primary strain became
dominant but levels of mtHRV remained relatively
high (5 - 8 units per ml). Significantly higher
levels of activity in the bacterial species
associated with HRV were also found in the blood
and lymphatic system of this specimen, and
cognitive ability as measured by standardised
reward/punishment tests was higher than in other
individuals. More research is needed to establish
a link between levels of mt virus, bacteria and
cognitive ability.

Attachment #2

To: G. Harman, New World Pharmaceutical Group,
Ramsey Island
Re: Horizontal Transfer of Skill-Sets Via Blood
Containing the mt Strain of the HRV Virus
R. Hopkin, T.R. Maggs, A Tyler-Smith

ABSTRACT
An activated dead individual (Ω) with high loads
(5 - 8 units per ml) of the meme-transfer strain
of the Human Reanimation Virus (mtHRV) in its
blood was taught simple tasks by
reward/punishment treatment. Three activated dead
individuals exposed to the blood of Ω
subsequently displayed part of these skills.
Controls exposed to blood from Ω that was virus-
free after passing through .22 μm filters did not
acquire any related skills. There was no change
in activity of bacteria associated with this
virus in either mtHRV-treated specimens or
controls. The authors conclude that mtHRV is able
to affect changes associated with skill-set
acquisition and memory, and suggest that these
changes may be associated with variations in the
base-pair sequence of core RNA of mtHRV.

Attachment #3

To: G. Harman, New World Pharmaceutical Group,
Ramsey Island
Re: Morphology of Bacterial Colonies in the
Nervous System of an Individual of the
Resurrected Dead
R. Hopkin and H.H. Chou

ABSTRACT
An individual infected with blood obtained from
Patient Zero subsequently exhibited high levels
of the mt strain of the Human Reanimation Virus
and high levels of the associated bacterial
species. We present evidence, including CAT
imagery and electron and scanning-electron
microscopy, that bacterial colonies formed
highly-differentiated structures parallel with
the sympathetic and para-sympathetic nervous
systems.

Sound file #1. Extracts from a conversation of 5 minutes 35 seconds duration.

Thomas Moreby: What is it you are you reading?
Alison McReady: Research papers.
TM: He gave them to you?
AM: On a thumb drive full of interesting stuff. You know what it is, Thomas, a thumb drive?
TM: Do not think me a fool. Do you believe that because I am from another century I do not understand yours? Since my rebirth, I see everything and I hear everything and I do not forget. I comprehend what computers are, and how information may be stored in a variety of formats.
AM: *You* store information in an interesting format.
TM: Ah, you have been reading about the so-called virus. I believe it is a better format than any of your computers.
AM: At least they don't kill people. Computers.
TM: But can they bring them back from death, and give them a new and better kind of life? Can they reproduce?
AM: Can *you*?
TM: I may prove it to you, by and by.
AM: And how will you do that?

[break]

TM: I pity you.
AM: Why is that?
TM: Because you are not yet dead. The dead have so many advantages over the living.
AM: Such as?
TM: The dead do not require possessions. They do not love and they do not hate. They are not slaves to passion. They have thrown off those chains. One must work, when one is alive, to earn a living. But you need earn death only once, and then you are free. You are as the lilies of the field. I could set you free, Alison. You are not

yet married. But if you will only put your ring finger in my mouth, I will marry you to death.
AM: Talking of the dead, how did your friends find you? The ones with guns.
TM: Did he ask you to ask me that?
AM: Your friends followed you to my camp.
TM: They are not my friends.
AM: What are they, then?
TM: Like you, they are my subjects.
AM: You're not the king of me.
TM: Did you not listen to what I said, Alison? I am King of the Dead. Everyone now living will in time come to serve me. Where is he now, by the way?
AM: Outside. Keeping watch.
TM: For my subjects.
AM: We'll deal with them if they come for you. Don't worry.
TM: And also for the Colonials. Did he tell you about them as we drove here? I thought I heard the two of you talking.
AM: I think you could hear us perfectly well.
TM: Did he tell you everything, I wonder. What do you think?
AM: I trust him. He trusts me.
TM: I would not trust him. He is a spy. Once an agent of the government, and now a turncoat.
AM: He still serves his country.
TM: Is that what he told you?
AM: He's protecting you.
TM: From the Colonials? There is no need. I *want* to go to the Americas.
AM: Why would you want to go to America?
TM: It seems that I still have blood-ties to the Colonies. Living relatives. The scientists compared my blood with theirs. I would like to meet them.

[break]

TM: When I was yet living, so long ago it seems now like a dream, we had dominion over the Americas. And we will do so once more.
AM: Death has no dominion.

TM: That was written before I ascended to my present position. *I* have dominion, Alison. Am I not risen?

AM: And yet here you are, our prisoner.

TM: The dead are patient. I may be your prisoner now. But even if you keep me prisoner until you die, my captivity will not be a significant fraction of my existence. So you see, all I have to do is wait for you to die, and I will be free. And then, because I am King of the Dead, you will be my subject. You will serve me gladly.

AM: It says here that the fleas you carried were in a state deeper than suspended animation. They were completely dried out, neither dead nor live, but they returned to life when exposed to sufficient moisture. Like brine shrimp larvae.

TM: Ah, my little friends.

AM: They made you what you are.

TM: *I* made me what I am.

AM: They turned you into a monster. The fleas, and the bacteria and viruses they carry.

TM: You think me monstrous?

AM: All of you are monsters. The living dead. Walking horror film clichés.

TM: I know about moving pictures. Also television. The Internet. The dead do not need such things, of course. We are in a pure state of existence that does not need ephemeral distractions.

AM: When you were found near that church you were infested with fleas. They were under your skin.

TM: You cannot understand me while you are alive, Alison. No one living can. But if you join me then everything will become clear. A bite, a kiss . . . You turn away because you are frightened. Or because you are repulsed. How foolish. Soon you will be like me, Alison. It is inevitable. You will be like me, and you will be in *my* dominion. And unless you give me due respect now, I will *punish* you. Is an eternity of punishment worth a moment of impoliteness?

[extracts end]

Dr Alison McReady's journal, 19/06 (continued):
Just come down from the silo where the Spook has been keeping watch. Scoped the countryside, had a conversation out of earshot of our guest. Ralph told me he saw a helicopter, a Black Hawk above Kidlington. Radio traffic suggests troops are doing a grid search and his friends can't safely travel yet. So we're locked down here for now. Luckily, few of the dead are about. None with guns. Ralph saw one a few fields away, being attacked by starlings – it caught and ate one and shambled off.

We're about twenty miles west of Oxford. On a farm at the top of a rise, with views of big fields full of weeds and strips of woodland and an empty stretch of dual carriageway. Not far, I think, from where I first met Ralph. The farm is deserted, of course. Boards over windows and doors, BAD DOG INSIDE spray-painted on the boards over the front door. Ralph drove straight into this big Dutch barn. When we lifted out our guest, a huge tomcat slouched off, pausing at a safe distance to hiss at us before disappearing. Straw bales on one side, what I hope are mice rather than rats rustling in them. A pen with a few dead cattle on the other, little smell despite the summer warmth.

Thomas Moreby said he liked the place. We propped him against the foot of one of the steel beams that hold up the roof. I set up another bag of whole blood. His third. He still looks like a corpse. Ralph gave us space to talk. He had given me a netbook and a thumb drive with files about research on Moreby, and I'd scanned a few while we drove. And he'd told me about the Americans.

The provisional government wants to give Moreby to the Americans in exchange for aid – arms mostly – and a share in anything their research uncovers. My old boss, Prof D, is involved, quelle surprise. Some people, including Ralph, thought rendition of Patient Zero was a bad idea. They extracted Moreby and were taking him to a safe place when they were ambushed. Ralph wouldn't tell me where. Told me I could get out when his backup arrives.

I said I'd think about it. I know this: I think giving Moreby to the Americans is definitely a Bad Idea.

I'm going to try to talk to him again. Just in case I can wheedle any more info out of him. Just in case things go bad.

Sound file #2. Extracts from a conversation of 22 minutes 15 seconds duration.

Thomas Moreby: You are a doctor.
Alison McReady: I was a doctor, then a medical researcher, and now I'm back to being a doctor again.
TM: And your mother was a nurse. It is in your blood, caring for people. The dead do not forget, you see. We remember everything.
AM: Although I'm thinking of taking up research again.
TM: On me?
AM: On your friends.
TM: You can come with me to America. We would have such fun together.
AM: I still don't understand why America, Thomas.
TM: I told you. I wish to visit my relatives.
AM: Right.
TM: Also, it is not an island.

[break]

TM: My parents were poor. My father a birdlimer. Do you know what that is?
AM: Tell me.
TM: He caught birds. Some to eat, but mostly songbirds. Lovely ladies in London loved to listen to linnets and larks.
AM: Were you born in London?
TM: I was born in Stoke Newington. I believe it is in London now but it was not in London then. We rented a two-room cottage held up by a tree of ivy. Every week I had to cut back ivy from the windows.
AM: What did your mother do?
TM: She died.
AM: I'm sorry.
TM: Do not be. I do not remember her. She died in childbirth a year after giving birth to me. And my brother died at the same time. How sad for me. No wonder I wanted to escape death *et cetera*. Or so the psychologists would want me to think.

AM: What about your father?

TM: He was an unpleasant man. A drunk and a lout. He abused me. He abused my sister. He died. And I made my way to London to make my fortune. I was eleven. By and by I became apprentice to Mr Hawksmoor, and then his assistant. We built churches.

AM: Including All-Hallows.

TM: I am not going to give up my secrets to you, Alison. Even if you do put me in mind of a whore I once had.

[break]

AM: It says here that your nervous system has been replaced by bacteria. "A network of highly differentiated colonies of bacteria." Do you find that interesting, Thomas?

TM: The devil-doctors who tortured me thought it interesting. I do not.

AM: Really? It raises all kinds of interesting questions, doesn't it? To begin with, are you still the same person who had a functioning nervous system? Or are you just a mess of bacteria dreaming about him?

TM: He was my larval form. I remember him, but I am not him.

AM: Then you are different.

TM: I am dead, to begin with.

AM: . . .

TM: I know that you stay silent to provoke me, not because you do not understand me. But I will explain anyway. The King has many houses. It does not matter which one he lives in. He is *still* King.

AM: I don't think it's an exact analogy.

TM: Analogies rarely are. Which is why philosophers will never go out of business. I will put it another way. You feel that you inhabit your skull. Yet "you" are merely the product of the activity of certain specialised cells. Does knowing that make a difference to who you think you are?

AM: Do you believe in the soul, Thomas?
TM: Do I believe I am some residue, and that the most important part of me has fled to a better — or in my case, worse — place, like a cockleshell fleeing a sinking ship? No. I will tell you exactly why. I have not been reduced by death. I have been *enlarged*.
AM: You mean you have special powers you didn't have before?
TM: You would like me to tell you about them, would you not?
AM: . . .
TM: I can outwait your silence, Alison.

[break]

TM: I can summon my friends. You know that, of course. But you don't know how. I can do it over a distance, invisibly.
AM: Like a hive mind? A collective consciousness?
TM: I will resort to another analogy. It is a little like your Internet. When we first arrived, I sent out a messenger. And that message will spread until it reaches the right people . . . Even now, The Seven are rising.
AM: You don't shed viruses. They don't stay intact outside of blood. Too big. Bacteria? They don't infect living humans, only those killed by the virus. Can your friends follow gradients of bacteria in the air, Thomas? Like a scent?
TM: I have already said enough.
AM: But you said *a* messenger. Not messengers . . .
TM: . . .

[break]

TM: Listen.
AM: I don't hear anything.
TM: I forget that your senses are not as keen as mine.
AM: Wait. Is that a helicopter?

[extracts end]

Dr Alison McReady's journal, 30/06:
They caught us, but now we're free.

When Ralph saw the Blackhawk and spotted military vehicles on the dual carriageway and troops in the fields he knew we didn't have much time. They'd been tracking the dead – Moreby's "followers" – who were straggling towards the farm from the west. I could hear the noise of the firefights between troops and the dead as I took samples of blood from Moreby. That was why Ralph had wanted me to transfuse him. The researchers had drained him, but the fresh blood I'd given him had quickly acquired his population of special viruses and bacteria.

We put the blood samples in plastic bags and buried them in various spots, in the surrounding fields. We hid the thumb drive and my Blackberry, too. And then we freed Moreby. That took some care: we hoisted him up and the stretcher by a rope around his chest, and Ralph threatened to blow off his kneecaps if he tried anything and kept his pistol on him while I (perched on a stepladder) dealt with the straps and the padlocks and chains that fastened him to the stretcher. Moreby was calm and still throughout. Dangling there in his backwards jacket, asking me to stay with him. Saying, when I told him I couldn't, that he'd see me again. Saying that he had all the time in the world to wait for me, and soon enough I'd enter his kingdom and know everything I needed to know.

I told him that I knew one thing. I knew how he communicated with his friends.

Then Ralph shot at the rope holding him up, and he dropped, and we piled into the Range Rover and got out of there.

The idea was to let the Americans chase Moreby, so we'd have time to escape, and come back for the blood and the rest later. It was our least worst alternative. That, or stay with Moreby and be captured, or try to make a run with him and be chased and captured.

They got us anyway. There wasn't time to get away because Moreby waited for the Americans to arrive. He surrendered.

I won't dwell on the subsequent unpleasantness, dear diary. Already done that at length, in the debriefing.

Prof D. turned up, at the end. Made me an offer. Join his team at NWP, work with the Americans on Moreby in a state-of-the-art lab in something called The Bunker somewhere in the mid-west. He looked genuinely upset when I declined.

I was released into British custody and Ralph's friends intercepted the small convoy taking me to a max security prison. It was no contest. They had a tank.

They'd already rescued Ralph. He had a worse time than me, but I'm taking care of him now. And here we are, in what my Spook would call an undisclosed location. We have Moreby's blood, and all the files on the thumb drive. The work goes on.

I'm going to chase down my idea about how Moreby "talked" to his friends. It has nothing to do with telepathy. I'm sure of that. I think it was his fleas. He was still infected. Or carrying eggs. He let one or two hatch in the lab, and the fleas infected the lab mice or rats or monkeys (they had a whole menagerie, according to Ralph). I like to think it was a monkey. Not killed by the virus, but made slightly smarter by the memes carried by the mt strain, or by the bacteria, or by both. Escaping, giving itself up to and being eaten by what would become the first of the new kind of dead.

And as in the lab, so in the barn. Starting with a mouse or rat bitten by one of Moreby's fleas, or maybe a bird.

We'll find out. We'll find out all his little secrets, and that's how we'll defeat the dead.

I'm with Ralph now. I'm part of the Human Resistance.

From: Evangeline Yates
To: Rob Buhner, Associate Editor, Rolling Stone
Subject: Article on the ADM
Date: 18 June

Here's a partial rough draft of the piece. I haven't worked in the interview quotes yet, so I've included the raw transcriptions of those. Do what you want to with it. My advice, kill it. Just kill the whole thing. Smack the Delete key on the whole bundle, like I'll be doing in a few minutes. I'd like to think that an article, at the very least, could stay justifiably dead in this world.

If you insist on running it, please, please, take my name off it. Credit it to anyone you want. Maybe Alan Smithee, the name film directors use when they've lost control of their movie and they no longer want to be associated with it.

This ADM organization . . . I'm sorry, but I can't stomach the thought of playing any role in promoting it, even by condemnation.

No such thing as bad publicity, remember.

Sorry,
Evvy

FRIGHT CLUB

by
Evangeline Yates

Forget most of what you know from the movies. The first rule of Fright Club doesn't discourage anyone from talking about Fright Club. Talk it up all you want. Everybody involved encourages it.

Instead, the first rule of Fright Club is this: The good guy always wins.

It's easy to tell the good guy at Fright Club. He's the one with glowing skintones who's *not* trying to eat his opponent.

On a humid June night at Louisville, Kentucky's Sprint Convention Center, the top-draw picture of health is Mark Vanderhoven, a one-time mixed martial arts contender familiar to fans of the now-dormant Ultimate Fighting Championship. But before he even squares off against the latest opponent trying to separate him from his face, his hands are full just trying to sort out a cock-up with his entrance music.

Reality check: It's not really called Fright Club. That's just the nickname whose source nobody remembers. Since its inception little more than a month ago, this impromptu fight league has been doing brisk business as Apocalypse Death Match. And while Rule Number One isn't necessarily made to be broken, it's impossible to enforce without blatantly interceding to rescue a fighter should he find himself in trouble. No fighter who wants to command the respect of an audience claims to want to be pulled out of the fire that way.

And, to be honest, the deck is stacked enough as it is.

Still, there's always the possibility of it all going wrong. The *world* has gone wrong, so why should cage matches pitting live fighters against the living dead be immune to catastrophe? It's this uncertainty that its fans find so compelling. It's why they drive dozens, even hundreds, of perilous miles to see this twice-weekly morality play in the flesh. It's why a growing global audience tunes in over the Internet to catch the carnage via streaming video. It's the same show going on outside their windows day and night, but with the ADM, they get something they can't count on in their streets and backyards: the hope of a happy ending, with life triumphing over death, and just enough of a lack of iron-clad assurance to give it suspense.

After all, when a fighter risking his life can't even count on the technical crew to get his ring music right, what guarantee is there, really?

Mark Vanderhoven has a superstitious reliance on the legendary Canadian power trio Rush to pave his way. In the corridor linking the locker room to the arena, word comes down over a compact walkie-talkie in his manager's hand: The sound crew can't find the CD his team has furnished. Any substitutions? Team Vanderhoven halts their progress halfway to the ring. It's Rush or nothing. You have to draw a line somewhere.

A voice crackles over the handset: "We've got somebody's iPod up here with a playlist that has 'Closer to the Heart.'"

Vanderhoven leans toward the handset. "Fuck that shit. It's gotta be 'Working Man.'"

They find another suitably high-energy track that mollifies Vanderhoven, and the ringwalk is back on. In what now passes for everyday circumstances, he looks like an amiable farmboy, with jug ears and an unruly cowlick and a face perpetually on the verge of erupting into a mischievous grin. But now he radiates focus and resolve, a transformation that reveals a side of him that only the dead could miss.

In the arena, the crowd greets him like a conquering hero, and even though the venue is far from filled to capacity, the cheer raises the roof. There's something different about its energy, a purity that could never exist when audiences were divided in their allegiance. Everyone here is his fan. No booing, no detractors, no one hoping to see him taken out in the first round. He fights on the side of every living soul here. Whether it lifts him or is an extra weight to carry is impossible to discern. Given the ability fighters have to block out everything except the opponent in front of them, he may be genuinely unaware of it.

In the ring, waiting for his next opponent, he seems alone and vulnerable to a degree that prizefighters never have before, when the most at stake was pride, a checkbox in the W or L columns, and maybe a championship belt. The history of pre-fight smack-talk is full of guys who said they were willing to die in the ring, but this was an outcome expected of exactly none of them. Here it's a distinct possibility.

So under the lights, he waits, with a champion's good sense not to showboat.

And he is a champion. He's done this nine times before. So when, traditionally, challengers await champions, what's he doing entering the cage first?

That's an easy one: Ravenous carnivores have never been especially good about observing formalities.

The entrance music for the combatant on the side of the dead is always the same. It's somebody's idea of a joke, and a pretty good one: a tune by British band of Goth-punk weirdoes Alien Sex Fiend, called "Now I'm Feeling Zombified." It's fitting, obviously, and morbidly amusing, but it's also functional. The song seems to have no end, exactly the kind of track you need when you have no idea how long it's going to take the wranglers to get a feral wreck of one-time humanity across the floor and into the cage. Like a fighter who's already taken too many shots to the head, they're slow on the uptake and easily distracted.

It takes at least two wranglers to get a zombie across the floor and into the cage. More, sometimes, depending on weight class. Each wrangler wields a staple of animal control agencies: an eight-foot pole looped at the end with a ballistic nylon collar. At minimum, the dead are secured from both sides. Bigger zombies may need a third collar, secured from behind; the biggest of all, a fourth in front. Pushing and pulling, the wranglers move as a unit. Once they've ushered the zombie through the cage doorway, they converge shoulder-to-shoulder, then loosen and remove the collars one at a time, until they can slam the door shut.

And the fight is on.

There's no referee to remind the fighters that they've gone over the rules in the dressing room. No shaking of hands, no touching of gloves. This is no ritual of combat. It's the real thing.

The dead may be aggressive, but they aren't especially crafty. They come straight at you, and this one, with the blue-collar look of an oilfield roustabout gone to ruin, is no different. For Mark Vanderhoven, he's easy to evade, using lateral movement to slip away, skipping sideways around the outside while the zombie constantly turns to find him again. It's more than drawing out the inevitable. It gives Vanderhoven time to track the quirks and particulars of the way this one moves.

And look it in the eye long enough to gauge its degree of cunning.

When Vanderhoven finally strikes, it's sudden. He stops and plants himself, and when his opponent shuffles into range, he throws a brutal low round kick. When it's done right, with the fighter stacking his hips and turning into it, the contact point is with the shin, which becomes the next best thing to a baseball bat. It connects just over the zombie's knee, and the entire leg buckles inward. There's no indication of pain, but its mobility is cut by about 40%.

Of course these fights are controversial. Criticisms abound. Not so long ago, in most sports, an HIV+ diagnosis meant the end of a career and a sharp decline in the number of people willing to compete with the afflicted athlete, especially in combat sports where blood comes with the territory. In comparison, when fighters like Mark Vanderhoven get in the cage with one of the walking dead, the match has exponentially higher odds of turning into a suicide mission, and much faster and surer than from AIDS.

Fighters—the living ones—are quick to brush off the danger. The zombies' mouths are secured with rubber bite blocks, courtesy of area dentists' offices, held in place with elastic straps. They're also outfitted with gloves that cover their fingernails. Because the dead and their clothes come in in less than pristine shape, they've also been hosed down and chemically disinfected, a process not unlike an old-time prison delousing. The fighters are fond of pointing out that the real danger is reserved for the wranglers who first make sure the dead can't bite or scratch. For the record, the prep teams wear chain-mail gloves over latex.

With its mouth unable to close, ropes of drool sway from the zombie's chin and jaw as it continues to stalk. Vanderhoven attacks the same leg one more time, then steps in to pepper his opponent with a flurry of punches. For anyone familiar with sport fighting's usual rhythms, a match like this looks unnervingly wrong. Zombies don't try to block an attack, or dodge out of the way. They're loose enough to roll with any number of punches. They absorb an astonishing amount of punishment. Few things can be as demoralizing to a fighter as seeing his opponent take his best shots and keep on coming, but in the ADM, this is the norm.

The zombie is all lunges and attempts to grab, and most of the time Vanderhoven finds it easy enough to spin and slip from its grasp. Not always, though. In one queasy exchange, it manages to hold on tight enough that Vanderhoven pulls it along for the ride, and only the leverage of a palm-heel strike to its chin forces them apart. A minute later, it lands a quick backhand across his face that sends him to the mat. He rolls to the side a couple of times, putting himself off the line of attack, and when he pops up to his feet, he needs another few moments to clear his head.

Again, the distinctions from orthodox prizefighting become obvious. Unlike knockdowns in boxing, there's no going to a neutral corner and waiting out a ten-count. And eventually the bell between rounds becomes conspicuous in its absence. There *are* no rounds.

Rule Number Seven of *Fight Club*: Fights will go on as long as they have to.

With two more round kicks to the legs, Vanderhoven drops his opponent to the mat, then follows it there. He plants a knee on its chest, then throws the other leg across the zombie's neck to clamp its head in place. He grabs its near arm, locking the back of its hand to his breastbone as he falls back and straightens his bent leg over the zombie's chest. He holds the captive hand tight while pushing up with his hips. It's a common submission technique called an armbar. Its usual goal is to motivate your opponent to surrender by forcing the elbow opposite the way it's supposed to go. A fighter who doesn't tap has months of physical therapy to look forward to.

Vanderhoven shows why. He doesn't wait for a tap-out. Surrender will never come. Instead, he goes straight for the break.

Even with an opponent that's universally feared and loathed, it's an excruciating moment when the elbow turns inside out with an audible snap. The zombie may feel no pain, but it plainly registers that something is wrong. It batters at Vanderhoven's leg, and a moment later, Mark has reversed his position to seize the other arm and give it the same treatment.

Within another two or three minutes, he's applied a similar technique, called a kneebar, to each leg. He's reduced his opponent to a limp puppet that can only crab around after him on broken knees and elbows. It's a Mark Vanderhoven trademark, and it's clearly exhausting work.

For a finale, like a victorious matador finishing off a worthy bull, he's given the honor of putting a spike through the head of the opponent that can no longer stand to face him. After a few exchanges with the ring announcer, he departs to a cacophony of cheers.

In another few days, there will be another opponent like the one he's just bested. And another after that. There's no fighting your way to the top of your division in this league. Here, there's always another challenger. They might as well be tearing the door off the hinges to get in. Even to a spectator, there's something dispiriting about that.

While Mark Vanderhoven's entrance song turned into a compromise, there was a glimmer of serendipity in it that could make it worth considering as a permanent fixture at his future matches:

Some lyric about learning that we're only immortal for a limited time.

If the ADM had to arise anywhere, Louisville, Kentucky, is as likely a place as any. Parked on a bend in the Ohio River, 378 miles upstream of the Mississippi, in the days of flatboats and paddle-wheel steamers, Louisville became a crucial inland port for a young nation striving to take shape out of the chaos of frontier life, revolution, and industrialization. Its earliest residents lived in a network of forts, whose log palisades were all that stood between them and the Indians and British soldiers who'd just as soon have seen them dead.

Human flesh as a commodity goes way back here, too. Louisville was perfectly situated as a staging area for rounding up surplus slaves from the Upper South and shipping them to the cotton fields of the Deep South. The expression "sold down the river" . . .? This is where it originated.

Generations later, boxing legend Muhammad Ali came from here, as did the premier gonzo journalist, Hunter S. Thompson, who coined the prescient phrase, "When the going gets weird, the weird turn pro."

Mix all that with a few zombies and stir, and the ADM seems an inevitability.

But will it last? *Can* it last?

Obviously, that comes down to nothing less than the survival of humanity. Yet strangely enough, it's not hard to see something hopeful in the ADM, and uniquely American: the unkillable impulse to make money and meaning out of circumstances that no one wishes had transpired. Not a single fighter steps into the cage expecting anything other than to walk out alive and healthy again, to see tomorrow, and most do.

But not all.

Only the naïve would think this isn't going on elsewhere. While they may lack the promotional muscle and Internet reach of the ADM, you can find similar spectacles occurring regularly in at least a dozen places across the country. One of them, held in Omaha, Nebraska, became notorious this past week for the gruesome in-ring death of a young mixed martial artist named Anthony Chappell. It wasn't broadcast to an audience, but it should surprise no one that his death was captured on cell phone video.

Of course it's tragic. Nobody disputes that. But the prevailing stoic reaction among nearly everybody connected with the ADM is that Anthony Chappell knew what he was signing on for long before he stepped into the cage.

Even if it's all consenting adults among the pugilists who've made an organized sport out of fighting the dead, there's also the don't-try-this-at-home factor. Parents groups, especially, have been quick to condemn the ADM because even though it's the end of the world as we know it, kids are no less prone to doing incredibly stupid things.

Backyard ADM tournaments are this year's rite of passage for the young, dumb, and hormonally addled. Can you smell the lawsuits cooking? Leading the pack is a wrongful death suit filed by the families of four teenage boys in Madison, Wisconsin, who, a few weeks ago, rounded up a terminally deceased neighbor with the intention of . . . well, you know. Not just any zombie would do, however. They held out for the fattest one they could find, on the assumption that it wouldn't move very fast. Give them two points for thinking of safety. Then deduct four for their failure to recall that temperatures and decomposition can result in a buildup of gasses that inflate a corpse from within until it's like a pressurized bomb. It didn't survive the first front kick to the midsection.

But, as has forever been pointed out, in America anybody can sue anybody for anything. Filing the lawsuit is one thing, and collecting on it another. With the judicial system in disarray, to put it mildly, and what's left of sheriff's departments busy with things more life-and-death than serving summonses, claimants may have an epic wait for their day in court.

It goes higher. ADM President Noah Carver keeps hearing rumors about how what's left of the federal government wants to shut down his growing operation, although the threats never actually seem to amount to anything. Which means they're either gossip, or the empty bluster of a government that has its hands full simply trying to establish order and keep people alive rather than worry about enforcing the hardline on a disagreement about mere bad taste.

TRANSCRIPT OF INTERVIEW WITH MARK VANDERHOVEN:

Evangeline Yates: Excuse the cliché, but you're not from around here, are you?

Mark Vanderhoven: No, I grew up in Washington. Bellingham. I ended up fighting out of Bettendorf, Iowa. With almost a year in-between down in Brazil, working on my ground game.

EY: You were in the UFC.

MV: Yeah, for about five minutes.

EY: Oh come on, more than that. You were on that last season of *The Ultimate Fighter.*

MV: Yeah. I didn't win, but you don't necessarily have to be the last man standing to get through the doors.

EY: So this, the ADM, does this seem like a few rungs down the ladder to you?

MV: Oh yeah, more than a few rungs. It's the whole ladder. But it was never about the money, if that's what you're getting at. The thing you learn quick about the UFC is, unless you're one of the top guys, what UFC really stands for is You Fight Cheap.

EY: Actually, it wasn't the money I was getting at. More the caliber of opponents, let's call it.

MV: It is what it is. They are what they are. It's weird, though. This is the first time that hate, real hatred, has entered into it. I've never hated my opponents before. A lot of the time, they're even guys you like. Sometimes you have to fight friends. That's part of the business. Other times, maybe you don't like the guy, maybe you think he's a douche, but you get over it. If you hit each other long enough, it clears the air. Whatever your differences, you've still got this one basis for respect in common. And sometimes, if a fight turns into a real ordeal, you and your opponent see more into each other than anyone else does, or ever gets to. "Full-spectrum humanity" is how one of my trainers used to put it. But these zombies, these Infected, what do they see? A buffet sign? And if there's anything to see in them, I haven't found it.

EY: You've heard the arguments, haven't you? That if you're keeping them from biting or scratching, it's not really a fair fight. And if it's not a fair fight, then it's just a drawn-out execution staged for entertainment.

MV: Fucking zombie-lovers, man, can you believe it? Doesn't matter how low a life-form something is, it's gonna have its advocacy groups. [sighs] Where do I even begin? Okay, how about this: I don't get to bite and scratch, so why should they? Plus if I bite you, at worst you'll need a tetanus shot. One of them gets its choppers into me, that's it.

EY: Which is possible. The Anthony Chappell death showed that it's possible for things to go totally wrong in there, despite all the precautions. Does that weigh on you at all?

MV: Uhhh . . . next question.

EY: You don't even want to touch that one? That's the elephant in the room.

MV: What do you want me to say? Okay, it can happen, but you can't let a thing like that linger in the back of your mind. You'll start making mistakes when it matters most. So me, and the rest of the guys, we don't talk about it. Not like it's real. So next question.

EY: Next argument against, then. That the dead aren't even trained fighters.

MV: No, but they're natural predators. Even without their teeth and nails, they've got advantages normal, trained, living fighters don't have. With one of the deadheads, on average I'm having to work harder than I did in at least half of my regular MMA fights. A lot of my tools are gone, out the window. Zombies, they don't feel pain, so they're not afraid of getting hit. They don't tap out. I can't choke them out. You can knock them out, but Jesus God it's hard to do. You know the big thing they've got on their side? Stamina. They don't get tired. Or discouraged. They just keep coming. You know the old rope-a-dope strategy, from boxing? You lay back on the ropes and cover up while the other guy pounds on you long enough to wear himself out, and he's got nothing left when you slip out and go after him? Well, they're the ultimate rope-a-dopers. And to top it all off, they're just plain stronger. Have you heard that?

EY: Not from anywhere I'd consider a credible source.

MV: I understand the skepticism. I mean, look at them, right? They're a mess. Stand them next to someone who keeps in shape, and the claim looks even more ridiculous. You wouldn't think there's any comparison. But it's not what's on the surface that matters. It's because they're fucked up all the way through that they're stronger. They're not held back by the checks and balances that normal people are subject to.

EY: Checks and balances?

MV: There's more potential strength in the human body than ever gets tapped. Part of the reason why goes back to the pain thing. If you or I hit something or grab onto something hard enough, it starts to hurt. So we back off. They don't. The other thing is, you know that saying about how for every action there's an equal and opposite reaction?

EY: Sure.

MV: That's true with muscle movement. We've got enough potential muscular strength to dislocate our own joints and break our own bones, but our nervous system overrides it. Let's say I'm doing bicep curls with dumbbells. I'm not just fighting the weight. I'm also fighting the fact that my triceps, on the other side of my arms, are pulling in the opposite direction. When athletes get stronger, it's not always because we're adding muscle bulk. Sometimes you don't want to add bulk. There are wiry guys that are freaky strong. Skinny girls that can deadlift three times their own bodyweight. That's not bulk. It's their nervous systems. They've overridden the override. Partially. You'll hear about it happening to regular people too, sometimes. You know, the woman who lifts the car off her kid. They can't repeat it, but it happens in the moment. Well, the zombies are in that place all the time. What's left of their nervous system doesn't care about holding them back. They're basically eating machines that'll rip themselves apart trying to get to you.

EY: That's an education. I never heard the rationale behind the strength claims.

MV: Normal people don't think about those things. Most people don't even know how their own bodies work. You have to talk to trainers, fighters, like that, to get the straight shit.

EY: Even if they are stronger, another argument against the ADM is that the dead are also somebody's family. Or they were. Somebody's father, brother, son. There are people who say that regardless of what's become of them, they should be dispatched as quickly and humanely as possible. That they shouldn't be exploited this way.

MV: If they want me to stop, I'll stop, just as soon as the geeks stop trying to exploit my tender vittles.

EY: What made you want to do this? You had a promising fight career underway with the UFC, and it's possible it could've continued in some form. Why walk away from it for what some are calling a freakshow?

MV: In the early days they called the UFC a freakshow too.

EY: True, but I don't think there's anybody who wants the zombie apocalypse to last long enough for this to become respectable.

MV: You got me there. Okay. Um. You'll laugh. Or think it's stupid.

EY: I promise I won't.

MV: It's like, you know how after 9/11, you had this flood of people enlisting in the military, because they wanted to go fight? For me, that's what it was like. Saw all that shit starting to go down in England, figuring it was only a matter of time before it hopped the ocean. Fighter by nature, by trade, I had to do something. The question was what. Picking up a gun, being part of a kill squad, that's the default move. But was that really going to be the best use of my talents? I decided no, it wasn't. I got wind of this and knew right away this was it. I'd rather serve by showing people that it's possible to stand face-to-face with these things and come out alive.

EY: Except most people aren't going to be facing the dead already outfitted with bite blocks and gloves.

MV: No, but they probably will be facing them with more than a pair of four-ounce MMA gloves.

EY: Most people won't be facing them one-on-one, either.

MV: Well, if it was a perfect world, we wouldn't have zombies in the first place, would we?

It's no different than with the beheading videos that became one more propaganda tool of 21st century warfare: As long as you know where to look online, it isn't difficult to find the cell phone video of Anthony Chappell's death.

Like most videos of its kind, its cold, distant, documentarian gaze seems to diminish the drama of the event. We've been trained by movies and TV to associate tragedy with camera tricks and editing, and music cues to make sure we know to be horrified or sad. Reality seems so much more anticlimactic.

At the center of the grainy, handheld video is a lithe young black man so light on his feet he looks as if he could bound out of the cage at the first sign of trouble. He appears confident without being careless, his performance a textbook example of that old boxing maxim: stick and move, stick and move. The woman who shot the video seems so assured of another victory over the dead that her attention starts to wander, along with her viewfinder. The frame increasingly whips to the left as she turns to talk to someone.

That all changes at just over the six-minute mark.

The explanation out of the Omaha club that hosted Anthony Chappell's death is that the elastic band holding the bite blocks in the zombie's mouth broke, or was dislodged. This makes sense. For a few unbearable moments, it's apparent that Chappell knows something is wrong before anyone else does. Until now, he's only evaded—he hasn't run. He hasn't panicked.

Watching, it's hard not to reach the conclusion that he didn't have to die. There's a margin of thirty-odd seconds in which things could've turned out differently. Someone could've fired a single bullet. Someone could've opened the cage door. No one did.

Fighters lead with their left or their right. The dead lead with their teeth.

The voice behind the camera blurts, with flat disbelief, "Ohmy*god*."

In movies, even the most harrowing, there's one thing they never get right: the sound of a scream of mortality. You could do nothing but watch films the rest of your life and never once hear the kind of sounds that come from a man actually having his head sawn from his neck, or being partially devoured in front of spectators. It isn't the actors' fault that they can't hit that pitch and timbre. Maybe no actor is capable of going to the place that sounds like that originate from.

In front of more than 200 paying spectators, and anyone else who wants to watch post-mortem, Anthony Chappell went to that place.

The peculiar thing about such a public death is that nobody seems to know what became of his body.

TRANSCRIPT OF INTERVIEW WITH ADM PRESIDENT NOAH CARVER:

Noah Carver: You don't see many women writing about things like mixed martial arts. Least of all our take on it.

Evangeline Yates: My brothers were MMA fans since Royce Gracie had hair.

NC: That explains a lot.

EY: Maybe you'd attract more women if you'd let them fight in the cage. It's not like you can't find women who want to do it. They're out there. They're practically on your doorstep.

NC: What, has Mia Mayhem been chatting you up? The audience isn't ready for that. For her. Trust me. They take their chances that a thing like Anthony Chappell isn't going to happen very often. If it does, they'll deal, as long as it's a dude. But if they see it happen to some tough little America's Sweetheart type, forget it, it's all over.

EY: The plaque you have on the wall over there. [Note: "Sport has only one task: to strengthen the character of the people, imbuing it with the fighting spirit and steadfast camaraderie necessary in the struggle for its existence."] It looks like a quotation, but it's unattributed.

NC: It's also edited. When I had that plaque made, I left out a couple words. Well, one word, two times. German. It's actually German sport, and the German people.

EY: It wasn't Hitler, was it?

NC: Joseph Goebbels. Hitler's Minister of Propaganda. Close enough.

EY: I can see why you edited it. So why are you even telling me?

NC: Because Google still works, most of the time. I saw you reading it, and it looked like you might've been copying it down. I knew you'd find out soon enough, and if it wasn't me that told you, then it would look like I had something to hide, when I don't.

EY: Why hang it up there at all?

NC: Because to me, the reminder is more important than whoever might get offended.

EY: And nobody asks about where it came from?

NC: If somebody's inquisitive enough to ask about it, they're usually the ones who get why it's up there. The ones who don't get it, they're not curious enough to ask.

EY: Well, it does put us, the living . . . I mean, it puts us—

NC: Uncomfortably on the side of the Nazis? So what? It's not a nationalistic thing, it's a human thing. We're in the same position as Germany was in the 1930s, which is when this quote came from. They'd been crushed and humiliated by World War I, spent the 1920s recovering, and in the early 1930s the International

Olympic Committee decided to make Berlin the host city for the 1936 Olympics. It was their welcome back to the world, and they had a lot to prove. They had their Aryan supremacy to prove. On a smaller scale, they had just as much of a vested interest in Max Schmeling, the boxer, especially when he fought guys like Max Baer, who had a Jewish dad, and Joe Louis, who was black. And the '36 Olympics, the biggest star there, our biggest star, was Jesse Owens. Black. To the Germans, these guys were two steps away from jungle savages, so if you can't beat them, what does that say about you, about your supposed superiority?

EY: But that was all bullshit.

NC: Of course you and I know that now. Then again, the typical rotten meatbags shambling down your average Main Street these days, do you feel superior to them?

EY: That's different.

NC: Yeah? Tell it to them. Listen, if they're the ones who get to decide what history is in the future, then how do you think they're going to view us? Us, who are trying to exterminate them at every turn, by any means possible? And rightfully so, in my opinion. So if that means I've got to get my inner Nazi on, so people who look and smell like you and me still have our place in the world a year from now, ten years from now, a thousand years from now, then so be it.

EY: Are they even capable of a sense of history? Or a need to preserve it?

NC: I have no idea. I wouldn't have thought so at first. Now? Nothing would surprise me. There are rumors about experiments . . . Did you see the movie with Will Smith, *I Am Legend*?

EY: No.

NC: Don't bother. Read the book, instead. Yeah, it's an old book, turns out. It's been filmed a few times, but nobody's had the balls to film it the way it was written. Especially the end, which is when the title finally makes sense. The main character, Neville, he's the last man in a world of vampires. It's been his mission to destroy them. Finally they catch him, and execute him, they're burning him alive. As he's on the pyre, he's looking out at the crowd, and he finally sees the terror they've always had of him. Imagine that. They, in their millions, are afraid of him. He realizes it doesn't matter that they've won, not to them. The memory of him is going to haunt them forever. He's going to be the bogeyman of their myths. That's Neville's last realization.

EY: Cold comfort.

NC: Yeah. And I don't want to be the bogeyman. I want to be the one still telling the stories to my kids at night.

EY: What would you tell your kids if they asked why you're willing to risk the lives of your fighters by sending them into the cage with something that could kill them even if they win, should they get infected?

NC: What's the alternative? Are you getting at the protective suit thing?

EY: It's been suggested as a way to make the sport safer for the fighters.

NC: Nobody wants to see that. Who'd pay to see that? You watch a fight, you want to see a guy going in there with shorts, his gloves, a knee-wrap if he needs it, and that's it. Anything else just gets in the way.

EY: Of the contagion, yes, wouldn't that be the idea?

NC: Whether a fighter's winning or losing or exhausted or smells blood, you need to see his face. It tells you everything. You can't see any of that if he's wrapped up like some fucking ninja. It could be anybody in there. And believe me, fighters have enough ego that they want people to see who they are.

EY: Regardless of the danger.

NC: Especially because of the danger. It's like . . . like porn. You don't really want to see people fucking with rubbers on. You'd rather see them going at it bareback.

EY: I don't watch porn, myself.

NC: You like to watch sport fighting, though, don't you? Some people don't hesitate to label any depiction of violence pornography. That goes double for the real thing.

EY: This wasn't something I'd been planning on asking, but I've heard a rumor.

NC: It wouldn't be the fight game without rumors. About what?

EY: That a couple of nights ago, a delivery truck showed up here all the way from Nebraska. With the body of Anthony Chappell. Except, you know, no one's just a body anymore.

NC: [6-second pause] Where did you hear that?

EY: People talk. I don't remember.

NC: Bullshit you don't. Okay, interview's over.

EY: If you told me about the Goebbels quote because, if you hadn't, it would've looked like you had something to hide, what do you think stopping the interview now looks like?

NC: I don't have anything to hide. There's a big difference between having something to hide, and something that's privileged business information. You don't see that? Can't you see that?

Forget the cage—the *real* action happens out in the field. So say the zombie wranglers who make sure that the cage has a steady supply of cannon fodder for the fighters. They have a point. One ride-along with them should be enough to convince anyone that this crew has the misfortune of being one apocalypse too late for their own reality show. In a medium that could make stars out of Arctic fisherman and truck drivers traversing icy roads, all the elements are there. Call it *The Rottenest Catch*, or *Road Kill Truckers*. They just need a camera crew.

The non-human star of the show would undoubtedly be Petunia. This is the crew's name for their former power company utility truck, customized into a kind of armored personnel carrier: Caged-over windshield and side windows. Reinforced side panels laced with barbed wire. Fenders beefed up into battering rams. Three mounted machine guns and a rack of rifles, shotguns, smoke grenades, and whatever else the crew can scrounge. The firepower is mostly there to thin the herd around the specimen they're after. For that, the key feature is the truck's cherry-picker, a hydraulic arm with a man-size bucket at the end. What used to hoist repair personnel up to fix troublesome transformers now swings out like a boom, to put lead wrangler Big Jake Holloway mere feet away from their quarry. Once he's up close and personal, Holloway closes the distance with an even heavier-duty version of the pole-and-collar contraption used to bring the zombies to the cage.

"It's not as easy as it sounds," says Mia Mayhew, the spotter. She has an uncanny knack for assessing prime fighting stock through a pair of binoculars. "The kind of deadheads we want, it's not like they just stand still for it."

Mia is the sole member of the crew who dreams of graduating from Petunia and becoming a cage fighter herself someday, just as soon as the ADM consents to admitting female combatants. A beguiling mix of dimples, tattoos, and a rock bottom body fat percentage, she has her *nom de guerre* ready to roll: Mia Mayhem.

Petunia starts her appointed rounds two or three days before an exhibition, a mutant mash-up of safari, military excursion, and old-fashioned autumn hayride. The crew of six—two in the cab, four in the back—bounces along with the same madcap enthusiasm that boaters feel for water choppy enough to give all aboard a steady drip-feed of adrenaline. As the truck patrols the streets, back-alleys, parks, and parking lots of Louisville, Mia pans-and-scans for potential candidates while everyone else watches for trouble. There's no need to be quiet about any of it. On this hunt, it's impossible to scare away the game. Noise draws them.

The wranglers reject a lot of what they encounter in the wild. They can afford to be picky, because, frankly, demand remains stable while supply is only getting better. The ADM's official policy discourages them from taking potshots at the wretched refuse, to avoid the possibility of collateral damage to the living, but the crew can't resist getting in some marksmanship practice now and then.

For Jake Holloway, it's a simple matter of economics: "Paper targets cost money. The dead don't cost shit."

After the first futile ninety minutes of their latest hunt, Mia spots a keeper outside a liquor store in an east Louisville strip mall. She trades her binoculars for a hunting rifle and helps isolate their deadhead of the hour: two shots, two kills. As the wheelman sends Petunia careening down the street and into the parking lot, Jake Holloway scrambles into the cherry-picker, like a lookout in the crow's-nest of a pirate ship. To lure the zombie closer, the buxom MILF-type in the passenger seat, who doubles as navigator, flashes from the cab window with the noisy zeal of a Mardi Gras reveler after more beads. Apparently it takes more than death to stop most men from lunging after the nearest pair of bodacious ta-tas.

With a whine of hydraulics, the cherry-picker swoops out near their target. Big Jake levers his pole closer and drops the collar over the zombie's head and cinches tight. Of course it fights. They wouldn't want one that didn't. Once Jake gives the signal that he's secured the pole in a makeshift oar-lock mounted on the rim of the bucket, the fellow manning the control panel levers the cherry-picker up and away, leaving the ADM's newest fighter dangling and kicking in mid-air, by the neck, for several vulnerable moments.

The question is inescapable: Have they ever had one come apart on them, like a botched hanging? Here's a hint: Do a YouTube search for "Zombie pops his top."

Fortunately, this one maintains structural integrity, and seems little the worse for wear while the cherry-picker swings around to position the bucket over the open top of the modified garbage truck that follows like a loyal dog. Petunia is continually shadowed by this second truck, with its own two-man crew. Pity them. There's no glory in garbage detail. Peering through their windshield at Petunia, they look a bit like boys forced into violin lessons, staring out at their friends playing baseball. As Jake Holloway opens the noose and lets the zombie drop into its mobile prison, the duo can barely even see what's going on.

It isn't all action out here. Most of the reality behind even an imaginary reality show is never seen—it's just people waiting for something to happen. Aboard Petunia, there's a lot of downtime, a lot of cruising, a lot of heading off to check out reported clusters of living dead that could turn a single stop into a trip to Wal-Mart.

After she's helped nab the liquor store zombie, Mia settles into her seat and passes the drive time by practicing her fighter's hand-wrapping technique, encasing each hand in 108 inches of stretchy cloth. Over and over and over again.

"You can never get this down too perfect," she explains.

Why does she want to get it down at all? If Mark Vanderhoven joined up with the ADM driven by a need to inspire, what is it that ignites Mia Mayhew's desire to become Mia Mayhem?

She glances around to see if any of the rest of the crew is paying attention, then leans close and keeps her voice low.

"I'd never tell this to a guy reporter," she says. "The way things are headed, how long's it going to be before a bunch of these would-be alpha males get together and decide to put all us surviving breeders into quarantine?"

She really thinks that could happen?

"Absolutely. For the good of the human race, is how they'll try to sell it. 'Lay back and spread your legs for the future.' That's exactly the kind of cage I don't want. I'd rather take my chances with the other. Maybe that'll make some of these guys think twice before trying to fuck with me."

Next stop is a community baseball field which, rumor has it, pings the homing instincts of several males who, despite being dead, might still be considered physically fitter than most pre-apocalypse videogame-addicted teens. Petunia and crew are in luck—they count eight, and Mia targets an imposing bruiser who could've wandered in from the nearest football field. The crew loves open fields: easy access, easy exit, and nothing but unobstructed, long-range vision.

At first their well-honed routine goes like clockwork. Right up until the point that Big Jake locks down the pole and the cherry-picker hoists the zombie off his feet. It could have played the bad-guy half in the most riveting heavyweight match-up the ADM has put on yet, but we'll never know. It never takes its eyes off Jake, an unnerving degree of focus from a dead man, then whips out a knife that might impress even "Crocodile" Dundee. Finally, a display of that fabled strength of the dead: With a roar, it slices through the thick nylon collar before the cherry-picker is halfway to the garbage truck, and drops back onto home turf.

Then stands its ground.

It's a surreal moment, nothing and no one moving, eight pairs of living eyes locked in mutual loathing with one dead pair. Does the zombie realize there's no point in running? It certainly seems to, which lends its challenge and defiance a strange kind of doomed poignancy. Eventually, though, gunfire will break any spell.

When asked if they've ever seen anything like this before, the crew mutters, mumbles, and demurs, until finally admitting that, yes, it's happened a time or three. That, one way or another, a surefire capture has slipped the noose. All in the past two weeks.

"There's a rumor floating around that they're getting smarter," Mia Mayhew says. "From what I can see, it's not just a rumor. They really are. And not just weird exceptions anymore, either, but as a rule. And it's happening fast. Somebody back at base said it was like the hundredth monkey effect."

For the uninitiated, this is the theory that postulates an almost supernatural spread of learned intelligence through a population, after a critical mass of its members has gained particular knowledge. The classic example: Once enough monkeys on one island learn how to wash dirt from their food, this knowledge is picked up by monkeys on the surrounding islands.

"Scary, huh?" Mia asks, and perfects her hand-wrap for perhaps.the hundredth time that afternoon. "One day they're going to really start working together. One day they're going to be waiting for us out here."

TRANSCRIPT OF INTERVIEW WITH ANTHONY CHAPPELL:

Evangeline Yates: Can you hear me? [24 seconds elapse] Anthony, do you understand anything I'm saying? [33 seconds elapse, broken by the sound of shuffling] Anthony, I don't have much time, I'm not supposed to be in here, I'm not even supposed to know about you, I don't think, so if you can understand me . . . [16 seconds elapse] What, does nothing compute in that three-pound lump of tofu up there rotting between your ears? [12 seconds elapse, then eye contact]
Anthony Chappell: If you don't work . . . you don't eat. [6 seconds elapse] If you don't work . . . you don't eat. [repeated 19 times before recorder turned off]

It's being billed as the biggest fight in the history of the ADM. That's a very short history, admittedly, but history isn't what it used to be, and you have to grab your hype wherever you can find it.

What puffs their chests in pride is the first official cage fight between a living professional fighter and a semi-pro dead one. In skill levels, at least, Mark Vanderhoven and Anthony Chappell make the most evenly matched pair of combatants that the ADM's audience has seen yet.

"It was inevitable. This was going to happen sooner or later. It was just a matter of time," ADM president Noah Carver said at the press conference. "It's where the sport was headed all along. The sport's always evolving. We're just fortunate enough to be the ones bringing this to you first."

It's been a week since Mark Vanderhoven's entrance was plagued by misplaced music, and this time he's left nothing to chance. He makes his way to the cage without hitch or glitch, before the biggest crowd that Louisville's Sprint Convention Center has entertained in the post-apocalyptic era. He's still the favorite, the reigning champion, the conquering hero on the side of anybody and everybody with a pulse, and the greeting he receives confirms it.

Mostly.

What a difference seven days make. He's never heard boos before. He's never had to wait in the cage and listen to cheers for an opponent that takes three wranglers to bring in. Few boos, and few cheers, but what Anthony Chappell's minority of fans lack in numbers, they make up for in volume. Fighters learn early on to ignore the hubbub of fickle crowds, but still, this is something new. There are now spectators who are openly rooting for a popular fighter, as alive as they are, to lose to a corpse.

That has to sting a little, and motivate a lot. And it's hard to shake the feeling that the display is one more sign of the capsizing of the natural order.

Welcome to Fright Club, version 2.0.

But like so many nights before, once the door is closed, Vanderhoven leaves everything else outside the cage and focuses exclusively on what's in front of him. This time, the fighter he faces appears to try to figure him out as much as Mark tries to get a sense of him. The stalking is more than mindless hunger. There may be a strategy here, and calculation. Maybe it's body memory, maybe it's instinct, or maybe it's evolution, but Anthony Chappell moves better than any dead fighter that Mark Vanderhoven has faced yet. When Mark throws a combination of punches, Anthony slips and evades. When Mark feints a left kick and instead snaps that murderous roundhouse right toward a knee, Anthony raises his shin to block.

And when Chappell lands a flurry of his own, Mark Vanderhoven clearly feels them

It's nearly ten minutes into a series of grueling clashes and separations before Mark, visibly tiring, gets a successful takedown and goes to work in his trademark style. His armbar is still a thing of brute force beauty, and breaks Chappell's left into a new configuration with such devastating power that it splits the skin across what used to be the inside of his elbow. Quickly, Mark disengages and rolls off to gather himself again, catch his breath, and plan the next assault.

The ADM has tried to make the sport safe, remember, with bite blocks to keep the dead from snapping, and full gloves to keep them from scratching. It's as if all their sharp edges have been filed away.

Is it instinct, or evolution, that one would finally improvise, and make new sharp edges? Is that inevitable too? Is this where the sport has been headed all along?

It's at least where the sport heads tonight.

When the fighter that was once Anthony Chappell straggles to his feet again, he stands still for a few moments, seeming to assess his limb as it flops and dangles from his shattered elbow. Without further hesitation, his gaze never once leaving Mark Vanderhoven, he torques the break against the cage fencing. The move coaxes ripples of confusion from the crowd, then waves of revulsion as the break worsens, skin and muscle shredding and peeling back to bare a jagged stub of bone.

Then, once more, he leads with his left.

Defensive cuts, forensics experts call them: slashes across someone's hands and forearms as they try to protect themselves from an attacker's blade. It's nearly always in vain, just postponing the inevitable. But Mark Vanderhoven sustains a lot of them before he goes down.

And while the bite blocks hold, Anthony Chappell still has his tongue, and one good hand.

The crowd surges to its feet, even the most vocal of Chappell's fans drowned out by the tsunami of protest and outrage. They think this isn't what they've paid for, when in fact that's exactly what it is. Some of them storm for the exits, others storm the cage, a brief but intense brawl breaking out between spectators and security guards, and while it rages, Anthony Chappell moves between his dying opponent and the cage door. He stays there crouching, poised and ready, and only God, if He's still watching at all, knows what the remnants of Anthony's mind make of what his unblinking eyes show him.

It looks for all the world like he's defending a fallen brother. It's a greater display of solidarity than anything going on outside the cage.

The ADM began, they say, as a ritual for the living to prove our superiority over the dead. But maybe the dead don't see it that way. Maybe the dead have as much or more of their own to prove.

As for Mark Vanderhoven, perhaps mourning is premature.

There can be no doubt that he'll be back.

Good fighters always learn more from their losses than from their victories, and come back stronger the next time.

From: Evangeline Yates
To: Rob Buhner, Associate Editor, Rolling Stone
Subject: One last thing re: the ADM
Date: 20 June

I don't know why it took an extra couple of days for me to realize this.
PTSD—post-traumatic stress disorder—gets my vote.

But they're keeping the fighters, right? Keeping the ones who die in the
cage. That's a given. Obviously it explains why Anthony Chappell
showed up in Louisville. It also explains why we don't see anybody
coming in to finish him off in Omaha, in that amateur video when he
first got turned. But why DIDN'T anybody come in to finish him?
Wouldn't you think that would be a contingency, just in case? So was
keeping these poor guys around to fight another day the grand plan all
along? If so, who's really behind it?

The even bigger question: What are they eating? If they're keeping the
fighters, they'll have to feed them. "If you don't work, you don't eat." So
what ARE they eating, where are they getting it, and most importantly
. . . who's supplying it?

"People say I should be banned. [waves his arms around and adopts high-pitched effete voice] 'Oh, hey, he shouldn't say that about the Pope, man.' And, you know, that's the [BEEP]ing American Way, man. You don't like what some [BEEP]er says then just go ahead and ban him. Me, somebody steps outta line – and I don't care diddly who the [BEEP] they are – someone steps outta line and I'll take him down, man: Jews, blacks, Indians, Catholics, Mormons, gays . . . I don't give a rat's [BEEP], man. They talk [BEEP] then they get wiped, leastways they do by Mrs Maughmstein's little boy."

—Bernie Maughmstein promoting his autobiography, *You Know What I'm Saying?* (Running Press 2012, $25.99) to Tamsel Fadal on WPIX, June 17, 2012.

[Voice Mail of Private Jolene Lindbloom, MIA]

"Jo, it's Raquelle. I'm leaving this so you'll know—*OK, I'm coming, gimme a minute!*—The soldiers say you already know, I'm not sure I believe them. Like, the right way, the wrong way, and the Army way? They showed up about ten minutes ago and told me to pack fast, I'm being evacuated. Except they just came in a van and they're not evacuating anyone else, just me. Only the families of soldiers in the field, they said, for their own protection. Protection against what, I asked; terrorist reprisals, they said. It sounds fishy to me—*I said, OK, I'm coming, gimme a minute!*—I'm taking the iPad so I can leave messages in the Cloud for you. Look in the Cloud, OK? Password is your old cat's name and your old address. Remember that!"

"*[unintelligible)]* . . . or so help me, ma'am, I will pick you up and carry you! *Now!*"

"All right, all right. The name's 'Rocky' LaFortune soldier—who the hell are you calling ma'am? I oughta . . . *[fades]*."

[distant sound of door slamming, tape ends.]

[Text Document: ro.lf@[redacted] uploaded to the Cloud]

Dearest Jo,

They won't tell us anything about the weird light in the sky. We saw it yesterday, a week after we got here in, god help me, Shamong, New Jersey. (I've lived most of my life in either this state or New York and I never knew there was a freaking Shamong, New Jersey.) "We're not qualified to explain weather conditions," is the party line they're giving us, but not even the eight-year-old is buying it. These soldiers must think we're morons. I'm sorry now I left with them. No, I'm not. I don't know, I am and I'm not. I guess I'm not sorry I'm an hour away from Perth Amboy right now.

The eight-year-old – she's a bright one, her father (Guy-Something-Italian) calls her Kitty and she keeps saying, "*No, it's* Kit, *like* Kit Carson, *Daddy*" – she announced it was a nuclear bomb. Her father & older sister (Deedee, I thought 12 but she's 14) tried to shut her up (they are the only other civilians, soldiers picked them up before me). The father kept apologizing – "Kitty's wild imagination, it's always running away with her" unquote – but the look on his face said something else entirely. The soldiers just laughed it off. Well, they tried. The older of the two sergeants, Wrenfrew (Christ, how the hell do you pronounce that? I keep waiting to hear someone say it but all anyone calls him is "Sarge") went into a big explanation about how a nuclear bomb emits an electromagnetic pulse that knocks out everything electronic. But seeing as how my iPad was obviously still working and so was that cute little Nintendo, so whatever was making the weird light in the east had to be something else.

I don't know what offended the kid more – his talking down to her or referring to her handheld as a "cute little Nintendo" (it may be a Nintendo, but it's one of the more rarefied models, nothing cute or little about it, never mind the *Hello, Kitty* sticker). Her father sat on her pretty hard after that. Poor kid's getting bored – she's got something like half-a-dozen cartridges she's been swapping between and I think she's exhausted her entire repertoire twice since we got here. Her sister Deedee's got a laptop; most of the time she just sits and pouts at the screen. She hardly says anything except "Shut up, runt" to her sister. Well, there's not much to do here. (Note to the committee in charge of planning for the next global apocalypse: kids bore quickly – videogames and movies are *not* luxury items.)

I've been pretending to do spreadsheets while I search the Cloud. Whenever anyone asks to look at my iPad, I pop one up on the screen; nice and boring. I said I was doing a home-study course to train as an accountant, so they think I'm nice and boring, too. Of course, the soldiers know I'm an Army wife, but when I asked if any of them know a Private Lindbloom, they all said no.

Weird how we all seem to be kind of playing our cards close to the (bulletproof) vest.

More later. I hope you remember to look in the Cloud. If you can. *When* you can. *When*, *When* when, oh, *please*, when

[Text Document: ro.lf@[redacted] uploaded to the Cloud]

Dear Jo:

Now I know how the people from New Orleans felt after Hurricane Katrina when they had to camp out in the Houston Astrodome. This place is nowhere near as big and there's just me, the man and his daughters (Di-something-Italian), and half-a-dozen soldiers staying with us – the sergeants Wrenfrew and Jameson, corporal Charette, privates Oh, Pappadopolous (sp?) and Rossi. Sometimes jeeps or transports stop here, but they never stay long.

I don't know what to call this – a shelter? A tent? It's inflatable, looks almost like it should be part of a bouncy castle. No bunk-beds, just military-issue coto. Very narrow, a couple of times, I've almost fallen out of bed just rolling over. I'm tempted to ask if I can push two of them together. There are enough extras – fourteen empty ones, to be exact. They thought they'd have two dozen people here. Bad planning? Or did something happen to them? I've tried asking – as indirectly as possible, of course, things like, *So, how long do you think we'll be here?* and *Think we'll have enough people for a game of touch football soon?* – but the soldiers aren't talking. The privates say they don't know anything more than I do and both sergeants tell me not to worry and to enjoy the space while I can because it could get crowded soon. The fact that it *isn't* crowded worries me more. Am I screwy?

At least we've got power and I can plug in the iPad. I want to keep it charged as much as possible, just in case the generator quits. I can't help thinking anything could happen at any time. Something's off. I mean, more than just the fact that we're in the middle of an unprecedented disaster. Why are we with the Army and not the National Guard? I haven't seen hide nor hair of the Guard. Something must have happened to them, but what?

Also, this doesn't feel like a well-run military operation. It's weird. I don't mean the soldiers are slacking off or anything. But I'm getting this feeling like they don't know much more about what's going to happen next than I do. Like they're making it up as they go along. It's not like being at Ft. Dix.

Every time I went to Ft. Dix, it was like being inside a machine in pretty much perfect condition, everything happening as and when ordained. That used to bug me but right now I miss it. I wish I felt it. Then I'd know there was still something left of the world I know. Okay, I'd rather it was the National Endowment for the Arts than the military. Hell, I wish it were cable TV instead of the military but I'm in no position to be picky.

(No offence, honey – I promised I'd support you in anything you want to do and I'm not going back on that. I just wish we'd wake up one morning and find out there was no longer any need for the military, and recruiting stations wanted to sign people up to be dancers and painters and writers instead. I so wish I would wake up tomorrow morning and that would be true. You know me – incorrigible romantic aspiring to irrepressible optimist. We always were the Odd Couple of Perth Amboy.)

Anyway. According to my map app, we're only 20 min. west of Dix but they're not going to take us there. I don't know where we're going or when. Every time one of us asks about that, they tell us they're waiting for instructions from command. But I've got this awful feeling that they're waiting for Godot. Like I said, making it up as they go along. Is that simply because this is an actual emergency and not a drill?

(Had this been an actual drill, we would be filling out survey sheets. How satisfied would you say you were with the conditions of your disaster? Extremely satisfied, very satisfied, neither satisfied nor dissatisfied, very dissatisfied, extremely dissatisfied. How likely are you to recommend the squad who dragged you out of your home? Highly likely, very likely, probably not, not bloody likely. I said *aspiring* to irrepressible optimist. The way things are going, I'll be lucky to reach semi-permanent-press-able fatalist.)

After I back up to the Cloud, I'm going to email these to you and copy myself – belt and suspenders. God, I hope you remember about the Cloud.

[IM Log: ro.lf@[redacted] uploaded to the Cloud]

[05:08:16 EST] **KC:** hello rocky? ipad lady?
[05:08:20 EST] **RLaF:** Kit?
[05:08:46 EST] **KC:** that WAS a bømb i NO it was
[05:08:56 EST] **RLaF:** But no EMP
[05:09:35 EST] **KC:** 2 far away. & 2 far 4 radiation, I hope
[05:09:59 EST] **RLaF:** Hope it's not a bomb, tho
[05:10:40 EST] **KC:** WAS we cant ever go home again, radiation
[05:11:00 EST] **RLaF:** Why are you so sure?
[05:11:05 EST] **KC:** Mushroom cloud
[05:11:06 EST] **RLaF:** ?
[05:12:49 EST] **KC:** file sent
[05:13:04 EST] **KC:** Did u c?

[05:13:12 EST] **RLaF:** Where did you get that?

[05:13:53 EST] **KC:** webcam balcony my cuz apt hoboken

[05:14:37 EST] **KC:** u there?

[05:14:45 EST] **RLaF:** Yes. Who else have you showed this to?

[05:14:48 EST] **KC:** no1

[05:15:13 EST] **RLaF:** Why did you show it to me?

[05:15:37 EST] **KC:** bcuz i cant sho any1 else

[05:15:52 EST] **KC:** ru mad @ me

[05:16:01 EST] **RLaF:** No. No, never. Just shocked

[05:16:27 EST] **KC:** im sorry

[05:16:35 EST] **RLaF:** It's OK. Too early to get up, go back to sleep

[05:16:21 EST] **KC:** OFF

[Text Document: ro.lf@[redacted] uploaded to the Cloud]

Jo! My Jo, I found you, I found you! Part of you, anyway – I found some of the video you uploaded when you were headed uptown. Oh, God, Jo. Oh, God. Please find this, please tell me you found someone in command or they found you and you're in Canada or something. Tell me you made it out before *that*. Send me some sign of life!!!!

[Text Document: ro.lf@[redacted] uploaded to the Cloud]

This morning as we were eating breakfast (powdered eggs and biscuits, awful), Pvt – Corporal? – Pvt. Oh asked if anyone was online. "Surfing the web, checking email? watching funny cat videos, looking at porn, ha ha?" He tried to sound offhand, like it was no big deal. We all said no. Deedee said she was writing in her journal. Kit said she was playing games. Their dad said he was reading a book on his phone. I showed her a spreadsheet.

Call it a lie for a lie.

Except I don't blame them for lying to us. I wish that little shit had never sent me that video.

No, no, that's not fair. I didn't mean to call her that. I'm not thinking straight. If anyone's a shit, it's the older girl, Deedee. When she isn't sulking, she's snapping at Kit. Although if I were fourteen, I probably wouldn't be any better. I was a real shit at that age, myself, barely human. I'm sorry I have to know what Kit knows but I'm even sorrier *she* has to. If Kit's since showed it to her sister, then no wonder she's snarling. Those poor kids. At least one of them knows too much and they both probably want their mom. God only knows where she is now.

[Videofile: ro.lf@[redacted] uploaded to the Cloud]

A woman's face barely visible in low light.

[inaudible whisper.]

[SMS Exhanchange: ro.lf@[redacted] uploaded to the Cloud]

thx 4 pword, wish I had mifi router like u.

We shld b careful. Yr dad always looks nervous when I sit w/u.

hes worried about my mom. U worried 2?

Yeah. Last word, Jo was about to be deployed nyc

ono – mayb my mom was 2!

Maybe not. Jo said some going 2 cape may. What's her brig, reg?

2nd brig 72 div

Pretty sure they're in Cape May

u just saying that?

No. Yr dad looks nervous again. Talk later, OK?

[Text Document: ro.lf@[redacted] uploaded to the Cloud]

Dear Jo:

Emailed convo w/Kit to myself & deleted from iPad. I feel sick. I can barely look at her, I'm afraid she'll see the lie about her mom all over my face. I'll probably delete this too. I just want to talk to someone, anyone. No, that's a lie, I want to talk to you, Jo. I'm going to take an extra Prozac, just to make sure I don't cry.

This morning I hid in the latrine & took inventory: Prozac will last three weeks. After that, I need a doctor or a pharmacy.

Or not. Maybe under the circumstances I'm no longer clinically depressed. Maybe there's no such thing as clinical depression any more. Maybe clinical depression is a disease from a different world. Another planet. I can't even remember what it was like to live there. Maybe I'd better wean myself off Prozac before I run out & avoid withdrawal. Then I'll be ready to take up arms against a sea of Infected and by opposing them, end them. Or end up ending myself. The end.

Why is there never anyone around to witness my wittiest moments? Please find this, Jo. Please be alive so you can find this.

[Text Document: ro.lf@[redacted] uploaded to the Cloud]

Dearest Jo:

The eight-year-old lit out for the territories today. I'm not really making light of her running away. The truth is, it's all my fault – she was heading for Cape May. A soldier bivouacked (what is that, anyway?) somewhere south of here brought her back looking a bit more than slightly worse for wear. She walked into a booby trap – the soldier found her hanging by one ankle from a tree. In movies or TV shows, it's usually played for laughs but the real thing isn't very funny. The poor kid has a pulled butt muscle, of all things. It's obvious that it hurts like hell – that's a big muscle. Just thinking about having a charlie horse in my ass makes me wince. Pvt. Ramirez (soldier who brought her back) said she was lucky she hadn't dislocated her hip, too. Then added she was *extremely* lucky she hit that trap & not the one a little farther on – she'd be impaled on spikes in the bottom of a ten-foot hole!!!!

Which would have been *my fault*. The lie I told that child about her mother almost killed her.

Now she's confined to bed with an ice-pack on her bottom. Sgt. Wrenfrew (how the *fuck* is that pronounced? I *still* haven't heard anyone say it) threatened to handcuff her to the bed-frame. He was laughing when he said it, but I could see he wasn't really kidding. The father was going to take away her videogame as punishment but I talked him out off it. The kid's in pain and the only thing anyone has is ibuprofen and there's nothing else to take her mind of it – no TV, no dvd player and no dvds even if there was. Worse, no books or magazines!!! (Right – a preview of the Tenth Circle of Hell, the one even Dante couldn't bring himself to write about.) All my books are on the iPad and I'm not too inclined to let it out of my hands, but I sat with her for a while and let her play with it. She let me fool around with her videogame. Surprised to find that it's got wireless capability. I wasn't going to let on about my MiFi but she already knew – her game had picked it up. So I gave her the password. She promised not to download prøn. Ha, ha. (Does prøn still exist?!)

But that's not the punchline. You want to know the punchline? They asked her why she wanted to go to Cape May and *she wouldn't tell them*!!! The kid didn't rat me out and she could have. Hell, I would have.

I keep searching the Cloud for some sign of you.

[Text Document: ro.lf@[redacted] uploaded to the Cloud]

Well, the people we've been waiting for are here.

The soldier who brought Kit back arrived with four more civilians today, two older women, fiftyish, sixtyish, one of them a doctor, a teenage boy – 17? 18? I don't know. He must be cute because although Deedee barely looks at him, she's slightly less sulky all of a sudden – and a fortyish man on a stretcher, heavily sedated and missing part of his right leg below the knee. An emergency amputation, done last night by the doctor. With an axe, in a hurry. I'd shudder but I'm way past that now.

They were about to bring the man inside when Wrenfrew (dammit, somebody say his name already!) stopped them. He and the doctor had a serious tete-a-tete and then two of the soldiers put up a pup-tent outside for him. Except for the doctor, we've all been ordered to stay away from him, until further notice. You can guess why. We certainly did, although we don't know most of the details. Except the doctor swears she took his foot off no more than fifteen minutes after he was bitten and she cut as high as she could without going above the knee. Above the knee, it would be too dangerous to move him, she said.

Dr. Bessette brought a supply of drugs with her. She and Wrenfew had a discussion about that, too. Apparently, he wanted her to turn everything over to him; she told him unless he was a licensed physician or a pharmacist, he wasn't getting his hands on anything other than aspirin or a roll of gauze, and even then he'd have to convince her he really needed them.

It looked pretty tense for a few minutes. The other sergeant, Jameson, took him aside and talked to him and then had a chat with the doctor. The two of them shook hands and the doctor agreed to give everyone physicals.

All anyone knows about the other woman is her name: Ruth. Pvt. Ramirez found her on the road, walking by herself and carrying a pitchfork. From the style of her clothes – i.e. home-made dress, drab and dark – I think she might be a Mennonite. Not Amish, I don't think – we're too far away from Amish country. Or are we? I don't know.

I overheard Ramirez telling Sgt. Jameson that they had a hard time convincing her to get in the jeep when she saw the man, even though he was unconscious. She was still clutching the pitchfork when they drove up; the tines aren't clean. Pvt. Oh took charge of her. He spent an hour trying to talk her down from whatever edge she was teetering on, with limited success. Which is to say, her eyes don't look quite as crazy but she still won't let go of that pitchfork (although Oh got her to wash it off – outside – before she brought it inside).

[Text Document: ro.lf@[redacted] uploaded to the Cloud]

The boy, Wesley, is 17. He lost his glasses and he's so nearsighted that he's all but blind. That's not the punchline, though. Here's the punchline: the doctor is diabetic and what insulin she has won't last a week. Two more things to put in the global apocalypse survival handbook: when foraging for supplies, hit as many pharmacies as possible and don't forget to loot optometrists' shops.

Jesus. Nobody had to put up with these inconveniences in George Romero movies.

[Text Document: ro.lf@[redacted] uploaded to the Cloud]

Oh, god, sometime during the night, Ruth killed the man in the pup-tent. She said he had turned into *"One of them"* (I swear, that's how she sounded). Dr. B could neither confirm nor deny – Ruth used her pitchfork and what's left is barely identifiable as human. Now Ruth is strapped down on one of the cots and heavily sedated. No one knows what else to do with her.

I don't think anyone knows what to do with the rest of us, either, except I'm prett

---

[Videofile: ro.lf@[redacted] uploaded to the Cloud]

Blurry movement.

[sound of automatic-gunfire, people yelling.]

Video cuts sharply several times, until POV from her lap shows woman looking up through a steering wheel.

LaFortune:
"What the fuck? What the *fuck?* What *is* this?"

Man 1 *[off-screen]*:
"You said you had a chauffeur's license!"

LaFortune:
"*Chauffeur*, not *pilot!* This looks like a 747!"

A small hand reaches from around the back of the woman's seat, does something on the dashboard. Sound of engine coming to life.

Girl *[off-screen]*:
"I watched when that soldier drove me back. He says they don't have keys. You don't want to be looking for your keys in a combat zone."

Woman looks down to her right, touches something, then grabs it. Sound of gears grinding. She does something else and the vehicle lurches forward.

LaFortune:
"Everybody hold on!"

Several minutes of bouncing; screams from back of vehicle.

[sound of more weapons-fire.]

Woman sees something, turns steering wheel sharply, stamps on accelerator. A few seconds later, several thumps as the vehicle bounces over something lumpy. Woman brings vehicle to an abrupt stop. Sound of passenger side door opening and slamming.

Man 2 *[off-screen]*:
"Go! Go! Go!"

[screams from back of vehicle.]

Man 2 *[off-screen]*:
"Shut the fuck up! I can't hear myself think! *[pause.]* Thank you."

Cut to black.

Same POV, sometime later. Vehicle traveling swiftly but less frantically.

Man 2 *[off-screen]*:
"—ive now, you can pull over anywhere."

LaFortune:
"No, Sergeant Jameson."

Man 2 *[off-screen]*:
"Ma'am, I don't think you're understanding me—"

LaFortune:
"Ma'am me again and I'll boot you out without slowing down."

Man 2 *[off-screen]*:
"Okay, *Ms. LaFortune*, pull over and let me drive. Please!"

LaFortune:
"What part of *no* don't you understand?"

Man 2 *[off-screen]*:
"Ma—Ms. LaFortune—"

LaFortune:
"You might as well call me Rocky."

Man 2 *[off-screen]*:
"Fine. Pull over, *Rocky*."

LaFortune:
"No, I need the experience."

Man 2 *[off-screen]*:
"Come again?"

LaFortune:
"I need to learn this monster. You can drive later. You got nothing to do, take a nap."

Man 2 [off-screen]:
"*Come again?!* In *these* seats?"

LaFortune:
"Switch with Oh in back."

Man 2 [off-screen]:
"That ain't gonna happen, lady, now pull over and let me drive."

LaFortune:
"No fucking way."

Man 2 [off-screen]:
"Why the fuck not?"

LaFortune:
"Because *I can't shoot and you can!*"

Man 1 [off-screen]:
"She's got you there, sarge!"

Man 2 [off-screen]:
"Can it and tell me what kind of ordnance we've got."

Man 1 [off-screen]:
[barely intelligible: something about M16s, clips, one(?) dozen grenades, grenade launcher.]

Man 2 [off-screen]:
"Okay, Mr. DiTommasso—"

Man 3 [off-screen]:
"Guy. My name's Guy."

Man 2 [off-screen]:
"Okay, Guy, you know anything about firearms?"

Man 3 [off-screen]:
"Some."

Man 2 [off-screen]:
"Enough to keep track of the ammo?"

Girl [off-screen]:
"*I* could do that!"

Man 2 [off-screen]:
"Good, but your dad's doing it for now. If I need your help, I'll ask."

LaFortune:
"You might yet."

Man 2 *[off-screen]*:
"God help us if I do."

[Text Document: ro.lf@[redacted] uploaded to the Cloud]

Dearest Jo,

We're in Bridgeton, NJ, at a farm with an airstrip. Airstrip, nothing else. I think Jameson was hoping to book a flight out (he won't say one way or another). No planes here, not even birds. Weird. But at least there aren't any dead people.

No live people, either. They left in a hurry. Maybe when they got wind of what happened to Manhattan. Speaking of wind: Kit's been asking Sgt. Jameson and Pvt. Oh about fallout – like, is the wind radioactive? They stonewalled at first then I guess Jameson's conscience got the better of him. He said, *if* there had been a nuclear event – a hypothetical situation – he thought we should be far enough away but anyone worried about something like that should probably stay indoors as much as possible. Hoping to put the kibosh on any ideas she might have about making another break for it, I guess. But I notice most of us seem to avoid leaving the barn.

A couple of hours after we got here, we heard a Jeep engine and two more soldiers from Shamong showed up, both covered in blood. Corporal Liza Charette (she's the one I thought recognized your name) and Pvt. Nick Pappadopolous. They only had a couple of M16s and not much ammunition. Jameson and Oh held them at gunpoint and made them both strip to see if they were bitten. They didn't hesitate. Dr. B examined both of them. Cpl. Charette was fine but Pappadopolous had what looked like several deep scratches on his thigh so now he's chained to a metal stake in the front yard, like a dog. It's awful, I hate it, but Pappadopolous went right along with it, saying it's the only way to safeguard the rest of us. If he's infected, we'll know within 24 hours. Sgt. Jameson said if he is, he'll take care of it. (If he's not, I feel like we'll all owe him a big apology. He and Cpl. Charette are all that's left of the soldiers who held the line while we escaped.)

"When your adrenaline's flowing, you don't question anything, you just *do*" – you told me that, remember? Well, I'm no soldier, but I guess some of you rubbed off on me because when we were attacked, I just *did* – got in that Humvee and drove like a bat out of hell.

Okay, I *do* remember that an 8-year-old girl had to tell me how to start the fucker. But after that, I was running on a direct current from the fight-or-flight zone. I haven't brought up to Jameson that he had the gall to argue with me about driving after I saved his ass from fucking zombies (!!!! I can't believe I'm using that word, I swore I wouldn't and here I am doing it anyway). I won't bring it up unless he starts something else. Ha, ha, joke: I know damn well I need him a hell of a lot more than he needs me, likewise the rest of us. That makes it a bad joke, I guess.

Not quite as bad as "What do you mean, where's Ruth? I thought she was with you". Which no one has made because we all know that at the moment of truth, not one of us even considered taking the extra time to undo the straps, pick her up, and carry her or drag her or demand someone else help get her to the Humvee. I don't feel as guilty about that as I do about the fact that, if I had it to do over, I'd still leave her there. To be bitten. Infected. Torn apart. Devoured. And I'd still be sitting here telling myself that there wasn't time, I couldn't have carried her even if I had put down my iPad because I'm not strong enough, and no one else would have stopped to help me so I just would have sacrificed myself for nothing.

Remember how the last time we IM'ed, I said I wasn't buying the zombie story, it had to be some kind of super-ebola-cum-rabies kind of thing? Well, so much for *my* future in medicine. I keep forgetting that just because I have the complete *E.R.* boxset, it doesn't mean I'm qualified to make a diagnosis.

(*Had* the *E.R.* boxset. It's too radioactive now for anyone except zombies and they don't seem to be much for the boob tube.)

Please be alive, Jo, please. Please have got out of Manhattan before the bomb fell. I'm begging you.

All the time we were on the road, we all kept asking Sgt. Jameson and Pvt. Oh, if those were zombies, where did they all come from? Because they didn't look like they'd burrowed out of a graveyard. That was my argument that they couldn't be dead people – there were so many of them. I know a lot of people die everyday, but I didn't think the death rate could be that high in rural New Jersey.

Well, I was right, it's not. The zombies that attacked us died of radiation poisoning. Some died right away, some died trying to get away. Then they got up

(I still can't believe I'm writing this)

and attacked people farther out from the detonation. And *they* attacked more people farther out, and so forth and so on. A frigging zombie domino effect.

Radioactive zombies. I swear to god, *I cannot believe I'm writing this*.

Oh started talking about how maybe radiation could actually make the zombies mutate, but Jameson shut him up. So I've been looking through the Cloud for something on god help me mutated radioactive zombies. I get a lot of stuff on George Romero. As if!!!!

I'm writing this so I can look at it in print and see if it makes any sense.

Uh-oh, Jameson's yelling

[Videofile: ro.lf@[redacted] uploaded to the Cloud]

POV is tilted. Someone is apparently holding an iPad in the crook of an arm, surreptitiously recording a confrontation between two men near a partially open door inside a barn.

DiTommasso:
"—isn't a military installation any more—"

Sgt. Jameson:
"Whether it is or it isn't, I'm still responsible for your safety and that of everyone else here."

DiTommasso:
"Yeah? Then you're responsible for his safety—"

Sgt. Jameson:
"I have to make sure they're not a threat—"

DiTommasso:
"Not by chaining a teenage kid up outside like an animal!"

Sgt. Jameson:
"By however I think best, now go—"

DiTommasso:
"Treating a soldier like that is one thing but a kid—I'm a father—"

Sgt. Jameson *[yelling]*:
"I'm a father too!"

DiTommasso stares, open-mouthed.

Sgt. Jameson *[lowers voice]*:
"Please go and look after your girls and be thankful they're alright. Keep them away from the front of the building. If it turns out the boy is alright, we'll bring him in. If not, we'll handle it."

DiTommasso:
"How long are you going to keep him out there?"

Sgt. Jameson:
"Till we know for sure. Now, please, sir—"

Pvt. Oh moves into frame, pulls DiTommasso by one arm.

Pvt. Oh:
"Come on. Your girls need you, sir."

DiTommasso lets himself be pulled away. POV moves closer to Sgt. Jameson, shifting to keep his face in-camera.

LaFortune:
"Do you really think he's infected?"

Sgt. Jameson:
"It's a matter of following safety protocols, not what I think."

[Text Document: ro.lf@[redacted] uploaded to the Cloud]

I should have guessed. Poor Wesley has some kind of injury. It might be from getting into the Humvee – he missed his footing climbing in and was dragged more than a few feet before Guy and Doctor B managed to pull him all the way in. Dr. B treated the road rash – not much to do except pick the gravel out of his shredded skin and clean the wound. Instead of getting better, he got feverish. Now he's outside, lying on a blanket, chained to the same stake Pvt. Pappadopolous was. At this point, he's so delirious, I don't think he knows where he is.

I want to ask Dr. B what she thinks but I'm afraid of the answer.

A man stands at a partially open door. He's watching something. POV moves behind him and he shifts position. Brief glimpse of a teenage boy lying on his side on the ground. His breathing is ragged, uneven.

Sgt. Jameson:
"This is how it spreads. HRV. The Death. People get in a car, one of them is infected and doesn't tell the others. As soon as the infected person turns, everybody gets bit. Then *they* keep going till they meet someone else. And so forth and so on. Hell, for all we know, zombies can drive themselves now."

LaFortune:
"The infection – whatever it is – just animates corpses. It doesn't seem to make them smart. I ran over three back in Shamong because they just stood there staring at me. The biggest moron I ever met had enough sense to get out of the way of a speeding car."

Sgt. Jameson:
"What if they don't need to?"

LaFortune:
"What do you mean? They can't get any deader?"

Sgt. Jameson *[laughs grimly]*:
"There's that. But you saw how they attack. What if they're not stupid, they're just—well, like a hive mind. They're not individuals like us, they're just a lot of bodies under a single intelligence?"

LaFortune:
"Then it's not a very intelligent intelligence."

Sgt. Jameson *[glances at iPad]*:
"Computers aren't intelligent, you have to program them. Even then, they won't do anything they're not programmed to do. But some programs can learn, right? Maybe the single mind or force or whatever that's moving all these corpses is learning from everything that happens to them. Trial and error, with an unending supply of bodies to use. Even when the bodies are damaged, they keep going. They don't stop till you cut the head off or burn them up."

LaFortune:
"Yeah, but sooner or later the bodies *will* run out. There's not an infinite supply of living people."

Sgt. Jameson:
"No, only seven billion. And as stupid as this thing might be, you gotta

figure that it'll learn *something* before it uses up half of them. Maybe by the time it gets to corpse number four billion, it'll know enough to dodge a speeding car. Or bullet."

LaFortune:
"That's assuming you're right and there's really some kind of mind, a— an *intelligence* behind this at all. But why should there be? There isn't a mind behind the Ebola virus."

Sgt. Jameson:
"Oh? You sure about that?"

[long silence]

"*I* ain't sure of anything any more, either, except what I have to do to stay alive and protect those in my care. Aw, *shit!*"

> POV moves position and is now looking through partially open door. The boy is up on all fours, trying to crawl toward them, making gurgling noises. Blood drips from his open mouth.

LaFortune:
"But you thought this would happen, didn't you?"

Sgt. Jameson:
"Yeah, but I was hoping it wouldn't."

> He draws a pistol.

"Stay here. Don't turn the camera off."

LaFortune:
"What? What cam—"

Sgt. Jameson:
"Look, you're not an idiot, right? Well, neither am I. I know you been taking pictures and videos on the sly—you're not as sneaky as you think. You been recording me just now. So record the whole thing, what I got to do and then upload it to the Cloud."

LaFortune:
"You want a video of you killing a kid?"

Sgt. Jameson:
"Destroying an Infected. I want it on record, what has to be done. The whole filthy, bloody thing. This ain't antiseptic."

> He marches out to the kid, kicks him over onto his back, puts his boot on the kid's neck and shoots him squarely in the face. Gore splatters his legs. He walks out of frame, comes back with a spade and hacks the kid's head off with it. He bats the head far away from the body, starts to walk back toward the barn, then pauses, staring thoughtfully

at the ground. He vomits twice, then straightens up, wipes his mouth and returns to the barn.

"You get all that?"

[Text Document: ro.lf@[redacted] uploaded to the Cloud]

Dear, dear Jo:

I got part of the video you uploaded from Times Square. Only a few seconds are clear. After that, it's all staticky and full of interference. I don't know that you're alive but I'm going to keep writing to you anyway. I saw the other video files, the ones from the people in the high-rise. One of them says something about how there has to be a witness to what happens. Well, I just uploaded a really horrible video. I hope you never see it. The weird thing, though, was all while it happened, I had that feeling I talked about before, how Dix ran like a machine. The machinery was functioning the way it was supposed to. Oh, god.

[Videofile: ro.lf@[redacted] uploaded to the Cloud]

Early morning, inside the barn. POV of a man shouting at a woman. A small girl is standing nearby, crying

DiTommasso:
"They kidnapped my daughter! They took Deedee!"

Cpl. Charette:
"You need to calm down, sir—"

[distant, single gunshot.]

Everyone freezes.

[second gunshot.]

DiTommasso:
"Omigod. *[screaming]* Deedee! Deedee!"

Kit *[tearful]*:
"Daddy, *shut the fuck up!*"

 [Text Document: ro.lf@[redacted] uploaded to the Cloud]

Dear Jo:

It's too awful. Deedee is dead. I don't know how she got infected, whether she went out to the boy in the yard or she got bitten or scratched somehow during the attack in Shamong – no one knows, no one'll ever know. She hid the wound and of course, it started to fester.

(Fester; that word used to make me think of Uncle Fester from *The Addams Family*!)

I don't know who caught on – I suspect it was the doctor, although it could have been anyone. Jameson told Pvts. Oh and Pappadopolous to take her away while we were sleeping, tie her up and wait to see if it was a garden-variety infection or *not*.

I guess they didn't have to wait very long to find out it was *not*.

Oh said he made sure she didn't feel any pain. Afterwards, they burned her body. Guy got hysterical. Doctor B gave him an injection and he's been asleep ever since. She says the combination of shock and drugs could knock him out for a whole day. She was going to give Kit something, too, but Kit begged her not to because she's terrified of needles.

She's more afraid of getting a shot than getting shot.

Frankly, I think she's more afraid of getting left behind. I would be.

Someone's here, a truck or

[Videofile: ro.lf@[redacted] uploaded to the Cloud]

POV of outside, seen through open barn door. Two pick-up trucks arrive with four men and two women.

First Man:
"—not here to harm anybody, we're just checking for survivors! Everybody okay?"

A man steps out of the barn, back to camera, sidearm holster unsnapped.

Sgt. Jameson:
"I'm Sergeant Jameson. What can I do for you?"

First Man:
"It's what we can do for you, actually—"

The man from the barn rests one hand on his pistol but doesn't draw it.

Second Man:
"Hold on, now, no need for anyone to get an itchy trigger finger. Where you from?"

Sgt. Jameson:
"Who wants to know?"

Second Man:
"Max Anderson. I'm a vet, myself. Saw combat with the 11th Armored Cavalry in Nam."

Sgt. Jameson:
"Blackhorse?"

Second Man:
"That's the one. I was on Operation Kittyhawk."

Sgt. Jameson:
"I am pleased to make your acquaintance, sir, and I know you'll understand I'm responsible for the safety of my people."

Second Man:
"I do, sergeant, and I—well, I'm not sure how to go about offering you help except, well—we're here to help. We've established a safe place with pretty steady power, running water, indoor plumbing and a good supply of food. Hot shower interest you at all? Or a hot meal or two? If you're on your way somewhere else, we won't interfere with whatever orders you have."

The man from the barn looks back over his shoulder at the camera. A woman moves into POV from the right.

Dr. B:
"How are you folks fixed for medicine?"

▮ The question seems to puzzle them.

Second Man:
"We have a doctor and a veterinarian."

Dr. B:
"And a pharmacy?"

▮ The second man frowns, seems reluctant to answer.

Second Man:
"Well, we got a doctor and he's in charge—"

Dr. B:
"I'm only asking because there's a diabetic among us and the insulin's running out."

Second Man:
"I'll talk to our doc."

 [Text Document: ro.lf@[redacted] uploaded to the Cloud]

Dearest Jo:

Jameson sent the visitors off, saying he'd consider their offer and they could talk tomorrow. Then he and Pvt. Oh went into the tower for a couple of hours. I think they were trying to make contact with their command or some other military – any other military? Maybe even book a flight out for us civilians. Ha, ha (humorless laugh). Anyway, either they didn't get the answers they wanted or maybe no answers at all. A little while after they came back, Jameson took me aside and told me that he was going to send Oh and Pappadopolous on a recon to check those people out. If they're okay, they'll leave us civilians with them.

I said, what if I don't want to stay there?

Jameson said he wasn't taking requests. If it's safe, he's dropping us there and if we have the sense god gave a goose, we'll stay put and ride things out in relative comfort, or words to that effect. (Actually the part with the sense god gave a goose is verbatim. It startled me – I thought for a minute I was hearing *your* voice. Or is this just something everybody says in the army?).

I said that I thought unless he had specific orders from someone in command, he and the other soldiers ought to stay there, too, as protection.

He looked surprised for a second and then told me that sounded like something his own wife would say. He said their duty as infantry was to find a company to hook up with and continue to engage the enemy. I argued – suddenly I really did *not* like the idea of them leaving us. Why shouldn't they have to stay and guard everyone from zombies or anything else, for that matter? I said as much, but he just rattled off a bunch of regulations about combat infantry and I don't know what. It was so weird hearing that. Combat conditions. No one in living memory has been in combat conditions *in this country*. The closest we've ever come are Pearl Harbor and the World Trade Center in Man
hat-00-=090
tan

I was typing that and all of a sudden I just *heaved*. Twice. All over the iPad. Good thing it wasn't a laptop. All I had to do was wipe it off and make sure nothing got into the plug or anything (obviously it didn't). Everyone was worried, asking me what I'd eaten – thinking some of the food was bad, I guess. That wasn't it and I'm okay now. I won't be eating anything till tomorrow, but I'm okay. It wasn't food poisoning. It was

Well, you know how I told you how I used to be an easy crier till I started taking Prozac? Thank god – it was so embarrassing! Prozac Woman doesn't cry. Anyway, when I was writing that about Pearl Harbor and the WTC, all of a sudden, something overwhelming hit me. But instead of bursting into tears, I puked.

Is that actually better than crying? Stay tuned.

(Please, please, please stay tuned. Please *be* tuned.)

[Videofile: ro.lf@[redacted] uploaded to the Cloud]

POV from the back of the Humvee, following the pickup trucks.

DiTommasso:
"—seem okay to me."

Pvt. Oh:
"They might be. But being careful doesn't hurt."

DiTommasso:
"None of them had any visible wounds. I thought it was pretty good of them to show us as much skin as they did—"

Pvt. Oh:
"Sir, there's more to be careful of than zombies. You can't trust anyone just because they're alive."

DiTommasso:
"One of those men is a veteran—"

Sgt. Jameson:
"So he said."

DiTommasso:
"You don't believe him?"

Sgt. Jameson:
"Didn't say *that*."

DiTommasso:
"Sounded like it."

Sgt. Jameson:
"It's like Oh said. These are strangers. When the standard conditions of society break down, some people take advantage, do things they couldn't get away with before."

DiTommasso:
"Worse than taking a 14-year-old girl away and shooting her in the head?"

Sgt. Jameson:
"Lots worse."

> Cuts to black.
>
> A suburban street. Five men are pointing rifles in the general direction of the POV.

Anderson:
"—old you what the local ordnances are here. We are god-fearin' people and we don't hold with *her* kind. The government says they can join the army now so sign 'er up. She can go with you because she ain't stayin' here!"

Sgt. Jameson *[off-screen]*:
"What you're doing is illegal—"

Anderson:
"Already explained to you what the laws are *here*. It ain't up to the army to tell us what's legal and what isn't. We're within our rights to live without worrying about degenerates walking around eyeing up our kids, planning to do god knows what to them."

Cpl. Charette *[off-screen]*:
"Mr. Anderson! It's a federal offence to—"

Anderson:
"Seen any feds lately? Me, neither. You find any, feel free to send them round to see us."

Kit *[off-screen]*:
"If Rocky can't stay, *I* don't want to!"

DiTommasso *[off-screen]*:
[barely audible unintelligible.]

Anderson:
"See? It's already too late for your kid! When you see her marching in some goddamned parade holding hands with something that don't know whether it's a boy or a girl, you remember *[fades]* . . ."

Sgt. Jameson *[off-screen]*:
"Wait a minute—what about the doctor?"

Anderson *[with heavy sarcasm]*:
"You got an appointment?"

Sgt. Jameson *[off-screen]*:
"Not *your* doctor, ours. She's diabetic and she's in a pretty bad way."

> POV swings around to the Humvee. A woman is sitting in the passenger seat, eyes closed, possibly unconscious. Up on top, a soldier has his weapon trained on the civilians. POV swings back to the group of men.

Anderson:
"Is she a lesbo, too?"

Sgt. Jameson *[off-screen, but very close, speaking under his breath]*:
. . . un-fucking-believable. *[raises voice]* I don't know, I didn't ask!"

Cpl. Charette *[off-screen, nearby]*:
There are *fucking zombies*—

LaFortune *[off-screen]*:
"Forget it. People like that would rather have a zombie bite them than someone of the same sex kiss them."

Cpl. Charette [off-screen]:
No, seriously—*zombies at ten o'clock!*"

Sgt. Jameson [off-screen]:
"We are *outahere!*"

[sounds of gunfire.]

> POV swings crazily, then running, blurry motion into the back-seat of the Humvee.

Sgt. Jameson [off-screen]:
"Mow 'em down!"

> Glimpse of zombies bouncing off the front of the Humvee or going down beneath the tires. One clings to the hood for several seconds. The driver leans out of the side window and fires a pistol. He scores a direct hit in the middle of the zombie's forehead.

[a beat, then the sound of Sgt. Jameson screaming.]

[Videofile: ro.lf@[redacted] uploaded to the Cloud]

> POV of a woman driving what appears to be a luxury SUV. Someone else is holding the camera on her. She glances at it from time to time, but mostly keeps her eyes on the road. It's a bumpy ride.

LaFortune:
"It's been five days since our encounter with the god-fearing folks of Bumfuck, Pennsylvania. Well, I *think* it's been five days—

Kit [off-screen]:
"Close enough. Four-and-a-half days."

> The girl is obviously sitting in the front passenger seat, holding the iPad. It's a very bumpy ride—trees are visible through the driver's-side window. POV pans to the back seats: A man and a female soldier are directly behind the front seats. Behind them are a black woman in a ripped and dirty State Trooper's uniform and an older man with a white beard and frightened eyes.

LaFortune [off-screen]:
"We've lost a few—"

Jump cut to a scene time-stamped four days earlier. Pvt. Oh is standing by the side of the luxury SUV. The Humvee seems to be gone. The area is a clearing in a wooded area, off-road. Behind the SUV, giant pylons holding power lines stretch far into the distance.

DiTommasso [off-screen]:
". . . far we are from the next—"

Pvt. Oh suddenly screams and tries to pull away from the SUV. The doctor has grabbed him through the open window and is gnawing on his neck. There is blood spurting everywhere.

Cpl. Charette:
"Oh, *fuck me*—!"

[sound of automatic gunfire.]

Pvt. Oh falls to the ground. Dr. B hangs limply out the window, most of her head gone. Cpl. Charette moves forward from behind the camera, making *stay back* gestures with one hand. She glances over her shoulder.

Cpl. Charette:
"And shut that fucking thing *off*—"

Jump cut back to woman at steering wheel of the SUV.

LaFortune:
"—told you to delete that!"

Kit [off-screen]:
"Delete it yourself. I uploaded it to the Cloud."

LaFortune:
"Whatever, I just don't ever want to see that again."

Kit [off-screen]:
"Maybe not, but the Sarge was right. Somebody's got to witness."

The woman glances at her unhappily.

LaFortune:
"Don't be precocious or you won't get any toys for Christmas."

Kit [off-screen]:
"There's no such thing as Christmas. Not any more."

Older Man [off-screen]:
"Yeah, now it's Easter, for everybody. Resurrection, all day every day."

State Trooper [off-screen]:
"They told us in Sunday school that when the dead rose, that made it Judgment Day."

| POV swings around to passengers. The soldier looks scornful.

Cpl. Charette:
"They also said there'd be signs and wonders in the sky. Anybody seen any of those? How about just a road sign telling us where to report for judgment?"

State Trooper *[uneasy]*:
"I didn't say I believed any of that stuff—"

Cpl. Charette:
"Doesn't matter whether you do or not. So far, I haven't seen any signs or wonders, just the dead rising. Except all they do after they rise is try to eat the living. I don't remember hearing about cannibal corpses in the gospels—"

DiTommasso *[abruptly, flat, dead voice]*:
"Take and eat, for this is my body."

[shocked silence.]

"Whoever eats of my body and drinks of my blood has eternal life, and I shall raise him up at the last day."

Kit *[off-screen, fearful]*:
"Daddy?"

Cpl. Charette:
"I think that's enough, sir."

| Hand covers iPad screen.

[Videofile: ro.lf@[redacted] uploaded to the Cloud]

| POV looking up from girl's lap at her and the woman, still driving.

Kit:
". . . look at it yourself if you don't believe me!"

[sound of paper rustling.]

Cpl. Charette *[off-screen]*:
"She's right. We're in Delaware."

▌ SUV slows to a stop.

LaFortune:
"So what do you want me to do? Find another pylon path? We've still got about half a tank of gas."

Cpl. Charette [off-screen]:
"We head for Washington."

▌ POV swings around to the soldier. Beside her, the man seems to be fast asleep in the shoulder harness.

LaFortune:
"Seriously?"

▌ POV swings back to her.

"Why? What's in DC?"

▌ POV swings back to the soldier. It continues to swing back and forth between the two women as they talk.

Cpl. Charette:
"Command headquarters."

LaFortune:
"Seriously?! You're still looking for someone to—to—to *tell you what to do?*"

Cpl. Charette:
"I'm still in the Army, no matter what and, so far as I still know, the President is the Commander-in-Chief."

Older Man [off-screen]:
"So, what—you want to drive up to the White House? There won't be anyone there, they'll have evacuated the whole goddam government—"

Cpl. Charette:
"There will be an organized command that I can report to. Tell them what happened. Get reassigned."

Older Man [off-screen]:
"And what about us? What are *we* supposed to do?"

Cpl. Charette:
"There'll be some provision made for evacuating civilians—"

LaFortune:
"Oh, yeah. That worked real well before, back in Perth Amboy—"

Cpl. Charette:
"It worked well enough that you weren't gridlocked on 95 South in sight of the mushroom cloud that used to be Manhattan."

[pause.]

LaFortune:
"It's gone downhill a lot since then."

[the two women suddenly burst out laughing.]

Kit *[off-screen, honestly puzzled]*:
"What's so funny?"

State Trooper *[off-screen]*:
"I think it's a geography joke."

Kit *[off-screen]*:
"Huh?"

State Trooper *[off-screen]*:
"You had to be there."

Kit *[off-screen, frustrated]*:
"I *was* there and I still don't get it! What's so funny?"

[the two women laugh harder.]

[Videofile: ro.lf@[redacted] uploaded to the Cloud]

POV of rolling countryside. Approaching sign reads: CHESAPEAKE BAY BRIDGE.

Cpl. Charette *[off-screen]*:
"There'll be a roadblock well before the bridge and another right at the bridge. If I still had my radio, I could've called and told them we were coming."

LaFortune *[off-screen]*:
"You sound pretty sure about that."

Cpl. Charette *[off-screen]*:
"It's only logical. They'll probably be MARSOC – United States Marine Corps Special Operations Command. Protecting the capital. And the Capitol."

LaFortune *[off-screen]*:
"What if you're wrong? What if there's no one at the bridge?"

Cpl. Charette *[off-screen]*:
"If there's no one guarding access at the bridge, all bets are off. Everyone's dead."

LaFortune *[off-screen]*:
"What do we do then?"

Cpl. Charette *[off-screen]*:
"Fuck if *I* know."

- -

- -

[Videofile: ro.lf@[redacted] uploaded to the Cloud]

POV of a military roadblock on an otherwise empty highway. A black female Marine in fatigues with a name-tag that says JACKSON holds up her hand as the SUV slows to a stop. She talks through the open driver's window.

Jackson:
"—tracking you folks since you left the airstrip in Bridgton."

LaFortune *[off-screen]*:
"You have? How?"

Jackson:
"Oh, *please*. Do you think you're the only person who knows how to access the Cloud? Thanks to people like you, we've got a pretty good idea of what's been going on. Better than satellite—satellite data comes in slower."

LaFortune *[off-screen, nervous laugh]*:
"So, uh, where is everybody?"

Jackson:
"If you're talking civilians, we evacuated everyone in this vicinity to the wildlife refuge and put some reservists on guard duty. It's kinda crowded and they're camping out with pretty basic amenities—they ran outa toilet paper a few days ago, but there's still plenty of food to go around. I think there's room for two-three more and I guaran-damn-tee you you'll be safe."

[brief silence.]

LaFortune *[off-screen]*:
"I don't know . . ."

Jackson:
"On the other hand, we've got more room and we need people a lot more than they do."

LaFortune *[off-screen]*:
"Okay."

Jackson:
"Yeah? You sure?"

LaFortune *[off-screen]*:
"I'm sure."

Jackson:
"Maybe you want to think about it some."

LaFortune *[off-screen]*:
"No, I'm good to go. And I might as well."

▌ Female soldier enters frame from left.

Cpl. Charette:
"What's the story?"

Jackson:
"Looks like we got another recruit. *If* she doesn't change her mind after a hot meal and a good night's sleep at Annapolis, that is."

Cpl. Charette:
"No shit?"

LaFortune *[off-screen]*:
"What about the others—Guy and Kit, the old guy, and the statie?"

Jackson:
"You don't worry, everybody'll be taken care of."

▌ POV follows the female soldier as she walks around the front of the SUV and climbs back into the front passenger seat.

Older Man *[off-screen]*:
"What's going on?"

State Trooper *[off-screen]*:
"Where are we going?"

Cpl. Charette:
"Okay, quiet down. We're going across the bridge to Annapolis. There's a naval transport from there straight down Chesapeake Bay to Norfolk and Craney Island. You'll be safe there."

Kit *[off-screen]*:
"What are you going to do, Rocky?"

LaFortune *[off-screen]*:
"I'll be staying at Annapolis, I guess."

Kit *[off-screen]*:
"Why?"

LaFortune *[off-screen]*:
"Basic training."

Kit *[off-screen]*:
"Daddy, I want us to—"

Cpl. Charette:
"Your dad's first duty is to take care of you, Kitty Carson."

Kit *[off-screen]*:
It's not *Kitty* Carson, it's Kit—"

[Text Document: ro.lf@[redacted] uploaded to the Cloud]

Dear Jo:

I'm in the Army now. I'll never get rich by digging a ditch. Can you believe it? I can't.

I figured Annapolis would be even more of a well-oiled machine than Dix, but it's kind of ragged here. They're trying to coordinate all the information coming in from the Cloud. It's a big mess. Charette says that's probably where they'll put me after some quick and dirty basic-intelligence.

OMG, military intelligence. Jumbo shrimp.

At least I'll learn how to use a weapon.

Saying goodbye to Kit and her dad was hard. The older man went with them, but the statie stayed on like me. The Marines took charge of her and I haven't seen her since.

If anyone had told me when I got evacuated from Perth Amboy that I'd end up joining the military – well, I dunno, maybe I'd've believed them. For one thing, I figure it's the only way I can find you, and for another, I think it's the only way I'll keep from going crazy until I do. I can't stand the thought of being one of a herd of refugees. Especially after what I heard tonight.

Washington's gone dark. For the last five days, there have just been tweets in bursts, bits of video, and maydays. No news about the President or her husband. The CO says there are a lot of bunkers in DC, water-tight, air-tight, impregnable. Anyone in them will be safe from the Infected . . . until the air and water runs out.

Then the bunkers will become tombs and then . . .

I don't know when I'll be able to send you another message, or even if. I'm still hoping you're out there, Jo. I'm uploading everything to the Cloud. I'm not going to give up looking for you, no matter what.

I just realized something: I can't remember when my Prozac ran out.

DEAD, AND IN PERSON!
ONE NITE ONLY!
SOLD OUT!

BERNIE MAUGHMSTEIN JOKE #1208

Hey, fuck all this PC shit, right? The only
good zombie is a live one. You know what
I'm saying?

NOTE	ACTION
It was generally felt that the temporary surveillance placed on the telephone[s] of Dr. Jason Willson had demonstrated some cause for concern regarding the health of and mental stability of Dr. Willson. The death of his wife in a tragic airplane crash seems to have blown him "off course." Although he has quieted down, his outburst at The Bunker (during which he requested synapse weepage to inject into Marianne Willson) boded badly and for a time it was increasingly felt that Dr. Willson may need to be withdrawn from the project. However, Dr. John Mwani had some considerable input into Dr. Willson's situation and we're back on the straight and narrow. Nevertheless, WLP feels that further surveillance should be considered depending on any serious deterioration. *Approved by WLP*	*J.W. Fletcher*

▼ [From the computer records of William Halloway. File name: "STORIES IN PROGRESS"]

Ebb and Flo
by Will Halloway

So we must keep apart,
You there, I here,
With just the door ajar
That oceans are,
And prayer,
And that pale sustenance,
Despair.

—Emily Dickinson (1830-1886)

LOOKING BACK at those far-off days, Ebbett Mehan was no longer able to say, hand on heart, that he had ever made it with Alice Baez. He had, of course . . . many times: Christ, for a good few weeks after Alice had broken the news to him that her father had been called back to LA, the pair of them had fornicated like rabbits in the hope that Alice would fall pregnant and thus her folks (neither of whom had much time for Ebbett and they made that pretty plain) would see reason and leave her to stay with Ebbett and his mom and dad. But it hadn't worked.

And now, some forty-some years later, sitting on his sofa with the printed-out e-mail from Neil Jakobson suggesting the big get-together, he was replaying key events from their brief—barely six months during 1968

▼ [The diary of Jeffrey Willson – entry for Monday June 17]

Monday, 11:15 pm

Found another partial in Gramps's computer files. I'm going to try finish one of these things sometime.

Dad isn't coping very well. Neither am I. The house feels busy around us though Ken Schroyce says we – that's me and dad – says we are extemporizing our grief. I don't think he knew what he was talking about. I looked it up and it didn't make any sense to me. But I think he maybe means that somehow, we are creating the activity around us. I prefer to think it's mom, fussing the way she always did.

▼ [Telephone conversation between Jeffrey Willson and Alexandra Leaf Spaulding, Wednesday June 19, 8:16 pm]

"How's your dad?"

"Not good."

"Tell him I said Hey, yeah?"

"Mmm. I found another story from my Gran'pa Will today."

"Yeah? Good?"

"As far as it goes. It's just a fragment."

"Yes, everything's a fragment of something else."

"Leaf?"

"Yeah?"

"You drinking or something?"

"Drop. Dead."

"It's a big day tomorrow."

"I know."

"Still okay for me to come stay?"

"Sure. Dad said this morning are you still coming over."

"Great."

"Hey, I'm looking forward to it."

"Me, too."

"Your dad going to be okay?"

"He'll survive. I think."

▼ [Extract from the eulogy given by Jason Willson for Marianne Willson (his wife) on Thursday June 20 and sent out to selected friends and family (see appendix 118b for full list). Recorded cassette in the Dictaphone of Jeffrey Willson]

Ladies and gentlemen, my thanks to you all for coming. These are difficult times for us all. I think you all know me well enough to accept when I say that Marianne was my world. And Jeffrey's, too, of course. But Jeffrey is young and for me personally – while I do not wish to minimize my son's loss – Marianne was my entire life, the air that I breathe, the smells that I smell, the sounds that I hear and the tastes that I taste. She was my wind and my rain, my warmth and my coolness. She was my spring, my summer, my fall and my winter. And now . . . now, ladies and gentlemen, she is my work. I shall not rest and I shall not relax; I shall not pause in any way whatsoever save to eat and to drink (and I do that only that I may keep the strength to continue) . . . and this shall be my life until a solution is found . . . a solution to what is increasingly the most savage blight levied against mankind in the history of human cognizance. In closing, I shall say only this: a small part of a stanza written by one of our greatest poets, Emily Dickinson.

> Parting is all we know of heaven,
> And all we need of hell.

Thank you ladies and gentlemen.

▼ [Minutes from a meeting between W. Leonard Paryder, Senior Controller (East) and Special Agent J.W. Fletcher, Thursday June 20]

NOTE	ACTION
It was resolved that permanent telephonic and audio surveillance should be installed in the home and vehicle[s] of the following with immediate effect:	*J.W. Fletcher*
	Jay Disbro
	Flip Carpenter
	Malcolm McKerry
Dr. Jason Willson	*Prof. M.T. Déesharné*
Dr. John Mwani	
Mr. Leo Holdstein (attorney)	
Professor Stephen Ming	
Rod Wardale	
Theresa Chumskor	
Professor Shalenka Vim	
Dr. Dick Spratton	
Dr. Bob Loader	
Professor Jacob Zeitner	
Mr. Fletcher to initiate a small team to carry out the necessary installations.	
Approved by WLP	

▼ [Telephone conversation between Dr. Jason Willson and Professor Jacob Zeitner, Thursday June 20, 6:16 pm]

"Jack, it's Jase."

"Jase . . . Jesus, man. How you doing?"

"Not good. Not good at all."

"Jesus, Jase . . . I just don't know what to say."

"We had the burial today."

"What was that?"

"What?"

"Something clunked. Is someone listening in on this, Jase?"

"Hah! Why would anyone want to listen in on my phone calls."

"Well, I heard a – there! I heard it again.

"Jase, are you drinking?"

"And eating. I'm being a good b—"

"I'm talking about booze, Jase. That was a glass banging against the telephone and ice clunking in the glass. Wasn't it?"

"I was thirsty."

"Jason, take it easy will—"

"I want her back, Jack."

"Jason—"

"I've been patient, Jack. I've given it a shot. Now I want her back."

▼ [Memo from the Office of Dr. Brewster Gilray to W.L. Paryder]

Mr. Paryder,

Doctor Gilray has recently been visited by the FBI. It would appear that the zombiefied (sic) body of Mr. Thomas Moreby has been forcibly removed from the custody of the british authorities. Doctor Gilray does not want any unnecessary attention centering on our work at the bunker to hamper our progress. He said it was a case of eggs and omelets and that you would understand. Please confirm receipt of this memo.

Cordially,
Lois Chappelle
Assistant to Dr. Brewster Gilray
NWP

Special Agent Philip "Flip" Carpenter: Please state your name for the record.

Thomas Moreby: Thomas Moreby.

FC: Welcome to the machine, Mr. Moreby. I hope you enjoyed your flight.

TM: It is interesting to be here, Mr . . .?

FC: Carpenter, sir. Interesting?

TM: Everything in this new world is interesting, do you not you think so?

Special Agent Malcolm McKerry: Can you open the gate, Flip?

FC: Sure. Press the gate, Mr. Moreby.

MM: Let me, sir. You can't with those manacles There.

TM: Thank you, and thank you, Mr. Carrier.

FC: Carpenter, sir. C-A-R—

TM: Whatever.

FC: Enjoy your stay, sir.

TM: Oh, I intend to. I am sure we shall meet again.

*[static]*lla? You there? Pick up the*[static]*am—

Nate? I'm here, you go on now. Over.

Bella, we're out on the*[static]*Pasture Road over to Old Man Penn*[static]*place. We got reports of a prowler over in the cemet*[static]*. You better send over*[static]*sics.

Over.

Nate, you're all over the dam place here. You got the handset down yore drawers again cos it sure-as-shootin' sounds like you're talkin' outta your ass? Over.

Love*[static]*too, Bell*[static]*

Me and my partner, Officer Joshua Deranjukl, received a call at 20:46 hours from Mr. Abraham Pennhaligan, whose home borders the property, that there was someone wandering around in the cemetery. We went to investigate and discovered Dr. Jason Willson. He was sitting beside the grave of his recently interred wife, Marianne Willson, and he was reading to her from the Bible. He apologized for causing any concerns and agreed to leave immediately. Officer Deranjukl and I thought we detected the smell of alcohol on Dr. Willson's breath and we felt it not advisable for him to drive home. So we took him in the patrol car. The doctor assured us that he would call Mr. Pennhaligan sometime tomorrow. We went around to put Mr. Pennhaligan's mind at ease.

Brew,

Our guest is in place. Feisty bastard, but we're dealing with him. Of the latest batch, 11 of the 17 are still with us but 2 are touch and go and Flip Carpenter says 4 more are deteriorating. But, of course, they don't have the longevity of our guest. The next test is to explore the frontal lobe sac, which means draining the sac through the nasal cavity. I need an okay for this because we cannot anaesthetize because to do so would destroy any efficacy of the weepage. This has been the case on other attempts, but this time there will be a degree more discomfort. An early response would be appreciated.

Paryder

Mr. Paryder,

Doctor Gilray has asked me to let you know that he authorizes you to proceed with all due haste.

Lois Chappelle
Assistant to Dr. Brewster Gilray
NWP

▼ [From the files of Professor M.T. Déesharné]

CASE NOTES

Patient #1: Mr. Arthur Burchamp
Patient #2: Mrs. Felicity Burchamp
June 22, 13:45: Permission received to proceed.

Prof. M.T. Déesharné

▼ [Transcript: Interview Room Log, The Bunker. Saturday June 22, 15:03]

Special Agent Philip "Flip" Carpenter: Good day to you, Mr. Moreby. Let the record show that the patient—
Thomas Moreby: Let the record show, Mr. Carrier, that I am neither patient nor a patient. The first suggests a weakness and the second an ailment. I am troubled by neither of these afflictions.
FC: As you will. Are you being attended to?
TM: I am being interrogated, sir. Constantly.
FC: I apologize.
TM: You apologize. How wonderful. I believe it was your Oliver Wendell Holmes who said apologizing is a very desperate habit and one that is

rarely cured. It is merely egotism wrong side out. In truth, it never pays dividends.

FC: Never, Mr. Moreby?

TM: Never, sir.

FC: Well, I can only say that the reason is that time is against us and—

TM: Never ruin an apology with an excuse.

FC: Holmes again?

TM: Johnson, my dear fellow. And Kimberly, not Samuel.

FC: I was going to finish by saying that there is much we need to know.

TM: And you shall, Mr. Carrier.

FC: Carpenter. That's Carpenter. C-A-R—

TM: And you shall, Mr. Carrier. In the fullness of time.

FC: And that is the one thing we do not have. Time.

TM: One of two things, surely.

FC: What's the other thing?

TM: Knowledge, sir. The other thing is knowledge. Just why is it that I am here?

FC: You are here to assist us in our investigations.

TM: Mmm . . . that sounds . . . intriguing.

FC: We want you to meet someone.

TM: Is this someone a he or a she?

FC: Yes. Their name is Burchamp. Felicity and Arthur. Our volunteers.

TM: You know what they say about volunteers, Mr. Carrier?

FC: Remind me.

TM: One volunteer is worth ten pressed men.

FC: Or women.

TM: Oh, surely not—that would be twenty pressed women.

FC: Tut tut, Mr. Moreby. I didn't know you were discriminatory.

TM: I will wager that there are several things about me you do not know, Mr. Carrier.

FC: Hmm.

TM: Did you know, for instance, that my middle name is James? Called after the young Stuart pretender. No? I thought as much.

FC: I'm not—

TM: You are not convinced? You still believe everything about me is on your little electrical device there?

FC: We're pretty thorough.

TM: Very well. My favorite color. Is that there?

FC: I don't think we—

TM: I asked you a question, Mr. Carrier. You might afford me the courtesy of an answer. Is my favorite color on there?

FC: Er, okay . . . favorite color. No, that's not here either.

TM: Do you want to know what it is?

FC: If you want to tell me.

TM: I do. It is red. Blood red. Not the namby-pamby red of a pricked finger, but a deep plasma burgundy straight from the vein. You are nodding, Mr. Carrier.

FC: That's Carpenter. You know what my name is. You're just trying to piss me off.

TM: Is that what you think?

FC: Yes, that's what I think.

TM: Is it working? Let the records show that Mr. Carrier is shaking his head. I take it this is being recorded on another of your infernal devices, yes? And now he is nodding.

FC: Yes, it's being recorded.

TM: You were nodding. You did not tell me why. Why were you nodding, Mr. Carrier? For the record, of course.

FC: Because what you said—about the blood—it's what I expected.

TM: You are a very clever man, Mr. Carrier.

FC: I don't think so.

TM: No, I do not think so, either. I was being ironic. I do not think that you are clever at all. [pause] You did not respond. Have I offended you?

FC: No.

TM: Good. I am pleased.

FC: Great. I'm glad you're pleased.

TM: Hmm. How about my favorite food, Mr. Carrier. Do you know what that is?

FC: No.

TM: No? Well, well—you surprise me. Despite the fact that your masters solicit my help, you do not seem to know very much at all, do you, Mr. Carrier?

FC: We know what we need to know.

TM: No, you only know what you think you need to know. There is a difference. Would you agree? Would you say that there is a difference between what you know and what you think you need to know?

FC: I . . . er, I don't know.

TM: [laughs] You really do not know much at all, do you Mr. Carrier?

FC: Okay, tell me. I've got my iPad ready. Tell me your favorite food and I'll enter it. Then we'll know.

TM: Very well, Mr. Carrier. Are you ready?

FC: I'm ready.

TM: Very well. It is three things, I am afraid. I love them all dearly and I just do not think I could choose between them.

FC: [sighs] Okay. Let me have them. Why are you leaning forward? Please remain upright in the chair.

TM: Are you frightened, Mr. Carrier? Frightened of me?

FC: No, I'm not frightened. There's no way you can break those chains, so you can't get to me.

TM: [laughs] Cannot "get" to you. How delightful. You think I want to get to you, Mr. Carrier? Let the records show that Mr. Carrier is nodding again. Perhaps you are correct, Mr. Carrier. I sense we could enjoy a . . . shall we say "a relationship." And you know . . . perhaps we shall. One day.

FC: Don't hold your breath.

TM: There is not a chance of that, Mr. Carrier. You do know that, at least. Surely?

FC: [sighs] Yes.

TM: Good. Then I see you are making progress. I was leaning forward merely so that I might whisper to you.

FC: The recording machine will pick up any sound so there's no need to—

TM: Oh, no . . . I was not trying to avoid anyone else hearing what I have to say. I was simply trying to achieve a spirit of . . . of intimacy.

FC: What did you want to say to me?

TM: Why, I wanted to tell you my three favorite foods.

FC: Tell me then. Don't whisper. Don't lean forward. Don't do anything at all. Just tell me.

TM: You are getting annoyed now, Mr. Carrier. And we were doing so—

FC: We're not "doing well," Mr. Moreby. We're not doing anything. Just tell me. Just tell me your favorite food. Or your favorite foods.

TM: Ah, very well. In no particular order then. Eyeball, tongue and ball-sack.

FC: Is that supposed to upset me?

TM: Upset you? Why would I want to do that?

FC: You're trying to . . .

TM: Trying to what, Mr. Carrier?

FC: It doesn't matter. Forget it.

TM: I certainly would not want to cause you distress.

FC: Well, you didn't.

TM: Good. I mean that. You know what they say about distress, don't you?

FC: [sighs] I reckon this is something else I don't know, Mr. Moreby. So, tell me . . . what do they say about distress? Should I make an entry?

TM: If you so wish.

FC: Okay, I'm ready. Go ahead.

TM: They say that distress toughens the meat. An animal that is calm is much more tender. Ah, you are shaking your head, Mr. Carrier. Do you not agree with that?

FC: Given our . . . understanding . . . Mr. Moreby, tomorrow you will meet our other guests.

TM: [the sound of a handclap] Oh, I do so enjoy meeting new people. I cannot wait for introductions.

FC: [click] Hello?

Voice on intercom: Yes?

FC: Agent Carpenter here. Can you make sure that our other guests are prepped and ready in Ops Theater #6 for midday tomorrow?

Voice on intercom: Will do. [click]

TM: Should I bring anything?

FC: Not really. Think of it merely as a party, Mr. Moreby.

TM: How splendid. I do so love a good party.

▼ [The personal diary of Dr. Jason Willson – entry for Saturday June 22]

Morning, Saturday, June 22

It's the nights that are the worst. Just looking at the bed is almost more than I can take. I can smell her . . . Marianne: I mustn't lose calling her by her name. Marianne. Marianne. Marianne. I can smell <u>Marianne</u>. Can smell her perfume. I'd forgotten what it was until I hunted it down in the bathroom, in her cupboard. It's Vent Vert by Balmain. I put it back where I found it, but then I had to go back and get it out again for another fix. I've now left the stopper out of the bottle—I took it downstairs with me. I put it in the kitchen and switched the radio on, so that it felt like there was life around the place again.

Later

It's nighttime, now. I brought the bottle back upstairs. It is now on the table on the landing, outside of our bedroom so that, whenever I step out there, I can still smell you. I'm in the bedroom. Our bedroom. It's like you've been here today. I can feel there's been another presence around the place. I wish you could come and say something to me. I was out most of the day—couldn't stand to be here. Did you wonder where I was? Do you miss me as much as I miss you?

I've picked up some comic books out of Jeffrey's room but looking at them—ghosts and ghouls and decapitations—I feel it's too much like work. (What a ridiculous thing for me to write.) Jeffrey left after the funeral. I spoke with him this afternoon: he's staying over at the Sheriff's place. He says he's thinking about joining the resistance movement. With Alexandra and her father (hereinafter Wyatt Earp). He's growing up fast.

I need to sleep. The problem is waking up.

▼ [Telephone conversation between Professor Stephen Ming and Dr. John Mwani, Saturday June 22, 11:16 pm]

"John?"

"Steve? What's up?"

"Sorry to bother you so late. You busy?"

"Hey, does the Pope shit in the woods? But I always have time to stop working and talk. What's up?"

"Jason Willson."

"Jason? What about him?"

"Did you get one of the eulogy CDs he's sent out?"

"Yeah. Poor guy."

"Yes. Did you know he wants to come back. To *work*."

[SILENCE] "And this is not good, why?"

"I don't think—we don't think—we don't think he's ready."

"Who's the 'we', Steve?"

"Well, it's me . . . and Rod, Theresa, Shalenka . . . and Dick Spratton and Bob Load—"

"Yeah, I figured they'd be in there. Dick and Bob . . . the fuckwit twins."

"They're only thinking of—"

"Steve, they're assholes. Assholes do not think. Trust me on this. I'm a consultant neurosurgeon: I know of what I speak."

"I think you're being a little unfair, John."

[PAUSE] "And you are ringing me why?"

"I thought you might reason with him. Tell him—"

"Bob Loader wants to take over the project. Dick Spratton wants Bob to take over the project. And if you subscribe to the Gaia theory, the whole planet wants Bob to take over the *project*, but—and listen to me on this, Steve—the human race wouldn't make it through to Thanksgiving."

"John, Jason's just buried his wife."

"Right. Yes, he has just buried his wife. So that right back at you, Steve. I'll bet he's going out of his mind and—"

"That's what we're—"

"Out of his mind and he would give his right arm to get back into the saddle. I know I would. [PAUSE] And so would you, Steve. I mean . . . Janet?"

"Yeah, I don't like to think about—"

"Well you should fucking think about it, Steve. I think about Marilyn. If Marilyn were dead? I mean, come on man. Don't be a stooge for the fuckwits. Really. Don't do it. [SILENCE] Steve, say something. Talk to me."

"I'm here."

"Okay, let me tell you this: you're gonna need some other patsy on this, amigo. Cos I won't do it."

"He would listen to you, John."

"Maybe he would. Maybe he wouldn't. We'll never know. Because I am not going to ask him to step down from the project."

"Not necessarily step down . . . just for him to take some extra—"

"Steve, you're not listening here. I'm not going to ask Jason to do anything at all. He's his own man. And he's in charge here."

"Okay, maybe the— Maybe Dick and Bob have got ulterior mot—"

"Maybe?"

"—some ulterior motives. But there's something else."

"Something else? Something like what?"

"Something about Jason."

[SILENCE] "Just spit it out, Steve."

"It's his face."

"His face?"

[SILENCE] "He's always smiling."

▼ [E-mail conversation between W. Leonard Paryder and Flip Carpenter, Saturday June 22, 5:00 pm]

From: W. Leonard Paryder <big_daddy@deadbolt.com>
To: Flip Carpenter <flipthebird.@deadbolt.com>
Sent: 22 June 17:00
Subject: DISTRESS

Flip, I have been playing your tapes. Let me know if you want to take a break. I don't think your recent talk with our guest was all that helpful. Drop me a line when you've got a minute.
WLH

- -

From: Flip Carpenter <flipthebird.@deadbolt.com>
To: W. Leonard Paryder <big_daddy@deadbolt.com>
Sent: 22 June 18:12
Subject: Re: DISTRESS

Sorry for the delay in getting back to you. I'm fine. Honestly. But a break would be good. It's been a bit of a slog. But I don't want to come over as being a wimp. I know we're all under a lot of pressure to get a breakthrough.
Flip

- -

From: W. Leonard Paryder <big_daddy@deadbolt.com>
To: Flip Carpenter <flipthebird.@deadbolt.com>
Sent: 22 June 18:19
Subject: Re: DISTRESS

After tomorrow's procedure take the next few days off. Consider that an order. And you're not a wimp.
WLH

5:50 am

I just woke up, shaking. Bad dream. I was living in that house in the Hopper painting—I don't recall the title. Dad was there and there was something lying on the kitchen table. And get this—Robert Duvall was there too, the way he was in Apocalypse Now. There was this noise—a farting noise—and the sheet over the thing on the table gave a little flutter. And Duvall said "I love the smell of corpse gas in the morning." And he and dad laughed. And then dad noticed I was there and he stood up and pulled me over to the table. He started lifting the sheet from one corner and he said, "Aren't you gonna say hey to your mom?" And I woke up. I just called dad and there was no answer.

"Mr. Pennhaligan?"

"Yeah, this is Abe Pennhaligan. Who's that?"

"Jason Willson, Mr. Pennhaligan."

"Call me Abe."

"Okay, Abe. I'm calling—"

"What can I do for you, Mr. Willson?"

"It's Doctor Willson. But call me Jason."

"Okay. What can I do for you, Jason?"

"I'm calling to apologize."

"Whatcha apologizing for, Jason?"

"Well . . . I think I may have caused you some concern? Last night?"

"Concern? How's that, Jason?"

"I was in the cemetery and I think you—"

"Oh, right, you're the fella."

"Yeah, I'm the—"

"Cops told me. They came around, told me I had nothing to worry about. Truth to tell, I wasn't worried. [PAUSE] I'm sorry to hear about your loss, Mr. Willson. I know better than most folks how you're feeling. Lost my own Marjorie some eight years ago now. I'm a sight older than you are, Mr. Willson—"

"Jason."

"Yeah, right—Jason. I'm a good sight older than you are so I guess I'm closer to the exit doors than the entrance, if you catch my drift."

"Yes, I know what you mean."

"A sight older and it's been a sight longer since my Marjorie passed across."

"That's a nice way of putting it, Mist— Abe. A real nice way of putting it. Makes it sound like she's just nipped out to switch on the Mister Coffee."

"Yeah, well, we know that's not the case, Jason. But we use this . . . this kind of shorthand to somehow make it more acceptable. But it's not, is it? It's not acceptable at all. [PAUSE] You still there?"

"I'm still here."

"You okay?"

"Not really."

▼ [Transcript: Ops Theater #6 Audio Log, The Bunker. Sunday June 23, 12:02]

Arthur Burchamp: What are you going to do?

Felicity Burchamp: Artie?

AB: It's okay, dear. It'll be okay. What's happening please? Can I see my wife?

M.T. Déesharné: In due course, Mr. Burchamp.

AB: That's Artie. Can you call me Artie?

MTD: If you wish, Mr. Bur— Artie, I mean.

FB: Artie, I can't see you.

AB: I can't see you either, honey. Sir? Sir, could you make it so my wife and I can see each other?

MTD: I'm afraid we must maintain the head in a static position, Artie. That's for the both of you.

AB: We wouldn't move it . . .

MTD: I'm sure you wouldn't intend to move your head—same with Mrs. Burchamp—but it could be just an involuntary reaction and—

AB: That like we couldn't control ourselves?

MTD: Something like that, yes.

FB: What's he saying, honey?

AB: He's saying—

MTD: It's to lessen the possibility of injury, Mrs. Bur—

AB: Lessen the possibility of injury? You said there was no danger.

FB: Artie, he said—

AB: You said there was no danger.

MTD: Yes, there is no danger, Mr. Bur— Artie.

AB: Well there must be some danger because you said—

FB: He said lessen the danger, Artie. He didn't say remove any possibility of danger. He just said less—

AB: I know, Fee.

MTD: I said lessen the chance of injury, not danger. You're putting words—

AB: Hey, Mr . . . Mr?

MTD: It's Professor. Déesharné. Like "day" and then "sharn" and then "a" again at the end . . . "a" as in day, I mean.

FB: So it's not safe? You're saying it's not safe? This thing we're doing? What is it we're—

MTD: Nothing is ever completely safe, Mrs. Burchamp. Nothing is 100%.

FB: Artie, I'm scared.

AB: I know, sweetie.

FB: What is it we're doing anyway?

MTD: Mrs. Burchamp, we're draining the sacs at the front and sides of your brainpan.

FB: You're doing what? That doesn't sound like—

AB: You said it was a simple extraction. You said you were going to do a simple extraction and then you would use the fluids you released.

MTD: You signed the—

AB: I signed up to have a tooth pulled. That's what I signed up for here.

MTD: A tooth pulled? You're joking, right? They told you that you were having a too—

AB: Hey, doc, get me out of here. I need for you—

FB: Artie, make him get us out.

AB: I am doing, honey. I'm doing—

MTD: I'm afraid that's not possible, Mr. Burchamp. Nurse? Now would be good.

Nurse Jasmine Ugamno: Right away, Doctor.

AB: Hey, lady . . . where you going with that needle. You put that needle down now, you hear? You hear what—

FB: Artie! Artie, she's gonna stick it in—

AB: Doc, make her put the needle down. Please make her—

FB: Oh, Artie, Artie, *Art—Aiiiiieeeeeeeeeeeiiii!*—

MTD: She'll be okay now.

AB: Is she asleep?

MTD: Er, no, Mr. Burchamp.

AB: Fee? You okay? Can you hear me, sweetie?

MTD: She's not asleep. What we have done is administer a drug that disables the cerebral cortex.

AB: Fee? She's not speaking, Doc.

MTD: No, Artie. She's not speaking because we have frozen her entire central nervous system. We had to make sure she wouldn't move while we begin the transfusion.

AB: Transfusion! Is she going to be okay?

MTD: Artie, what you and your wife are doing is for the benefit of humanity.

AB: Doc, I don't give the scab off of a rat's poisoned dick for humanity. I just want— Hey, now where you going with that needle, Doc?

MTD: I'm going to inject it into you.

AB: And then . . .? What is that stuff? The stuff in the needle?

MTD: That is—

[a door opens and closes]

Flip Carpenter: Good afternoon, Doctor. I take it you already know Mr. Moreby?

MTD: We met briefly while his transportation was being arranged. Mr. Moreby.

TM: And a good afternoon again to you, sir. I regret that I cannot presently shake your hand but, alas, as you can see . . . Are we ready to begin?

AB: Begin the hell wh—?

TM: Patience, sir. All in good time. I take it we have frozen the cortex? Good. And you are about to administer the—

MTD: As you can see.

[sound of struggling accompanied by guttural grunting]

TM: Indeed. And that activity is with the cortex disabled. Hmm. It beggars belief.

[the struggling and grunting—now high-pitched—intensifies]

I feel we must make haste. What is—?

MTD: Burchamp.

TM: And that is—?

MTD: His wife.

TM: Good. Mr. Burchamp?

AB: Call me Artie.

TM: I would just as soon not, Mr. Burchamp, for reasons that will become all too clear. The relationship we are about to embark upon is hardly what one might call "cordial."

AB: What's happening to my—?

TM: Let us press on. Do you know why you are here, Mr. Burchamp? I will take that as a no. I am aware you are unable to move your head. These people have charged me with helping them find a serum that will combat the plague currently ravaging the world outside. But first we need to give you the disease. That was administered to your wife a little while ago. She has now turned. The sound you can hear is her body reacting to a transfusion of my blood.

AB: Oh my Go—!

TM: I am afraid that your God has no part in any of this, Mr. Burchamp. It is my god that rules here now. But pray let me continue, if I may. The first injection was recently administered, yes nurse?

NJU: About five minutes ago, Mr. Moreby.

TM: Thank you. Mr. Burchamp, that injection is supposed to freeze the cerebral cortex, from which all instructions with regard to movement are made. As you can hear—

[the struggling and grunting are now loud]

—that hasn't been too successful. And we need that success because the frozen cortex means absolute minimum movement. We need minimum movement because the way we intend to administer the test serum is through the eye socket. This will entail popping the eyes out onto your cheeks and injecting directly into the frontal lobe through the rear membrane.

AB: What?

TM: I shall assume that your response simply reflects your dismay at the process I have identified, rather than a lack of understanding on your part.

AB: *What?*

TM: Indeed. Professor Déesharné, I think the answer lies in the speed with which you follow the contamination. I propose a slight deviation. Clearly your other volunteer—Mrs. Burchamp?—it is clear that she is going to be of little if any use to us. I see you've popped one eyeball but—

AB: *Fee!* What have you done to my wi—?

MTD: Mr. Burchamp, please try to remain calm. We're doing—

TM: Nurse, please prepare another shot of the cortex injection.

NJU: Certainly, Mr. Moreby. I have it ready.

TM: Now, Professor, be ready to pop the eyeballs and syringe the membrane through the left socket—that's the easiest side.

MTD: Very good, Mr. Moreby. Er . . . what are you doing?

TM: I am going to bite a chunk out of Mr. Burchamp's shoulder, just where it meets the neck. That should ensure the virus has the shortest distance to travel to reach the brain.

[in addition to the struggling and grunting from earlier, there is now the sound of a man's hysterical voice and some crashing of metal equipment, followed by a tearing sound and additional noises . . . the sound of someone chewing]

NJU: Oh my God!

MTD: Jesus Christ!

FC: Moreby, stop . . . !

AB: *Arrrgggggghhhhhhhhh!*

▼ [The personal diary of Dr. Jason Willson – entry for Monday June 24]

It's just after 3:00 in the morning as I write this. The house feels busy. It's you, baby, I know it is. You want me to do something. I don't know if I'm up to it. God I'm so tired. I just had a dream. Jesus Christ, it was so real. So fucking real. I know—I'm sorry about the language. No, I'm not really fucking sorry . . . not about saying "fuck" anyway. You remember that pizza and pasta place we used to go to when we lived up on Riverside Drive? Times Square? Well, we were there.

Tonight. You were as large as life and just as beautiful as ever. We sat in the booth just inside the door. You remember? The waiter was called Brendan and he downloaded Captain America onto a blank DVD. Well, he served us tonight. I ordered mushroom alfredo on crostini to start followed by a salami pizza. You had that blue cheese big mushroom—the one I don't like and you always used to feel guilty about ordering, cos I never wanted to try a piece but you always wanted to try a piece of mine. Remember? Anyway, we were there tonight, back in New York. I watched you walk away from the table to go to the bathroom. The big wooden fan-things were whirring around above you and everyone was watching you. I thought why shouldn't they, and then I saw they all looked really sad. You gave me a wave as you pushed open the door to the bathrooms and, just for a second, I wanted to call you back, tell you not to go. I remember thinking I'd tell you just to pee in your pants but, whatever else you did, I wanted to make sure you didn't leave the table. Then you were gone. They were playing Bobby Vee's Take Good Care of My Baby over the PA, and Brendan came up to me and he leaned over the table and he put his arms around me. I thought it was a little strange, but you know how you accept stuff in dreams? Anyway, he—Brendan—he said to me, She isn't coming back, you know. And I said to Brendan, I know that. And we just nodded to each other. And then Brendan, he says to me, You still want your food? And I shook my head. And then I opened my eyes and I was in bed with my arms wrapped around your nightdress sobbing into your pillow. I'm going to make a cup of chamomile. I need to sleep.

▼ [Telephone conversation between Professor Stephen Ming and Dr. John Mwani, Monday June 24, 2:38 pm]

"John?"

"Yeah, this is John. Go ahead."

"John, it's Steve Ming."

"Jeez, Steve . . . I didn't recognize you."

"Well, it's me."

"You got a cold or something?"

"I'm whispering."

"You're whispering? Why you whispering, Steve? There somebody there? Somebody with you? Hey, where are you any—?"

"There's nobody here with me. I'm here at The Bunker."

"Oh. Okay. So—?"

"I was just worried someone might come in. I mean, while I'm talking."

"Oh. Right. Steve, are you okay?"

"I'm fine. Listen to me. Have you . . . this is a tough one."

"Go ahead, Steve—spit it out."

"Have you . . . have you been to see me today?"

"To see *you*?"

"Yes."

"Why would I want to do that?"

"I don't know that you would want to see me. It's just—oh, wait. John, forget it."

"Forget it? Forget what?"

"Just forget it."

▼ [Telephone conversation between Professor Stephen Ming and Dr. John Mwani, Monday June 24, 2:47 pm]

"Hello?"

"John, it's me."

"Steve, what the hell—?"

"I couldn't talk. Before, I mean."

"Somebody come in?"

"No, nobody came in. It just suddenly occurred to me that my phone could be bugged."

"Who would want to bug your telephone, Steve?"

"I dunno. Same people who came out to my house?"

"Somebody came out to your house?"

"I think so. There were little things that were changed. Things only I would spot. Doors open to a certain mark on the carpet, papers placed at a certain part of the sofa arm or the table. Stuff like that. It used to work for James Bond, right?"

"You're a long ways from James Bond, Steve."

"Yeah, well . . ."

"Where you calling from now?"

"My son-in-law's Blackberry."

"So who do you think has been visiting?"

"And bugging me."

"And bugging you."

"CIA? FBI? Homeland Security?"

"Harper Valley PTA?"

"Yeah, you may laugh, John but I aim not to take chances."

"Well, you've certainly not done that."

Later

I fell asleep in front of the TV and had the mother and father of all dreams. Marianne, you were there, looking as beautiful as ever, and there were some people from work, and Jeffrey was there—he was with Leaf, Alex, the girl from next door . . . and they were making out. There was a single bed downstairs in the living room and they were going at it under the sheets, grunting like a pair of rutting dogs. You asked me if I was okay and I told you I didn't know. You patted my hand then—I could feel it, baby—still can. (I'm smelling it right now, wondering if you really did come to me.)

And there was this woman, sitting all by herself at the big table. She wore dark clothes that didn't show much skin, all gathered together at the neck with a brooch. I asked you who she was and you looked at me as though I was crazy. "Why," you said to me, "that's Emily Dickinson." Then we were sitting there at the table with her and she patted my hand—I saw her reaching out and I withdrew the hand that you had patted. And she said to me "The eyes glaze once, and that is death." You frowned at that and turned to me. And you said to me, "Am I dead sweetie?" Emily Dickinson smiled and covered her mouth with her hand. I told you that you weren't dead, only sleeping. And you said you wanted to wake up. "Wake me up then sweetie," you said to me. And what was worst of all was that you sounded cross with me. And as I watched, your mouth just kept on getting bigger and your eyes got like little black beads . . . like a shark's eyes.

And then I woke up.

"Jack, it's me."

"Thank God, Jase. I've called you a couple times, but you never picked up. Didn't send a text, didn't—"

"I've been busy."

"You still drinking?"

"A little. Not much. I'm not bingeing, put it that way."

"Are you back at work?"

"Well, yes and no."

"Pick one."

"They don't want me back yet. They say I'm not ready."

"I think that doesn't sound too unreasonable. Who's 'they'?"

"Spratton and Loader."

"Ah, the Cheech and Chong of neurological medicine."

"That dates you."

"I thought you liked Laurel and Hardy—what does that make you? Anyway, that'll mean Steve Ming is also lined up with a rifle pointing at your heart. You know what John Mwani calls them? The Fuckwit Twins. It's just so apt. But is Ming involved?"

"I'd guess so."

"So you're on gardening leave."

"At least they didn't tell me to spend more time with my family."

"Ouch. You said 'yes and no' when I asked if you were working?"

"They don't want me back at The Bunker yet so . . . so I'm doing a little moonlighting."

"Yeah?"

"And I want to hypothesize with you."

"Lucky me."

"According to Jim Staniforth and some of the other guys from New World Pharmaceuticals, the whole thing goes—"

"Whoa, hoss. New World whatity what?"

"Pharmaceuticals. They're all over The Bunker. Almost seems like they're the ones running things these days . . .

"That sounds—"

"Jack, I trust you like a brother but I'm on a limb here . . . difficult terrain. I need to restrict information on a need-to-know basis."

"Okay. Go on."

"According to those guys, here's how it goes down. There's a break in the skin—be it rip, tear, bite, cut, etc., but it's usually a bite with the removal of flesh as a standard add-on—and then there's inflammation, always assuming the victim survives, leading through a sequence of physiological alterations culminating in altered macrophages attacking healthy tissue. The macrophages invade the nervous system and fuck the brain."

"Is that a medical term, 'fuck the brain'?"

"Too right it is."

"Jase, it's good to have you back."

"Thanks, Jack. But—"

"But? There's a 'but'?"

"You don't need to know the 'but'. Trust me, I'm—"

"You're a crazy bastard."

"Yeah, crazy may well be right on the button. I want to ask you a question. If, as we now suppose, this surfeit of proteins required by the process creates, in turn, a ravenous appetite that effectively powers the body then—"

"Jason, think about what I think you're about to say. Think about it carefully."

"'Jason'? What happened to 'Jase'?"

"I have no idea. I think he just left the building and I'm now left talking to his looney-tuney doppelgänger. This is about Marianne, isn't it?"

"Jack, don't do this. Just talk to me, okay? I pray to God that you never find yourself in the same situation with Kath—"

"Jase, that's not playing fair and you know—"

"Fuck 'fair,' Jack. I've had it with 'fair.' New World is at the cutting edge, but my contact there has dried up. Last I heard before I left, they were bringing us a visitor."

"A visitor? Who?"

"Some kind of VIP."

"You don't know who?"

"All I heard from one of the guards was that someone was going to be coming in from the British Isles."

"And you don't know who?"

"Uh-uh."

"So what do you want?"

"Well, in a nutshell—"

"In a nutshell, Jase."

"In a nutshell, could we siphon from the brain pan of one of the plague victims and inject the macrophages straight into the brain of a deceased person?"

"To do what?"

"To kick-start the whole neurological process when—"

"When the intended recipient is dead."

"Right. Yes."

"You're going to try bring Marianne back. That's what this is all about, isn't it?"

"Jack, you owe me on thi—"

"I owe *you*? Since when? What was the occasion that would warrant your asking me this?"

"Jack, just answer me and I'll go away. Might that work? Just answer me."

"It might."

"And now I need to ask you where the Golden Pathway is."

"Jase—"

"Jack, just tell me. I've read your references to it in the past and heard you mention it off-hand. Where is the traditional skull weak spot that'll allow me to syringe into the brain direct through the skull?"

"You'll never do it through the skull. The Golden Pathway lies behind the ear. You'd need to drill into the soft spot behind the upper ear."

"Thanks, Jack."

"Don't thank me. Jase, one other thing."

"Yes?"

"There's an old saying. Never bite the hand that feeds you. I'm not sure the recipient of your efforts would necessarily agree with that. Always assuming it works, of course."

"Of course. See you in Hell, Jack."

"You can pay the Ferryman!"

"The eyes have it, right? Oh, hey . . . someone's at the door."

"Stay well."

"You too."

▼ [Conversation between Central Dispatch at Precinct 14 (Germaine Shutz) and Patrol Car #17 (officers Nathaniel Melansky and Joshua Deranjukl), Monday June 24, 23:35]

What's up, Nate? Over.

Germaine! Hey girl, what's happening? Over.

Nothing much. You gonna piss on my fire now? Over.

Nah. Old man Pennhaligan next to the boneyard saw another prowler; could have been two this time, he says. He let fly with a twelve-gauge . . . thinks he may have winged one 'em. We're here now, me and my man—say hey, to the Germ, man!

Hey, Germaine. Over

Hey yourself, Stilts. So where you boys heading now? Over.

We're gonna double-check in the graveyard, but it's difficult to see too good and I don't wanna go around with blazing lights. We may need to wait until tomorrow. Over.

Okay, stay in touch. Over and out.

Over and out.

From: Malcolm McKerry <madasahatter@deadbolt.com>
To: W. Leonard Paryder <big_daddy@deadbolt.com>
Sent: 25 June 07:01
Subject: HAIL, THE GANG'S ALL HERE

The lady is here. We can begin the party proper.
MM

- - - - - - - - - - - - - - - - - - - -

From: W. Leonard Paryder <big_daddy@deadbolt.com>
To: Malcolm McKerry <madasahatter@deadbolt.com>
Sent: 25 June 07:08
Subject: Re: HAIL, THE GANG'S ALL HERE

Malcolm, I sometimes wonder whether you're actually taking all of this as seriously as you might. Where's the other package?
WLP

- - - - - - - - - - - - - - - - - - - -

From: Malcolm McKerry <madasahatter@deadbolt.com>
To: W. Leonard Paryder <big_daddy@deadbolt.com>
Sent: 25 June 07:10
Subject: Re: HAIL, THE GANG'S ALL HERE

In the slammer.
MM

- - - - - - - - - - - - - - - - - - - -

From: W. Leonard Paryder <big_daddy@deadbolt.com>
To: Malcolm McKerry <madasahatter@deadbolt.com>
Sent: 25 June 07:12
Subject: Re: HAIL, THE GANG'S ALL HERE

How's Flip?
WLP

- -

From: Malcolm McKerry <madasahatter@deadbolt.com>
To: W. Leonard Paryder <big_daddy@deadbolt.com>
Sent: 25 June 07:13
Subject: Re: HAIL, THE GANG'S ALL HERE

Still picking lead out of his hiney :-)

MM

- -

From: W. Leonard Paryder <big_daddy@deadbolt.com>
To: Malcolm McKerry <madasahatter@deadbolt.com>
Sent: 25 June 07:15
Subject: Re: HAIL, THE GANG'S ALL HERE

A tragedy. But then life is full of them.
WLP

▼ [Transcript: Interview Room Log, The Bunker. Tuesday June 25, 08:00]

Special Agent Malcolm McKerry: Doctor Willson. I'm special agent McKerry.
Dr. Jason Willson: What am I doing here?
MM: You're being retired, Doctor.
[sound of door opening]
MM: Ah, Doctor Mwani. Join the party.
Dr. John Mwani: McKerry. Jason.
JW: John? What's going on?
JM: Jason, we're going to try rebuilding someone using the macrophages. I
know you spoke with Jacob Zeitner about—
JW: Jack? Is he—?
MM: Professor Zeitner is dead, Doctor.
JW: Dead? Jack's dead?

MM: Not before he told us all about your theory of injecting the macrophages directly into the brain.

JW: You—

JM: We'd like you to help us, Jason.

JW: Do I have a choice?

MM: What do you think, Doctor?

JW: What do you want me to do?

MM: We want you to die, Doctor. Heh, I always wanted to say that.

JM: And then we're going to bring you back.

▼ [Telephone conversation between Alexandra Leaf Spaulding and Jeffrey Willson, Tuesday June 25, 4:25 pm]

"You heard from your dad yet?"

"Nope."

"I'm sure he's fine."

"We'll see."

"Don't be so pessimistic."

▼ [Notes on the treatment of Dr. Jason Willson – Wednesday June 26]

The transfusion of Moreby's blood was a success, and we "lost" Dr. Willson at 11:46 this morning. The patient's son will be informed through normal channels. I immediately removed the eyeballs and injected macrophages directly into the frontal lobe. Then, assisted by Dr. John Mwani, I began a series of further reconstructive procedures. Firstly, I removed cartilage and muscle from the patient's lower back and inserted them into upper thighs. Shoulder muscles were then removed and threaded into calf muscle. This was an attempt to improve the stiff-walking gait, but it was of only limited success. The patient was still given to drifting to one side and was still prone to extending his arms at 180 degrees to his body. The eyeballs were then fitted with transmitters. At least the patient is now conscious. He's not happy, but he's conscious.

Prof. M.T. Déesharné

Thomas Moreby: Ah, Professor Déesharné. Welcome to my humble lodgings.

Prof. M.T. Déesharné: Why did you just do that?

TM: Do what, Professor?

MTD: Wave your hand at me.

TM: It wasn't at you, Professor. It was at the little spying gadget up there on the wall, nesting there like an insect, waiting to pounce.

MTD: Why did you wave at it?

TM: I was being neighborly. Now, more to the point: I trust that you are comfortable?

MTD: Er . . . should I not be asking that of you rather than you of me?

TM: Why is that?

MTD: Well, you're behind that wall of reinforced glass and I'm here and—

TM: Behind glass.

MTD: Excuse me?

TM: You are there, behind glass.

MTD: Well, heh, I'm on the other side of the glass, yes, but—

TM: From where I am sitting, you are behind the glass, dear fellow. I, on the other hand, am in front of it.

MTD: I'm not sure—?

TM: You are not sure where you are, Professor?

MTD: No, I was going to say that I'm not sure what you—

TM: You need to get out, Professor. Is that not what you say?

MTD: Pardon?

TM: *Has any one supposed it lucky to be born? I hasten to inform him or her it is just as lucky to die, and I know it. I pass death with the dying and birth with the new-wash'd babe, and am not contain'd between my hat and boots. And peruse manifold objects, no two alike and every one good. The earth good and the stars good, and their adjuncts all good.*

MTD: What are you talking about? Is that some—?

TM: *I am not an earth nor an adjunct of an earth. I am the mate and companion of people, all just as immortal and fathomless as myself. (They do not know how immortal, but I know.)*

MTD: Oh, you mean, "You need to get out more."

TM: No. I mean you actually need to get out. Out from where you are now.

MTD: I'm afraid I really don't— Please . . . please sit down, Mr. Moreby.

TM: Can you not bring yourself to call me Thomas, after all that we have been through together?

MTD: Mr. Moreby . . . please—

TM: I am afraid that we have what you might call a situation here.

MTD: Mr. More—Mr. Moreby . . . your straps . . .

TM: Yes, they are not fastened. As you see. No, there is no point in pressing the alarm button, Professor. The gentleman on the other side of your televisual device is asleep. And he has disabled the alarm.

MTD: Please—

TM: *I lift the gauze and look a long time, and silently brush away flies with my hand. The youngster and the red-faced girl turn aside up the bushy hill, I peeringly view them from the top. The suicide sprawls on the bloody floor of the bedroom, I witness the corpse with its dabbled hair, I note where the pistol has fallen.*

MTD: Hello? Hello up there?

[the sound of a metal security door being rattled in its frame]

TM: *The city sleeps and the country sleeps. The living sleep for their time, the dead sleep for their time. The old husband sleeps by his wife and the young husband sleeps by his wife. And these tend inward to me, and I tend outward to them. And such as it is to be of these more or less I am. And of these one and all I weave the song of myself.*

MTD: Can anyone hear me up there? *Hello!* Please answer me!

TM: *I am of old and young, of the foolish as much as the wise. Regardless of others, ever regardful of others. Maternal as well as paternal, a child as well as a man. Stuff'd with the stuff that is coarse and stuff'd with the stuff that is fine.*

MTD: What do you want?

TM: Why, only for us to be together. Truly together.

[the sound of a click]

MTD: Please . . . please go back from the— It's open! How did you do that? The glass partition . . . you've— Hello? Help me . . . please . . . somebody.

TM: *Space and Time! Now I see it is true, what I guess'd at. What I guess'd when I loaf'd on the grass. What I guess'd while I lay alone in my bed. And again as I walk'd the beach under the paling stars of the morning. My ties and ballasts leave me, my elbows rest in sea-gaps. I skirt sierras, my palms cover continents. I am afoot with my vision.*

[the sound of a slap, followed by a sliding noise and then a thump]

MTD: Please . . . please, I'm hurt. I thought you were here to help us?

TM: To help? Do I contradict myself? Very well then, I contradict myself. *Soy grande, contengo multitudes.*

MTD: Wha— What?

TM: *Jeg er stor, jeg indeholder Skarer.*

MTD: I'm sorry . . . I'm sorry but I don't—what are you doing?

TM: *Je suis grand, je contiens des multitudes.*

MTD: No . . . no, please . . . what are you going to do? No, no . . . not my trousers . . . please, no! Help! Help me, somebody!

[the sound of a struggle, followed by a zip opening]

MTD: Please—!

TM: Eyoballs, tongues and . . . and *ball-sacks*!

MTD: Oh, Jesus H. Christ . . . for the love of—

[the sound of eating, slurping and tearing, coupled with a high-pitched scream]

TM: *Eu sou grande, contenho multidões. I am large, I contain multitudes.*

▼ [E-mail sent by J. W. Fletcher to W. Leonard Paryder, Wednesday June 26, 6:06 pm]

From: J.W. Fletcher <straightarrow@deadbolt.com>
To: W. Leonard Paryder <big_daddy@deadbolt.com>
Sent: June 26 18:06
Subject: HOUSEKEEPING

Dear Leonard,
I thought you should know. Your Mr M. is out of control. This for your eyes only.
Cordially
JW

- - - - - - - - - - - - - - - - - - - -

From: W. Leonard Paryder <big_daddy@deadbolt.com>
To: J.W. Fletcher <straightarrow@deadbolt.com>
Sent: 26 June 26 18:09
Subject: HOUSEKEEPING

JW —
Mr M. does not BELONG to me. We are only subcontracted. What's up?
W. Leonard Paryder
Senior Controller (East)

- -

From: J.W. Fletcher <straightarrow@deadbolt.com>
To: W. Leonard Paryder <big_daddy@deadbolt.com>
Sent: 26 June 18:13
Subject: HOUSEKEEPING

You still got your old cell? Call mine as soon as you can.
JW

▼ [Telephone conversation between Special Agent J.W. Fletcher and W. Leonard
Paryder, Wednesday June 26, 6:27 pm]

"That you, Leonard?"

"Who the hell did you think it was? This is like something out of a Cold
War potboiler."

"Ah, the Cold War! Those were the days."

"JW, I have neither the time nor the inclination to reminisce. Where
are you?"

"Doesn't matter where I am. We have a problem and I thought you
shou—"

"What's the problem."

"Your Mister Moreby. He's the fucki—"

"I told you: he is not 'mine.' He does not belong to me. I may be my
brother's keeper—"

"I don't give a rat's arse who owns him, but someone's—"

"What has he done?"

"Killed the Burchamps."

"Who the fuck are they?"

"Volunteers."

"How?"

"Moreby came in and played God."

"Great."

"It gets worse."

"How worse?"

"Now he's killed that stuck-up Brit professor. What's-his-name . . . Déesharné.

"Excuse me?"

"You heard. He killed him. Professor Déesharné."

"How?"

"You don't wanna know. *Do* you wanna know?"

"Go on. Spit it out."

"That's an unfortun—"

"Just fucking tell me, JW."

"He ate his genitals, eyeballs, tongue—plus most of his face—the right side of his waist, right side of his shoulder and neck, and . . . and then he broke open his head."

"Fucking hell, fucki—"

"His brain isn't there."

"Who's?"

"Déesharné's."

"Great. Just fucking wonderful. Where is it?"

"He ate it."

"Well, I guess that's no surprise. That's what they do, they—"

"No, Leonard, he didn't just eat it—he *absorbed* it . . . absorbed everything in it. That's what he does . . . what he's been doing for—for Christ knows how long! Maybe he was around when the first wannabe man crawled out of the Piltdown gloop, when they plotted the movement of the stars and built the pyramids, when the three wise old men followed a star . . . maybe he has always been here. Eating people and ingesting them. And from that, he—"

"—he becomes them."

"Not exactly becomes them, but accumulates all of their knowledge. And he's speaking . . . he's talking like . . . like in a variety of voices. It sounds like some kind of stand-up routine. He says he's multitudes. That mean anything to you? Keeps on saying it."

"*I am large, I contain multitudes.*"

"That's it. That's what he keeps saying . . . sometimes in different languages, but you can tell it's the same thing because it always ends up 'multitudes' . . . something like that."

"It's from a poem by Walt Whitman."

"So now he's a poet?"

"Uh-uh. Now he's *everyone*."

▼ [Transcript: Cell #9 Audio Log, The Bunker. Wednesday June 26, 19:14]

Thomas Moreby: Good evening, Dr. Willson.

Jason Willson: Who's there?

TM: My sincere apologies, doctor. My name is Thomas James Moreby.

JW: Mr. Moreby. I can't say I'm pleased to see you . . . mainly because I can't see anything.

TM: I believe that situation will improve.

JW: Why are you here, Mr. Moreby?

TM: Why, my dear fellow . . . this is where the future starts. Where else should I be if not here, on the very threshold of everything that is to come about. Are you not excited? Are you not liberated? If I were to release your arms from their bindings, then would you not delight in the absence of a pulse in your wrist or of the movement of blood in your veins?

JW: It's hard . . . hard to close my eyes.

TM: That will improve. All discomfort will pass. You are, Dr. Willson, the start of the future. You are tomorrow today. Soon to become now. And I am the figure on the horse, waving its broadsword as I lead the charge.

JW: What are you charging, Mr. Moreby? What—?

TM: I am . . . how should one say . . . I am reborn.

JW: Do I detect the voice of a man with a mission?

TM: Perhaps a man with a purpose would be more accurate.

JW: You're playing semantics, Mr. Moreby.

TM: No, Dr. Willson. A purpose is that thing one was actually created for—not something that one might aspire to during the latter course of one's life . . . or something that one might have thrust upon oneself.

JW: Christ, you make it sound as though you're here as God's emissary.

TM: I am a god's emissary, I have no doubt of that. But I am also on the side of righteousness, my good doctor.

JW: Like so many others before you.

TM: Ah, the sin of hubris. Guilty as charged, I fear. But is there not a need for self-belief in the person who one day will rule not only this land, but all those others that span this tiny globe?

JW: What about our President?

TM: My dear doctor, even as you and I are speaking, your Government is collapsing. The walls of the old America are coming down. It is time. Time for change. And I fear one is either a part of the problem or a part of the solution.

JW: Tell me, where are the doctors who did this to me?

TM: Alas, I regret that they are no longer amongst us—not since the unfortunate Mr. Carrier took on the nomenclature that I anointed him with.

JW: So why—?

TM: So why have I gone to all this trouble, Dr. Willson? Why, for knowledge, of course. The greatest boon that man can ever crave. Your techniques combined with my own have shown me the way forward. A new dawn for my people. And you have, perhaps somewhat inadvertently, provided me with the perfect subject upon which to test my theories.

JW: Why have you done this to me?

TM: You? Oh, forgive me doctor, but I did not mean *you*.

JW: Who—?

TW: But now it is time for us to leave this place. Our destiny awaits elsewhere.

JW: "Us"? Mr. Moreby, is there someone else there with you? I can hear some—

Unidentified Female Voice: Hello, Jason.

JW: *Marianne?*

Eloise
by Will Halloway

> Then, methought, the air grew denser, perfumed from an unseen censer
> Swung by Seraphim whose foot-falls tinkled on the tufted floor.
> "Wretch," I cried, "thy God hath lent thee – by these angels he has sent thee
> Respite – respite and nepenthe from thy memories of Lenore!
> Quaff, oh quaff this kind nepenthe, and forget this lost Lenore!"
> Quoth the raven, "Nevermore."
>
> —Edgar Allan Poe, *The Raven*

The long grass that served as the middle age of Samuel Lewis Dortmund was a lonely environment, particularly since the death of his beloved Eloise. Many were the nights when he would sob himself to sleep, repeating her name like a mantra.

Marianne
Marianne
Marianne
Marianne
Marianne
Marianne
Marianne
Marianne
Marianne
Marianne
Marianne
Marianne
I will find you . . .

Mr. Paryder,

Doctor Gilray has requested that all operations at the bunker are terminated immediately and any remaining traces be eradicated. Please confirm receipt of this memo.

Lois Chappelle
Assistant to Dr. Brewster Gilray
NWP

DEAD, AND IN PERSON!

ONE NITE ONLY!

SOLD OUT!

BERNIE MAUGHMSTEIN JOKE #1249

I have nothing against zombies, okay?
Some of my best friends are dead.

BERNIE MAUGHMSTEIN JOKE #1263

You wanna know how to tell for sure
someone ain't a zombie?
Look up his ass. You know what I'm
saying? If all you see is cobwebs then he's
already on the bus, man.

BER

LOCATION

The LakeView Resort & Spa, 3534 Lake Tahoe
Boulevard, South Lake Tahoe, CA 96150 (hereinafter
designated "LVRS"). LVRS was a popular hotel and
condominium resort on the shore of this key
vacation and recreation destination until its
desertion a month ago. Founded in 1962 and
regularly upgraded, in its final form LVRS
consists of twenty-two blocks each holding four
small wooden townhouses, arranged around paths in
pinewoods leading down to the lake. Six additional
one-story beach houses flank a facility at the
shore consisting of a pool, children's paddling
pool, and hot tub, formerly serviced by a small
café and surrounded by a terraced area. From this
a wooden jetty reaches eighty feet out into the
lake. On either side of the foot of the jetty are
arranged a number of informal barbecuing
facilities, along with picnic tables on a small
grassy area leading to a narrow sandy beach.

LVRS remained sparsely inhabited for several
weeks after the initial incursion of HRV onto
United States territory—primarily by former staff
members, people either aware that their homes
elsewhere in the state had already been overrun,
or those who believed that the resort would
provide an easily defensible location. This hope
proved unfounded. The second major wave of
Infected exiting the Bay Area overran LVRS during
the weekend of June 15-16. All remaining human
inhabitants of the resort perished during that
two-day period.

Since that time LVRS, along with all other
previous habitations and businesses along the
south shore of Lake Tahoe, has remained deserted.
A few generator-supported functions such as
motion-sensitive lights and some low-voltage
digital CCTV security imaging remain active;
otherwise the resort is a dead facility.

RECON OBJECTIVE

To ascertain whether LVRS can be reconditioned and held as a forward base for counterattack against NZO forces and eventual retaking of the Bay Area and surrounding area by MARSOC.

TRANSCRIPT

Following is a transcript of CCTV footage recovered from a security-imaging camera in grounds of LVRS. Footage is in black and white, with sound. Camera shows a fixed viewpoint of the edge of the terraced area associated with the spa café, a portion of the grassed area on the other side, and the beach, which is approximately twenty feet in depth. A basic cinderblock barbecue facility stands on the grass. The beginning of the jetty is also visible, stretching out into darkness. Initial sound consists of lapping sounds of water against the jetty supports. Visibility is limited.

Recorded events commence at 20:38, according to time code, although there is evidence that the motion-sensitive CCTV camera failed to trigger at some earlier point, as MAN 1 is already in vision at the start of the recording. He is visible from behind, sitting against the edge of the terrace. At 20:39 MAN 2 enters the field of view. He is bulky, wearing denim jeans and a plaid shirt, and in middle age. He is carrying a supermarket paper sack under each arm, with some difficulty. When he gets close to the barbecue, one of the sacks starts to slip. He elects to place both hurriedly on the ground.

MAN 2: Fuck *me* that's some heavy shit. I never realized how heavy all this shit is. You could have helped, man.

[MAN 1 grunts.]

MAN 2: Yeah, right. Wear the young ones out first, huh?

[Man 2 puts his hands on his hips and looks out into the darkness over the lake.]

MAN 2: Fuck, bro. How long has it been? I mean . . . how long? Seriously. I was trying to work it out on the way here. But it's like, I'm driving, and it's dark and actually I'm pretty fucking drunk. Course we don't have to worry about traffic on the roads, right? That's one thing. But let's work it out. I'm forty-seven, which is a fucking joke in itself. How did *that* happen? And the last time I remember us all being here, the entire family and cousins and dah dah dah, is . . . It was the year before I moved to Chicago, right? I was twenty-nine. Which is like . . . a zillion years ago. No, hang on, come on. Forty-seven. Twenty-nine. Twenty-eight? No way. It can't be nearly thirty fucking years. Oh, okay. *Eighteen* years. Shit. That's still long, man. That's still really fucking *long*. Seems like it was, okay not yesterday, but, you know, not . . . *that* long.

[Man 2 is silent for a few moments, swaying slightly.]

MAN 2: That's some pretty easy math I was fucking up. I'm amazed we got here in one piece.

[*Man 1 grunts again. Man 2 turns back to look at him.*]

MAN 2: Right. Whatever. Let's do this.

[*He squats down and starts removing things from the bags he put on the floor. He takes out a large bag. He takes out a smaller bag wrapped in white plastic.*]

MAN 2: Burgers, plain and simple. Steak? Ha. No fucking chance. When's the last time you saw a steak? Right. Steak would have not been . . . realistic. Suits me fine. I always thought burgers kicked steak's ass on a barbecue anyway.

[*He peers down at the barbecue.*]

MAN 2: Basic fucking barbecue, man. Guess you got to make the best of what you got though, right? If it was enough for Dad to work his magic, it's good enough for us.

[*He takes out another, lighter bag.*]

MAN 2: Buns. Uh, right. Yeah. Buns. Fuck. Did I remember mustard?

[*He leans down to search through the second bag. Loses his balance and keels over until he is lying on the grass.*]

MAN 2: [*Muffled.*] Crap.

[*After a moment he moves his head, peering.*]

MAN 2: Ha. Found the mustard, though. And the JD, halle-fucking-lujah.

[*He pushes himself up to a seating position and pulls a bottle of Jack Daniel's from the nearest* bag. He takes a large gulp, and holds it out toward Man 1. No response.]

MAN 2: Good call, man. You're wasted enough. Okay. Let's get these burgers rock and rolling.

[He gets up surprisingly fluently, and starts unpacking bags onto the support area around the barbecue.]

MAN 2: Duh. Might want to start the fire, right?

[He picks up one of the larger bags, tears at one end, and eventually opens it. He pours charcoal into the barbecue. Then brings up a small tin, which he up-ends and squirts liberally over the coals. He pulls a box of matches from his pocket. Lights one, and tosses it in. The fuel ignites noisily, momentarily whiting out the image on screen.]

MAN 2: Whoops!

[The image settles and the sound of flames dies down, to show Man 2 lighting a cigarette off another match. Man 1 grunts again, louder this time.]

Man 2: Are you kidding? You're giving me a hard time about *smoking*—when the world's fucked to shit? Fuck it. Not to mention we're in the fucking outdoors, dude. Lake fucking Tahoe, man. First cigarette I ever *had* was by this lake, matter of fact. Your eighteenth birthday, did you ever know that? I remember . . . I remember you were standing with Mom and Dad, must have been pretty much right *here*, and I'd got this half pack of smokes somebody had given me at school, who was it: yeah, Jimmy Garwhen, fucking asshole he turned out to be. And I'm fifteen and Dad's let me have two beers because it's a *special* special occasion and I'm thinking fuckin' A, this is the life. *This* is the grown-up thing, right here. And I went around the back of . . .

[He indicates vaguely with his hand toward the beach houses outside our POV.]

MAN 2: . . . and lit one up. Coughed like a fucking maniac. Had two more later, though. I worked at it. You've got to work at that shit, right? Even bad habits don't come easy.

[He regards the fire for a moment.]

MAN 2: You know what, I'm just going to put these babies right on there. Going to take forever otherwise. I'm hungry. You hungry?

[MAN 1 grunts, louder this time.]

MAN 2: Right. Bet you are.

[He opens the white plastic bag and takes out a couple of patties. Dithers for a moment, then holds both in one hand.]

MAN 2: Dude . . . the *barbecue sauce*. Dad's special blend, the secret recipe, made by my own good self. But you got to *remind* me of this shit. If we're relying on me to get this thing done right, we'd be better off chewing on twigs.

[He picks up a plastic bottle. He squirts the contents onto the burgers. And his hands, by accident. And his jeans. He slaps the burgers on the grill portion of the barbecue. There is a hissing sound and flames leap up, whiting out the screen again. He rears back, staggering slightly.]

MAN 2: Guess they're going to be pretty fucking chargrilled.

[He picks up the bottle of alcohol and comes to sit on the wall fairly near Man 1. He takes a drag of his cigarette and flicks it out toward the lake. Thinks a moment.]

AN 2: Ah, shit.

[He gets up, trudges into the darkness out of sight. There's a faint splashing sound. Then he trudges back into vision, holding something, slumps back down next to the other man.]

MAN 2: Still can't do it. Nobody here, whole world's gone to shit, and I can't flick a butt in the lake. Not this lake. You know, in my whole life, I never smoked in front of Mom and Dad? Not once. Even at Dad's funeral, I'm shaking and totally fucked up and I still went and hid behind a tree so Mom wouldn't see, even though I was forty-two years old. But *you*, you used to do it right there at the table. And then you gave up smoking and they're all, "You rock". Though of course I didn't give it up. Ha. Looking back, I really do *not* regret the decision not to give up. That turned out okay for me. But I still remember you smoking the first time some year, you were like seventeen or something, right at that picnic table over there, and it's another Fourth of July and everyone's hanging out and you just pull out the Marlboros and light up. Nobody bats an eyelid. That was cool, man. You're good at that shit. Seen you pull that all your life, but I never learned the lesson. And now . . . nobody . . . gives . . . a . . . damn. I could drop my pants and go fuck a dog in the middle of the street and nobody . . . would . . . care.

[Man 2 takes another pull off the bottle of alcohol—holds it out to Man 1, who grunts, but doesn't take it.]

MAN 2: Burgers starting to smell good, though, right?

[He laboriously gets to his feet and lurches toward the barbecue. He picks up a burger and turns it over.]

MAN 2: Holy *fuck* that's hot.

[Nonetheless, he does the same with the second. Then flaps his hand about, before slowly stopping. He is silent for a full minute before speaking more quietly.]

MAN 2: You know what I regret? Not coming that year. When I was twenty-fucking-nine. I don't even know what the fuck that was *about*. Okay, I'd gone to Chicago and it would have been a lot further to come, but . . . I don't actually know why I didn't do it. I could have got on a plane, whatever. I guess it was an age thing, maybe. You think you're getting too old for the family-all-together shit. Plus Julie didn't get why I'd do it and she didn't want to come and . . . I really wish I'd come, man. And the next year too. I remember you calling me that second time, you were standing here with Mom and Dad and eating burgers and I was . . . I don't know, in a bar, I think, drinking away the fact the dumb bitch had left me in the end, I guess, and you called and I didn't pick up because I was wasted and I figured you'd be wanting to give me a hard time for not making it to the big rah-rah family event . . . and in fact you just left a message saying, "Wish you were here."

[He turns back to look at the seated man.]

MAN 2: I got back into it after that, but then Paul started skipping every other year, and Marie did the same the other way around, and the cousins stopped making it for good, and it just seemed like it was never the same as it had been when we were kids except for Mom and Dad were always here. Feels sometimes like it was my fault it went that way. Like I fucked the whole thing up. Did I? Was it down to me? If I hadn't skipped those two years, would it have kept . . . shit. Whatever. I don't know. You think you know every damned thing when you're twenty-four. You think great, thanks for all the years and I love you still, but I'm out here on my own now. Big fucking mistake. If you got a family and it likes being together once a year . . . *just fucking do it*. Bite the bullet and get on the fucking plane. There's plenty of time and a hundred different ways to be an asshole. Don't feel you got to get them all done at once.

[He leans forward and peers at the barbecue.]

MAN 2: Getting there, bro. Getting there. Better get the rest of the road on the show. And at least we're here *now*, right? That's something. And that's down to me. If I hadn't come got you, it wouldn't have happened. Score one point to me. Course getting there earlier would have been even better, but that'd have meant getting my shit together and not being a fucking asshole, and it's too late for that now.

[He starts pulling stuff out of the bags on the floor. Buns, a bag of lettuce, tomato, ketchup, mustard, two paper plates. Lays them out on the side. He starts moving items around, trying to get things in a particular order.]

MAN 2: You not going to do this? You *always* did this part. Me, I'd've probably just picked the meat up with my fingers, left to myself. You were always up in it with the got-to-be-just-so and just-do-it-right. And you were right, as I came to appreciate in the fullness of fucking time. And you know what? You know . . . what?

[His hands stop moving. He has started to cry.]

MAN 2: This shit changes nothing. You were right.
Do everything just so. Do it *right*. If the rest of
the world can't be fucked, then fuck 'em. Do your
thing. *Do it right.*

[He stands, no longer trying to do anything,
shoulders heaving. Then he sniffs, wipes his
sleeve across his face.]

MAN 2: Okay then. Glad we got that straight.

[Then suddenly he looks off to his right. Stands
absolutely still, and silent, for twenty seconds.]

MAN 2: [Quietly.] You hear that?

[He's silent again, staring off into the
darkness.]

MAN 2: You hear 'em now? Off down along the shore.
Seems like maybe there's braindeads still in these
woods after all. I knew there would be. Told you
so. I never thought those things were as dumb as
everybody makes out—and they're getting goddam
smarter, too. *Lots* smarter. And they gotta be
loving that smell, right? Burgers cooking in the
open air. Cooked by someone you know, in a place
you've been to so many times it feels like home.
There is no food in the fucking *world* tastes like
a burger eaten sitting with people you've known
your whole life. That, my friends, is the word of
God.

[He grabs the bottle of alcohol and takes another
big gulp, before shouting into the darkness.]

MAN 2: You *like* that smell? Course you do. That's
meat cooking, and it's meat done right. Old Man

Stegnaro's special sauce. Fucking shitheads just gnawing dead shit. That's not how it's *done*, don't you fucking get it?

[*He's quiet for a moment, looking off along the shore.*]

MAN 2: Fuck, dude. There's a *lot* of 'em. Not sure we got enough to go round all these dead fuckers. Course, you probably won't be eating yours and, be honest with you, I don't really want mine, what with the ground round having come out of your actual fucking *leg*. But that's the kind of joke you would have loved, bro—say it ain't so. You make do with what you got, right? You were always telling me that. *And* you'd have made me bring all this other shit if you'd been alive to have a say-so, and so that's what I done. Standards must be maintained. You can turn the Stegnaro brothers' world to shit, but we ain't coming down to your level. Still here, still standing, still doing it right.

[*He looks off along the shore and cackles triumphantly—gesturing towards himself as if instigating a fight. He addresses people out of frame.*]

MAN 2: You want some? You fucking *want* some? If you're going to eat, you dead fucking *assholes*, then do it *right*.

[*He holds the barbecue sauce bottle above his head and squirts it liberally over himself.*]

MAN 2: Fucking deadheads.
[*At the left and right extremities of the screen, we can make out shadows of human size, lurching toward Man 2. The fire is unsettling them, but they are neither retreating nor halting their progress.*]

MAN 2: Yeah, yeah—"Oh, look at us, we just keep on coming." Assholes. And don't forget the mustard.

⟦The encroaching shapes are now within a few feet of him. He picks something else up from the ground. He holds it, flips the cap, looking over at the slumped other man.⟧

MAN 2: Sorry I didn't get there sooner, bro.

⟦He holds the thing in his hand up and squeezes, squirting something else all over his clothes and head and body. Then pulls another item out of his pocket, as he squirts the fuel over the shapes now closing in on him.⟧

MAN 2: I love you, man.

⟦He flicks a lighter and holds it to his chest. The flare of the flames whites out the screen. The surrounding figures flail around, now also burning.⟧

MAN 2: Gonna be pretty fucking chargrilled, huh?

⟦A blazing shape reaches out towards the camera.⟧

⟦Screen goes black.⟧

BERNIE MAUGHMSTEIN JOKE #1287

So I'm walking along the street, man . . . you know . . . and this fucking zombie comes up and starts with the growling, and I'm like, "What the fuck you trying to tell me, man?" You know what I'm saying? So I go, "Hey, man, you're coming on like out of <u>Scooby-Doo</u>!" And that's the

problem right there, man. I mean, they're coming on and giving it "<u>These folks have rights, too</u>!" Zombies have rights? What the fuck . . . most of 'em can't even <u>talk</u>, man.

BERNIE MAUGHMSTEIN

The worst thing would be this. To feel the bite
growing inflamed, the poison spreading through
your blood. You lose your mind; your body too
becomes a stranger. And of course you fight.

Remember strawberries' crush on your tongue,
Sing Mozart to yourself – La Ci Darem
La Mano. Plead with friends and then watch them
recoil in horror. It will not be long.

The virus eats you. And then you eat brains.
You shamble and you groan and you decay.
You have no longer anything to say
with all that wit and charm. And of the pains

you feel, the worst as beauty, brilliance go
to rot, will be to be that thing, and know.

To have the Formerly Alive to tea
is awkward. Wire his jaws, so he can't bite
your other guests – is forced to be polite.
You chain him up, and hang on to the key

so no one sets him loose. Make a puree
of brains and blood and feed him through a straw.
Toast it on crumpets? He prefers it raw.
Let your friends try it - tell them it's pate.

Your special guest will moan and toss his head.
Put down some paper towels to catch the drips,
and best not talk of the Apocalypse
to someone who is risen, but still dead.

Observe these rules, take a good hostess' pains.
Once guests have left, blow out his stinking brains.

Some of them run at you - you must be fast
to hope to get away. And some are slow.
The key to your survival is to know
which ones are which. There was a time, now past,

when they all shambled, all stank of the grave
that they'd left recently. And they were made
by hand, by craftsmen. You were still afraid,
But they were tame, somebody's household slave.

The quick wild ones are feral, a disease
that you'll catch if they catch you. Yet they treat
the old slow kind politely if they meet.
Offer them bits of people. On their knees.

The dead are snobs. The stench of long decay
outranks the slick young beast who rose today.

The army comes in tanks and jeeps. You wave
then duck as bullets whizz close to your head.
You cheer - they mow down acres of undead.
Then learn it isn't you they've come to save.

Their bodies armoured, goggles on their eyes
You can't tell where they look, or if they smile.
You sense they plan to be here for a while.
They bring in trailers. Men in suits and ties

arrive by car, seem to be in command.
They catch your neighbour's children in a net.
Look at them briefly. Club them. You forget
to stay down. And they shoot you out of hand.

The last thing that you hear is someone shout
"Let God sort live and undead vermin out!"

You chop its head off. Takes you seven tries
to cut through gullet, vocal chords and spine.
It groans and growls. Perhaps this is a sign
that it is conscious, even though its eyes

are bloody, blank. The head will try to bite
as it rolls on the ground. Will break a tooth
chewing at stones and soil. You see the truth
but hide from what you know. These creatures might

in their dead way be more alive than you.
The fingers you cut off swinging your knife -
each one of them has its own wriggling life.
Cut off its ear - that will start creeping too.

Blast them to bits - see how each bit behaves.
The chunks will fight to stay out of their graves.

The dead are always at it. Like to kill,
 and tear and eat. But even more than those
They like to fuck. The moment that you close
huge oven doors on them, be sure they will

be screwing as they burn. Each black charred bone
is wrapped around another, charcoaled tongue
 thrust into burned lips. They can fuck so long
 because they do not breathe. You hear them moan

out in the night. It's not to terrify.
 It's not all about you. They make the beast
with two backs. Or with five. Say two at least.
And when they catch and eat you, as you die

the ones whose teeth you feel don't lead the pack.
He's busy with three dead blondes round the back.

The blank expressions, dull eyes, of each face
 May lead you to believe they have no soul,
 whereas their death and rebirth made them whole
 united corpse and spirit in one place.

Their bodies punish sinners, free them too
to see the living God and serve His will.
It's Him who pulls them from the grave to kill
to tear apart, and bite, and gnaw, and chew.

His servants work their fingers to the bone.
Killing the clock around. It's how they pray
watching the movements of His face each day
He whispers that he knows them for His own.

And we pray too – we hope they'll pass us by
that only unbelieving sinners die.

We love, but do not love the flesh beneath,
our lover's skin – the subtle flow of veins
the net of nerves through which our love takes pains
should we require it. We may love their teeth

but not the pulp or gums; the blue-green eye
but not its socket. They are all too real –
it is a half-measure of love we feel –
Touches the fingers' tips and does not pry.

into the quick. I know a girl whose skin
is lace and tatter. Her unbeating heart
is on display, and naked. Torn apart
her ribs its broken cage. Her brain within

her shattered skull is blue-green with decay.
Perhaps I'll give her my own heart today.

If, shambling past, they smash a porcelain bowl,
a marble faun, perhaps embed a shard
inside their putrid foot, it may be hard
to understand their sudden frenzied howl

is ecstasy not pain. They all love art
but not as we do. Their long drawn out screams
are gorgeous music. Sometimes in your dreams
you hear it and it terrifies your heart.

That's just a fragment of its dark effect
on their decayed and very different brains.
Eyes drop out, ears fall off, but there are gains
refined and subtle senses. They select

the finest brains to eat. For them a taste
so fine, that, in our skulls, it's just a waste.

Their bodies are a war zone - death and life
fight over them. Their bodies writhe and twitch.
Live cells kill rot - they moan because they itch.
It's like they burn. If you could take a knife

and slice into their flesh, it seethes and boils
like ants in civil war. Their burning bile
corrodes their guts and lights and liver while
digesting what they eat. Their guts in coils

knotting like rutting vipers. Mildewed eyes
are wet but not with tears. They may seem slow -
they are fermenting fiercely as they go,
They snatch our flesh - each bleeding handful buys

a moment. Soon their flesh falls off the bone -
each one will lie, and deliquesce, alone.

They are so many. Stand on a high place
and watch them shamble. Grey as winter cloud
the sea of faces, and they moan so loud
it's like a scream. And every single face

is marked with all the signs of quick decay
and yet they still stand up, and wander round.
It's like a flood. Those standing on high ground
watch each last bit of dry land fall away

and know there's no way they can stop the tide.
Sooner or later tides will always turn
but meanwhile there's no wood for you to burn,
no food to eat, and no friend at your side.

They are all dead. Don't tell yourself the lie
that you'll survive. Just walk down there and die.

She is the walking dead. No matter who
she was before, you must burn her with flame
because the dead can never be the same
as they were once. And she will make you, too,

a thing that rots and staggers. Take a blade
and cut her head off. And ignore her moan.
She let them bite her. Left you all alone.
What sort of love was it that she displayed

by dying? Rotting? Soon her lovely face
will fall away; and soon her matted hair
will drop in clumps. You never knew despair
before you saw her die and rise. No trace

of her is left in it. And through your head
this thought runs - though I live, I too am dead.

And some are children. Thin, and fierce, and fast.
It takes them quickly, and it dries them out.
The old ones moan; the small dead children shout
and yell as if in playgrounds. They'll run past

you, double back. You see their teeth
and their dead eyes, and open bloodless wounds.
Their shrieks are wordless, just unthinking sounds.
And through their wounds you see dried bone beneath.

They're many. You can fight them off. You cut
them down, and trample them. Something will break
inside you. Once you thought it for hope's sake
you went on fighting. Bitter in your gut

an acid sense, that hope has told you lies.
The future's vicious jaws and mad dead eyes.

They eat as many of us as they can.
And then they slowly start to fall to bits.
It's a slow process. Cell by cell it hits.
Bones disconnect. They stumble. In a span

of weeks they will be rot, tatter and shard.
Some of us live. We hide. We eat cold food
from cans. Snare and kill rabbits. In a wood
we have a cabin. Our survival's marred

by what we've lost. The cities turn to dust,
take art books music with them. We forget
all that we were, or loved or hoped for. Yet
the worst of all the things we lose is trust.

All strangers are the dead returned. Our fear
will go on killing, year by bloody year.

DEPARTMENT OF THE ARMY
2ND INFANTRY DIVISION
SOUTHERN CALIFORNIA COMMAND BASE
CAMP PENDLETON
MAJ. GEN. HARLAND DAWSON, COMMANDING

10 SEPTEMBER

Operation New Zombie Order Southwest (ONZOSW) Phase IV Report (IOR)

FOR OFFICIAL USE ONLY

1. SUMMARY Since setting up base camp in what was formerly USMC Camp Pendleton, approximately 46 miles north of San Diego, California, the New Zombie Order Army Southwest (NZOASW) 2nd Infantry Division (2ID) has been successful in using intelligence supplied by New America's Zombie Intelligence Service (ZIS), as well as its own risk assessment, and has moved to Phase IV of the original ONZOSW plan. Early estimates of approximately 10,000 armed members of the Human Resistance Movement (HRM) in San Diego County (SDC) were revised upwards after initial assaults encountered heavy resistance. However, the SDC HRM was weak in logistics and supply, since Phase III of ONZOSW had successfully severed supply lines, via land, air, and sea. In all areas, HRM has consistently maintained an effective supply of small arms, consisting largely of former home handguns and hunting rifles; their ammunition supplies, however, are limited, and few of their weapons are effective at long range.

Explosive ordnance is largely lacking, and the HRM has no air support or mechanized mobile units. 2ID forces have encountered only one HRM light tank used in a combat situation—a 1968 Sheridan, which the HRM very likely acquired from a museum or other exhibit. The Sheridan was easily disabled, and the HRM has shown nothing else to match our MRAP (Mine Resistant Ambush Protected) transport vehicles.

NZOASW has achieved consistent victories in the field against the HRM by employing large numbers of fast-moving troops. With the new NZOA combat helmet SR-6, we've been able to avoid head trauma casualties that made our operations in the past difficult, and the HRM has been slow to develop counter-measures against our "rush" strategy. Our use of BDA (Battle Damage Assessment) has allowed us to continue to respond to HRM tactics by generating new TTP (tactics, techniques, and procedures).

2ID has successfully set up four major HICs (Human Internment Camps) in SDC, with approximately 2,000 insurgents safely and securely detained. SDC is now considered neutralized and under NZO control, and the 2ID now prepares to advance north.

2. GOALS 2ID now turns to the ultimate goal of OZASW: The neutralization and annexation of Orange County (OC) and (in Phase V) Los Angeles County (LAC). Despite early reports that these areas had fallen under NZO control, they are in fact still heavily-populated by living insurgents, and ZIS believes the OC HRM to be organized, armed, and led by experienced military commanders from MARSOC (United States Marine Corps Special Operations Command). Success in OC and LAC will depend on rapid deployment of large numbers of NZOASW troops via our MRAPs, on engaging the HRM quickly and neutralizing opposition, and on capturing the HRM leaders alive for immediate consumption by General Harland Dawson in order to obtain intelligence regarding HRM TTP.

3. TIMELINE On 13 September, at 0800 hours, 2ID will send the 1st Brigade (1B) north to acquire the San Clemente and Mission Viejo areas, where ZIS intelligence suggests little-to-no opposition will be encountered. On 16 September, 2nd Brigade (2B) will secure the Interstate 5 freeway, providing a line via which 2ID's BOO (Base of Operations) will be relocated from Camp Pendleton to the former Marine base at El Toro, located near Irvine in OC. From there, on 19 September, 1B and 2B will proceed north along an inland route, acquiring Santa Ana, Garden Grove, Anaheim and Buena Park. 3rd Brigade (3B) will proceed along a coastal route, neutralizing Newport Beach, Huntington Beach, and Seal Beach. Combat conditions are expected to continue for one week before all areas are considered secure and under NZOASW domination. On 26 September, TSC (Tactical Support Corps) will follow, constructing HICs at locations in Anaheim, Westminster, and Fullerton. By 3 October, HICs will be fully operational and confinement of living insurgents will begin. On 13 October, administration of all San Diego and Orange County HICs will be transferred to the FDA (Food Distribution Agency). On 14 October, NZOASW forces will enter LAC and Phase V of ONZOSW will begin (see separate IOR).

4. COMMAND

A. Major General Harland Dawson is in command of 2nd Division. General Dawson previously oversaw 2ID during neutralization of the states of New Mexico, Arizona, and Nevada. Prior to his HTZT (Human-to-Zombie Transformation), General Dawson was a 24-year-old graduate of West Point (ranked #1 in his class) and was serving as a Major in the former United States Army. Dawson's battalion fought during the Battle of Washington, but although his battalion fought with honor (and withstood longer than any other during that conflict) they were finally overcome by sheer numbers and Dawson suffered a mortal shrapnel wound to the chest. After his HTZT, Dawson was integrated into NZO's Operation Darwin, in which he was allowed to feed only on captured human military leaders. Dawson responded well to this program, and was soon placed in charge of 2ID. (NOTE: Dawson continues to participate in Operation Darwin.)

B. Serving as Special Aide to Major General is Captain Drew Hatch. Little is known of Captain Hatch prior to his HTZT. After HTZT, he was first assigned to the New America Zombie Intelligence Service, where he assisted in the early development of Operation Darwin. He was assigned to General Dawson on 12 August.

C. The three brigades that comprise 2nd Division are overseen by Colonel Marisa San Juan (1st Brigade), Colonel Kelvin Tang (2nd Brigade), and Colonel Harrison Delvecchio (3rd Brigade).

This document has been prepared for the Department of Human Neutralization by the New America Zombie Intelligence Service.

MARTIN S. CHARLES
Major, NZOA

SPECIAL FIELD REPORT

CLASSIFIED

22 September

As previously detailed in NZOIA-1130-240-02, NZOASW is currently operating five STFs (Special Task Forces) in the Southern California region specifically dedicated to acquiring targets from Capture/Consume Lists prepared by ZIS.

At 1530 hours today, STF387, under the command of Lt. Michael Kowalski, located the #1 target on the list: HRM leader David Ankstrum. Ankstrum is a decorated military veteran (Lt. Colonel) with experiences in both the Afghan and Iraq human conflicts of 2001–2009, and has made NZOASW incursions into OC difficult. STF387 has been in the field for ten days trying to locate Ankstrum, who was found yesterday in a temporary but heavily guarded HRM base camp. Lt. Kowalski is to be commended for leading his five soldiers in a covert mission which removed Ankstrum alive from the camp with no casualties to NZOASW troops.

STF387 returned Ankstrum to NZOASW's base at El Toro, where he was presented to Captain Drew Hatch, who currently oversees Maj. General Harland Dawson's participation in Operation Darwin. After performing a brief interrogation of Ankstrum (which proved fruitless), the HRM leader was presented to General Dawson for immediate consumption (and was afterward permanently terminated to prevent HTZT). General Dawson was then able to use knowledge acquired from Ankstrum to pinpoint key locations of the HRM. The general also obtained new knowledge of certain key HRM strategies, and is said to have benefited overall from Ankstrum's knowledge and skills. We now anticipate a close to combat in OC by 4 October, only slightly behind the original timeline provided in NZOIA-1130-235-14.

DREW HATCH
Captain and Special Aide de Camp
to Major General Harland Dawson, NZOA

6 October

ONZOSW is proceeding well in the Southern California theater, with construction of Orange County HICs now underway and preparation being made to launch the Los Angeles County attack on 8 October.

However, I'm going on record here (in a *strictly* confidential way) to express some concern over Maj. General Dawson's commitment to Operation Darwin. The STFs in the field have been unable to locate other HRM leaders from our Capture/Consume List, and this is (naturally) creating some difficulty for the General, who currently hasn't eaten in four days, despite a plenitude of human captives in our camps. As we all know, hunger clouds judgment, and I believe that General Dawson is on the verge of breaking protocol and consuming one of the normal human captives. ZIS and those of us who designed Operation Darwin from the ground up are, of course, well aware of the potential dangers should the General choose to consume one of our non-military prisoners; those chosen for inclusion on the Capture/Consume List were thoroughly researched and found to lack backgrounds that might prove distracting to the General. General Dawson, however, remains (or so I believe) completely unaware of this aspect of the Operation, and I still advise against informing him.

I will continue to work with field commanders and emphasize the urgency of pursuing and acquiring targets from the Capture/Consume List, but I would also like to urge ZIS to consider investing more resources into pursuing intelligence that would allow us to expand the list. Otherwise, the entire war here in the southwest could conceivably begin to tilt back to HRM control.

DREW HATCH
Captain and Special Aide de Camp
to Major General Harland Dawson, NZOA

SPECIAL FIELD REPORT

2ND INFANTRY DIVISION
SOUTHERN CALIFORNIA COMMAND BASE
MAJ. GEN. HARLAND DAWSON, COMMANDING

CLASSIFIED

26 October

Phase V of ONZOSW is now in its 18th day. I will shortly send an estimate for a revised timeline. Let me state now that as Commander of the entire 2nd Infantry Division, I accept full responsibility for the delays.

We are encountering difficulties here in Los Angeles County with extremely well-organized HRM forces. Specifically, the humans seem to be adapting their TTP to repel all zombie incursions, to retain control of key areas, and to evade capture. Today, Special Task Force 267 acquired a human commander who ranked highly on the Capture/Consume List, but the commander committed suicide before he was brought to me; he apparently had hidden a cyanide capsule somewhere on his person, and managed to swallow the capsule and self-terminate before he could be consumed and his knowledge acquired. I would like to commend STF267 leader Major Angela Hamilton, who attempted to consume the human commander after she realized he'd poisoned himself.

I would also like to request a special leave from Operation Darwin. I haven't eaten in seven days now, and will be unable to function should this continue beyond another two, possibly three days. I am encountering severe opposition from Major Hatch, and I find myself increasingly concerned about his real motives and goals. While I do not question the Major's dedication to the ultimate goals of ONZO, some of his methods—such as his steadfast refusal to allow me to consume targets outside the Capture/Consume List—seem counterproductive and detrimental to our ability to function. I am therefore requesting that a special unit be chosen for me from among those humans we already have in captivity, and that this be done within the next twenty-four hours. We've reached a critical juncture at this point in the execution of Phase V of Operation New Zombie Order Southwest, and I believe it is in the best interests of the entire zombie nation to have a commander who is clear-headed and functioning to the best of his abilities.

HARLAND DAWSON
Maj. General, NZOA

SPECIAL MEMO

CONFIDENTIAL — FOR ZIS EYES ONLY

29 October

Phase V of ONZOSW may have encountered an extremely severe difficulty today, in the form of its commander. ZIS erred in estimating the amount of time General Dawson would be able to endure hunger.

Specifically: Yesterday, General Dawson ordered the return to base of the 23rd Battalion, even though the battalion had been making some (limited) headway in the La Mirada area of Los Angeles County. I questioned the order at the time, and General Dawson informed me that he wanted to redeploy that battalion to assist the 32nd in Lakewood.

At 0530 hours this morning, General Dawson directed me to check on a communications problem, which required me to leave command office for a short time. I now suspect that the General manufactured this "communications problem", because I found no such issue and returned to the command office to find that the General had gone. At 0545, General Dawson personally assumed command of the 23rd Battalion and led them into the field in the area of Norwalk.

The next five paragraphs of this timeline are reconstructed from interviews with soldiers who were in the 23rd and witnessed Dawson's actions:

General Dawson led the battalion north on the Interstate 5 and then along the streets of Norwalk, encountering only small pockets of human resistance which were quickly neutralized. The situation remained calm until Dawson and his soldiers encountered a secured and heavily armed HRM camp set up on the grounds of a former elementary school.

Before launching the attack on the HRM camp, Dawson informed the members of the 23rd that, due to the recent shortage in food supplies, the NZOASW Commander-in-Chief (President Moreby) had approved an immediate AAC (Attack and Consume) operation. This, of course, was not in fact the case.

The General acted with considerable bravery as he led the 23rd into battle. The new SR-7 combat helmets proved effective in repelling head trauma, but the insurgents were also armed with home-made explosives ("Molotov cocktails").

Fighting continued until approximately 1100 hours, when the 23rd broke through the HRM's defenses and commenced the AAC operation.

While the enlisted soldiers were allowed to consume freely, Dawson and the officers of the 23rd withheld as they sought out the HRM commanders. They were able to locate and capture two leaders; one succeeded in self-terminating before she could be halted, but the other was deprived of the lethal cyanide capsule and was consumed by General Dawson. This HRM commander was later identified at Hector Robles.

At approximately 1400 hours, the General and the 23rd Battalion returned to base camp. I immediately requested a debriefing with the General, which he granted. During our interview, he admitted to consuming a human target not on the approved Capture/Consume List, but insisted that he had acted in the best interests of the NZO and had consumed only an HRM commander, similar to those who appear on the official list. This was confirmed by eyewitnesses.

General Dawson seemed rejuvenated by having fed, and I detected no immediate cause for concern, but I nonetheless feel that it's possible that General Dawson's commitment has been compromised and that he should be observed carefully and with all due concern.

DREW HATCH
Captain and Special Aide de Camp
to Major General Harland Dawson, NZOA

DEPARTMENT OF THE ARMY
2ND INFANTRY DIVISION
SOUTHERN CALIFORNIA COMMAND BASE
EL TORO
MAJ. GEN. HARLAND DAWSON, COMMANDING

30 October

REQUEST FOR STAFF TRANSFER

I am hereby requesting that Captain Drew Hatch, currently serving as the Special Aide de Camp to the Major General of the NZOA Southwest, be transferred from this assignment.

Although Captain Hatch has served satisfactorily in this capacity, I believe his particular skills and experience are far better suited to intelligence missions, and that he would best serve the NZO by re-assignment to ZIS or another intelligence agency. The NZOASW General's office would function at peak performance levels with a Special Aide de Camp who is superior at administrative and organizational tasks.

I request that Major Hatch's transfer be immediate, and that I be allowed to review and approve his replacement.

HARLAND DAWSON
Major General, NZOASW

CONFIDENTIAL — FOR ZIS EYES ONLY

31 October

I was ordered to keep ZIS updated on any suspicious behavior I observed on the part of Major General Harland Dawson.

Two days ago, I reported on how the General led the 23rd Battalion into combat and encountered and consumed HRM leader Hector Robles, who did not appear on the ZIS Capture/Consume List. Yesterday I requested and received from ZIS a background file on Robles, who was essentially a family man with no military experience. This is exactly why we initiated Operation Darwin—by consuming Johnson, I believe that Dawson may have acquired information that will actually be a detriment to his ability to lead this division.

Since returning from the field two days ago, Dawson's behavior has been questionable. He has performed routine duties in an acceptable fashion—directing units in the field, approving supply requisitions, etc.—but he has noticeably made no plans to act on any intelligence gained via Robles. When I attempted to question the General on any such data, he informed me that he believed Robles was on drugs and the information received was so fractured that he's still trying to process it. While there is some history on record of similar incidents involving information obtained from addicts, there is nothing in Robles' records to indicate any involvement with drugs. It seems especially unlikely behavior for a middle-aged man with a wife and two children in a combat situation.

I was also informed yesterday by ZIS of the General's attempt to have me transferred. Since I have performed all duties for the General in a more than satisfactory fashion (and since he has never given me any indication that he was dissatisfied with my work in any way), I believe he may have requested this transfer because he (rightly) suspects my ZIS connections and wants to avoid close observation. This would only be the case if—as I believe—his ingestion of Hector Robles has had negative effects on him.

I will continue to observe and report back.

DREW HATCH
Captain and Special Aide de Camp
to Major General Harland Dawson, NZOA

[The following e-mail message was obtained from General Dawson's
personal phone approximately two days after it was transmitted,
and was translated from the original Spanish.]

e-mail message
Date: Fri, 1 Nov 06:33:19-0700 [06:33:19 AM PST]RM
From: hectorrobles@freezom.net
To: alejandrarobles@ztel.mobi
Subject: I need you to hear this

Dear Alejandra:

I'm sure you know by now that your husband, Hector, was killed three days ago in an
attack on the Norwalk HRM base.

I know this, because I am the one who killed him.

My name is Harland Dawson, and I am the Major General in command of the New
Zombie Order Army forces currently attempting to annex Southern California. On 29
October, I personally led an infantry battalion into Norwalk. After we encountered the
HRM camp, we neutralized all human insurgents discovered there. Your husband
attempted to self-terminate before we could capture him, but he was unsuccessful. My
soldiers consumed the humans under Hector's command, and I consumed Hector.

I assume you have some familiarity with how HTZT—the process of transitioning from
human to zombie—works, and as a result you would thus understand that, by
consuming your husband, I gained his memories and experiences. This, of course,
explains why I am contacting you via this private e-mail that you kept only for
communication with your husband. I know—or, perhaps, more accurately, I remember—
your life together with Hector. I remember your first meeting, fifteen years ago, at your
mutual friend Devon's house party. I remember the wedding day, the birth of your first
child (Maribel, now 14), the arrival of your son Maximiliano two years later, the tenth
anniversary trip to New Orleans, and how Hector left his job at a chain hardware store
to join the HRM. I know how you last saw him a week ago, how you kissed him and told
him to be careful as he left, and he told you the same. I know about the Day of the Dead
altar you've set up to celebrate the coming 2 November by remembering all those
you've lost in this war. I know you and Maribel and Maxi are not at an HRM camp, but
are instead sheltering in the storage area of that hardware store where Hector once
worked as an assistant manager. Hector was right in believing that it was a safer place
for you.

You need to understand something about me: I made a critical mistake in consuming
your husband. I understand now why I have always been ordered to consume only
HRM leaders investigated and approved by Zombie Intelligence—because those men
and women have all been completely dedicated to their lives in the military and were
chosen because they left little or no family.

I have never consumed anyone like Hector. I've never known what would undoubtedly be thought of as a "normal" human life. Even before my own transformation, I was urged—no, I was *ordered*—by my father to pursue a life in combat. As a child, I was beaten if I questioned father; as a teenager, I let him choose the direction of my life; as an adult, I agreed with whatever he said and continued to seek his approval.

As a zombie, I ate him.

And he was bitter.

Hector, though, wasn't a soldier; he was an extraordinarily brave (and, I suspect, charismatic) man who was a natural leader and who accepted his role as a leader when the time came. He fought to protect you and your children, not because he believed in country or principle or even paycheck. He cared only for you.

I've never known commitment to anything but ideal and duty. And now knowing it, I find myself shaken.

Why am I violating my primary orders and committing treason by telling you, an enemy, all of this? Because for the first time in my life (lives?) there is a war raging within me. I now question if NZO really needs to exterminate and imprison all humans, especially if we replace your commitment to each other with nothing but our hungers.

What you need to know is this: We will be coming for you. Tomorrow I will personally lead a squad into that store, and if we find you, you will be captured or consumed. And if this happens, the part of me that is now Hector will be devastated, and I choose not to endure that.

But I'm also—somewhere, in some core I can barely access—*me*, Harland Dawson, a committed career officer, and so I will follow my directives and pursue all intelligence leads acquired as a result of consuming Hector. My battalion will leave shortly. I'm giving you this chance to run. As soon as you finish reading this.

RUN.

Sincerely,
Harland Dawson
Maj. Gen., NZO

SPECIAL MEMO

CONFIDENTIAL — FOR ZIS EYES ONLY

2 November

I request an immediate trace be put on all calls, e-mails and text messages sent to and from General Harland Dawson's private smart phone (you have the number in his personnel file).

At approximately 0630 hours yesterday morning, General Dawson retired to his office, closed the door, and engaged in some private business. Approximately fifteen minutes later, General Dawson left the office and informed the 23rd that he would again be assuming command of them in a mission to follow up on information obtained from the consumption of HRM leader Hector Robles.

That mission will occur today. It is currently 0730 hours, and I am sending this before I leave with the General and the battalion.

The General seemed anxious to be sure that I accompanied him on this particular mission, which is unlike his behavior from 29 October, when I believe he misdirected me so that he could embark on a mission without me.

I believe it is possible that the General used his private phone to convey information to the enemy. I realize this is a severe accusation, one punishable by court martial and execution, and so I request this additional surveillance to obtain proof that can be used to publicly relieve Dawson of his duties.

Should ZIS choose to fulfill this request and find that General Dawson is indeed in violation of the strictest principles of combat, then I recommend that we promote 3rd Brigade commander Harrison Delvecchio and assign command of the 2nd Division to him immediately. I have interviewed Colonel Delvecchio and believe he is more than capable of accepting this responsibility and continuing Operation New Zombie Order Southwest's successful advance into Los Angeles County. He has also indicated to me his willingness (and, indeed, eagerness) to participate in Operation Darwin.

> DREW HATCH
> Captain and Special Aide de Camp
> to Major General Harland Dawson, NZOA

SPECIAL FIELD REPORT

2ND INFANTRY DIVISION
SOUTHERN CALIFORNIA COMMAND BASE
MAJ. GEN. HARLAND DAWSON, COMMANDING

CLASSIFIED

2 November

This morning at 0730 hours, 2nd Division Major General Harland Dawson assumed command of the 23rd Battalion and led them on a field mission to utilize information obtained from previous consumption of HRM leader Hector Robles.

The information regarded several pockets of survivors spread throughout the LAC communities of Norwalk and Santa Fe Springs. The battalion encountered minimal resistance en route, with approximately ten members of the HRM terminated and an additional seven captured alive for transferal via MRAP to the Fullerton HIC. No serious NZOASW casualties were reported.

However, as the battalion reached the parking lot of a hardware store where General Dawson reported that Robles' family—his wife, Alejandra, is also an important figure in the HRM—would be found, heavy resistance was encountered. HRM soldiers driving four armored Humvees appeared, circled our troops, and hurled a variety of explosive devices from their moving vehicles. NZOASW soldiers were able to terminate two of the four vehicles, but not before the explosions had led to final deaths of 49 members of the battalion. A full list of the casualties will be found appended to the end of this report.

The remaining two vehicles parked approximately 300 yards away, and almost immediately produced and fired two rocket launchers (ZIS has been informed that their intelligence regarding a lack of such weapons among HRM forces was incorrect). One rocket successfully destroyed one of our MRAPs; all twelve soldiers aboard were incinerated in the attack. The other rocket detonated in a pocket of infantry, and eighteen troops were destroyed.

General Dawson ordered an immediate withdrawal of all NZOASW troops. Infantry and remaining MRAPs retreated to a safe distance of 500 yards, where the MRAPs were arrayed to form a defensive shield. NZOASW's own explosive ordnance was deployed, including airborne drones which successfully damaged both of the remaining Humvees. Drone cameras revealed the surviving humans fleeing into the hardware store.

General Dawson personally selected a squad of nine men to accompany him on a search-and-destroy mission into the store. Captain Drew Hatch objected, stating that the General was too valuable to participate in such a risky venture, but Dawson persisted. He did agree to allow Captain Hatch to accompany the squad.

All squad members, including General Dawson and Captain Hatch, were outfitted with the latest issue bomb suits before attempting to enter the store. Squads were positioned around the perimeter of the building, to prevent human escape attempts and also to deter potential ambushes from additional HRM troops outside the store.

At 1415, General Dawson led the squad into the building. They encountered several primitive booby traps, but fortunately the bomb suits were effective in preventing injury. The squad reconnoitered the front of the store, but found no sign of the human survivors

Dawson then led the squad into the offices and storage area located at the rear of the store. Almost immediately the squad was embroiled in a firefight. HRM ordnance included SAPHE shells, which were successful in penetrating the armor and SR-7 helmets of the NZOASW soldiers. Nine of Dawson's ten men were terminated in the firefight by SAPHE shots to the head before the HRM combatants were disarmed. Only General Dawson and Captain Hatch—who had taken shelter during the firefight and refrained from participating—remained.

[NOTE: The following account is a transcription of events recorded by a live videocamera on the scene. General Dawson was apparently unaware that Captain Hatch's helmet was made to the Captain's specifications and included a videocam that was retrieved shortly after the events described below. Although the videocam was destroyed, technicians were able to salvage the memory chip and retrieve the recording.]

All but two of the HRM combatants were also terminated during the firefight, and the two still alive were mortally wounded. General Dawson stepped forward and shot one in the head, thus preventing HTZT. The remaining enemy soldier was a woman wearing a Kevlar vest, but she had taken multiple shots to the arms and legs, and was now incapacitated. As Dawson approached her, she attempted to lift her weapon. Instead of defending himself and following protocol by terminating her, Dawson instead removed his helmet and called the enemy soldier by the name "Alejandra".

The soldier responded by lowering her weapon. Dawson approached and knelt beside her. Although the videocam's audio was unable to record a whispered exchange between the two, the resulting conversation caused the enemy combatant to completely set her gun aside and to display an intense emotional response. At one point, she and the General both gestured at a primitive altar set up nearby which held photos, flowers, and small plaster skulls (experts have since identified this as part of a Mexican celebration called *El Dia de los Muertos*, held each year on 2 November).

At this point, Captain Hatch, who had left cover to record this exchange, called out to the General. The General responded by taking the enemy's dropped weapon. The audio clearly records him asking her, "Loaded with armor-piercing rounds, right?" She nodded.

General Dawson then turned, pointed the gun at Captain Hatch's forehead, and pulled the trigger.

The camera position then changes abruptly, which is presumably the result of Major Hatch falling to the floor, permanently dead as a result of Dawson's head-shot.

What follows consists of audio only (the video is blocked by an unknown object that Major Hatch had fallen behind), and the audio can't be clearly made out. There is a further, brief verbal exchange in Spanish, presumably between General Dawson and the enemy soldier, who was later determined to be Alejandra Robles, an important figure in the HRM. Following are several minutes of cries on the part of Robles, accompanied by the sounds of chewing.

The last sounds on the audio recording are a gunshot, then footsteps and a door opening and closing. Cleanup teams later confirmed that Alejandra Robles had been partially consumed and then shot in the head.

At 1450 hours, the NZOASW troops Dawson had stationed behind the store reported that the General appeared, told them he required the use of their MRAP, and ordered them to remain where they were. They said General Dawson was covered in fresh human blood, but seemed calm. After commandeering the vehicle, Dawson headed north from the store.

General Dawson would of course have known that the MRAP contained anti-theft tracking devices, and he abandoned the vehicle approximately ten miles from where he'd taken it. It was recovered at 1620 hours. The General's combat apparel and personal phone were also found in the vehicle, but all weapons had been removed.

General Dawson's whereabouts remain unknown as of this writing.

MARTIN S. CHARLEŞ
Major, NZOA

e-mail message
Date: Sun, 3 Nov 06:33:19 -0700 [06:33:19 AM PST]RM
From: deadgeneral@freezom.net
To: zispao@mi.army.mil
Subject: From Harland Dawson

This is a message to the entire upper command of the NZO from former Major General Harland Dawson:

As you know by now, I have abandoned my position and forsaken my duties to the New Zombie Order. I have committed the highest of treasons and will expect the most severe judgment to be passed upon me should I be captured.

But before then, I ask President Moreby, The Well of Seven, and all NZO military personnel to hear my words:

If NZO continues to move along its present path, it will fail. Probably within less than two years.

We have always depended on consuming humans to acquire new information. As a participant in Operation Darwin, my meals were confined to those who—like me—had led human lives dedicated strictly to duty to their country. I was not allowed to experience human traits such as love, grief, or creativity.

But recently, driven by severe hunger, I disobeyed the imperatives of Operation Darwin and consumed two non-military humans. Now Hector and Alejandra Robles—husband and wife, father and mother of two children—live within me. Hector, who played guitar and wished he could sing better; Alejandra, who wrote music for her husband. They worked together as a single unit, and as one they created entirely new things. They created children, a family, strategies, songs.

We—the members of the New Zombie Order—can do none of these things. We can only acquire thoughts that are already old by the time they reach us. We are incapable of invention or innovation, and this means that we are incapable of ever progressing. We can never be anything more than a stagnant nation.

A truly dead nation.

Yesterday was an important day for Hector and Alejandra—Day of the Dead, for which they made an altar that celebrated their deceased loved ones. Now Hector and Alejandra live inside me, and I am like that altar—nothing but a collection of memories that won't change.

As are all of you zombies reading this.

We must cease actions against the humans immediately. We must recognize that *they* are our future, and we must learn to live side-by-side with them.

I know you won't heed this warning, and that you already have ZIS agents hunting me down. And that's why I'm going in search of Maribel and Maximiliano—Hector and Alejandra Robles' two children. I know where Alejandra took them when she received my warning, before she returned to organize the ambush that almost took my life permanently. I'm going after them now, and when I find them, I will do whatever I must to protect them and keep them safe. I do this not for Hector and Alejandra within me, but for the future of humanity and zombiekind both.

Don't bother trying to track me via this message, which I'm typing from an abandoned laptop I found in a store in Hollywood. Fifteen seconds from now, I will destroy the machine, retrieve the vehicle I left outside, and disappear.

It's a fate that I fear awaits us all.

Sincerely,
Harland Dawson

Menu

Our goremet chefs prepare only the freshest produce, and our dishes reflect this city's international clientele. We are firm believers in organic, home-prepared food crafted with love from fresh, locally sourced produce. All our dishes are processed "just in time", and our suppliers personally select our product to order, ensuring ultimate freshness.

Appetizers

Carpaccio

Thinly-sliced and richly aged, ensuring exquisite flavor of the delicate flesh

Yukhoe

The traditional Korean delicacy, using only the most tender meat, thinly julienned, and seasoned with a mixture of *bae* (Korean pear), soy sauce, sesame oil, spring onion, minced garlic, sugar, salt and sesame seeds

Mett

Low German specialty of minced meat and lightly seasoned with salt and black pepper. As is traditional, this dish is prepared fresh to order only

Mains

Classic Tartare

A generous serving, made to order.
Please indicate the age of meat desired to your server

Tartarmad

A variation on the above, this mainstay of Danish smørrebrødn is furnished on rye bread with or without the traditional toppings
(served with a delicate side salad of jellied eyeballs)

Kachila

A distinct dish from Nepal of wonderful raw minced meat mixed with mustard oil, ground fennel and minced garlic. When ordering, please be aware that our sources may be limited, depending on availability

Kibbe Nayyeh

Lebanese specialty with highlights of minced raw meat, mixed with fine bulgar wheat and spices. Served with mint leaves and olive oil. Proffered with or without finger sandwiches

Gored Gored

Eritrean dish of pure unmarinated and cubed flesh.
We serve this stunning dish with a bowl of *jus natural*, for full enjoyment

---

Desserts

Trio of Truffles

Liver, brain and heart, served with a beautifully reductive *effusion de sang*

Sweetbreads

A traditional end-of-meal delicacy. Please let the server know if you wish for additional pancreas (extra charge)

Cervelles en gélatine

Sumptuous bone marrow jelly, encasing a full-sized brain.
This makes a stunning end to any meal

Please note that a discretionary service charge of 20% will be added to all parties of six or more.
This is to help with the clean-up afterwards.

FROM: Lt. Colonel W. Edwards,
NZOASW Field Office #14,
San Diego, CA.

TO: Dr. Daniel Ashcroft,
New America Zombie Intelligence Service,
Washington, DC.

PRIVATE AND CONFIDENTIAL

Dear Dan,

Congratulations on the appointment. Given that my own recent elevation to the brass was strictly a field-promotion after the Dawson debacle in SoCal, I know I'm way too dumb to understand what the hell a "Department of Psychological-Variants Control" *does* exactly, but I figure that if you're in charge then it's probably doing it right.

Look, I'm not sure if the enclosed falls strictly within your purview, but it was brought to my attention by one of our field transcribers and, I don't know, I just thought it might be something you should take a look at.

Technically, the papers haven't been declassified yet, but there's nothing in there of any strategic or military significance so I'm going to trust to your discretion regarding them (and, in cover-my-ass mode, from where you may have obtained them).

The bulk of the material is a transcript of a relatively informal Internal Affairs debriefing following a routine investigation into some killings, but I'm going to interleave some extracts from the killer's personal journal to provide context where necessary. There are a couple of anomalies in procedure that I thought might prompt the ZIS's interest. Anyway, see what you think.

Sincerely,

Waldo

[TRANSCRIPT OF AUDIO DEBRIEFING: MONDAY, DECEMBER 9]

Interviewee: Detective Sergeant James Bertrand
Interviewing Officer: Detective Lieutenant Consolata Meadows

CM: Good morning, Detective.

JB: Lieutenant.

CM: You need anything? *[pause]* Verbally, please. Headshake's not going to record.

JB: I'm fine, Lieutenant. Thank you.

CM: You mind if I smoke?

JB: No. But I didn't know you—

CM: Habit I picked up recently. Very recently. From a perp we obtained. You know how it is.

JB: Yes, Ma'am. I do.

CM: Okay. Background data first. Your original DOB?

JB: November 4th, 1982.

CM: And your HTZT?

JB: October 17th, Ma'am.

CM: Recruitment to Security Enforcement?

JB: October 31st.

CM: Happy Halloween.

JB: Ma'am?

CM: Sorry. Humor. Something else I inherited from someone.

JB: Strange, isn't it?

CM: What is? Humor?

JB: No. No, that thing. The . . . picking up of—

CM: The YAWYE Syndrome, they're calling it. You Are What You Eat. You might want to remember that if you talk to a lawyer.

JB: Do I need a lawyer?

CM: Don't know. What do you think?

JB: Do we even *have* lawyers?

CM: Second oldest profession, Detective Sergeant. New Order or old. Now, shall we get on with why we're here?

JB: Ma'am? With respect, I don't know why we're here.

CM: It's just a debriefing. Pretty routine.

JB: Is it?

CM: Isn't it?

JB: I don't know. I was given an assignment. I completed it. Filed a report. I'm not sure what the problem is.

CM: You think there's a problem? *[pause]* Detective Sergeant?

JB: I don't know, Ma'am. Like I said.

CM: Like you said.

[the tiny sound of a cigarette being stubbed out]

JB: You only smoked half of it.

CM: Yeah, I know. It's weird. I feel the urge, act on it, but the smoking itself doesn't give me much of anything.

JB: So why do it?

CM: Why not? What's it gonna do? Kill me?

JB: Huh. That was humor, wasn't it?

CM: Graveyard humor, Detective Sergeant. Best kind. Now, let's talk about Martin Gifford and his odd little hobby.

[Extract 1 from Martin Gifford's journal, Exhibit #B478.]

Here's the thing; they make it easier than it used to be. When girls were girls, they were suspicious sometimes. Now they're eager to be approached. Because they're hungry. Silly things. They're not as hungry as me.

CM: I'm going to give some background for the record. Correct me at any point if your recollection differs. Following the successful pacification of Los Angeles, the strict military supervision of sectors NW4, NW5, and C2 was replaced by a less numbers-intensive defense policy, and responsibility transferred to local Security Enforcement. Not much to disagree with so far, right?

JB: Right.

CM: Right. Over the course of a month-and-a-half, various patrols in those sectors discovered six bodies. Well, I say "discovered," but it's not like the bodies were *hidden* or anything. Not hidden at all. More like they were displayed, wouldn't you say?

JB: Judging by the reports, Ma'am, yes.

CM: Left in plain sight for us to find. Correct?

JB: Correct.

CM: Like somebody was having a bit of fun with us.

JB: You could put it that way, Ma'am, I suppose.

CM: Well, certainly we could say someone was showing a blatant and insolent disregard for the New Zombie Order we were in the business of imposing, couldn't we?

JB: Central Command seemed to think so.

CM: Indeed. Sensing a pattern to the killings that produced those bodies—wonder how long it took 'em to work *that* out?—our superiors initiated an investigation, and the docket landed on your desk.

JB: That's right, Ma'am.

[Extract 2 from Martin Gifford's journal, Exhibit #B478.]

Look, I know I'm fussy. I know I don't take every opportunity that presents itself. But I have certain barriers of taste. And—especially in this changing world—someone's got to maintain standards. That's what I say. So while that means I can sometimes go a long time without a playmate, it also means that I don't bring home someone unsuitable for Mother.

CM: So, given your experience with the LAPD before your HTZT, you were assigned to investigate and, depending upon the results of that investigation, to take any appropriate action. Correct?

JB: Yes, Ma'am.

CM: I'm getting tired of my own voice, Detective Sergeant Bertrand. Talk me through it, would you?

JB: Okay, Ma'am.

[pause]

CM: Whenever you're ready.

JB: Yes, Ma'am. Sorry. *[pause]* Well, there were certain inescapable conclusions from the get-go. For one thing, it was clear that the killings weren't the work of any of us.

CM: Us? You mean Security Enforcement?

JB: No, Ma'am. I mean . . . our kind. First, the victims weren't human, but recent transforms. Extremely recent, in fact.

[Extract 3 from Martin Gifford's journal, Exhibit #B478.]

It's impossible to find one completely unmarked of course, but what I try and find is one with a single wound. Someone who was, for whatever reason, abandoned after the killing bite.

Best of all, as I'm sure you can guess, is when I can get them before they wake. That's only happened once before. Last night's was even better.

JB: Second, the final dispatch of the victims—after the . . . activities . . . that preceded it—was the driving through the forehead and frontal lobes of a sharp and heavy metal object. I verified with the M.E.'s office that the actual implement was an industrial chisel-blade.

CM: A-ha. Someone's little variation on "shoot 'em in the brain." Someone who thought guns just weren't intimate enough.

JB: Precisely, Ma'am.

CM: But, gun or no gun, brain-trauma execution was the M.O. So you figured the killer you were looking for was human.

JB: Correct.

CM: A human was hunting down newborns, destroying them, and displaying them ostentatiously for us to find.

JB: Correct.

CM: You know what I call that, Detective Sergeant?

JB: No, Ma'am.

CM: I call that uppity.

JB: I don't believe the motive was insurgency, Ma'am.

CM: I was joking, Detective Sergeant. But, please, clarify.

JB: The victims were all female. The nature of the mutilations was clearly fetishistic. And the bodies were attired in various costumes that indicated psycho-sexual obsession. We weren't looking for a member of the resistance movement, Ma'am. We were looking for a predator.

[Extract 4 from Martin Gifford's journal, Exhibit #B478.]

The Zees usually work in packs, so I was very conscious of my good luck when I came across my latest friend. As usual, I'd been hunting on the fringes of the Echo Park ghetto, where the unconverted still feel free to wander, and the dumb ones feel free to wander alone. I spotted a certain foolish little miss—young, pretty, ripe—who was just about to learn her lesson: She'd got herself cornered, but only by one of them. I enjoyed her screams as he herded her into an alley, biding my time. I let him take his first bite—happened to be from her stomach, could've been anywhere, not something I can control—and then stabbed him through the back of the head. She looked really grateful, until I knocked her out.

By the time she woke up, I'd been able to get everything ready. She was already strapped to the table and, more importantly, I'd been able to take my time selecting her wardrobe for our date.

JB: By triangulating the locations of the bodies and using a series of surveillance operations, I was able—

CM: I've read your report, Sergeant. Your police-work was frankly exemplary, but we don't need to rehash the details. That's not what this is about. Let's move on to what happened once you'd determined who and where the perp was.

JB: Yes, Ma'am.

CM: You found that our guy was a human male, 24-years-old—later identified, once you discovered his journal, as Martin Gifford—who'd escaped the military sweeps by taking up residence in a former industrial location at Melrose and Gower.

JB: Yes, Ma'am.

CM: Now, help me out here. You were fairly convinced this was your killer? Beyond a reasonable doubt, say?

JB: Yes, Ma'am.

CM: But you kept him under observation for quite some time.

JB: I did. I . . . *[pause]*

CM: Go ahead, Detective.

JB: I was trying to understand what his trigger was. Where the hunger came from. What sent him out. But after a couple of weeks—

CM: And two more victims.

JB: Yes, Ma'am. After a couple of weeks, I realized I'd been overthinking it. It was just . . . it was just something he did. Something he did on Monday nights.

CM: Every Monday night?

JB: Yes, Ma'am.

CM: You verified this by surveillance?

JB: I did.

CM: Just something he did on Monday nights. Like a poker game.

JB: Or Karaoke.

CM: Just a way to pass the time. A way to have a bit of fun. They really are strange creatures, aren't they?

JB: I'm not sure. Are they really any different from us?

CM: Can't you tell anymore? We only consume living flesh because we must to survive. Gifford was a monster. Look, Detective Sergeant, what we're having trouble understanding—what I'd like you to help me out with—isn't *his* behavior. It's *yours*.

JB: Ma'am?

CM: I understand your curiosity, I really do. But, nevertheless, you identified and located him on—let me check my notes here—the Monday of what would turn out to be his penultimate attack, the fifth of six victims . . .

JB: Yes, Ma'am.

CM: Did you have reason to assume he was unfit for the meat farms?

JB: No, Ma'am.

CM: But nor did you immediately terminate him.

JB: No, Ma'am.

CM: No. In fact, you didn't apprehend and detain him until the day after the killing of his *sixth* victim.

JB: That's correct, Ma'am.

CM: And you chose to detain him in his own base of operations rather than bring him in?

JB: Yes, Ma'am.

CM: And—besides not notifying your Supervising Officer that to all intents and purposes you'd closed the case—it was apparently a further ten days before you took appropriate disciplinary action.

JB: *[small grunt of laughter]* "Appropriate disciplinary action."

CM: Am I amusing you, Bertrand?

JB: No, Ma'am.

CM: But you find my choice of words . . . what? A little bureaucratic? A little clinical?

JB: Euphemistic, I'd say. Ma'am.

CM: Oh. How very precise of you. Then by all means, Detective, let's call a spade a spade. You didn't eat the little fucker for a week and a goddam half. 'Sup with that?

JB: Not entirely accurate, Ma'am.

CM: How so?

JB: I didn't *finish* eating him for a week and a half.

She was even younger than I'd thought and quite remarkably pretty. Mother and Father were delighted by her, and quite entranced by the Victorian Maiden look I'd selected for her to wear. It suited the newborn pallor, of course, and lent an engaging sense of outrage to her screams. It really was one of our best nights together as a family.

JB: You mentioned the "industrial location" where he'd based himself. It was what used to be a movie studio. He'd set up home in what they used to call a back-lot, this particular one being a simulacrum of a middle-class street. In one of the houses, he'd created a mock family for himself. Mother and father—long dead, you understand, and I mean dead, not like us—were sat at a fully-dressed dinner table. Gifford would bring his dates home to meet the family and then make his parents watch as he . . . consummated . . . the relationship. In various ways. And then they'd all—in his head, at least— partake of the family meal.

CM: The dates were dinner.

JB: Yes, Ma'am. Parts of them, at least.

CM: Perhaps not so very different from us after all, Bertrand.

JB: It's different, Ma'am.

CM: Is it?

JB: Yes. You see that, don't you?

CM: What I see isn't the issue here. *[pause]* But if it helps, yes. Yes, it's different. Was that why your eventual execution of him was so punitive? So fucking *thorough*? I mean, you didn't leave a single morsel, am I right?

JB: I didn't.

CM: Let's change tack a moment. Gifford's last killing was Monday, November 11th. And he himself—after his nine-day adventure with you— finally departed this world on a Wednesday. So you can imagine our surprise, I'm sure, when another body turned up the following Monday?

JB: Bodies are always being discovered, Ma'am. It's a jungle out there.

CM: Yes, but not bodies dressed in a cheerleader uniform and mutilated in ways familiar to anyone with a passing knowledge of this case.

JB: That does sound . . . specific.

CM: I agree. And yet the one person we can be sure isn't responsible is Martin Gifford. Because there isn't a single physical trace of Martin Gifford left on earth, thanks to you. "Some of them just don't deserve to come back," is that what you were thinking?

JB: I suppose I must have been.

CM: You were feeling anger, maybe? Perhaps even empathy for his victims? It's possible. YAWYE syndrome. You could have picked those things up.

JB: I could have.

CM: But you don't feel them now, do you?

JB: Not in the slightest.

CM: You feel differently?

[pause]

CM: Detective Bertrand?

[pause]

CM: Is it you that's having a bit of fun with us now . . .?

[Extract 6 from Martin Gifford's journal, Exhibit #B478.]

It is not enough to kill. It is not enough to eat. I want to hunt. I want to trap. I want to terrify. The meat is seasoned by its fear.

BERNIE MAUGHMSTEIN JOKE #1301

Okay, okay . . . hey, okay. Ease up now.
You people are like to piss your pants at
this rate. Place is going to be awash, man.
But I'm okay, yeah? I'm up on the fucking
stage, man. Okay, okay . . . let's go easy
now. Okay. I wanna talk to you about . . .
I wanna talk to you about sex, man.

Right? I mean, am I fucking right, man?
But . . . hey, I'm talking here lady. I'll come
listen to you when you appear someplace
lady but until then, just shut the fuck
up. Okay? Okay? Okay. I wanna talk to
you about sex . . . about sex . . . between
zombies.

I remember the very first time I was taken to the theatre. My father didn't want me to go. He looked unhappy about it. It was my mother's idea — she said, "Dickie, you have to take him to the theatre sooner or later," and my father stared down at me critically, the way he would analyse everything, not blinking, not moving his head, giving me a once over assessment. And I stood up straight and tried to look well-behaved, and adult, and whatever else he might want me to be. He then nodded curtly, and said that my perspective as a seven-year-old might come in useful. And I had to put on my best clothes, the ones I only ever wore when Grandma came round; he put on, as always, his work clothes — that brown tie, those brown trousers, that tweed jacket he liked.

There was a certain allure to the theatre even then. This was where my father went to work, and it seemed to me that therefore this would be a place rather like him, quiet, a bit forbidding, and very mysterious. And I knew that it involved people dressing up in funny clothes and saying things that weren't true, but that they hardly ever got told off for it. If anyone ever told them off, it was my father; at this stage he was the third most senior drama critic on The Sunday Times — which wasn't terribly senior, really, and meant he rarely got to review any of the top West End shows but instead the lesser things on the fringe or in the provinces. Still, he took it all very seriously, and once in a while, when one of his critiques was published, he would present the newspaper to me and my mother at the breakfast table. "Look at that," he'd say, and we'd see his name at the top of the article, RICHARD HARDY, and in a thick font, and that was exciting — my father was famous, he was almost as famous as the actors he was criticising! — and then he'd proceed to explain why this particular evening at the theatre had been joyless or disappointing or starved of all cultural merit. Showing us his reviews were the only times that I ever saw him properly smile. He told me he loved theatre. "Theatre is the life blood of any healthy society," he said. "That's why it has to show the very highest of aspirations. That's

why I have to complain when it's found wanting." And he
ruffled my hair as he said this, a rare sign of affection,
as if I'd been admitted to a secret important truth, as if
now, like him, I was one of an elite.

There was no hair ruffling that first day we went to the
theatre together. I'd never seen before how tense my father
would get before a performance started, as he settled down
grimly in the auditorium with his notebook and pen at the
ready, as if the pressure was on him, as if he would be
the one required to declaim a speech or break into song.
There were children all around us, calling out to each
other, spilling out of their seats, and my father said he
hoped they wouldn't make too much noise during the play
itself. They were all drinking lemonade and eating
Maltesers, and I asked my father if I could have lemonade
and Maltesers too, and he said no. "Now, hush," he said to
me, as the house lights went down.

It's impossible for me now to appreciate how good, bad, or
indifferent that production of Aladdin and His Magic
Lamp really was. Probably it was all a bit passé — in
retrospect I certainly don't recall anything original
being done with the source material, and I suspect the
costumes and set design were gaudy and cheap. But it
seemed fresh to me, so new, that there were all these
strangers on a stage and I was allowed to stare at them
and keep right on staring and that it wasn't rude — and
that they were talking to each other, but they were also
sort of talking to me. The plot was easy to follow, and
the songs simple enough so that all the kids could join
in when required. At one point Wishy-Washy threw some
sweets into the audience, and I got some Maltesers after
all.

And throughout my father would tut, and shake his head,
and scribble things down in his notebook.

Afterwards, my father asked me if I had enjoyed myself,
and I said I had. And he did that assessment thing on me

— he stared down at me unblinking and unmoving. "Why?"
he said. And I suppose the main reason was that I was
with him, I was with my father for once, we were doing
something together — but I couldn't tell him that, that
wasn't what he wanted to hear. I told him I'd thought the
show was funny. And what it really was, I think, was that
there was such a sense of community in that auditorium —
that when the panto was working, there were two thousand
eyes all trained in the exact same direction, and we all
held our breath as one, and laughed as one. And at the end
we all applauded as one, Aladdin and all his friends came
out to take a curtain call, and everyone in the audience
clapped — even my father clapped — and I didn't really
know what clapping was, but it seemed like the right
thing to do, it was fun to be a part of that barrage of
noise offering thanks and approval for the evening's
entertainment. And the curtains came down and the lights
came up and we all filed out of the theatre as strangers
once more — but for a couple of hours in the dark it was
as if we'd all been family, all been one, sharing the same
thing.

My father's review took my reaction into account. He
damned the direction and the acting and the script and the
stagecraft. But he also wrote, It may be engaging enough
for children without taste or much ambition. And he
pointed out the review to me, and it was the first time I'd
been mentioned in a newspaper, even tangentially, and I
felt so proud.

And that's the reason I became a playwright, I think. That
first taste of the theatre had given me the desire to tap
into that community I'd felt, I too wanted to make an
audience bond together like that. And I suppose, too, I
wanted to create a piece of theatre that my father would
like. Something that would make him write a good review.
Something that'd make him ruffle my hair again, and smile.

- - - - - - - - - -

The greatest casualty of the zombie apocalypse was the arts. It's typical that in times of national crisis that arts funding is always the first to be slashed, and that's because we live in a philistinic society which sees culture as essentially bourgeois, and irrelevant to the needs of the ordinary man. It quite makes me fume. The government pumped all their money into the emergency services, of course, into the police and the hospitals and the army — and I don't pretend there wasn't a need for them, but let's be honest, from this vantage point, where we can see quite clearly that there was no cure to be found for the plague that turned the population into living—dead monsters, and that there was no law enforcement or defence force strong enough to resist the ravening hordes, all that money seems to have been rather wasted, doesn't it? We might as well have had a few million siphoned off towards the galleries that proposed an exhibition of new sculptures and multimedia tableaux inspired by the outbreak, or towards some questing agit prop theatre productions that would have inspired thought and debate.

What my father said was true. Theatre is the lifeblood of a healthy society. And by closing the theatres we denied that blood a chance to flow. It happened with Oliver Cromwell, it happened with World War II. It's happening now, and I tell you, the consequences will be devastating. Let's face it, what we saw on the streets of London was one of the greatest social upheavals since the Industrial Revolution or the Poll Tax riots. It's my job as a playwright to document it, and the tools with which I can do so have been taken from me.

I'm not arguing this for my own sake. Revolutions in theatre occur every twenty years or so, and I think that's essential — believe me, if the zombies were espousing some new artistic movement of their own that would render mine outmoded and quaint, I would welcome it with open arms. Any true artist will be prepared to tear down to the foundations the tired structures of the now, so he can

build something in its place more urgent and inspiring.
But all I see going on is a lot of tearing down. The
zombies don't seem interested in expressing themselves,
just in killing people and eating their brains. And here
in my garret at night I hear them out on the street
keening at each other, and I try to detect in it the signs
of music — but I think instead it's probably just wails of
hunger.

I knew that the zombies would come for me eventually. I
was holed up in Watford, and it seemed so far I'd been
lucky — I'd look out of the window and see that
neighbouring houses and shops were being gutted, but that
they were leaving my block of flats alone. One night I
heard screams from the floors below, and I knew then that
the end would only be a matter of time. They took the
family from across the hall, and the woman in the flat
above went two nights later. And when at last they
battered down my door I was almost relieved. I'd been
living off baked beans for months, and my supply was
running out. And I had put in a strong box under the bed
all twenty-six of my plays (seven produced, nineteen
pending), in the hope that future generations might
discover them and commit them to posterity. I was ready.

There were three of them; a man, and a woman, and
something too rotted for me quite to tell. And they looked
so hungry, and I couldn't help it, I felt a wave of such
pity for them, it seemed to me that all the brains in the
world wouldn't be enough to feed those poor souls. I hoped
the woman would be the one to get me, she looked the best
of the bunch, and I moved closer towards her to give her
first dibs. But she didn't step forward; neither of her
partners did. Instead they flapped their arms at me,
gesturing at the door. I couldn't work out what they
wanted at first. "Should I follow you?" I asked, loud and
clear, as if to infants, as if to the OAPs in the dress
circle seats on Thursday matinees, and they nodded; and
they looked so unhappy about it, as if the only thing they
really wanted was to tear chunks out of me, and the woman

in particular gazed at me so longingly, and her mouth drooled. Anyway, they kept on flapping their arms like that for a while, it was quite clear they weren't going to leave without me. "Hang on," I said, "I'll get my coat."

There was a sea of zombies on the streets below, and when I reached ground level I was quite sure they would attack me — now, en masse, I could hear their keening as a constant thing, their teeth were chattering with the need for food, and their lips smacked thick and wet. But as I walked they fanned away from me, and I began to feel like a prophet, like the waves were parting for Moses — or a bit like a pariah, actually, it was like when all the actors avoided me at the party after that particularly poor press night.

They took me to their leader. There was nothing special about the leader, nothing about him that suggested charisma or statesmanship. He dared to come quite close to me, and I could see that it was a real effort, he so obviously wanted to give in to his primal instincts and chow down.

"You write us play," he said.

I had no idea that zombies could talk. It came out slow, as if language was something he had to remember, as if all that was very far away.

Bearing this in mind, it seemed cruel that I said, "I beg your pardon?", and forced him through the effort of saying it again. A look of very human irritation passed over his face as he did so.

"Of course," I said. Because you should never say no to a commission. "What sort of play? I have lots of plays."

"Celebrate. Victory."

Well, I could see why the zombies might want that. They'd done so well, and now they wanted to kick back and relax and enjoy themselves with a show. I asked about cast size, and box-office sales, and how long an interval he wanted, and he just sort of glared at me as if these were matters of great irrelevance.

"Friday," he said.

"You want me to deliver a draft this week?" Because that wasn't my method at all. I liked to workshop scenes with the cast first, see if anything helpful came out of improv.

"Performance. Friday," he said. And that was that. I should have realised. Zombies are all about hunger, the need for immediate satisfaction. Why would it be different whether they wanted fresh brains or a three act light comedy?

I was allowed to choose the venue. I had always wanted a play at the National Theatre. They had rejected my manuscripts too many times. Amazingly, most of it was still standing, no doubt due to its bunker-like construction. I said I'd need paper, and I was promised it. I said I'd need more food. I was given all the baked bean tins I could carry.

"You'll get your play," I said. "But what do I get in return?"

He didn't say I'd get my life. I was glad of that, because I knew it wouldn't be true. He didn't insult me with a lie. He said, "Your father."

I went home right away, and set to work.

- - - - - - - - - -

I am an experienced dramatist. Indeed, I am probably the
most experienced dramatist working in Britain today. And
so I can tell you that one of the greatest traps you can
fall into when writing a new script is to anticipate your
audience too much. Who are these people, "the audience"?
You don't know them. You don't know their particular
concerns, their likes or dislikes. They arrive at the
theatre to see your play from a thousand different lives,
they're as disparate a group as can be. And your job as
writer is not to find some unifying factor amongst them
and play upon that — rather, your job is to celebrate their
diversity and channel it for your own ends. They should
come to the show a random ragbag, and leave bonded by the
clarity of your vision, your single vision, your vision as
author and artist.

But in the case of zombies. Well. It's different. They all
seem to have one specific thing on their minds from the
outset. And I think it's perfectly possible to second
guess that and write for them directly.

And that's where I first went wrong. I looked at my zombie
producers, and decided that they wouldn't understand the
innovations of modern drama technique, they wouldn't
appreciate what I had learned from new wave productions
in Eastern Europe, or the little moues I liked to make
towards the nouveau avant garde. I looked at my zombies,
and I patronised them. I admit that now.

I decided upon a plot. I decided upon a love story.
Everyone loved love stories. Everyone could get that.

Two star-crossed lovers. One boy, one girl (no need to
challenge sexual orthodoxy). Brought up on different sides
of the tracks. He's a zombie, she's a living human being.
Both families disapprove. Oh, it's Romeo and Juliet. It's
West Side Story. It's intimate, but also epic. It's perfect.

It took me hours to come up with names for them. Any
writer worth their salt will tell you that you can't rush

into these things, names are important. At last I fixed on
Sally and Steve. Sally and Steve sounded good. And then I
decided I'd written enough for one day — if there weren't
any words actually on paper yet, I was sure they would
flow tomorrow. And I went to bed.

I couldn't sleep. I made the mistake of thinking of my
father.

Because suddenly the audience wouldn't be anonymous at
all. There would be one man there I knew I had to impress.
Assessing my words in that cool emotionless way, all
brown and tweed. What would he think of Steve? Was the
name too populist? Would he think its combination with
Sally too alliterative, not alliterative enough?

I had realised long ago that my parents must be dead. It
wasn't that we hadn't spoken since the outbreak of the
virus. The truth was, we hadn't spoken for years — and I
realise now that was my fault, it had all been my fault.
Every Christmas, every birthday, I had thought of giving
them a phone call, to see how they were, to see whether I
could maybe apologise and put things back the way they
should have been. And when the news of the zombies came
out, and it was clear so quickly that there was no hope, no
way of beating them back, our civilisation was being swept
aside and the reign of mankind was over and a new order
of walking dead had begun, I thought, this is it, this is
my last chance. I must make peace with my mother and
father, and I must do it now, before it's all too late —
because what do old feuds matter, we're family, we're
family, there is more that connects us than keeps us
apart. It has always been that way, and I've been too proud
and too stupid to admit it — call them now — I must call
them now, and we can say our goodbyes. I knew my father
would never run from the zombies. He wouldn't hide away,
as I had, like a rat. He had too much dignity. And Mother
— my mother wouldn't fight a zombie, she wouldn't fight
anyone, if a zombie came to the door she'd invite it in and
offer it cake. Both of them would be amongst the first to

fall, as the zombies advanced they would stand their
ground and face their fates with equanimity. As the crisis
spread, as reports filtered in that entire swathes of
Britain were being wiped out, I knew that every moment I
hesitated to find my parents would cost me dear.

And I hesitated. I admit it.

The play I offered my father would have to be worthy of
him, and make up for the silence of the last eight or nine
years. I needed his forgiveness. No, I needed his pride. I
needed this play to be a masterpiece, something bold and
true, and I couldn't worry about what any other zombies in
the audience might make of it.

Steve and Sally and their little romantic entanglements
seemed so trivial to me now.

I got up from bed, and went to the window.

Outside I saw the zombies thronging the streets.
Indefatigable in their search for food. Unsleeping,
tireless, pushing on as one single body of men, an army, a
beautiful army — and I thought, that's it, there's the
unity I've always tried to inspire in my audiences, there's
your community theatre. It's there beneath my feet. These
are people who aren't held back by ego or neuroses or
father issues — these are people better than I am, more
determined, focused. These are the victors. How dare I
patronise them, how dare I even think of that.

And if they could work all through the night, then so
could I.

I sat down and wrote the first act. It was the best
writing I had ever done. It poured out of me, my hopes, my
love for a better world, my new belief in walking dead
superiority. I took a break then, a single half-hour
break, and cooked myself some baked beans. Then I wrote
act two. Act two was even better still. Act two was

soaring and majestic, it was a triumph. Sally and Steve
conquered all in the name of love, and their fathers at
last accepted their love, they embraced it. Living and
living-dead came together as one, forever more, accepting
and constant.

Exhausted, I collapsed upon my bed. And I could still hear
outside the march of the zombies, their feet slouching in
an unending rhythm that sent me soon to sleep.

- - - - - - - - - -

When I woke up, Sir Andrew Lloyd Webber was leering over me.

And it still looked like Sir Andrew Lloyd Webber. There
was a pallor to the skin, and the eyes were whitened a
little, and not quite looking in the same direction maybe.
But he looked reasonably fresh for all that. Maybe he'd
only recently been turned. Or maybe, even in death, he'd
got the cash to keep his corpse nicely manicured. There
was an expensive sheen to his rotting flesh, and the bits
of skin that were drooping off his face did so with a
monied languor.

I'd never liked Sir Andrew Lloyd Webber. His populist
approach to theatre was against everything I'd held dear.
Not that I'd ever seen a production of his, mind. "It's an
honour to meet you," I babbled.

Sir Andrew held up one withered hand to shut me up. "I've
come for the script," he said. So I gave it to him.

He began to read it. Slowly at first, but then with ever
increasing and disdainful speed. "Where's the music?" he said.

"There isn't any."

"No music! But I have a cast ready. I have an orchestra. I
have my dancers. What will they do without music?"

I told him that the story of Steve and Sally wasn't a
musical, it was a vibrant and soulful exploration of
themes of identity and social . . .

"Yes, yes," he said. "Like Phantom of the Opera. But it has
to have music. There has to be a melody to the dialogue.
With melody you can find emotion, no matter the banality
of the storyline itself."

I refused to accept my story was banal. Sir Andrew raised
one dead eyebrow at that, most ironically, and a part of
his forehead snapped off.

He made me read my dialogue aloud. It sounded clumsy and awkward. I told him it was the clumsiness and awkwardness of real living people. He told me that no one wanted that — they didn't want truth, they wanted something that was better than truth.

He told me that there were precious few real living people out there anyway.

"We must do rewrites," he said.

So we sat down, the two of us. He showed me how to soften the dialogue, how to make sure that Steve and Sally no longer hid what they were feeling but spoke it out good and loud and clear. It wasn't subtle, but, by God, you knew what was going on. Once in a while I made a rhyme, and Lloyd Webber seemed to smile approvingly. I wrote the lyrics, he wrote the music, lots of it — all quite catchy, but none of it exactly memorable. We worked through the day. I was fuelled by my baked beans, he by a packed lunch of raw kidney and lung.

It was long dark when Sir Andrew Lloyd Webber said, "At last." And it was done, and I had written a new script, and it was covered with staves and treble clefs. "We must get this to the theatre at once so rehearsals can begin!"

We went to the National Theatre in his limousine. Even undead, Sir Andrew still employed a chauffeur.

When we entered the rehearsal room, the zombie cast shuffled to some sort of attention. Some were dressed as cats, some as steam trains, a handful of them hippy Biblical characters. They gathered around for a read-through. Most of the actors couldn't speak at all, and those that could delivered my lines in a slurred monotone. Then Sir Andrew got them all up on their feet, and they improvised a dance, and quite a few of them fell over.

Sir Andrew said, "I know a hit when I see one!" And then
said that this was in no way a hit. "It's a disaster! The
show opens on Friday, and the singers can't sing, the
actors can't act, the dancers can't stand up!" A couple of
his cast had collapsed and had never got up again — their
fellow thespians devoured them.

Privately Sir Andrew said to me, "I've seen a lot worse.
You should have been here for the first few weeks of
Cats!" And he smiled, and offered me his hand. I had never
touched a zombie before, and I was afraid that the merest
contact would turn me into some diseased brain-munching
fiend. But it didn't, and though his skin was leathery, it
was warm and surprisingly soft. "It's a pleasure working
with you," he said.

- - - - - - - - - -

And in the morning there were three more zombies standing over my bed.

"We've come for your script," said one, in an Irish brogue. I explained my script was finished, and had been approved, and was now in the swing of rehearsals. "We'll be the judge of that," said another, and his accent was Irish too.

The tallest of the corpses was George Bernard Shaw. Even sixty years dead he was a formidable figure: he had a beard so thick that he was not so much wearing it as it was wearing him — it was matted and mildewed, but it masked how much of Shaw's upper torso was decomposing, so was therefore clearly a good thing. He scoffed at my script. "It's all about the heart, but there's nothing for the brain." He kept breaking off from his stentorian admonishments to nibble at a brain of his own that he had brought along. An outspoken vegetarian in life, he was addicted to brain in all its forms now. "I don't care how your characters feel about being dead," he said. "I want to hear them reason it through in intellectual discourse!"

"Poppycock," said Oscar Wilde. Of the three zombies his body was in the worst state. Everything he said was delivered with ironic detachment, no doubt accentuated by the fact most of his face had ironically detached, and his mouth was fixed in a mocking grin. "What your script needs is to be lighter, more trivial. 'We should treat all the trivial things of life seriously, and all the serious things of life with serious and studied triviality'."

"What's that even supposed to mean, you dilettante?" snapped Shaw.

"You great big bloody bore," grinned back Wilde.

Shaw bit a chunk out of Wilde's leg. Wilde clawed at Shaw's face with long nails and produced blood and white gunk.

I had to separate them. It was agreed that Shaw would
stay in the kitchen and rewrite act one. Wilde, meanwhile,
would be sequestered in the bedroom and inject some
frivolity into act two. Shaw produced long aching speeches
of social conscience. Wilde put in jokes about handbags.

For all this time the third zombie hadn't said a word. I
thought maybe he couldn't speak at all, that in death his
tongue had atrophied. But when at last he talked, his
voice was clear and authoritative. I asked him who he was.
He took a long pause, and thought about the question, and
said, "Harold Pinter."

"And what does your work stand for, Harold Pinter?"

And he took an even longer pause, and thought about the
question harder still, and said, "Mind your own fucking
business."

And when Shaw and Wilde had delivered their rewrites,
Pinter looked the script over, crossed out anything which
looked like an explanation, and stuck a few long pauses
in.

I took the new script over to Sir Andrew in rehearsal.
"Thanks," he said. He'd got most of the cast on
rollerskates now. Some of them were doing acrobatics, and
some of these acrobats were even able to keep all their
limbs intact. "Got to have spectacle," he said to me, "and
by God, this is going to be spectacular."

- - - - - - - - - -

The last time I saw my parents was the opening night of my first play. I lie, it wasn't my first play, it was my eleventh. I mean it was my first play anyone had wanted to produce. I'd been sending scripts out all over the country, to big power houses like the RSC and the National, to the repertory theatres, to the touring companies. This new play was received most enthusiastically by a small troupe I'd never seen but had heard good things about. It'd be put on in a fringe theatre in London, right above a pub, and there wouldn't be any money — the cast were getting travel expenses only, and I was asked if I could contribute something towards that. It was one of the well-respected venues, though They didn't put on any old rubbish.

By this stage my father had long lost his job at The Sunday Times. He was still writing reviews, but doing them on spec. He'd buy a seat for any play that took his fancy, and write a crit, and send it around on the hope that someone might find his disapproval worth publishing. Nine times out of ten they didn't. I felt sorry for my father, but I was pleased in a way too — I thought this meant we were both in the same boat, I thought this would bring us closer together. It didn't, somehow.

We had an awful dress rehearsal. Some of the actors kept forgetting their lines, and then laughing because they'd forgotten their lines, and this made the other actors laugh too, even the ones who hadn't forgotten their lines. The pace was sluggish. The lighting cues were all mistimed, the one sound cue I'd wanted didn't happen at all. We had scant hours before we let the audience in for the first performance, and I felt sick. The director bought me a pint and told me that a bad dress rehearsal always meant a good opening night. I couldn't quite see why that should work. But then the girl from the box-office found us, and she said there was a sudden rush on ticket sales — it was unbelievable, she'd never seen anything like it! There was a sudden new buzz in the air, and I went to the auditorium, and almost all the seats were filled, it was a miracle! Forty people, there must have been at least forty people in there. And in there, too, I saw my father and mother. My mother wearing her best clothes, frills and bows, as if she were at a wedding, and looking so proud. My father in his theatre critic garb.

I couldn't sit with them. I couldn't sit at all, in fact — adrenaline kept me out of my seat, I spent the entire evening pacing up and down in the wings! And I think it was adrenaline that got us all through. The performances that had been so flabby at the dress now seemed sharp and precise — the actors hit their lines exactly. There was laughter, too, but at all the bits the audience were supposed to be laughing at. And the director gave me the thumbs up, and I thought — this is good, I'm not pretending this is great theatre, but it's good, everyone out there is enjoying themselves and no one has walked out or heckled or died. This is the beginning of something, this is what I want to do for the rest of my life. And at the curtain call the audience applauded — and it's hard to get a fringe audience applauding for very long, by God, it's cold and lonely out there, but the cast had to take bows twice! "Author! Author!" called the director, and "Author!" came from a few members of the audience too. "Go on, then," said the director, and laughed, and he pushed me out on stage. And the lights felt so warm on my face, and the audience were all in shadow but I could see on the front row that everybody seemed smiling and sincere, and I enjoyed the moment as the clapping built at my arrival, and I took a bow too.

I bought my parents a drink, and thanked them for coming.

"Oh, darling, it was so good," said Mother. "Though I'm not sure I understood all of it."

"Yeah, it's not really meant to be understood. What did you think, Dad?"

And my father stared down at me. Then, slowly, he took his
notebook from his tweed jacket pocket, cleared his throat,
and began to read.

"The greatest pleasure afforded any theatre critic is to
be at the debut of a new writer of talent," he said.

I blushed, I think, and thanked him.

"But not every maiden voyage can be destined for success.
And, sadly, Richard Hardy Jr. is to theatrical flair what
J. Bruce Ismay was to the Titanic."

I appreciate now what he was saying, of course. And, too,
that by refusing to flatter me, by treating me not as his
son but as any other professional playwright, my father
was paying me the very greatest of compliments. And
looking back I know it hadn't been a good play, and it
hadn't been a good evening, and no one really had enjoyed
themselves after all, and my father had been spot on. But
I'm afraid I didn't see it that way at the time. And I'm
rather afraid I punched him.

- - - - - - - - - -

I wish I had had the door to my flat fixed, but I dare say
the zombies would only have broken it down again. The
next morning I had Richard Brinsley Sheridan turn up,
full of advice about how to turn my play into a copy of
his eighteenth-century smash hit, The Rivals. Later in the
afternoon a whole gaggle of Restoration comedians turned
up — I thought Sir John Vanbrugh was there, and maybe
George Etheredge, and I only know because I looked them up
afterwards in an encyclopaedia — but they didn't have
faces left at all, and they had no conversation either.
They put into my script lots of cross-dressing, and Steve
was left spending most of act one wearing a large floppy
hat.

When on the Friday I woke to find yet another corpse in
the bedroom with me, I wasn't horrified, just annoyed.
"That's enough," I said. "No more rewrites. For God's sake,
the play opens this evening!" And I turned on the light.
I didn't think it was even a man at first. This was the
remains of an animal, a bottled spider — there was a
skull balanced on top of a skeletal frame, but most of the
bones supporting it had long since decayed, and so the
skull wobbled precariously as the zombie moved towards
me. I kept thinking it would soon snap and fall off. The
merest sliver of a heart quivered away behind the ribs,
like a startled budgie in a cage.

"Are you Shakespeare?" I said. Because, impossibly, for
all that the skin had long since melted away, the creature
was wearing an Elizabethan ruff.

"Ack," said Shakespeare. He didn't say it, in fact — the
bottom half of his face was missing. But he found that
noise inside him, somewhere, somehow, and let it out.

"Did you want to see my script?" I asked him. And I
handed him the latest draft, covered as it was with the
handwriting of a dozen different dead playwrights. He
looked it over for a few moments, his one remaining
eyeball rolling over the pages. And then he threw up over

it. I don't know where the effluence came from, but it
didn't matter, it was dark green and it stank, and it was
now all over act one, scene two.

He let back his head and gave an ack of frustration.

"It's all right," I said. "It's okay." I took the script back,
and wiped the pages clean. "I bet you want me to rewrite
it all in iambic pentameter, don't you? And put in the odd
sword fight. Of course you do. Well, that's fine. You can
watch me if you like. You can watch."

And I scribbled away for a few minutes. Shakespeare's eye
never settled on me. Once in a while he squawked another
ack. They sounded increasingly plaintive.

"Are you hungry?" I said. "Of course you're hungry. I'm
sorry. I'm sorry. I've nothing to feed you." He could have
had me, he could have taken me, I would have let him too.
But how he was going to chew, this little stunted genius,
there wasn't enough of a mouth left to bite, there wasn't a
throat with which he could swallow.

And he took my hand. William Shakespeare took my hand.

The eyes rolled one last time, the little bird in the
ribcage stopped moving and was still.

I held William Shakespeare close. "I'm sorry," I said, I
put my arms tight around my poor broken bard, and I don't
know why, I cried.

- - - - - - - - -

"Where have you been? We have a crisis!" And Sir Andrew
Lloyd Webber's face looked as hungry as I have ever seen
it. There was spittle at his mouth when he spoke, and his
eyes were bright and feral. And I backed away, I couldn't
help it, I thought he was about to go for my throat — and
then I realised this was not his hunger for flesh, but a
hunger for the thrill of theatre.

"What sort of crisis?" I asked, and I admit, I was weary,
there was not an ounce of adrenaline in my body. I had
spent the afternoon burying Shakespeare's body in the
garden, and if I had had my way I would have skipped this
opening night altogether and gone straight to bed. Would
have done so, too, had I not been sure that the zombies
would have dragged me to the show regardless.

"Most of the actors can't talk," said Lloyd Webber. "I
pushed them too far in dress rehearsal, most of their
mouths broke."

"And?" I said, but I could already see what was coming.
And Lloyd Webber said I would have to be the one to speak
the lines for them. I would stand in the wings, and the
actors would lip-synch. Those of them, at least, that had
lips to synch.

Sir Andrew busied himself with the orchestra, threw into
the pit from buckets assorted chunks of flesh and organs
to keep the musicians happy during the show. I peered out
at the audience as they entered the auditorium. It was a
huge space, two thousand seats, and at least four thousand
zombies sitting in them, crawling over each other's laps,
wedging themselves into every spare crevice — it was like
looking out at a wall of dead meat.

I had never played to such a large audience before. The
most had been a hundred, tops. And now I wondered what
was wrong, why this felt different, why for all those
bodies crowding every last inch of the stalls and the
dress circle this suddenly struck me as smaller and more

inconsequential. And I realised it was because they were
silent. There was not the slightest murmur of
anticipation. Not the scrunch of a single Maltesers bag.

I could see no sign of my father anywhere.

The lights went down. The actor playing Steve stepped out
on to the stage. He looked the part, the zombies in the
wardrobe department had clearly thrown themselves into
the costume store with something like enthusiasm. But
this close up I could see that Steve had barely got a jaw
left at all, presumably I'd just given him too many lines
to say and the effort had caused his entire chin to cave
in. I would have to be his voice. I would be all the voices
of the dead.

Steve spoke of his passion for Sally. His love of being a
zombie. I put in more energy to his twin declarations of
joy than he ever could have. He did a little zombie dance,
and sang a little zombie song, and made some jokes about
handbags.

There was not a sound from the audience. They were just
concentrating, that's what I told myself. But I knew that
was rubbish. Hushed quiet in a theatre is always a good
thing. Stone silence never is.

But the silence gave me a new confidence. A confidence I
hadn't felt in ages. Not since the apocalypse, for sure.
Not since my first play had opened, and I'd hit my father,
and the police had been called.

I had the confidence of knowing that, in that silence,
there was no one listening, and no one cared.

I began to edit the script. I could clear away all the
rewrites I hadn't approved of. No more Pinteresque pauses,
no more Sheridan quips, no more songs. I began to reinstate
my original lines. The play was the better for it. Why
couldn't the dead just stop interfering? Why couldn't the

dead accept that their time was done, and the living would
be so much better off without them? They'd made their
mistakes already. Now let us make ours.

And I realised that I was beginning to say this sort of
stuff out loud. And no one could stop me. I took my script,
my stupid compromised script, and threw it aside. I
wouldn't need anything from those pages any more. I felt
inspiration.

What did I talk about? I don't know. I talked about my
father. I remember that. I talked about how much I missed
my father. I talked about how much I loved him, in spite
of all, no matter how much I really deeply couldn't stand
the miserable old bastard.

And the actors on stage just sort of stopped, really, they
didn't even bother to mouth this stuff. And the orchestra
got bored, and began gnawing at their oboes and clarinets,
then began gnawing at each other. And Sir Andrew Lloyd
Webber just stared out into the wings at me with a look of
utter hurt, as if I'd betrayed him, as if I'd stabbed him in
the back. But, Andrew, if I stabbed you in the back, you
wouldn't feel a thing, you walking sack of death. I think
I may have said this out loud too. I think I'm pretty sure
I did.

I talked about the brave new world I had dreamed of for
them, a bold civilisation of the living-dead just waiting
to happen. And how they'd never achieve it. Because they
were just walking sacks of death, and if they had any
capacity for sense or feeling they wouldn't be sitting so
placidly in their seats watching my play, no, they'd be
standing up and jeering and throwing things on to the
stage and tearing up the seats, because my play was
really a piece of shit. It was shit. This was shit. They
didn't deserve a brave new world. Not if they meekly
accepted such mediocre entertainment.

There was a unity in the theatre that night. And I had always wanted to inspire a unity. But this wasn't a unity I understood, and I wanted no part of it.

And still they wouldn't boo, still they wouldn't shout at me to shut up or get off or to bring the singers back on so they could listen to more plinky-plonky tunes from Sir Andrew Lloyd Webber's stale back catalogue. And so I stepped out on to the stage. I stepped out, knowing their zombie celebrations were in tatters, that I was walking to my death. That at the sight of me thousands of hungry mouths would tear me apart.

I went out for my curtain call.

And stood there. The zombie actors really didn't know what to do with me there. They hadn't rehearsed this. They looked confused. They shuffled to one side, a bit embarrassed.

I stared out at the audience. I couldn't see them for the bright lighting. They were still so silent, deathly silent of course, but I could feel those eyes all staring back. "Come on!" I cried out. I tried to strike as defiant a pose as possible. I stuck out my arms, as if I'd just given them a showstopper musical number. I imagine I looked pretty silly.

My eyes began to adjust, and at last I could see them, all the dead. And all they'd wanted was a good night out.

They began to applaud.

Wild, proper applause. I had never heard anything like it. If they didn't have hands to clap with, they used other parts of their bodies. And once their own bodies were tired, once their rotting flesh had taken all the slapping it could take, they turned to their neighbours in the seats beside them, they began beating upon them, beating out their appreciation, eagerly, desperately, they weren't

going to stop, they couldn't stop — and the sharp staccato
of the applause began to sound wetter somehow, as they
beat past the skin and at the vital organs underneath, the
clapping began to splash.

And I enjoyed it, in spite of myself — this applause, for
me — nothing polite about it this time, nothing middle-
class and safe and slightly equivocal (because they hadn't
liked the set, or the jokes, or the twist in the second act,
because the seats had been too hard, because the drinks in
the interval had cost too much, because the play had been
too long or hadn't been long enough, because they didn't
frankly like theatre in the first fucking place and had
been dragged there by their wives) — this was the sound of
madness, the sound of frenzied animals. I couldn't help it,
I even took a bow. But then. But then, somehow. Somehow the
clapping just never stopped, and it became more ordered,
and then they were clapping in unison, all of them, every
last one of them, never missing a beat. And not a face was
smiling. They all wore the same expressions, and not one
had anything that resembled a smile.

"Is my father here?" I shouted out. "Where's my father?"

At first I thought nothing was happening, that after all
my rewrite hell the walking dead had still cheated me.
And then I saw a figure stand up. And walk towards me.
And up on to the stage. And into the lights.

And he was wearing tweed.

My father stared at me. He, alone in that amphitheatre,
wasn't clapping.

And I knew what had to happen then. That he had to
forgive me. That he had to accept me, and consume me, and
eat me down.

"I'm yours, Dad," I said. "You must be so hungry."

He continued to stare. His dead eyes narrowed in
assessment. Then he made a little noise of contempt, just a
pff! — and he turned around.

"Hey!" I said. "Hey!"

He started to walk away.

"Don't turn your back on me! Get back here. Eat me, you
shit!"

But he wasn't having any of it. He didn't want me.

That was when I leaped upon him. That's when I forced his
mouth wide open. With one hand I grabbed at his nostrils
and pulled upwards, with the other I took his chin and
yanked down — and I felt something give — and I heard a
splitting sound, a ripping, as his face was torn open. And
his mouth was so big now, and my entire head could fit
inside a mouth like that, I could put it in and he could
bite down and he could eat me whole and I would be like
him, I would be like my Daddy, it would be over. At last I
would be like them all.

And they jumped me. I was dragged off before I could force
a bite, and I was howling at them to let me go, please let
me go, please, just give me the end I deserved. But they
weren't listening — they weren't listening, their bastard
ears were dead to me. And still all about me, still, the
clapping went on.

– – – – – – – – –

They've brought me baked beans again, and some writing paper.

I told them I don't want them. And the zombies smile, because what I want has really very little to do with anything.

They said that they liked my play. It was quite good, <u>very</u> good, actually, well done. Everyone was most amused. Especially once all that silly romance stuff had stopped. So, more like that, please. They would expect another production within the week.

And they were sorry about the clapping. They'd been out of practice. They'd get that right next time.

Noël Coward and Terence Rattigan sometimes drop by. But not to offer me advice on my script. The mere idea! A playwright like me doesn't need advice, they say, not after my last show, I am world class. They just visit as fellow men of the stage, and share with me theatrical anecdotes. I hate them, I wish their dead bones would turn to dust. I tell them this sometimes, and they just grin. I ask them to eat me, and they laugh, as if I've made the very wittiest of jokes. "You should write that down," trills Noël. "You could use that!"

I'm their laureate. "But why can't you write your own bloody plays?" I say. But they don't reply to that.

"What do I get in return?" I ask. "I write you some plays, what do I get out of it?" And they don't tell me they'll kill me, because that would be a lie.

"We'll keep your father away," the leader promises. And he rolls his rotted eyes, and he shrugs his rotted shoulders, as if he hopes that'll be enough. And I suppose it is.

So I eat my baked beans, and I set to work on a new play. And, feeding and writing, I wish I had something meatier to get my teeth into.

BERNIE MAUGHMSTEIN JOKE #1322

But we shouldn't laugh now should we? I mean, "These folks have rights, too!" Zombies have rights? Oh really? And folks? They're not folks, man . . . they're meat that's gone off, man . . . a big 200 pound piece of not-so-choice rump that's been left in the trunk of your car a couple

weeks in the middle of summer. Or something you just drove over out on the highway, man. Roadkill - you know what I'm saying? And we shouldn't laugh at that concept, man? Roadkill has rights? Hey, I think the fuck not. Roadkill don't got no rights, man. You know what I'm saying?

BERNIE MAUGHMSTEIN

Dearest Laura,

Where are you tonight, I wonder; are you with your friends? Are you safe? Are you happy?

This was always your favourite day of the year, more than Christmas itself because, as you told me solemnly (I think you were six), presents were even better before they were unwrapped, when you could imagine all the things they might be – "even an octopus!" You've always taken so much pleasure in your imagination, I was surprised you didn't turn out to be a writer like me.

In my mind you are celebrating with your dearest friends in a cosy country pub with a fire crackling in the open hearth, a strand of coloured lights twinkling across the bar, the air redolent with delicious scents, the loud buzz of conversation and occasional roar of raucous laughter drowning out Susan Boyle singing traditional Christmas carols from the speakers.

It's a pathetic fantasy, I know, a scene from the dead past, but somehow my mind flinches away from accepting the sheer scale of what has happened. Even if London was almost totally destroyed, Glasgow and Edinburgh now desolate, depopulated wastelands, I cling to the belief that somewhere normal human life must continue, and that you are as safe in your cosy (metaphorical) island, as I have been on this real one.

Most of the Hebridean islands managed to survive quite well; at least, for a while.

Not Skye, of course – that was the first to fall, as you might imagine. Everyone who expressed their deep opposition to the bridge may now feel righteously justified . . . if any of them are still alive to feel anything at all. But I spoke to folks on Lewis a week ago, and to Jonty and Catriona on Colonsay only two days ago, and all was well . . . we islanders have managed to keep in touch, scattered as we are — who needs phones or the Internet when you've got short-wave radio?

For months I prayed you would think of that; I realise short-wave radios probably aren't so common on the mainland, but surely, if you made an effort—?

Sorry, sorry, sorry! I am not trying to guilt-trip you, darling! It's just, I am so desperate to hear your voice again. I'm sure you're fine, but I want to hear you tell me so.

As for me, well, life goes on, much as you remember it. Being so remote, cut off from all the changing fads and fancies of the day, which was so frustrating to you as a teenager, is what kept us from harm. Anyway, you will have no trouble imagining me baking bread and pies, tending the garden (not so much this time of year, of course), going out for walks with the dog, reading by the fire, and, yes, still writing.

Why bother? I'm sure most people would wonder why I'd write another book when there are no publishers, no booksellers, and no way even to reach whatever potential readers may still survive out there. But the simple truth is: I like making things up. Few things in life have ever given me the satisfaction of catching hold of a slippery little idea — a stray thought, an image from a dream, something overheard or misunderstood — and turning it into a story.

I've just finished a new one — I'd call it a YA fantasy if there were still marketing departments, booksellers, librarians or reviewers who cared — and for once, I don't have to worry about where to send it, or if it is too long or too short, too bleak, not bleak enough, too old-fashioned, too adult, too childish for my intended audience . . . because I don't have an audience. I only wish you could read it, dearest Laura. I suppose if I wrote it for anyone but myself, I wrote it for you.

It would be your Christmas present, if I knew where to send it

After the summer had passed without another word from you, your father said we had to accept that the worst had happened. But I knew you weren't dead; I know this the same way I know my own heart is still beating. Tommy could not believe it, such a resolute realist, but the spiritual connection between us is so profound, I would feel it instantly if it broke. It hasn't broken.

I think you must have managed to escape from Glasgow with the friend who had a boat, but you went somewhere else instead of coming here. Maybe your radio broke. I wonder if you joined the community on Iona? I can imagine you there. Everyone talks about that lovely, ancient, holy place; it's said that anyone who lands there will be safe; that the very ground has such power it can even heal the Infected, and as soon as one of them touches the soil, they become normal corpses, naturally dead; or even that they are restored to perfect health, normal life, their souls revived—

But, no, I don't believe that; I've written too many fantasies to believe them myself.

I don't think ancient religion will save us, nor modern science. I no longer believe that scientists somewhere must be working on a cure, and eventually everything will return to normal. I wish I could.

"I won't lie to you," said Mrs. Lully. "The operation *may* be painful." Like most of the teachers at the School of Perfect Light, she prided herself on straight speaking. "But you're a brave lad, and surely a little pain is a price worth paying for perfect freedom in the light forever?"

"It might be," said Giles, cautiously, when it became clear she expected an answer. "It depends on what you mean by perfect freedom."

He tried to sound respectful, but her expression hardened.

"If you paid attention in class, young man, you would know exactly what I mean. Freedom from fear! Freedom from evil! Freedom from the encroaching Shadows that plague us. There can be no safety for anyone until every shadow has been eliminated."

Giles knew he ought to pretend he agreed, but he just couldn't.

"But – my shadow is just a shadow," he protested. "It's not *evil*."

She looked shocked. "After the Plague – after everything that's happened, you tell me to my face that shadows aren't evil? The only way we can fight this thing is to destroy every shadow, starting with our own. Only then will we be safe."

Giles wondered if she really believed that. Shadows, as he had learned when much younger, were areas where light could not reach, being blocked by an object. Shadows were the absence of light, not *things* that could be cut off, like hair. Although people referred to "the Shadow Plague" as often as they called it "the Plague of Darkness", the menace was almost certainly, everyone agreed, some sort of alien invasion.

But he had promised Tansy not to argue, so he stared down at his feet and mumbled, "I'm sorry, Mrs. Lully. Of course, you're right. It's just scary, that's all."

She patted him on the head, like he was a dog. "That's all right, dear. I know the truth can be hard to accept. But we'll remove that nasty old shadow of yours tomorrow, and then you'll be free."

"Free to leave here?"

"Of course, if that's what you want."

Tommy always expected something like this to happen — not exactly this, but economic collapse, war, the rise of an oppressive government — whatever happened, he figured we'd be safer with our own small-holding on an island than in an urban jungle. And he was absolutely right.

We were very cut off here, with very little idea what was happening elsewhere, but that was a good thing. No contact meant no infection. Newcomers arrived with bits of news, people with boats who remembered our location from summer sailing holidays in the past — our population more than doubled. Luckily there was no problem with being "swamped by refugees", and we were able to accept everyone who came. Most of them had familiar faces and brought goods, information and skills to contribute. There was a little silliness at first about quarantine for new arrivals — we hadn't realised that "rapid onset" in this situation often meant minutes, not days.

I suppose I ought to be ashamed to admit it, but those early months were rather wonderful. Apart from my worries about you, they were the best days of my life. Everyone pulled together — we were a real community, even more so than during those years of fund-raising to establish the Island Trust — and there were so many things to plan, so much to do, and it was important — genuinely a matter of life or death. Self-sufficiency was no longer a "life-style choice". Tommy was in his element, as you may imagine! He knew how to convert the wind-farm, now that there was no longer a national grid, so that it would provide all our electricity. We could freeze surplus food, cook, keep our houses warm, watch DVDs — I could still work on my computer! — and never worry about running out of power. The liquid fuel for the boats and tractors would have to be rationed while Tommy and Dr Munro figured out how to convert the engines to run on something other than diesel or petrol, something we could produce here on the island — we were confident it could be done. Really, change is not so difficult, not when everyone is committed to it; what a pity it took a holocaust to prove that point!

Right here on our little island, we changed society. People with houses shared with those who needed shelter, and as far as work and supplies were concerned it was "from each according to ability, to each according to need". No one would have to suffer because of age or illness or bad planning in the past — nor would a few be allowed to profit at the expense of others. Individually owned boats became the island fishing fleet. No one was rich or poor — we were all equal. And everyone agreed to this radical social arrangement! Would you believe it — not even your old b te noir "Tory Ted", not even Marjorie Hunt, raised a peep of objection. It turns out that we're all communists under the skin ... or more accurately, recognising that "the end was nigh" we chose to live like the early Christians.

Like the cloistered religious communities of the dark ages, we would keep civilised values and culture alive until our children's children might eventually reclaim the Earth.

As time went by, we had to consider the possibility that the next boat that arrived would carry armed, dangerous raiders, like Vikings of old, rather than polite, middle-class families with their own yachts. So we had to plan how to protect ourselves.

So — we worked out strategies, had a volunteer militia, arranged a system of watches. (I use the royal "we" — as you know, I am useless with weapons and terrified of violence.) From the dun behind our house — I'm sure you remember — all the approaches to the island can be seen, and as there are only two safe places to land a boat, as long as we stayed vigilant we would not be taken by surprise.

Peter Lee was on guard duty the morning of September 30th, and saw a large vessel in the distance, which he recognised as a CalMac ferry. His guess that it was the MV Lord of the Isles turned out to be right. You probably remember the size of it from our trips to Islay for the Mod when you were at school — huge; big enough to hold at least 50 vehicles on the car-deck, and up to 500 passengers inside; no way it could dock safely here!

We hadn't heard anything from Islay for over a week, and feared the worst. Our attempts to hail the ship — Ted was in place at Comms Central (the hotel bar) asking for identification — but there was no response. Someone had to be on the ship, but was it a few desperate survivors with a malfunctioning radio, or a party of raiders intent on conquest? We had to assume the worst. Tommy went off with the Major to man the battle station.

"Maybe it's a ghost ship," said one of the children as Ted's questions were met by silence. Lucy Grieg said, "There's an idea. My son Ben told me that even though the captain is technically in charge, he doesn't have much to do nowadays, as the course is pre-set and the whole thing is automatic. Maybe there's no one on the ship at all, and this is entirely accidental..."

Peter Lee, who knew considerably more than she did, having worked as a motorman on the Islay run for several years, told her it could not be an accident. The course must have been set by someone, who must be monitoring it now. The ferry courses were set and controlled automatically, and while corrections could be made, to avoid unexpected obstacles, coming full-tilt at an island not equipped with a landing dock was hardly a "correction" and could not have been done automatically. If the automatic system had been disabled, at least two members of crew would be needed to steer it manually. If that was happening, they had chosen not to respond, so, clearly, they were up to no good.

Lucy seemed to think that her son (who had only worked a couple of summers in some lowly capacity on ro-ro ferries) was a font of all knowledge, and refused to let Peter have the last word:

"My Ben says..."

She got no farther than that before the radio crackled and a man's voice said: "Mum." Then again: "Mum? Is that my Mum? Lucy Grieg?"

I saw the colour of Lucy's face go from pinkie-brown to greenie-white before she staggered closer to the radio, pushing old Ted aside, and cried, "Ben? Ben, is that you?"

Like most of us with family off-island, Lucy had no idea what had become of her son — he'd been in Edinburgh doing post-grad studies when disaster struck.

The voice from the radio said, "Yes. This is Ben. I'm coming home now, Mum. I'm coming back for you."

He said nothing more. He did not respond to Ted's questions, nor to Lucy as she begged him, her voice wobbling with tearful emotion. "Ben, please, Ben, we have to know … who else is on board? How many people? Ben, please, you must answer; they've got weapons, and will use them! Tell them to hold fire! I can't stop them!"

Was Ben a survivor? The transformation was so rapid, if he had been infected before embarking, he would not have lasted long enough to speak to us. But if there were Infected on board, and he'd only just been attacked, the ability to recognise his mother's voice might have been the last gasp of his humanity before the virus extinguished his consciousness entirely. Lord of the Isles might have set out as a boat of refugees looking for safety, but over the course of the past two or three hours it had become a plague ship, a zombie-carrier we could not allow to land.

I thought of our last conversation with the people on Jura. They told us about a man who'd disappeared while sailing the year before, presumed drowned after his ketch was found drifting and empty. His body had never been found, until it turned up, more than half-rotted away, as you might expect after being immersed in the sea for some fourteen months, but also, most unexpectedly, re-animated, and ravenous.

He had infected two people, and they in turn each infected one or two more, and they — well, according to the new Laird (so John McNab styled himself, although in his previous existence he'd owned nothing grander than a B&B in Craighouse), the island's population was down to 67 living souls. He insisted the situation was "under control" but would not, or could not, explain how the threat had been contained.

CalMac didn't serve Jura, but Islay was separated from Jura by less than a mile of sea.

When we had thought of protecting ourselves from invasion, we had thought of human beings, against whom trickery and psychology, appeals to reason or emotion might work as well as physical weapons. We had thought ourselves safely out of reach of the Infected, imagining the ocean like a gigantic, unbridgeable moat. We certainly hadn't imagined a ship full of the living dead.

The light outside, after so long underground, was dazzling, almost unbearable, but Giles exulted in it, thrilled to see the sun and feel the wind on his face, and smell the open air, even if the tang of rotting fish and petrol fumes in the old boat weren't entirely pleasant.

The islanders welcomed them. There was no cowering underground here, and no nonsense about "perfect light" or the danger of shadows. They had been working on a plan to repel the dark invaders that utilised a new branch of physics.

While everyone else was talking excitedly with their hosts, and the younger ones began to run madly with the relief of having escaped, Giles saw Tansy still cowering at the back of the boat. No matter how he told her they were safe, she didn't seem to believe him.

"I told you we should have left her," said Daniel. He didn't back off at Giles' look, but muttered, "Sorry, mate, but it's just too late for some. I mean, *look* at her."

Taking her by the arm, making her walk with him, Giles tried to ignore his friend, but in the natural sunlight, away from the odd, diffuse, shadowless light of the school, he could see all too clearly what was wrong with his sister. She looked pale and listless, but that was not so disturbing as the fact that he could clearly see, whenever he glanced back at the ground behind them, that she had no shadow.

His own was perfectly dark, like a reflection of his body. But Tansy, for all that she felt solid to the touch, allowed the light to pass through just as if she had been a ghost.

It was true, then, although his mind flinched away from the horrible thought. There really *was* an operation that could separate the shadow from the body – the shadow *was* a thing – and if the staff at the school had been right about that, rather than playing mind-games with the students as Tansy and he had believed – then maybe they were right about other things . . .

Without access to any really useful modern weapons like missile-launchers, grenades and flame-throwers, our strategists had looked to the past for inspiration, and then built a trebuchet. Instead of hurling boulders, it would be used to launch Molotov cocktails onto the car deck. If a fire could be set there, it would quickly rage out of control. Car fuel tanks would begin to explode, and very soon the entire ship would go with it, for directly underneath the car-deck were the fuel tanks, which, as Peter had informed us, should be carrying up to 50 tons of marine gas oil. In other words, the ferry was one tremendous, moving fire-bomb just waiting for a fuse to be lit.

With any luck, the fire would end all threat. If any of the Infected survived and managed to get ashore, we'd fight them on the beaches. Able-bodied citizens were to repel any attempted invasion with shovels, spades, scythes and other implements of destruction.

Non-able-bodied citizens, or the terminally wimpy (like me), were under orders to remain barricaded in the hotel or otherwise well away from the fighting until the all-clear signal went.

Since the look-out hill was actually on our property, I had volunteered to keep watch and report whatever I saw to Tommy by walkie-talkie. (Yes, we still have that set we gave you one Christmas, and very useful it has proved.)

By the time I got to the top of the hill the ferry was near enough that I could see the car-deck quite clearly through my binoculars. I counted eighteen cars, one caravan, a couple of lorries and — the real bonus — a fuel tanker. A shame we couldn't salvage any of that useful oil for the fishing fleet, I thought, but it ought to speed up the destruction.

There were moving figures on the car deck as well, and from the way they shambled and stumbled into each other, fell over and got up again, it was clear they were no longer human. I hoped there weren't any living, uninfected people hiding out somewhere on board, because I hated to think we might be killing innocents, but there was no point in thinking about it: the ship had to be destroyed.

With agonising slowness, the ferry moved closer and closer, accompanied by the sound of warning sirens as it continued on an obviously dangerous collision course, directly for the white beach and the rocky cliffs. I wanted to run and hide, but made myself keep watching. I saw no lifeboats launched, saw no one jump overboard. They must all be Infected on board, deadly, lifeless creatures who couldn't think or plan but would destroy us if allowed to get close enough. That was how I thought of them then; that was how we all thought of the walking dead.

I watched as the first missile went whizzing out in a high arc, came down, crashed against the side of the ferry — the wrong side; the outside. I saw a line of flames run along the petrol, but it was a harmless little fire that quickly fizzled out

But the second landed perfectly, on the car deck, and began burning merrily; the next missile — in a plastic bottle that had once held six litres of Irn Bru — spilled its highly flammable contents across more of the deck, and I'd scarcely had time to sigh with satisfaction when the first car, an old Renault, burst into flames. Another missile shattered the windscreen of a Land Rover. With astonishing speed, the fire spread out of control, and petrol tanks began exploding.

The ship began to pitch and wallow; I could hear alarms going off, and guessed that the automatic sprinkler system must have activated in response to the flames. Peter had told us this would happen — and that it would be not only too little, too late, but could make things worse, as something called "the free surface water effect" made the ship unstable.

As the ship began to burn — it was oddly beautiful — I saw four or five flaming figures go over the side. Surely they hadn't jumped? Surely a zombie would not, could not, make the decision to try to escape immolation by jumping into the water? It must have been accidental, the force of the pitching ship sending them over the side, I told myself, and as I stared harder, I saw another figure, not in flames, quite distinctly, deliberately leap over the side . . . but no matter how I searched, fixing the binoculars more carefully, I could not see where — or if — it surfaced.

The ferry exploded. It was a raging fireball. Despite my distance, I felt the heat of the blast like the opening of an oven door. The crumpled boom of the blast seemed to echo for a long time before it died away. Then the Major gave the measured blasts of his horn to signal "all clear".

I felt a spasm of alarm, recalling the figures I'd seen going into the water. They wouldn't drown, they were dead already, and could continue their relentless journey towards us beneath the sea with no more difficulty — perhaps less — than they encountered above it.

I shared my concerns with Tommy via the handset, but he told me not to worry; we still had hours of daylight, and were well-armed against anything that might come staggering out of the water.

Pretty soon practically everyone, except the most elderly and feeble, was either down on the beach or on the cliffs congratulating the lads for their good work with the trebuchet. It was a nice afternoon, no rain, and quite warm. A mood of celebration bloomed and spread. Someone began building a bonfire. I could hear music and laughter, and feel the party atmosphere even from my distant perch. But although I was tempted to go join the others, the memory of that leaping figure — the non-burning one — still worried me, and so I continued to gaze out to sea, watching for a head, for movements of a swimmer even after so long.

But I saw nothing until suddenly the figure of a man emerged from the sea, rising out of the shallower water: a tall, slender man dressed in sodden jeans and shirt clinging to his body, walking so casually, steadily, he obviously felt no difference between walking in the air and walking underwater.

People fell silent, gaping at him. Then Lucy gave a glad cry and ran towards her son. Later, I was told that he said, "Hello, Mum, I told you I'd be back," and leaned down as if to kiss her. But that was no kiss he bestowed, but a large, voracious bite out of her upper arm, and she screamed like one of the damned.

Her dogs — did she have those two Rottweilers when you were here? — rushed to defend her, but of course it was too late. Although they managed to get a few bites in, Ben threw them off with casual brutal strength, breaking the spine of one

– which then lay motionless on the ground – and causing the other to yelp and squeal before it hobbled away as best it could, limping and dragging at least one damaged leg.

It was all terribly confused by then, with some people running away, others rushing – foolishly – to try to help Lucy – despite all the planning and drills, few people seemed to remember they had weapons, or how to use them. Only your father kept his head and did exactly what had to be done. He smashed in the head of the weirdly intelligent zombie Ben. Lucy, even in as much pain as she was, would have attacked Tommy if the Major hadn't stopped her. After Tommy took her head off, the Major held out his hand, displaying the ragged bloody marks of Lucy's fingernails, and said, with great dignity and courage, 'You had better finish me off as well, old son" – so Tommy raised the bloody scythe

I can't go on. Oh, darling, I hope you haven't seen as many terrible things as I saw that day – and in days to come. I know that wherever you are, and however you got there, it can't have been easy for you, but still, I hope, it wasn't _too_ hard.

Your father did what had to be done, he did it for the good of all; Lucy's end, like the Major's, was inevitable, and he did her a kindness, really – at least, that's what we all agreed. Although, afterwards, as we puzzled over Ben's behaviour and wondered how the zombie had even remembered her, let alone wanted or known how to find her, we realised that our understanding of what happened to people infected by this plague – the idea that they became corpses animated by a mindless virus – could not be the whole story. The whole business was far more complicated than it had seemed. So maybe our response to it was wrong, or at least, too simple.

Anyway, the smashing of those heads, the destruction on the beach, all that horror only bought us a little more time. Maybe it was all for nothing.

No one really thought about the dogs; I don't know why. The human bodies were taken away to be burned, but by the time anyone thought to look for Lucy's dogs, neither one could be found. This should have been a clear warning signal, but I guess anyone who noticed assumed, as I did, that someone else had taken care of putting down the badly-injured animals. I know it never occurred to me that dogs might be affected by the same plague that had nearly wiped out the human race.

So, in the end, it was the dogs, our beloved pets and helpers, who destroyed our community. Oh, yes, there were a few charred and mangled rotting corpses of long-dead humans who continued to drag themselves out of the sea, searching for live flesh, in the days and weeks to come, but they were easy enough to avoid, slow and stupid and hideous, not like the creatures we had shared our lives with, known and loved and trusted for so many years.

Within days of Lucy's Rottweilers going missing, so did nearly every other dog on the island, apart from that odd little creature belonging to Jean that never gets let out of the house, and our own Bella. But it was still another week before one of them attacked one of us, and we finally understood that we'd lost; our haven, no longer safe, had fallen to the invaders, and our fate was sealed.

I don't know why Bella didn't go the way of the rest of the dogs, but it must have had something to do with the corpse we found her eating on the beach. That happened before the ferry attack, so I have no idea where it came from, but it must have been dead for a very long time, because there was almost nothing left of it but bones. It was a moving skeleton when Bella leapt gleefully on it and knocked it down. Tail wagging in delight, she began to crunch and chew. You know that dog will eat anything, but that's got to be some kind of record. Tommy shouted "leave it!" but she wouldn't; when he went to try to pull her away, she chomped down all the harder, and then ran off with the skull and trailing vertebrae, to consume it in peace.

When she came home that night, she was like a different animal. Not aggressive, not to us, but... strange. She wouldn't come into the house, but she stayed close by, and although she still ate the food I put out for her, she had developed a taste for Infected flesh. It made her the most excellent guard dog, as any unsuspecting zombie who wandered onto our property became her prey. If they managed to do her any damage in return, I saw no sign of it.

They called them "lightstones" and they had been placed about the island to create safety zones. It was better than at the school of course – no need to live underground – but Giles felt uneasily aware that it was not so very different. Just as at the school, people were hiding from the Shadows, not fighting back.

Whatever the Shadows were, Giles thought, they were not going to go away. Defending a few small zones against them was not good enough. For long-term survival, not just protection, real weapons were needed.

Of course, people were working on the problem. He was pretty sure they'd already manufactured a few prototypes. There were people who knew much more than Giles about what worked and what didn't, and why should they tell *him*? For all that they were nicer to him on the island than they'd been at the school, he still didn't have any power.

They weren't going to lock him up, or threaten him with horrible punishments when he said he had to go outside the safety zones to look for Tansy. They let him go. They tried to talk him out of it, of course: they advised him against it; they told him he was throwing his own life away, and she was surely dead already, but if he wanted to die for nothing . . .

Of course he didn't want to die! Not even to save Tansy. But he did mean to save her, as well as himself. That meant he needed a weapon – that was obvious. But they refused to arm him in any way, even after he'd volunteered to test any experimental models they might have, at any risk to himself. Since they wouldn't give him a weapon, he made up his mind to steal one of the lightstones.

I have been trying to build up to the worst news gently, but there's no easy way to say it. Your father died on the 22nd of November. He survived the zombies, human and canine both, only to succumb to what was, I suppose, the most common cause of death in a man over 60, back in the old days. He had a heart attack.

Actually, he had two. I think he recognised the first one, but I believed him when he told me it was just indigestion (the bean and rabbit casserole was not my finest culinary creation) — we both wanted to believe it, because we still had some anti-acid medicine and pain killers in the medicine cabinet, but of course nothing at all to fix a bad heart. Even if the doctor had not had her throat ripped out by one of the dogs a week earlier, she couldn't have done much for him by herself.

I told Tommy how much I loved him and managed not to cry, and we went to bed, and when I woke a few hours later, he was lying dead beside me. He looked very peaceful.

Donny MacDonald came with his son, and helped me bury your father, and said prayers over the grave. I invited them to stay, but he insisted they'd be all right to get home: he had a gun and his son had an axe, and they'd watch each other's back...

But two people against a pack of zombie dogs? No chance. I heard Donny screaming... and that was it. They may have tried to come back to the house after dark — judging from the sounds Bella made, someone did — but I did not see them again. I don't know how many people are left alive on the island, but I think I may be the last survivor.

What is the point?

There is no point.

I don't want to be the last person alive.

When Tommy was alive, I had a reason for going on. But now—

Now, he's not even dead, not in the old-fashioned way of resting in the earth. Tommy has come back, like the others. How, I don't know. Is the virus or whatever it is in the very earth now? Or did someone dig him up — maybe the dogs? — and transmit the zombie-bug to his dead flesh?

It doesn't matter. I can imagine various scenarios, but why bother? Whether it was the bite from a flea or a bite from a dog or just what these days passes for the "natural course" of things, the end is the same. Somehow, he got out of the ground, out of the graveyard, and across more than a mile of rough ground to wander around what used to be his home, shambling and stumbling uncertainly as if, having made it this far, he has forgotten what he came for.

Bella watches and follows and dogs his heels, but makes no attempt to drive him off or eat him. She must recognise him. I think she is glad to have him back. I think I am, too. It makes things a little easier for me.

I keep thinking of Ben, piloting the ferry all the way from Islay, intelligent enough to set the course, emotional enough to want to be with his mother again. After his death, after his resurrection, he was still her son and he still loved her.

Is that how it is, darling? I think we were all wrong about this plague. I still feel an absolute certainty that you are alive, but now I think that you may be alive in a different sense than I had imagined. You may have become something else while still remaining my beloved daughter. Still Laura, but a new and different Laura who will never die. That has to be good, right? Especially if we can all be together again.

Giles was tired, but he could not rest. He dared not shift his attention from the Shadows he was fighting to glance at his watch, but the position of the sun told him it was still late afternoon. He should have been safely back by now; could make it in ten minutes if he ran flat out, but to do that he'd have to leave Tansy. He'd already found that she would not follow him unless he kept a firm grasp on her; he almost had to pull her along. It is very difficult to rescue someone who doesn't want to be rescued.

However, he had discovered something important. The lightstones were good not only for defence, but could be used in an offensive weapon. He'd managed to steal only a very small piece of one, but, embedded in a cricket bat, it was enough.

At first, he had only used it to ward off the Shadows, waving it about to keep them at a distance, but as he'd grown more desperate, he'd been forced to use it more aggressively, and had discovered that if he thought of it as a sort of broadsword, and rammed it straight into the darkest bits of darkness around him, he was sometimes rewarded with a result: the dark mass would shrink slightly and at the same time he could hear a sort of distant, tiny wailing sound. The shrinking back of the dark was only very slight, and the sound was so distant he might almost have imagined it, but both those things encouraged him to believe that he had managed to wound his enemy.

He was eager to bring the news back to the others. He didn't know how much longer he could hold out, especially as he was trying to protect not only himself but his sister, who stood there like a lump.

"Tansy," he gasped. "We have – to run – for it. Please! Run – I'll be right behind you—" As he spoke he lunged, holding the bat like an awkwardly-balanced sword, and this time the wail was much louder – it took him a split-second to understand he was hearing it in stereo. His sister shrieked as if she had felt the cut, and then she scrabbled at him, clawing and crying, and nearly made him drop his weapon.

This was the first real outburst of emotion he'd had from her since they'd left the school.

"Don't hurt them!" she shrieked. "You're hurting them!"

"What? Ow, Tansy, let go, I'm trying—"

"Stop it, stop it, you mustn't hurt them!"

"Who—?" But even as he tried to ask what she meant, he had an unexpected answer from the crowd of Shadows overhead. Somewhere in the shadows, someone spoke his name. It wasn't Tansy, although the voice was as familiar – more familiar.

"Mum?" he said, in wonder and terror.

"Oh, Giles . . ."

"Mum, oh, Mum, I didn't know! Where are you? Did I hurt you? I never meant to . . ." He dropped his weapon.

The Shadows rushed down and filled him, and lifted him, and took him in. It was nothing like they'd said it would be at the school, it was nothing like anything he had imagined. There was no pain, only a blissful darkness, and he didn't have to fight anymore, or be afraid, and he wasn't alone. His mother was there, and his father, and his grandparents, and their next-door neighbours, and all his old friends from primary school, and almost everyone he had ever known.

The only person missing that he cared about was Tansy. That was the one sad thing – and it was only a very small regret – as he rushed away into the swirling dark company, he was only sorry that the Shadows couldn't take her, too, and she would be left behind, to live alone forever.

BERNIE MAUGHMSTEIN JOKE #1358

Hey, apologies to Garrison Keister, right, but it's been a funny old fucking week in Lake Woe-Is-Me, right? No, really. Hey, no . . . listen up. Turns out some jolly old English guy has put together a fucking book, man . . . a book! All about us zombies, man. Like diary extracts, e-mails, transcripts

from TV and radio, maybe even fucking cake recipes . . . shit like that! You know what I'm saying? Like, we need all that current affairs shit, right? Cos, like, we can't open our fucking windows and see what's going down out there? I mean, "Hey world, I'm mad as hell and I ain't gonna

take this no more!" You know, I mean . . . eat your fucking heart out Paddy Chayefsky. "Hey, man, eat your heart out"? You betcha by golly, man . . . I'll have me a piece of that action!

A LETTER FROM THE REAL PRESIDENT OF
THE UNITED STATES OF AMERICA

My Fellow Americans,

This is your President, unbowed and uneaten. I send you via this leaflet my greetings and prayers that you are all weathering this terrible national crisis with the indomitable spirit that lives, moves, and breathes through these United States (and Guam, Puerto Rico, the U.S. Virgin Islands, American Samoa, and various other islands and atolls). I've never been prouder to be an American than I am today, as I watch our courage and resolve blaze through the dawn's early light. For I promise you, The Dawn is coming. The Dawn of the *Living*. Sitting here inside my subterranean bunker, I can't actually see it, but I know it is rising—but not like a zombie. Like a human being— proud, unchewed, and unchewing.

I also send greetings to all of humanity, including our intact allies in the great nations of the world. I fervently believe that the final hour of this worldwide catastrophe has struck, as millions of humans are fighting back to reclaim their freedom—

freedom from oppression, and tyranny, and basting. It is true that these are times that try men's souls, but we are the ones who have souls, unlike the godless monsters who have attacked us. Attacked not only Americans, but the animated, the quick. America pledges that we will not rest until everyone is safe, and free, and in pursuit of happiness and material gain; and the exchange of goods and services among our peoples, even under NAFTA, has resumed.

Global warming, imperial encroachment, the withholding of life-saving drugs due to political machinations—these are small matters, lesser issues that we can continue to resolve, as once we were doing, as soon as the greater threat has been removed. No one dissatisfied emerging nation or disaffected special interest group must take advantage of the rendering of established order to take up arms for selfish personal reasons. Remember, a house devouring itself cannot stand. There are no borders in this struggle against HRV. We human beings must put aside our differences of national concern and enmity if we are to destroy these walking dead and obliterate their WMCs—Weapons of Mass Consumption. America takes her role seriously as the leader of the free world, and we will employ all our resources—which are still considerable, and were expensive—to ensure that no one takes advantage during this time of chaos to push through a destabilizing agenda.

And now let me address you, my fellow citizens: I was duly elected and have sworn to protect you, to stand by you, and to defeat this great foe, as we as a nation have defeated so many others before. Difficult as it is to digest, it is a zombie, the so-called James Moreby, who has occupied our great White House. But he and his Cabinet of Seven will not stain its upholstery for long. I assure you that America is in this fight to win. We have mobilized the forces of the Human Resistance Movement, a living, breathing, army of might, and I have taken my Congressionally-approved place as Commander-in-Chief. I stand with head unbowed and firmly attached, leading a great body of fierce American patriots as we assail the zombie forces in the field, in the air, and underwater. We will disembowel this despicable enemy and fillet Moreby and his minions, grinding their bones into dust beneath our boots. Several times, if necessary, to ensure that he does not rise again. And again.

Even these so-called "smart" zombies that you see are abominations, and I have never heard of a repugnant mutation that was not ground out of existence by American resolve sooner or later. Are we not *real* men? And women. And transgender. Are we not free and undaunted, willing to expel the last breath from our lungs—even if they be gnawed upon—to preserve not only the freedoms and blessings bestowed on us by our Founding Fathers to this great nation, but given by our Creator to all villages, tribes, and nations of people the world over?

After Washington fell more than six months ago now, and the White House was taken, brave minutemen and women struck back at the rotten heart of our enemy, as we once did our warmongering British oppressors, who are now our dearest friends, dissecting his squadrons and companies and battalions. Using the finest brains among us—in a figurative sense—we have organized and armed ourselves, and we are launching counteroffensives all over this great nation of ours against this festering malignance. Rumor and innuendo will have it that California has fallen, but I'm here to tell you that that is a lie. The zombies are losing ground, and legs, and elbows, and we are beating them back with every engagement. Along Interstate Five, they have knuckled under, and in Mission Viejo, we have picked the military meat from their bones. San Diego, once considered local zombie headquarters, is now zombie hindquarters. Loyal Human Resistance Movement troops have gutted their strength after wave after wave of full-frontal assaults. We have much to cheer about, my fellow Americans.

There are widespread reports of zombies who have realized the grave error of their egregious assault on humanity. High-ranking zombies such as Major General Harland Dawson are losing morale in addition to noses, teeth, and tendons, and have begun to shamble into our embassies, consulates, camps, and foxholes, requesting sanctuary, amnesty, and refrigerated storage. They have reported that Project Darwin has been thoroughly compromised, as many of the finest minds absorbed by these wretches shout out for them to lay down arms. They see themselves for the maggot-infested corpses that they are, and not the "next step in Manifest Destiny," as has been claimed.

We are engaged in a great, uncivil war, testing whether our nation, or any nation so conceived and so dedicated to the body of humanity, can long endure. The false government that has gut-punched the very solar plexus of our democracy most certainly cannot endure permanently half-zombie and half-free. The summer soldier and the sunshine patriot will, in this crisis, shrink from the service of their country; but he—and she—and those others—who stands by it now, deserves the love and thanks of every uninfected man, woman, and child. Zombism, like Hell, is not easily conquered; yet we have this consolation with us, that the harder the conflict, the more glorious the triumph.

Zombism has been defeated in many partial battles. But it remains a considerable force in the world, and we cannot expect its final defeat save through effort and sacrifice on the part of us all. Many of us have made the ultimate sacrifice. It pains me greatly to confirm to you that my own dear husband, the First Spouse, met his untimely end when the White House was taken. He gave his life protecting a young intern he had barricaded inside the Lincoln Bedroom with himself, not realizing that she had already begun the terrible transformation that has destroyed the lives of so many Americans. The Vice

President, too, has seen his share of gore, losing a treasured family member as well.

But this is not the time to grieve. It is the time to act, swiftly and harshly. The human revolution is not weakened by attacks. On the contrary, it waxes and gains strength, for this is the revolution of those who possess the stomach to live free or die. Preferably once.

Now is the time for all good women and men to come to the aid of their species. To arms! Join the fight! Be strong, and courageous, and remember that one flame-thrower *can* make a difference. Our Human Resistance Movement front lines are throwing up a living wall of tough, seasoned fighters. Fall in behind them, and add your numbers to The Cause. We can win this war. We can cleanse the earth of this nightmare. Together, arm-in-arm, we can make it happen. Remember: a zombie dies a thousand deaths; valiant humans die but one. The HRM pledges to fight until no zombie is left standing, or staggering, or crawling. We will lay waste to The Death, HTZT, NZOA, and HICs. We will fragment the entire zombie order PDQ, and ASAP.

The next time you hear my voice, it will be raised in the heat of battle. Will you fight with me? As the First Spouse said, just before his unspeakable devouring, "We'll have their guts for garters." Will you have their guts for garters? Will you bleed the New Zombie Order dry with me?

In my husband's honor, and in the honor of all those who have fallen, and will fall, I know you will. I know your heart, America. To paraphrase the great General Sherman: "We would make this war as severe as possible, and show no symptoms of tiring till the zombies beg for mercy." And when they beg, we will show them none. If they sue for peace, we'll consign them to eternal torment. If they offer terms, we will intern them. There will be no surrender; there will be only death and dismemberment for these monsters among us. As hundreds of thousands of our enemies die, they'll curse the name of Thomas James Moreby with hatred equal to our own. For by occupying the Oval Office, he united us in a common purpose. By organizing his military, he presented us a clear target to smash. We are coming for you, Moreby, and for every flea-bitten footsoldier on this great battlefield of Earth.

And when the last zombie corpse blazes on the bonfire like the sunrise that I promise you, America; that I pledge to you, our allies; that I swear to you, the human race—then I'll stand proudly wrapped in the American flag and cry, "We have won. What victory has wrought, let no monster seek to rend asunder. We are one world, indivisible. Let us renew our appetite for liberty and freedom, and sate our thirst for glory. Let us be *humans*.

"Proud. And free."

God bless you, and God bless the true United States of America.

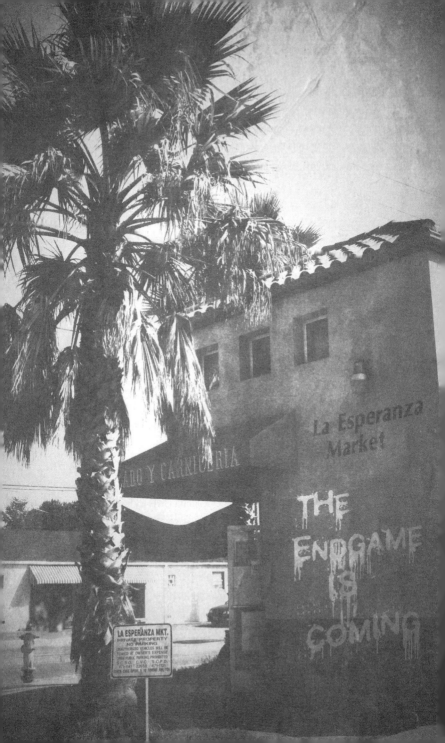

ACKNOWLEDGEMENTS

Many thanks to Duncan Proudfoot, Dorothy Lumley, Nicola Chalton, Pascal Thivillon, Joe Roberts, Roy Pinborough, Mandy Slater, Uli Meyer, Matt Sexton, Michael Marshall Smith and all the contributors for having the, er . . . brains to begin the fightback against the Zombie Apocalypse! Special thanks to Harlan Ellison, M.R. James, Nigel Kneale, Val Lewton, Edgar Allan Poe and H.G. Wells, for those who know . . .